HIDDEN KILLERS

ALSO BY LYNDA LA PLANTE

Jane Tennison series

Tennison

Prime Suspect

Prime Suspect 2: A Face in the Crowd

Prime Suspect 3: Silent Victims

Anna Travis series

Above Suspicion

The Red Dahlia

Clean Cut

Deadly Intent

Silent Scream

Blind Fury

Blood Line

Backlash

Wrongful Death

Lorraine Paige series

Cold Shoulder

Cold Blood

Cold Heart

Other titles

The Legacy

The Talisman

Entwined

Sleeping Cruelty

Royal Flush

Twisted

Quick Reads

The Little One

The Escape

Lynda La Plante

HIDDEN KILLERS

ZAFFRE

Copyright © La Plante Global Limited, 2016, 2017

Cover design by Alex Allden,
cover image © Dace Znotina / Alamy Stock Photo
Typeset by Scribe Inc., Philadelphia, PA.

Originally published in Great Britain by Simon & Schuster UK Ltd, 2016
First published in the United States as an ebook by Zaffre Publishing, 2017
This edition publishing by Zaffre Publishing, 2018

Zaffre Publishing, an imprint of Bonnier Zaffre
Ltd, a Bonnier Publishing company.
80-81 Wimpole St, London W1G 9RE

10 9 8 7 6 5 4 3 2 1

Trade paperback ISBN: 978-1-4998-6138-9

Also available as an ebook.

For information, contact 251 Park Avenue South,
Floor 12, New York, New York 10010

www.bonnierzaffre.com / www.bonnierpublishing.com

To my many loyal readers. Your support through e-mail
and social media has been a constant encouragement
to me, and makes all the hard work worthwhile.

GLOSSARY

A&E	Accident and Emergency
ABH	Actual Bodily Harm
CID	Criminal Investigation Department
CRO	Criminal Record Office (number)
DC	Detective Constable
DCI	Detective Chief Inspector
DCS	Detective Chief Superintendent
DI	Detective Inspector
DS	Detective Sargent
GBH	Grievous Bodily Harm
IRB	Incident Report Book
NSY	New Scotland Yard
OBO VAN	Observation van
OLD BAILEY	Central Criminal Court of England and Wales
OLD BILL	Slang for The Police
PC	Police Constable
PLONK	Slang for a female police constable
QC	Queen's Counsel
SECTION HOUSE	Residential accommodation for unmarried police officers
SOCO	Scenes of crime officer
THE MET	The Metropolitan Police
VDU	Visual Display Unit
WDC	Woman Detective Constable
WPC	Woman Police Constable

PROLOGUE

For WPC Jane Tennison, the months following the bank explosion, which caused the tragic deaths of DCI Len Bradfield and WPC Kathleen Morgan, were a difficult and painfully sad time. The truth was the incident deeply affected everyone in the Met, but most notably at Hackney Police Station, where many officers found their colleagues' deaths hard to deal with and all too raw to discuss. The imposing four-story redbrick-and-white-stone building had numerous stone-flagged corridors and winding staircases. The cells were located in the cold and dingy basement, and there were small cramped offices on the ground and first floors. The whole place needed redecorating and the station was long overdue for a refurbishment. But no changes had been made since the abortive bank raid involving the death of two loved and respected officers. It wasn't as if it had never happened or would ever be forgotten; it was just rarely, if ever, spoken about. However, the likes of Sergeant Harris ensured the daily routine and hard work continued, and a new DCI gave the detectives a strength and determination to continue working at the station.

DS Spencer Gibbs was placed on sick leave to recover from the burn injuries to his hands. Several detectives had tried to get in contact with him, even leaving messages at his home address, but to no avail. It seemed he didn't want any visitors and it soon became common knowledge, through the new DCI, that DS Gibbs had asked for a transfer to another station. Sadly, the whole incident left the young DC Mike Hudson, who was also injured in the explosion, too traumatized to return to work, and after attending the funerals of his colleagues he handed in his warrant card and resigned from the Met.

Despite her emotional and professional involvement in the devastating events, Jane was now even more determined to complete her probation and be confirmed as a fully-fledged police constable. As the weeks and months passed, she made admirable progress, not only in the classroom at her continuation training exams, but also on the streets where she made a number of good arrests. By anyone's standards, it was an impressive array of both male and female suspects, for various offenses such as shoplifting, criminal damage, drunk and disorderly, and handling stolen goods. Most notably there were two occasions, after a call over the radio, when Jane was first on the scene and had caught the burglars red-handed.

It was toward the end of her probation, in the last week of August 1974, when Jane spent a week on compulsory attachment with the Traffic Division. Although it was a great adrenalin rush racing around London at high speed with blue lights and sirens, to a variety of personal injury and vehicle accidents, being a Traffic officer was not a future she had any desire to pursue in the Met. She was crossing off the days in her pocket diary, longing for Monday, September 9th, which marked her final two weeks of probation and a plain-clothes attachment to Hackney CID.

Jane had already contemplated directly approaching DCS Metcalf who, shortly after the bank explosion, had given her his word that if she continued performing well as a probationer he would give her a personal recommendation should she desire to become a detective. His promise had been made well over a year ago now, and although she had seen Metcalf numerous times at the station, he had never raised the subject. Jane decided that it would be best to show a keen interest during her CID attachment and perform well, then she would be in a better position to approach him.

CHAPTER ONE

On Wednesday, September 4th, Jane was on the 2 p.m. late shift as Sergeant Harris inspected and posted the C Relief uniform officers to their beats and panda car duties for the shift. As Jane was about to be given her posting Detective Inspector Nicholas Moran entered the room and, as was the norm, everyone stood to attention for a senior officer. Harris had a look of disapproval on his face as he didn't like his parades interrupted, least of all by the CID. Moran nodded his approval at the officers' show of respect then gestured for everyone to sit down as he turned to Harris.

"Please finish posting your officers to their duties, Sergeant Harris, then I'd like to address them regarding some indecent assaults that have occurred on the ground in the last few weeks."

"I've finished, so you can address them now. But if you could make it brief I'd be obliged as *my* officers need to get out on patrol," Harris said, in a pompous manner.

"Thank you," Moran replied with a skewed smile that conveyed his displeasure at Harris's attitude.

DI Moran was an experienced and well-respected detective, having worked on the Vice Unit at Scotland Yard prior to his recent promotion and transfer to Hackney CID. He was in his mid-thirties, with blond hair that was neat, tidy and collar length. He wore a dark navy blue suit and white shirt with a button-down collar, blue tie and black ankle boots that made him look taller that his actual five feet ten inches. Jane had seen him on a few previous occasions but being a probationary WPC she had not come into direct contact with him; the word around the station was that he was on the fast track and going places.

Moran told the officers that over the last few weeks a number of young women had been indecently assaulted after dark, in both the Victoria Park and London Fields park in Hackney, and he strongly suspected the same man was responsible for all the attacks. He explained that the majority of the assaulted women had been prostitutes, probably because they were easy targets who would be least likely to report an assault. However, the last two victims were not prostitutes and the fear was that the suspect was becoming less discriminating about whom he attacked. As Moran spoke, all the officers present, apart from Harris, wrote down the information in their force-issue note books.

"The suspect is about five feet eight inches tall, with a deep-voiced London accent. He wore all-black clothing, which consisted of a waist length bomber-style jacket, black turtle neck jumper and trousers." Moran paused to let the officers write down the details.

"What about his color and facial description?" Harris asked, in a manner that implied Moran was lacking in his information on the suspect.

"Don't know, Sergeant Harris," Moran said, and deliberately paused while Harris sat back with a smug grin. He then continued: "Sadly none of the victims would recognize the assailant again as he had his face covered during each attack."

Harris kept quiet as Moran went on to say that he and some of his detectives would be carrying out undercover surveillance, with a decoy, at London Fields for the next few nights. He wanted two officers patrolling Victoria Park just after dark and the station panda cars should, if possible, make a sweep round the park at least every half-hour. This, Moran informed them, was a deliberate ploy to entice the suspect over to London Fields where there would be no uniform presence. Harris made an entry in the parade book, which was on the desk in front of him, and informed PC Jackson and PC Oliver that they would now be patrolling Victoria Park for the shift.

"However, should the officers patrolling Victoria Park see anyone acting suspiciously, or matching the partial description of the suspect, they have my permission to stop and question the person about their movements. If you're not happy with any explanation or answers they give, arrest them and radio the CID office. One of my detectives will be manning a radio and they will be on a different frequency to you. Are there any questions?"

Harris promptly closed the parade book and stood up. "Right, you all know your postings so book out your radios and vehicles, then get out on patrol . . . and no cups of tea beforehand."

Jane raised her hand, attracting Moran's attention.

"Yes, officer?"

"Sorry, sir . . . it wasn't about your case or the suspect. It's just that Sergeant Harris hasn't posted me to a beat yet. I could cover Victoria Park as well, Sergeant, or relieve the officers for their refreshments break?" Jane asked, hoping that she might get the chance to stop and arrest the suspect in Victoria Park.

The frown on Harris's face said it all. Jane was well accustomed to his condescending, chauvinistic attitude.

"I've done the patrol postings . . . you're in comms on the radio and VDU, Tennison."

DI Moran gestured to Jane. "Ah, yes, you're Jane Tennison? I'd like to have a chat with you about bringing your CID attachment forward to—"

Harris interrupted. "She needs to be on comms to relieve the early turn officer."

"And I need a female officer to act as a decoy tonight, Sergeant Harris . . . unless you fancy putting on a wig, skirt and high heels yourself," Moran said, in a tone that sounded as if he was being serious.

Harris ushered everyone out of the parade room, then slammed the door and turned to Moran.

"May I have a word, sir?" Harris said, indignantly. He walked a few steps away from Jane, followed by Moran.

Jane couldn't believe that even now, with only a few days of her probation left to serve, Harris still acted like a petulant child when it came to female officers' career opportunities. She also knew he was not a fan of the CID and often stated that young detectives didn't have much brawn or brains and depended on experienced uniform men like himself to get them out of trouble. Although Harris pretended to whisper to Moran it was obvious he wanted her to hear every word.

"You do realize that Tennison is still a probationer and inexperienced, and when it comes to the ways of the CID she may not be up to scratch, evidentially, if you make an arrest?"

"If you are suggesting my detectives would encourage a uniform officer to fabricate evidence then I very much resent your remark, Harris. Rest assured, her well-being will be paramount throughout the surveillance operation."

Moran looked at his watch before continuing. "You'd better get a move on . . . the early turn duty sergeant will be waiting for you to relieve him."

Harris gritted his teeth as he left the parade room. Moran gestured for Jane to sit down. He pulled over a chair for himself, using the back of it as an arm rest and swinging his legs either side. Although she didn't know Moran, judging by his cheeky smile and snazzy suit, Jane had formed an early impression that he reckoned himself as a bit of a charmer. Moran pulled a pack of Players from his pocket, took two cigarettes out, put the pack back in his pocket, and offered one to Jane, who declined. He tucked the spare cigarette behind his ear and lit the other with a Zippo lighter. For a fraction of a second Jane remembered DCI Bradfield using a similar lighter. But the moment passed as Moran flicked his Zippo closed, inhaled on the cigarette and blew out a ring of smoke.

"You obviously heard what I said to Sergeant Harris?"

Jane nodded. "Yes, sir, and I'd really like to work with you on your operation."

"A WDC from Dalston nick was going to act as the decoy tonight, but she went sick an hour ago and I need someone to replace her. A couple of the lads in the office recommended you as a bit of a looker, with a good arrest record," he said, in a serious voice.

"Thank you, sir," she replied, slightly embarrassed.

"There are obviously risks involved, but I can assure you that we will be watching you discreetly from an obo van. There will also be further backup nearby. But the choice is yours . . . if you don't want to be a decoy, I totally understand and you'll still be welcome on your two-week CID attachment."

"I'd be honored to be a decoy, and I know your detectives will watch my back."

Moran sat upright and slapped his hands on the back of the chair.

"That's great, darlin' . . . and whether or not we arrest the pervert you can add the next three weekdays with us as additional to your CID attachment."

"Thank you, sir, I won't let you down."

"I'm sure you won't, but first you'll need to get the right outfit together."

"OK," she said, wondering what he was going to say next.

"You'll need to tart yourself up a bit . . . You've got to look sexy . . . sort out your hair and makeup, maybe get a long wig or something and look like you're up for a good time . . . You all right with that?"

Jane nodded and Moran asked if she had any "scanty" clothing to wear for the job. When Jane replied that she didn't Moran pulled out a leather wallet from his suit jacket and handed Jane two ten pound notes.

"Here's a score. Use it, but get receipts so I can claim the dosh back as expenses for the decoy operation."

Moran looked at his watch and stood up. "Right, it'll be dark by 8 p.m. so you go get yourself sorted and be back here for a half-seven briefing in the CID office."

Jane nodded and Moran used his foot to shove the chair back against the wall before leaving the room. Jane sat for a few moments trying to think what clothes she had that might be suitable, but nothing came instantly to mind. This was a big opportunity and she didn't want to blow it. Looking at the money Moran had given her Jane wondered if she'd find anything suitable at shops like Chelsea Girl or British Home Stores, but she doubted it. And Carnaby Street shops would be too expensive.

She was relieved that she had nearly five hours to get ready. But first she had to inform the miserable Sergeant Harris that she was now officially on her CID attachment. She headed out of the briefing room and down the stone-flagged corridor with its peeling green paint and fading notices. Eventually she tracked him down in the snooker room and explained that DI Moran had said she needed to buy the appropriate clothes for her undercover assignment.

"No doubt you'll have the 'appropriate' clothing at the section house, Tennison, so I won't be authorizing any cash for you to buy anything."

He wafted his cue for her to leave, then bent down over the snooker table to line up for a shot on the black ball. Jane walked to the door then smiled as she turned back to Harris, who was just about to take his shot.

"That's fine, Sarge . . . DI Moran gave me a score." Harris pushed his cue forward and his hand slipped, causing the tip to scrape into the green baize, almost tearing it.

"Whoops!" she said, closing the door quickly behind her.

Jane took her uniform jacket and hat from her locker and left the station to get the 253 bus to Ede House, her home now for almost two years. Ten minutes later she was hurrying up the stairs to her room. She took off her uniform skirt and hung it in the wardrobe. Pushing the coat hangers apart one by one she looked through her clothes, even though she knew she didn't really have any that fitted the term "scanty." She thought about the money DI Moran had given her, but felt bad about spending it on something tacky that she would never wear again. In desperation Jane pulled on a pair of jeans, a white T-shirt and short jacket, but looking in the wardrobe mirror she realized she would definitely need to buy some suitable clothes.

There was one person she knew who used to wear tube top, hot pants, miniskirts and long boots on a night out to the disco. Jane laughed, remembering how her sister Pam would sneak out of the family flat with her outfit in a shoulder bag, so that her disapproving parents wouldn't see. She would then nip to a friend's house to change before going out to places like the Empire Ballroom in Leicester Square. One time Pam had arrived home after midnight and as she let herself into the dark hall she had fallen over on her high wedge boots, and their mother, hearing the commotion, had hurried from her bedroom.

"Do you know what time it is?" she had said so loudly that Jane had come out of her room. Pam had very obviously been drinking as she swung the bag with her clothes that she intended changing back into and had to prop herself up against the wall.

"I am only late cos I have been sick, I had a prawn cocktail at Norma's."

Mrs. Tennison had shaken her head, and told Jane to get her sister some Bisodol for her upset stomach, and, looking ashamed, she had returned to her bedroom.

"How much have you had to drink?" Jane had demanded as she had helped her sister to the bathroom and taken off her coat.

"Just a few Babychams, s'nothin', but I stayed on dancing and didn't get time to change back into . . ." She hadn't finished as she had started to retch and Jane had to help her to the toilet. As Pam had bent over Jane couldn't believe that she was wearing a miniskirt so short she could see her knickers, and even more shocking, was that Pam was not wearing a bra under her silky frilly blouse.

"You are not wearing your brassiere," Jane said in a harsh whisper.

"Oh for goodness sake, get with it, I haven't worn one for ages, nobody wears them now."

"Well, I do," Jane said, taking from the medical cabinet the pink Bisodol bottle and holding it out just as Pam was violently sick.

Jane took a bus toward her parents' home in Maida Vale, stopping off at Pam's salon, which was only a short distance from the family flat.

Pam was surprised to see her and Jane briefly explained that she was going on an undercover operation and needed to change her appearance. Pam made her wait until she had finished her client's tint, and then said she only had twenty minutes before she would have to comb the tint through as the other hairdresser wasn't in until later.

In the small back annex of the salon there was a bag full of wigs. Pam explained that when they were training junior stylists the wigs were pinned to a head stand and would be cut or colored. There were short bobs, long straggly blondes, and frizzy permed wigs, none in very good condition. Jane tried some of them on but they looked so false, until she put on a curly dark chestnut-colored wig.

"Can I borrow this one, Pam?"

"Yes, but you'll have to return it . . . that's real hair. What else do you need?"

"Do you have any makeup here?"

"Yes, cos sometimes I'm in so early I don't have time to do my face. I've also got a lot of samples as I do the makeup for the hair models when I'm doing one of the stylist events."

Pam tipped out from a cardboard box an array of foundations and lipsticks, eyebrow pencils, liquid eyeliner and false eyelashes. Jane checked herself in a mirror, still unsure about the wig.

"If you wait around I can do your makeup for you and comb out the wig and put some carmen rollers in it. You could do with a trim as well."

"No, I have to go, but another time. I really appreciate this."

Jane eventually left with the wig and some of Pam's spare makeup in a paper carrier bag. Pam had rather enjoyed helping and showing her how she could change her appearance, demonstrating how to stick on the false eyelashes. The sisters hadn't even discussed how long it had been since they had seen each other, or how things were going with Pam's new husband, Tony. A sixteen-year-old assistant was sweeping up and washing around the basins; she couldn't help overhearing Pam and Jane's conversation. As soon as Jane left she asked Pam what it was all about. Pam tapped the side of her nose conspiratorially.

"Can't say, Cheryl, but my sister's a police officer, going undercover."

She turned away and returned to her client who glanced at her watch, indicating that she had been waiting too long.

"Right, let me just comb this through for you, that extra ten minutes will give a better overall color."

If Pam had been surprised to see Jane, Mrs. Tennison was even more so. She immediately thought something terrible had happened, and it took a while for Jane to calm her down and explain that she was only there for a quick visit as she fibbed that there was a patrol car waiting, and she just wanted to give her mum a hug and a kiss. Mr. Tennison was out playing lawn bowls, which was fortunate, as it meant that Jane could see her mother, get what she needed and leave. Her bedroom was always just as she had left it, and it made her feel quite emotional. Everything was neat and orderly, although that soon changed as Jane rummaged through her wardrobe and overhead cupboards.

"Why don't you tell me what you're looking for, dear, and maybe I can help you find it?"

"It was just a costume I had years ago, when we did a school play . . . and some things I had for a Halloween party," Jane said, standing on a stool and rifling through an assortment of her clothes in the cupboard.

"They might be in Pam's old bedroom . . . I put lots of things in there for the Salvation Army. There's some of her clothes she doesn't want in there as well. Daddy and I were going to drop them off but haven't got round to it yet. Do you want me to look for anything special? Is it for a party?"

"Yes, it's for one of the officers that's leaving . . . but don't worry, Mum, I'll go and have a look."

Jane stepped down from the stool. There was no way she was going to tell her mother exactly why she needed to find the costumes.

Jane could not believe how many plastic bags were stacked in Pam's old bedroom. Mrs. Tennison started opening one after another.

"Is it fancy dress, dear? Here's that pair of thigh length boots Pam wore for her Dick Whittington costume . . . they cost a lot of money because she bought them from Biba . . . they're not real patent leather, and fit up over the knee."

Jane and her mother sorted through old clothes, most of which were Pam's and were things she wouldn't be seen dead in now that she was a qualified hairdresser and ran the local salon. Jane selected the clothes she wanted and put them into an empty plastic bag. She hugged her mother and left her refolding and packing up the discarded items. Mrs. Tennison wanted her to stay for an early dinner but Jane was eager to get back to the section house and try everything on.

"I have to go, Mum, but thanks for all your help."

"Well, I hope it's a fun party, dear . . . Daddy and I will get all these other things to the Salvation Army . . . not that I think any of their people would want to wear some of Pam's clothes. She used to worry me so much . . . all those flared trousers and skimpy tops."

"Bye, Mum."

Jane stuffed the wig and makeup into the same bag as the clothes and left her mother still packing everything else away.

By the time she returned to the section house it was almost 6 p.m. On her bed she laid out a miniskirt, a sequined stretch boob tube, a maroon padded bra, a pair of fishnet tights and the awful fake patent leather boots. She had also taken a frilly blouse, some blue plastic hooped earrings and an array of bangles and beads. Jane brushed the dark auburn wig to get some of the tangles out, then pinned back her own hair and pulled the wig on. It hung down to her shoulders and, looking at herself in the mirror, she couldn't believe how different it made her appear. She put on the frilly blouse and then discarded it for a red boob tube, pulling it down to put on the padded bra and eventually showing a lot of cleavage. She smiled, thinking how her mother would have had a heart attack if she could see what she looked like.

After Jane had pulled on the fishnet tights and zipped up the leather miniskirt, she had to stand on a chair to see herself in the sink mirror. She decided against the miniskirt and tried on a pair of dark green velvet hot pants instead. Climbing back onto the chair to check the outfit, she had a déjà vu moment. When she had first started her probation at Hackney, there had been the wretchedly sad investigation into the murder of a young prostitute called Julie Ann Collins. It was strange for Jane to recall how she had reacted when she had first seen the Polaroid crime scene photographs of the murdered girl. The seventeen-year-old Julie Ann, a heroin addict, had been wearing boots and hot pants when her body had been discovered.

The memory triggered a sudden wave of sadness as images of Kath and DCI Bradfield sprung back into her mind. Jane had to clench her hands into fists to fight back unexpected tears. She didn't want to remember them, not now, not when she was about to begin undercover work. It could jeopardize her chances of gaining a much longed-for place in the CID. She became angry with herself for being emotional, and as she had done so often before, she refused to let herself cry. It felt as if someone was squeezing her heart and she had to force herself to take slow, deep breaths until the pressure subsided. She had told no one about these "attacks," which were now less frequent, and she was certain she was capable of controlling them.

Jane stepped down from the chair and took out all of Pam's makeup, spreading it out on her small writing desk: the pale pink lipstick, the rouge and pots of eye shadows, and sticks of pan makeup. Pam had been quite a rebellious teenager, and Jane couldn't help smiling at how different they were. Perhaps it was just as well that Pam had started work in the salon straight from school and had met her husband and married so young, or she might have ended up going off the rails. Sisters they may be, but they had very little in common. Since Pam had got married and Jane had moved into the section house, they rarely saw each other.

It took Jane several attempts, using a small magnifying mirror, to stick on the false eyelashes. She had never worn them before, and found the tiny tube of glue very fiddly. She used one of the darker sticks of pan to cover her face and work into her neck as Pam had shown her. There was no makeup brush, so she had to apply the rouge with a tissue. Jane chose a blue eye shadow and then wet the mascara from the tap at her wash-basin and applied two thick coats, being careful not to unstick the eyelashes. She spent a long time checking her reflection and then lastly put on the pale pink lipstick.

It was nearly 7 p.m. and Jane realized she'd better get a move on as she didn't want to be late for the briefing in the CID office. She began to feel almost satisfied with her appearance until she realized that it was going to be quite cold as she would be out late, so she tied the blouse she had discarded in a knot around her waist. She realized it wouldn't be warm enough but she reckoned the adrenalin rush of working undercover would keep her from feeling the cold. Finally, she clipped on the big hoop earrings and pulled the cheap bracelets onto her wrists. She rather hesitantly looked at her police issue shoulder bag, but knowing she wouldn't be using it, she picked up the plastic makeup bag that belonged to Pam and popped her warrant card inside. It had a floral print and a zip and she could use it as her purse.

Jane practiced walking up and down the length of her small room. The boots made it difficult as the plastic kept rubbing her knees, and she had to constantly pull up the flap at the top. They were platform and had a stacked wedge heel, making it very hard to walk properly and mimic a confident "hooker's stride," swinging her hips and turning her head as if looking for punters.

Jane continued to increase her confidence by practicing her new role on the bus journey from the section house back to the station. To begin with, she was very nervous and self-conscious, wondering if anyone would recognize her or try to approach her. In recent months she had arrested several toms for soliciting and she remembered how they gave a "cold shoulder" steely eyed look when questioned. For her journey to work Jane had taken off the earrings and bracelets and was wearing her black raincoat over her disguise. She went into the station via the back entrance in case anyone saw her walking in by the front counter. As she walked along the corridor to the locker room two uniform officers stopped to question her.

"Oi, what d'you think you're doin' on police premises, luv?"

"The same as you, luv . . . it's me, WPC Tennison . . . want to see my ID?"

One of them muttered "Fuckin' 'ell," as they both moved off sharply down the corridor. The fact that they had not recognized her gave Jane a boost.

While storing her coat in her locker Jane had another moment of déjà vu. It was over something completely unconnected, but after being confident about controlling her emotions, this came on so strongly she had to brace herself. Jane had forgotten to spray on any perfume, and she had a visualization of Kath and her heavy French scent, which all the men used to tease her about. Kath had once sprayed Jane with it to get rid of the smell of Dettol from the first post-mortem she had attended.

Her recollection was suddenly interrupted by a loud knock on the locker room door, and DI Moran's voice.

"Two rather stunned uniform lads just said they'd seen you in the corridor . . . all right if I come in and have a look?"

"Yes, sir," Jane said, brushing herself down and shaking her head so the wig would look better.

"My God, you look the part . . . especially the sequined boob tube, which is very revealing," he said, his eyes transfixed on her, adding, "This is for you." He tossed her a pale blue waist length rabbit fur coat. "It'll be pretty cold out there so you'll need something to keep you warm that goes with the rest of the gear. It's evidence in a handling case, but for now it's yours." Jane gratefully put on the cheap rabbit fur jacket, which reeked of patchouli oil.

"I'll just check my makeup and then I'll be up for the briefing, sir."

"Your makeup's fine. I'd like to get out on the plot, so I'll brief you in the obo van. Get the duty sergeant to book you out with us . . . the obo van is in the yard."

Jane clipped on the earrings and went to the front office where Sergeant Rodgers was sitting at the duty desk. She liked Sergeant Rodgers. Unlike Harris he had a sense of humor and didn't bark out orders. He nearly fell off his seat when he saw Jane, but she was quick to identify herself to him and reassure him that she was not a trespasser in the station.

"Bloody hell, you look lovely, Tennison. Harris said you were getting dressed up for a UC job, but I never imagined you looking anything like this."

Jane smiled, but realized he wasn't joking as he stared at her in admiration.

"Fancy me, do you, Sarge?"

"I dunno how you done it . . . you look like a movie star. Pity I got a wife, three kids and a cross-breed Alsatian at home. Listen, good luck tonight, be careful and don't go sticking your neck out. You'll have plenty of backup out there, so use it."

"Thanks, Sarge. Can you book me out with the CID, please?"

Rodgers nodded and watched as Jane sashayed off down the corridor before booking her out in the station duty book. He noted that WPC 517 Tennison had left the station at 7:45 p.m. to work with CID on an attachment. Closing the duty book he tapped it with his hand and sighed. He knew how young Tennison was, and doubted that she had any concept of what she might have to face. Looking like a tough street-wise Tom could get her into a nasty situation.

CHAPTER TWO

Jane felt nervous in the obo van as they made their way over to London Fields. DI Moran gave her a small concealed radio, which he placed in the pocket of the blue rabbit fur coat. He had already made a small hole in the pocket for the earpiece and a small hand-held mic. He ran the wire for the speaker down the inside of the left sleeve of the jacket and the earpiece to the middle of her neck, up into the wig and into her left ear. Moran explained that it worked the same as a normal police radio and all she had to do was hold the mic in her left hand and press the small transmitter button whenever she wanted to communicate with him.

"Here, take this just in case you need to use it," he said, as he produced a truncheon from his inside jacket pocket and handed it to her. "Self-preservation always comes first so you hit 'em where it hurts most, as hard as you can if anything happens. OK?"

Jane nodded as she held the truncheon in her hand. "Where am I going to put it? It's too big for my coat pocket and I don't fancy trying to squeeze it down the back of this boob tube or these hot pants."

Moran laughed and pulled a rubber band out of his pocket. "Up your right sleeve, and use the band to hold it in place." He helped her with the truncheon and instructed her to make a radio test call to him once she was dropped off.

"You still up for this?" he asked, in a serious tone.

"Yes, sir. If I'm honest, I'm just a bit nervous."

"That's to be expected . . . but I've got plain clothes backup cars nearby, covering both sides of the Fields. The uniform officers are aware of what's going on should we need them as well.

DC Ashton is driving the obo van and we will be the nearest to you at all times. I'll be running the show . . . my call sign will be Gold, yours is Silver and the rest of the troops, should we need them, will be Bronze."

Jane gave a small nod of recognition to Ashton, a pale freckle-faced twenty-eight-year-old who had recently married. Like many of the CID officers, he had also been on Bradfield's team.

Moran smiled at Jane reassuringly. "Not many Toms are working the patch after what's been happening, but with less foot traffic we can tail you more easily."

Arriving at London Fields' west side entrance Moran told Jane to follow the path past the outdoor pool and hang around there for a while, "as if touting for business." They would park up in a suitable vantage point to watch her, and after ten to fifteen minutes she was to follow the central path through the park to the south entrance at Lansdowne Drive, then turn back on herself and walk through the park to the north entrance at Richmond Road. Moran said that if nothing had happened within the next hour or so she could jump back in the obo van to have a hot coffee, before repeating the route through the Fields.

From the front of the obo van DC Ashton called out that it was all clear. Moran checked the rear, then opened the back door to let Jane out, telling her that rather than looking for punters she should let them come to her.

The cold outside air mixed with Jane's nerves and she felt a shudder down her spine as she started to walk toward the Lido. She raised her left hand to her mouth and pressed the transmitter button on the mic.

"Gold to Silver receiving, over," she said, without at first realizing her nervous error.

"You're Silver, and yes, Gold is receiving . . . Over."

Jane could have kicked herself and responded, "Silver received."

Moran was joined in the obo van by the young and relatively inexperienced Detective Constable Brian Edwards. Edwards was a rawboned six-footer with thick dark curly hair, and usually looked as if he had just fallen out of bed. Tonight, however, both men were dressed in dark turtleneck sweaters and black trousers. Moran wore a black leather jacket and Edwards a black bomber jacket. It was too dark to use the spy holes and they had a better view looking out of the rear window, which had a reflective foil-like sheet on it so no one could see in.

London Fields was virtually desolate. There was hardly anyone about and nobody who could be described as acting in a suspicious manner. Jane kept on walking. By now she was feeling very tired and cold when over the radio came Moran's voice.

"Gold to Silver, white male, late sixties coming toward you, approach with caution."

Jane tensed as he moved closer, she took a deep breath, and felt the adrenalin rush of nerves. She could smell the alcohol as the man weaved and tottered toward her.

"Which way to the Cat and Mutton, my darling one?" he slurred.

In the obo van Moran became alert and told Edwards to stand by.

"I'm sorry, mate, I dunno," Jane said in a dreadful attempt at a cockney accent as she passed him.

"False alarm," Moran muttered. "He's pissed out of his head. I'm beginning to think this is a waste of everyone's time."

He opened a can of beer and lit a cigarette while Edwards had a cup of coffee from his flask and ate his sandwich.

It was now just after 10 p.m. and Jane made her way along the tarmac path, past the Lido yet again. She was struggling to walk in the thigh length boots that were by now really hurting her feet and had given her a blister on her right heel. But she had to keep up appearances, even though she was continually having to adjust her hot pants as they rode up her thighs. The cold night air penetrated through the frilly cheesecloth shirt that was tied tightly round her waist.

Jane couldn't believe that she hadn't even come across a "legitimate prostitute" having sex up against a tree, or a park bench, as she had seen before when out on uniform patrol. But she realized that the fact that there were no prostitutes about was actually in her favor. It meant she avoided any angry confrontations with local Toms questioning what a new girl was doing on their patch. Jane knew that an angry prostitute, or worse still a drunk prostitute, could be a real handful to deal with.

She carried on walking along the path, the pain from the blister getting worse, when she was suddenly aware of someone approaching quickly behind her. She gripped the radio mic in her hand, ready to press the talk button if she needed to. She could hear the sound of deep breathing and panting coming nearer. Jane's heart was pounding as she turned her head slightly, to look over her left shoulder, and saw the figure of a man in a hooded black tracksuit within inches of her. She had a sudden urge to scream but controlled herself as he jogged on past her.

Jane felt an incredible sense of relief as she looked to her left along Martello Street, on the east side of London Fields. In the distance, she could see the obo van moving slowly with its lights out. She was really glad she hadn't jumped the gun and radioed in for assistance, and taking a deep breath she walked on. The fact that neither Moran nor Edwards had radioed her about the jogger made her wonder how visible she was to them.

Jane's heart was still beating faster than usual. As she passed under a large tree she was startled by some conkers falling from the branches of the chestnut tree above her. Relieved, Jane smiled, but then she heard a much heavier thud behind her. Before she could turn around a black leather-gloved hand was clamped over her mouth while the other hand grabbed her round the chest, pinning her left arm to her side. The sudden attack caused the mic in her left hand to fall loose from the sleeve of the rabbit fur jacket, and dangle like a kid's glove on a string.

Jane's assailant groped and squeezed at her right breast with his left hand and started to drag her backward toward the covered entrance of the Lido. Jane struggled to break free and desperately tried to look over her shoulder toward where she had last seen the obo van. She attempted to scream, but the leather-gloved hand tightened around her mouth. A man's voice whispered harshly in her ear.

"I've got a knife . . . so keep your mouth shut, you fucking thieving whore . . . or I'll cut your throat wide open this time."

Jane nodded vigorously to indicate that she understood, and the leather-gloved hand relaxed its pressure slightly. Jane then realized that he couldn't be holding a knife as there was one hand over her mouth and the other was groping her breast. Her instinct took over and she opened her mouth wide and bit down as hard as she could on the gloved hand. As the assailant released his grip Jane screamed loudly and spun around quickly to confront her attacker. The man had a stocking over his head, making him unrecognizable, and he was wearing a black roll-neck sweater and black trousers. Jane understood exactly what he was intending to do to her when she saw his erect penis sticking out of his unzipped trousers.

In an instant Jane kicked her attacker hard in the groin. She pulled the truncheon free from inside her sleeve and hit him on the side of the head with all her strength, knocking him to the ground. The force of the impact against his skull made her lose her grip on the truncheon, causing it to fly out of her hand and onto the grass a few feet away.

Enraged, the assailant was growling and moving slowly. Like a bear about to make its final move on its prey he gradually stood up, the growling getting louder and louder as spittle foamed through the stocking mask. Jane managed to retrieve the radio mic, and pressing the transmitter screamed, "Urgent Assistance!" and yelled at the top of her voice that she was a police officer. The attacker, as if confused by the revelation, froze momentarily before turning to run. Jane lunged at him, grabbing his right shoulder from behind. In his desperate effort to escape, the assailant elbowed her in the mouth causing her lip to split and bleed. He started to run, and although Jane was determined to give chase she knew she'd never be able to catch him in the boots she was wearing.

Suddenly she saw DI Moran and DC Edwards running at speed toward the assailant and together they tackled him hard from behind, knocking him heavily to the ground. As he tried to get up Moran pulled his head back by his hair and smashed his face down onto the pathway, causing his nose to split and bleed profusely. The two detectives then pinned him to the ground, pulled his hands behind his back and DC Edwards handcuffed him.

Jane felt a mixture of fear and relief as she heard the two-tone sirens of the police cars making their way to the Fields. Moran spoke into his portable radio.

"All units from Gold, stand down. Suspect has been arrested and WPC Tennison is safe and well. We only require a uniform van for the prisoner to be taken to the station."

"You were supposed to be covering my back! Where the hell were you?" Jane shouted.

Moran calmed her down, explaining that their view from the obo van had become partially blocked as Jane had passed between some large trees.

"It wasn't until we heard you scream that we realized something was wrong. I mean, where on earth did he come from? It's as if he appeared from nowhere."

Jane's hand was trembling as she pointed to the chestnut tree. "Up there . . . he must have been up there, and jumped down. He grabbed me from behind, covered my mouth with his hand and said he'd cut my throat if I screamed. I couldn't get to the radio transmitter or shout for help until I bit him and he let me go."

The attacker now started shouting that he'd done nothing wrong, earning him a well-aimed kick in the side of his ribs from DI Moran. He pulled the stocking up off his head revealing a man in his early thirties, clean shaven and with neatly cut hair.

Moran looked at Jane as he put the stocking in a plastic bag. "He's your arrest, Tennison, so go ahead and caution him."

Jane licked at her split lip, tasting the blood as she spoke. "I'm arresting you for an indecent and serious assault on a police officer. You do not have to say anything unless you wish to do so, but what you say may be given in evidence."

"I've done fuck all! That bitch suddenly attacked me and started screaming . . . Look at my head!"

Moran gave him another kick in the ribs to silence him. He pulled the attacker up from the ground and noticed with disgust that the man's now flaccid penis was hanging out of his trousers. He glanced at Jane who glared straight back at him. By now her fear had been replaced by the buzz of adrenalin from making an arrest.

"Don't look at me—I'm not putting that thing back in his trousers!"

Moran laughed, surprised by her ability to make a joke after what she had been subjected to. DC Edwards roughly zipped up the assailant's fly, and hauled him away screeching in agony.

The prisoner was placed in the back of the police van, flanked by two officers and with DC Edwards sitting opposite him. DI Moran drove Jane back to the station in the obo van, and asked her to go over everything that happened and what her assailant had said.

She was still energized as she repeated how she had been attacked from behind and how he had threatened to cut her throat.

"I bit down on his hand as hard as I could so he released his hold."

"Good girl . . . sorry you had to go through that, but you did well. Are you all right?"

"Yes, sir."

Her heart was beating rapidly and she suddenly felt unable to stop shaking. Taking a few deep breaths she managed to calm herself down, forcing back the feelings of fear. In some ways she was more concerned that DI Moran might notice she had been panic stricken.

He had noticed and gave her a sidelong glance. As he concentrated on the road ahead he spoke quietly.

"You know, at some stage in our careers we've all had the guts kicked out of us. I don't mean literally of course . . . but once you've had to face that fear and been able to deal with it, the next time isn't nearly as bad. It's not just the adrenalin rush that helps you get through something like tonight, but the satisfaction that you caught the bastard."

Jane had not expected Moran to be so understanding. She smiled bravely and even attempted to make a joke.

"You been dressed up as a Tom to make an arrest, have you, sir?"

He chuckled, shaking his head.

"I never put a bad guy away that didn't deserve it, that's all you've got to know about me, Tennison."

Back at the station Jane asked to be excused so she could sort out her split lip. Moran nodded, instructing DC Edwards to find the duty officer. Jane went to the ladies', then after washing her hands she inspected her cut lip in the mirror. It wasn't as swollen as she thought it would be, but she knew it would take at least a week or so before it healed. That meant not visiting her parents for a while. She put on some makeup and lipstick to conceal the cut, and thought about what Moran had said to her. She was more confident that she had handled the situation well under extreme pressure, but there had been a moment when she had really feared for her life. When the stocking had been removed from her attacker's head she had been surprised to see that he was actually quite a good-looking man, and not the ugly, vicious person she had envisaged.

Jane thought about taking off her wig, but decided against it as it made her feel even more like an undercover officer working with the CID.

As she stared at herself in the mirror above the cracked washbasin, it triggered another memory. She was in the wash-room standing by Kath Morgan as she was getting ready to go on her first plain-clothed assignment; she had been so excited and eager to catch a burglar robbing old-age pensioners. Kath had been such a feisty woman, not afraid of anyone or anything, and regaled everyone by describing how she had brought the burglar down with a rugby tackle. She had been laughing in the incident room as she told everyone how she had grabbed him by his hair and discovered that he was in fact wearing a Marc Bolan-style wig. She missed Kath—Jane was the only woman at Hackney, apart from clerical staff. As she left the washroom she noticed that there was a laminated "LADIES TOILET" sign on the door. Smiling, she remembered the notice that Kath had handwritten and pinned to the door, which some of the male officers had then adorned with phallic cartoon drawings. A proper sign would have pleased Kath.

Jane headed down the corridor toward the small B Relief tea kitchen that officers used when the canteen was closed. She had a key to the cupboard for the tea bags and tins of instant coffee, which was kept locked as the contents were always disappearing.

Her head ached and she was hunting for a bottle of aspirin when DC Edwards hurried toward her.

"You'd better get back to the charge room . . . I've got to go and find Sergeant Harris . . . he was supposed to be there ages ago. The guv is getting so fed up he wants to shove a snooker cue up his backside if he doesn't appear soon."

"That's where you'll find him, he's usually in there having a game. If you like I can go and find him?"

"No . . . no . . . it's fine, I'll do it. A couple of uniforms are with the prisoner and he's handcuffed, so he's not going anywhere. But DI Moran has gone walkabout as well."

Edwards ran his fingers through his mop of unruly hair. His arms seemed too long, even for his size. He had always had a disheveled appearance. Sergeant Harris had complained about his untidiness on several occasions and Jane had even over-heard him asking Edwards why his trousers never had a crease in them. The following day poor Edwards had turned up for work with the burnt imprint of an iron on his flared trousers.

Jane continued along the corridor into the B kitchen annex. Unlocking the cupboard she pulled out a bottle of aspirin and filled a glass of water from the tap.

Edwards banged on the door.

"OK, I tracked him down . . . see you in the charge room. Hey . . . I couldn't have a couple of those aspirin, could I? I've got a terrible headache."

Jane handed him a glass of water and watched as he tipped four aspirin into his palm. She noticed that his hand was shaking.

"Are you all right, Brian?"

Edwards swallowed all four tablets in one mouthful and gulped down the rest of the water.

"Yeah, I'm fine . . . It's just that DI Moran makes me nervous. You know it wasn't my fault that bastard got you tonight. He clipped me one . . . I'm sorry you were put through that, Jane."

She gave him a friendly pat on the shoulder as he left and said she would see him in the charge room. She poured a fresh glass of water and took two aspirin, sipping the remains of the water before she rinsed the glass under the hot water and left it on the draining board.

Jane had been alone for a few minutes with the handcuffed prisoner when Sergeant Harris walked in, clearly irritated at being dragged away from his game of snooker.

"Where's Moran? I thought he was in charge of things?"

"He just went out to look for you."

"Well, he obviously didn't look hard enough, did he?" Harris replied sarcastically, sitting behind the charge desk. He took out a large custody sheet from the drawer, clipped it to a board, and removed a pen from his top pocket, as DC Edwards walked in.

"Right, who's the arresting officer and what are the facts?"

At that moment Harris took a second look at Jane, causing him to shake his head in disbelief.

"What on earth do you think you look like, Tennison?"

Jane gave him a cheeky grin. "A prostitute on the game, Sarge. I thought you'd know that . . ."

Edwards laughed but Harris was not amused. DI Moran walked into the room just as Harris chastised Jane for what he felt was as an impudent comment.

"Don't get funny with me, Tennison . . . I've got your final probationer's report to do in the next couple of weeks." He turned to Moran. "Ah, good, you've decided to join us . . ."

"As it happens, Harris, I needed a leak, which is a much more pleasurable experience than talking to you. Now, can we get on with booking the prisoner in?"

Harris grunted but he knew he was pushing his luck with Moran who, although much younger than him, was senior in rank. Harris asked for the facts of the arrest and Moran asked Jane to recount what had happened.

"I was working on attachment with the CID as a decoy in London Fields this evening—"

"I already know that, Tennison. I don't need chapter and verse, just get to the nitty gritty, please."

Harris's mockery was making her feel nervous. "Unseen by me the suspect jumped out of a tree, grabbed me from behind, covered my mouth and fondled my breasts—"

Harris interrupted, while writing on the charge sheet. "So he's been arrested for indecent assault, I take it?"

Moran didn't relish getting into a slanging match with Harris, least of all in front of a prisoner. From his pocket he pulled the plastic bag containing the stocking mask and threw it down onto the desk.

"I think you should know that this scrote wore that mask. It would have scared the shit out of most women, but not WPC Tennison. He elbowed her in the face while trying to escape, and also had this knife in his pocket when I searched him at the scene."

Moran took the flick knife, also in a plastic bag, from his pocket and placed it on the table next to the stocking.

Jane was confused. She had not seen Moran find the knife, and DC Edwards hadn't mentioned it. She glanced toward Edwards with a questioning look, but he was staring at the knife.

"I didn't let Tennison see this at the scene as she was obviously shocked by what happened to her. The attacker threatened to cut her throat if she screamed. Suffice to say, Sergeant Harris, he wasn't trying to drag her to London Fields Lido for a midnight swim! He is also suspected of a number of other sexual assaults and a recent rape."

Jane knew that a teenage girl had been raped about two weeks ago on Hackney's ground, but she had no idea that the indecent assault suspect was believed to be responsible for it.

The handcuffed prisoner, who was standing to one side listening, reacted angrily for the first time since he'd been brought into the station.

"This is bullshit! I never had a knife on me! That officer already searched me before he left the room for a piss . . . This is a fit up!"

The expression on Harris's face was one of pure contempt as he glared at the prisoner before turning to Jane.

"Did he say he had a knife, and did he cause that cut to your lip?"

Jane nodded. Harris stared at the prisoner harder. "What have you got to say for yourself?"

The prisoner took a deep breath as they all waited to hear his reply.

"I was walking through the park minding my own business when she asked me if I wanted sex . . . I told her I wasn't interested, then she started attacking me. She kicked me in the bollocks then hit me round the head with a truncheon—"

Harris interrupted. "In nearly thirty years' service I've heard every lie and excuse in the book from sick perverts like you. For your information WPCs aren't issued with truncheons."

"Well, she had one in her hand! And those two bastards smashed up my face and used me for football practice! I swear before God, I am telling the truth . . . I've been set up!"

Harris told him to shut up and looked at Jane. "Did you have a truncheon, Tennison?"

Jane was now becoming worried about the fact she'd used a truncheon on a suspect and glanced toward DI Moran for support. He raised his hand slightly to calm her.

"I loaned WPC Tennison my truncheon, knowing that she was acting as a decoy in an area where other women had been attacked. It was for her own protection," Moran said quietly.

Harris hesitated, then turned with a cynical smile toward the suspect.

". . . Which was good thinking as this pervert not only assaulted her but he was carrying a knife."

Harris glanced toward Jane. "I take it that, being in fear of your life, you used the truncheon within the law to protect yourself?"

Jane realized he was asking a leading question and hastily agreed that was the case.

"Yes, Sergeant, and then—"

Harris interrupted, leading her again. "You would have aimed for his shoulder, as per the Police Instruction Book, but this was literally a matter of life and death so you realized you had to incapacitate the suspect and hit him on the head as hard as you could, being a female."

Jane smiled. "Yes, Sergeant, that's exactly what happened. And before I hit him on the head I kicked him in the groin and—"

Harris cut her off. "As is standard procedure, I need to inspect the truncheon that was used."

Moran had picked up the truncheon and now pulled it out from his inside jacket pocket. He was about to hand it over but Harris just glanced at it.

"Looks fine to me . . . no blood on it. I take it the rib and facial injuries to the prisoner occurred when he slipped and fell trying to escape, correct?"

Moran and Edwards spoke in unison. "That's correct."

The prisoner, now extremely agitated, tried to interrupt, but Harris pointed a finger at him, making it clear he had better keep his mouth shut. He then asked the prisoner for his name, date of birth and address. The prisoner replied that he was John Allard, born February 20th, 1941, living at 33 Hall Road, East Ham.

Harris was still recording the prisoner's property on the arrest sheet as DI Moran checked his height against the measuring stick. He told the prisoner to remove his clothing, which he bagged up for forensics, and gave him a prisoner issue overalls to wear. As the prisoner undressed, both Harris and Moran noticed how athletic and muscular he was.

"Do a bit of weight training, do you?" Harris asked, and the prisoner replied that he liked to keep fit and work out.

Moran cynically replied, "Yeah, but obviously not enough to escape from a female police officer! I think you're lying because you've been nicked before and are probably wanted. I'll call you Allard for now, but we'll take your fingerprints so we can get them up to the Yard tonight to be checked against criminal records, then no doubt we'll find out who you really are."

"Allard" became increasingly sullen and demanded to speak to a solicitor. Harris refused him a phone call unless he gave his real details, but he insisted he had, so Harris denied the call on the grounds that it might interfere with the course of the investigation.

Harris stood up. "You three go and write up your arrest notes. I'll take the pervert's prints and we'll also have a little chat as to why he shouldn't hit police officers . . . especially female officers."

Harris grabbed the prisoner by the scruff of his neck and literally lifted him off his feet, hauled him toward the fingerprint room and slammed him up against the wall while he opened the door. As Allard cried out, Harris looked over his shoulder at Jane. "The results of the probationer's final exams are in envelopes on the duty desk."

Jane hurried to the duty desk and, finding the envelope with her name on it, tucked it into her pocket and joined Moran and Edwards in the CID office.

Moran handed her a CID pocket book and said that while she was on attachment any arrests, interview notes, etc., were to be recorded in it. Jane felt honored to be given the book. "Thank you, sir," she said.

"You're welcome. It would be best if you write the notes, then myself and Edwards can agree and countersign them from the point where we tackled the suspect. Edwards, help Jane, will you? I'll write up the notes from our perspective in the obo van." He pointed to the kettle in the corner and asked Jane to make him a coffee, then left the room.

As Jane wrote up the arrest notes Edwards said he'd make the coffee. She took the results envelope out of her pocket, placed it on the table and stared at it. When Edwards asked why she wasn't opening it she replied that it wasn't because she thought she had failed, it was more that she was worried about getting a good mark. She decided she would open it when she got back to the section house later.

Edwards snatched the envelope from the table and Jane tried to grab it back, but he held it up high out of her reach. As soon as she backed off slightly he quickly opened the envelope, pulled out the paper inside and unfolded it.

"Bloody hell! You passed with flying colors . . . ninety-four percent! You little nerd—you'll be a sergeant before we know it!"

Despite being annoyed by Edwards's antics, Jane was thrilled with the result. "I've only just about completed my two years' probation, so I don't have enough service to sit the sergeant's exam."

"Anyone with two years' service can apply to sit the exam, but you'll need the recommendation of a senior officer to do it."

"I'm not really interested in uniform promotion at the moment, though. First and foremost I'd like to become a detective."

"Well, your good work tonight will help, that's for sure," Edwards replied, as Moran returned.

"You two should be getting on with your notes, not yapping. When you've finished bring them to me in my office, Tennison, and I'll check them."

With Edwards's assistance it didn't take Jane long to write up the notes on her arrest. Edwards pointed out that although Harris had "led" her through why she used the truncheon it was best, in accordance with the Met instruction book, that she say she aimed for the suspect's elbow, but he suddenly ducked and she unintentionally hit his head.

"Also, don't write anything about the kicks to his ribs or how he got the cut to his face, or the nosebleed. He fell while trying to escape, OK?"

Jane felt a sudden chill. It was as if she was back sitting at home with DCI Bradfield when he had asked her to tell a similar lie after DS Gibbs had assaulted the black drug dealer Terrence O'Duncie during the Julie Ann Collins murder investigation.

"You all right, Jane, you look a bit pale?"

"Yes, fine. I know the score about the injuries . . . I've been down that road before. You know, I didn't actually see a knife in the suspect's hand."

"He told you he had one, so what's the problem?"

"Did you see DI Moran find that knife?"

Edwards frowned.

"No . . . but if he said he found it in the suspect's pocket then that's good enough for me. Hang on, are you suggesting he might have planted evidence?"

Jane could tell he was upset by her insinuation. "No, not at all. If he did actually have a knife on him then I am even more worked up about what could have happened to me. I didn't realize he was suspected of the rape as well . . . I thought it was just indecent assaults."

"There is no strong evidence. The victim had been out celebrating her seventeenth birthday and was attacked from behind on her way home. She didn't see his face, but she did see a flick knife, and the suspect even said he had a knife and told her not to scream. DI Moran's been dealing with it and he wanted to see how the prisoner would react when told he was a suspect . . . It certainly got him fired up, so you never know, Moran might be right."

"Why didn't he mention that he suspected the same person to me before the operation?"

"He told me not to mention it to you as he didn't want to make you worried about being a decoy. In hindsight, after what happened tonight, maybe he should have told you . . . But as I said he's got no evidence the same man committed the rape. It's just an assumption based on some similarities to the indecent assaults."

Jane didn't reply. She read through her notes again and then went to Moran's office and handed him the note book to read. She watched with interest and observed that he had a habit of nodding as he was reading. She hoped it was a sign that he was agreeing with her notes.

He smiled and looked up at her. "Good explanation for the use of a truncheon, but a defense lawyer will accuse you of intentionally aiming for the head. The bit where the suspect said 'I've got a knife . . . so keep your mouth shut, you fucking thieving whore'—is that, and the rest of what he said, word for word?"

"Yes, as far as I can recall, sir."

Moran had a look of contempt in his eyes, but not for Jane. "Nasty piece of work, isn't he? These notes are good, Tennison. Brief, yet concise and covering the relevant points about his attempted escape. You can elaborate further about the operation and how scared you were in your statement . . . but do that tomorrow, as I'm sure you'll want to get off for some shut-eye soon."

"Not really, I still feel wide awake."

"That's the adrenalin still pumping after making such a good arrest," he said, as he countersigned the arrest notes and handed the note book back to Jane.

"You'll need to get Harris to sign them as well, as he's the duty sergeant and he booked in the prisoner. Oh, and the rabbit fur jacket . . . can you leave it on the chair there? It's evidence in a case, so I need to put it back in the property store."

Jane removed the jacket. "Thanks for letting me use it, sir, it kept me warm." She placed it on the chair and left the room.

As she went downstairs to the front office she was surprised to see Sergeant Harris at the duty desk, though he was reading *The Sun* while drinking coffee and puffing away on a pipe. Jane asked him if he would sign her notes and handed him the pocket book.

"Oh, CID notebook now, is it? Uniform IRB not good enough for you now?" he said in a jovial manner that made Jane apprehensive, as it was unusual for him. "Has DI Moran checked and countersigned these?"

"Yes, Sarge, and DC Edwards helped me write them."

"Well, no doubt everything is tight as a duck's arse when it comes to the evidence of arrest." He flicked briefly through the pages, stopping longer to read and take in the bit where Jane was initially attacked and threatened. He looked her in the eye and spoke softly.

"How are you feeling? D'you need to take a couple of days' leave?"

"No thanks, I'm fine, Sarge. Especially now Allard, or whoever he may be, is in a cell and going nowhere."

"Well, that's mainly down to you, young lady. If you hadn't smacked him one he'd probably have got away before the cavalry turned up. So, what was your final exam result?"

"It was good, Sarge . . . I got ninety-four percent."

"Congratulations."

"Thank you, Sarge. Is it right you can sit the sergeant's exam after your probationary period is over?" she asked, because she thought that DC Edwards was wrong.

Harris cocked his head to one side, then gave her a cynical grin.

"Yes, if authorized by the Divisional Commander, who would of course seek the advice and wisdom of an experienced sergeant like me . . . But even if by some miracle you were allowed to sit the exam, and passed, you can't be made sergeant until you have five years' service. Now, even though you have nearly finished your probation you will still be under my supervision and I will be responsible for your Annual Qualification Reports. I think you could say that your future regarding any promotion is in my hands."

In the last year and a half Jane had learned not to let his demeaning attitude annoy her, as that was what he wanted. She wasn't the only person he belittled, it was just his nature. She smiled, refusing to be rattled by his attitude. "I'm not really interested in promotion yet. I'd like to become a detective constable first."

"Listen, Tennison, although your arrest tonight is commendable I doubt you would make the grade yet as you need more uniform experience. Being a decoy for one night is very different from being a detective and investigating major crime."

Jane looked him in the eye. "Will you be putting that in my final report?"

"I need to be frank with you. In my honest opinion, as your reporting sergeant, I feel you might be better suited to something like mounted branch or maybe even being a 'black rat,'" Harris said, referring to what many officers called the traffic police.

Harris handed Jane the fingerprints he'd taken from the suspect and told her to give them to DI Moran. They would need to be passed on to C3 Fingerprint Bureau at the Yard for comparison to prints on record, especially those wanted for crime and outstanding marks at crime scenes, particularly sex crimes.

"D'you intend wearing that wig and looking like a Tom all night? Go and get cleaned up," Harris said, and dismissed her with a wave of his hand.

Jane went to the ladies' locker room and removed the heavy makeup before returning to the CID office. She had been to DI Moran's office with the prints but he wasn't there. Edwards looked up from his paperwork.

"Moran went downstairs to put the rabbit fur jacket back in the property store, and release another prisoner he had in on suspicion of dishonest handling, then he was going home."

Jane held up the set of fingerprints. "Harris said I was to give him these prints so—"

DC Edwards interrupted and explained that Moran had already instructed the night duty SOCO to take the suspect's fingerprints to the Yard. Jane asked if he and DI Moran would be interviewing the suspect in the morning. Edwards replied that Moran had suggested she could sit in on the interview for experience, and he was to take the suspect's clothes and other evidence to the forensic lab. He explained that they might find fibers from the other victims' clothing on them, or vice versa. Jane said it would be a fantastic result if they found anything that linked him to the rape. Edwards said he hoped so too as there was no real evidence to charge him with the rape unless he admitted it.

"I doubt he'll ever do that . . . seems he's going to fight this case all the way, and the only thing we've got on him so far is the attack on me."

"Well, even if it is, Jane, there's no way out for him. Judges detest people who assault police officers so he'll get a long stretch for that alone."

Edwards yawned and said he was going to get some sleep on the armchair in the snooker room, and go straight to the forensics lab first thing in the morning. He suggested to Jane that she should go and get some kip too, as Moran wanted to start interviewing the prisoner at 10 a.m. about the other assaults he was suspected of committing. Jane asked him what time she should come in. Edwards said Moran was an early bird and would probably be in at 8 a.m. to prep for the interview, so Jane said she would be in at 7:30 a.m. As she thanked Edwards for coming to her rescue he asked if she was OK, as it had been a tough night.

"I was pretty shaken up at the time, but I'm fine now."

"Listen, you did a good job. I'd have been shitting myself if I were in your shoes . . . even more so if he'd pulled the knife to my throat."

Jane joked, "He technically had two offensive weapons . . ."

Edwards looked puzzled.

"The knife . . . and his erect penis!"

Edwards laughed.

"You'd make a good detective, Jane . . . Go on, bugger off and get some kip. Don't walk back or you might get arrested as a Tom! Get the night shift to drop you off at the section house."

Jane suddenly realized that she'd forgotten to tell Harris that DI Moran had said she could start her CID attachment as from now. She wished Moran was still there to tell Harris himself. She considered just not telling him, but knew that would probably annoy him even more. She headed back to the desk to find Harris.

Harris frowned at her. "When I said get cleaned up, I meant the clothes as well . . . your attire is totally inappropriate in the station and far too revealing."

Jane turned to leave. She was feeling really tired and certainly not in the mood for any of his caustic remarks.

"Hang on, hang on, Tennison . . . what did you want?"

"It was about my CID attachment, but it doesn't matter now."

"DI Moran spoke with me while I released his other prisoner. I agreed with him about your extended attachment, even though it will leave me one short on late shift for the rest of the week. That was a good arrest and you'll learn a lot assisting Moran with the interview. I don't always see eye to eye with him, but he's a good and respected detective by all accounts. But for Chrissakes don't come in wearing all that ridiculous gear . . . and pull that glittering boob tube thingy up over your tits."

"Thanks, Sarge." Jane smiled, deliberately over-accentuating the action of adjusting her boob tube.

As Edwards had advised, Jane got a ride back to the section house. Once in her bedroom she removed her wig, revealing her own hair plastered to her head. Her eyes stung as she pulled off the false eyelashes. Her split lip was now very swollen on one side, and a vivid dark bruise had spread onto her cheek. She took a long shower, relishing the hot water as there was nobody else using the communal bathroom. She washed her hair and, returning to her room, gently applied some antiseptic cream to the cut on her lip. She was totally exhausted. Looking at her shocking reflection she said to herself, "My God, I look as though I've just done two rounds in a boxing ring."

She hesitated as she recalled Moran's rough treatment of the prisoner, and the way he had controlled the whole situation, including her. He was so different from Bradfield, the only other DCI she'd worked with, who had been a gentle giant. Moran behaved like a street fighter and Jane was unsure if she was impressed by that or not.

It was 2 a.m. by the time she actually got into bed, and she'd have to get up in four hours. Lying curled on her side she found it hard to stop her brain churning over the events of the night.

She went over and over in her mind the sort of questions they might ask the suspect. She realized he would probably deny everything, but knew he would go down for a few years for the attack on her. Despite her bruised face and swollen lip, she had to admit that she had enjoyed the evening's events. The rush of adrenalin made up for the fear of being attacked and she'd liked being part of the team. Now, more than ever, Jane was determined to join the CID.

CHAPTER THREE

Feeling nauseous from lack of sleep Jane went to the canteen and got a strong black coffee and a bacon sandwich, which she carried to the CID office. The office was empty, so she sat at DC Edwards's desk and ate her breakfast.

"That looks good." Glancing up, she saw a dapper-looking DI Moran coming out of his office.

"Oh sorry, sir, I didn't mean to be late on parade."

"You're not . . . I'm early. And we don't have parades in the CID, just nine to five and two to ten shifts, and a rotation of one DS and a DC on a week's night shift. We've had some good news . . . Fingerprint Bureau got a match for the prisoner . . . he's not John Allard, he's Peter Allard, with one previous conviction for ABH in his late teens, in a pub fight. The address on his arrest sheet from back then is just up the road, in Stoke Newington. But his name isn't shown on the current Voters' Register."

"That's good that you got him identified, sir. Maybe he'll tell us where he lives now?"

"I doubt it, there might be evidence at his address that he doesn't want us to find. So that's why I want you to visit the last known address for Peter Allard to see if the current owners knew anything about him, or where he moved to." Moran handed her a bit of paper with Allard's details and his last known address.

"Will that be before or after the interview, sir?"

"Before. If we get something positive then we can use it to put him under pressure. In the meantime, I've got a meeting with DCS Metcalf about Allard's arrest."

Jane didn't want to ask Moran if he was going to tell Metcalf that she had been the arresting officer. She hoped he would as it would help when it came to asking him about joining the CID.

Moran handed Jane the log book and keys for one of the CID cars. "I haven't been given the five-week basic driving course yet, so I'm not authorized to drive police vehicles," she said.

"OK, well, go and see if you can get a lift in a panda car, or go by bus."

Jane hurriedly finished her coffee and went to the comms room to book out a radio and ask about getting a lift to Stoke Newington. There were only two panda cars on patrol, and they were both dealing with incidents, so she caught the bus to Stoke Newington High Street and walked the rest of the way to Kynaston Road, a quiet street lined with terraced houses built after the war. After repeatedly knocking on the door of number 23 and getting no answer, Jane felt it had been a wasted journey. She posted a note through the letterbox for the occupier, giving a phone number, and asking them to contact her at Hackney CID regarding a previous occupant of the premises. Before leaving she decided to see if any of the neighbors were in. An elderly lady answered the door of one of the small terraced houses and, after she had seen her warrant card, invited Jane in.

The narrow hall was lined with cat litter trays. The carpet looked as if it hadn't been vacuumed for years, and was thick with balls of cat fur. Mrs. Walker introduced herself and asked Jane if she liked cats. There was little Jane could say. The pungent smell of cats was overpowering in the hall, but in the living room it was almost suffocating. There were felines perched on every possible surface, even the piano keys.

Jane took out her notebook and perched perilously on the arm of a cat-clawed sofa. Mrs. Walker was standing next to a small, tiled fireplace. On the mantelpiece was an array of cheaply framed photographs of cats.

"Thank you for letting me in, Mrs. Walker. I just have a few questions—nothing serious."

"That's OK, dear, you ask away, and call me Eadie."

"Did you know the Allard family, Mrs. Walker?"

"Eadie . . . Yes, I knew them very well. There was John and Hilda and their children Peter and Cherrie. The daughter had something wrong with her. I used to babysit when they were nippers."

"Do the family still live there?"

"No, they moved out at least twelve, or more, years ago. The parents divorced and sold up . . . I don't know where they went, or where the children moved to."

"Mrs. Wal . . . I mean Eadie, do you know what job Peter did?"

"Oh, he was about eighteen when they left. He was very nice and bought me some flowers when he came to say goodbye. He was such a lovely handsome boy. I was so surprised when he got in a bit of bother for punching a lad in a pub, but his mum and dad said it was in self-defense. He used to do all kinds of different jobs, anything so he could pay his way really. I remember laughing when he was a nipper as I'd ask what he wanted to be when he grew up and he said that he wanted to be a cabbie, like his dad. He loved going out with his dad in the taxi. I think the divorce upset him . . . but that's life for ya, innit?"

"Thank you . . . you've been very helpful."

"That's all right, love. You get to my age an' yer glad of a bit of company. Is Peter in some kind of trouble?"

"No, we just need to trace him about something. Thank you for your time."

Jane left the house and, turning left at the end of the street, called into Stoke Newington Police Station, which was a ten-minute walk away, unaware that the back of her jacket and skirt were covered in cat hairs. She showed her warrant card to a PC at the front counter and asked if she could use a phone to make an urgent call regarding an investigation she was carrying out for DI Moran of Hackney CID. The officer showed her the way to the PCs' writing room and said she could use the phone in there. Jane called the Public Carriage Office at Penton Street, Islington and asked if they had a licensed cab driver under the name of Peter Allard. The lady at the cab office replied that she was very busy, but would do her best to look in their card index within the next hour. Jane gave her the phone number of the comms room at Hackney and asked her to leave the details with them.

Jane then spoke to Hackney and explained that she was expecting an important call from the Public Carriage Office and asked if they could radio the result straight through to her when it came. Satisfied that she'd covered all bases, she thanked the PC at the front counter and caught the bus back to Hackney, but rather than going straight to the station she decided to return to the scene where she had been attacked, as she wanted to have a proper look at it in daylight.

It was hard to get a clear view from the spot where Allard pounced on her, because of the trees. But from what she could see there were no black cabs parked up in London Fields' east or west side. Jane decided to walk down Martello Street, following the path of the main railway line above it, as it had quiet side roads that ran underneath the arches.

As she turned left into Lamb Lane Jane noticed a black cab parked up by the junction with Mentmore Terrace. She stopped to take a closer look and jotted down the license number on the rear of the cab. As she was doing so a man dressed in greasy overalls, carrying a wrench, approached her.

"Is there a problem?"

"No, I'm just checking something . . . is this your cab?"

"Why do you want to know?" he asked, with an inquisitive stare.

Jane had totally forgotten she was in plain clothes and quickly took her warrant card out to show the man.

"I'm a mechanic at the garage. This cab is one we're repairing," he explained politely, pointing to the large dent and scratches above the rear offside wheel arch.

It transpired that around the corner in Mentmore Terrace, out of Jane's view, there was a cab repair garage with a number of taxis parked up that were booked in for mechanical or body-work repairs. Wondering if any of the parked up cabs weren't there to be repaired Jane asked if the mechanic had a record of which cabs he was working on. The mechanic led her into the office and handed her a list attached to a clipboard. The list had the black cab license numbers of all the vehicles that were being booked in at the garage. Jane began checking the cabs in the road until she discovered one that was not on the list.

With a mounting sense of excitement, Jane radioed through to the station. The information she was waiting for had been received but the comms operator had been busy and had for-gotten to contact her. According to records at the PCO a Peter Allard was a registered cab driver and his license number was 7614, with an address in Walthamstow. Jane told the comms officer that the license number matched a cab she was looking at and that the owner, Peter Allard, was currently in custody at Hackney.

"Allard had a car key on him which was put in the prisoner's property locker in the charge room. Can you get the key booked out and brought down to me so I can see if it fits the cab, and inform DI Moran? Over."

"I'll get DI Moran's approval first. He may want to send a driver down with the key to bring the suspect vehicle to the station yard."

Jane waited anxiously, pacing the pavement next to the parked cab, but it wasn't long before the reply came that DI Moran wanted the vehicle brought to the station for exam-ination by a SOCO. The comms officer told her that as soon as the area car driver had finished the call he was on he'd collect Allard's car key and be with her as quickly as he could.

Jane kept checking her watch every five minutes. Nearly half an hour had passed and she was anxious to get back to the station, fearing that DI Moran may start interviewing Peter Allard with another detective. Eventually an officer arrived. The key fitted and he towed the cab to Hackney while Jane was driven back to the station in a patrol car. She hurried to the CID office and brought Moran up to speed with the latest developments.

"Bloody good work, Tennison. Job well done ... but I should have been informed about the developments as soon as you spoke with the Allards' old neighbor." He paused. "I'm not sure if you realize, but you've got cat hairs all over the back of your suit ..."

"Sorry, sir." Jane brushed self-consciously at the fluff covering her skirt.

Having just returned from the lab DC Edwards joined them and reported that Paul Lawrence, the lab liaison sergeant, would let Moran know as soon as they got any positive results.

"He's the best lab sergeant in the force. Brilliant eye for detail, so we're lucky to have him working on this for us," Moran said as he walked out.

Jane nodded in agreement. "DCI Bradfield said the same thing about him." The recollection of Bradfield filled her with momentary pain.

Edwards sensed her reaction and patted Jane's shoulder gently, which she acknowledged with a small smile.

"It's been hard to adjust to working alongside someone like Moran ... he's very different. He doesn't play rugby ... we all used to be in the police rugby team and have a few jars afterward, and a laugh. Have you seen Spencer Gibbs at all?"

Jane shook her head.

"No, I haven't."

"For the first few months after it happened the station was so quiet . . . Nobody wanted to talk about it. Gibbs used to be singing in the showers all the time, and playing with his rock band . . . I've phoned him a few times, and written to him, but I've had nothing back."

"I remember you emulating him, the way you used to slap the suspects around."

"Yeah . . . yeah . . . Gibbs was a bit of a naughty boy, but he was a good cop. It's not the done thing now. I leave that to the boss."

Moran walked back in.

"Leave what to the boss, Edwards?"

"Er, to get the forensic results from DS Lawrence, sir."

"Bollocks to that. You two, get SOCO and go over that cab with a fine tooth comb. While you're doing that I'm going to type up a search warrant for the suspect's address, and I want you, Edwards, to take it to the magistrate for approval and signature."

"Sorry, guv . . . Do you want me to do the cab over, or go to the magistrate?"

"For Chrissakes, Brian, get on and do both of them!"

The cab at the station yard was as clean as a whistle inside, but they found a fresh shirt and jeans in a plastic bag on the back seat. Underneath the driver's seat was a cabbie's cash bag with money in it, and in the glove compartment was a wallet containing money and a photograph of two young children with a pretty, dark-haired oriental woman. There was also a set of house keys and a cab driver's green badge, with a license number on it that matched the one they had been given by the PCO for Peter Allard. Jane and Edwards left the SOCO to take fiber tapings from the driver's seat, although he said that he didn't hold out much hope as the vehicle had obviously been carefully cleaned.

On their return to the station they updated Moran and showed him what they had recovered from the cab. Moran suspected that Allard had probably been using the cab as a cover to travel to and from the scenes of his attacks, on the basis that police officers rarely stop black cabs. He decided that he wanted to interview Allard before they visited his home address, which they now knew was 45 Grove Road, Walthamstow. Jane asked Moran if he thought the suspect would keep silent as he knew none of the victims could identify him because he wore a stocking mask.

"Admittedly with the others there is only circumstantial evidence due to the similarity in the attacks . . . but now I've got some leverage on him."

"What leverage, sir?" Jane asked.

"You'll find out during the interview, darlin' . . . so let's get cracking."

Jane and DC Edwards went down the stone-flagged corridor to the basement level where the cells were situated. The duty officer unlocked Allard's cell. Allard seemed very depressed and was unable to make eye contact, especially with Jane. As he held his wrists out to the duty officer to be handcuffed he turned and, for the first time, looked directly at Jane. He spoke softly.

"I am so sorry for what I did . . . I feel very ashamed . . ."

Surprised, Jane nodded. Edwards led Allard out of his cell, along the corridor and up the narrow concrete steps to DI Moran's office on the first floor.

Moran got straight to the point and asked Allard if he was responsible for the recent spate of indecent assaults in London Fields and Victoria Park. Allard remained head bowed and flatly denied involvement in any assaults of any kind, even the one on "her," he stated, pointing to Jane. He claimed that he heard the detectives saying at the time that they didn't see what had happened between him and the woman because their view was blocked by the trees.

Jane couldn't believe what she was hearing. Allard had just apologized to her, and now here he was shamefacedly denying it to Moran. She watched, incredulous, as he insisted that Jane was lying.

Allard stated that the male detectives believed her lie, and that they had planted a knife on him. Moran sat back and stared into Allard's dark, angry eyes.

"Come on, we both know you're lying, John. Oh sorry, forgive me . . . I mean Peter . . . It is Peter Allard I'm speaking to, isn't it?"

The use of his proper name caused a visible nervous twitch in Allard's face. Moran leaned across the table.

"Bet you're wondering what else we know about you, Peter?"

Allard shook his head and stupidly denied that was his name. Moran laughed.

"Peter, you're digging a bigger hole for yourself—your prints have been matched to a set held at the Yard from your previous arrest for ABH during a pub fight. You hit a young woman, didn't you?"

Allard once again demanded a phone call. Moran casually remarked that he wasn't allowed to call anyone until he admitted his true identity and told them where he lived. Then he could call whoever he liked. Allard looked worried as Moran pulled the green license tag from his pocket and started to swing it like a pendulum in front of Allard.

"We found this in a black cab that was parked up by London Fields, which is currently being forensically examined in our yard. This tag, and the license number on the cab, are both registered to you."

Allard hung his head. Moran pressed on.

"WPC Tennison here, who you state is a liar, did a little digging . . . she even went to your old home address and spoke to a neighbor who remembered you, as well as your dad, who was also a cab driver. WPC Tennison checked with the Public Carriage Office and obtained your home address in Walthamstow. Take a look at this photograph, Peter . . . nice-looking woman and two kids . . . look at it. Chinese, is she?"

Allard pressed back in his chair.

"What . . . you married to a slitty eyed chinky woman, are you?"

Allard was now shaking. "I'm not married, I don't have kids, and my name is *John*."

Moran slapped the desk hard with the flat of his hand. "Start telling the truth . . . the more you lie, the worse it gets. There's no way out for the attack on WPC Tennison—you'll be going to prison."

Allard said nothing. Moran swung around in his chair, then rocked back and forth for a moment before continuing.

"You gave a false name because you needed time to think about what you were going to tell your chinky girlfriend. In fact, the reason you asked to make a phone call, before we found out who you really were, was not to contact a solicitor but to call your chinky woman with a fabricated story."

"She's not Chinese . . . ! She's Filipino!"

"Ahhhh, Filipino eh? Are these two kids yours?"

"Yes . . . And her name is Marie. I want to tell her the truth before you bastards lie about me to her. She'll know I've been fitted up!"

"Fitted up? Look what you did to WPC Tennison's face!" Moran exclaimed, pointing to Jane.

She stared toward Allard as he lowered his head. His fists were clenched and Jane could feel the animosity and rage in him as he fought to maintain control.

"At last we get the revelation that Marie is your wife, and you are obviously Peter Allard? Well, for me it's all a bit late in the day . . . you've lied to me, Peter. So, when we execute our search warrant at your home WPC Tennison will be telling your wife that you are a pervert, and that you attacked her and split her lip. Then there's all the other defenseless women whose lives are in a mess because of what you did to them."

Allard started to open and close his tight balled fists and tilted his head sideways to look toward Jane. He stared at her, his eyes shifting as if unable to recognize her as the woman he had assaulted.

"You can deny everything at the Old Bailey if you want, but no jury in the world will believe you over us. If you're found guilty you will go down for a long time, but for how long is in your hands. Admitting all the indecent assault offenses will be a plus for you in the judge's eyes, and I'll even put in a good word about how you helped us before he sentences you."

"I keep telling you, I've got nothing to admit to—"

Moran pushed the picture of Marie and the children closer to Allard.

"Take a good look at your children, because you won't be seeing them for a long time . . . probably not even after you're eventually released. Not once your wife sees you for the pervert that you really are. But, if you admit all your crimes I may not have to tell her every sickening detail about what you did. I might even let her visit you in the cells . . ."

There was a long pause. Moran glanced toward Jane who was making copious notes. He picked up the photograph and tapped the desk with the edge of it, waiting. Eventually Allard sighed and slowly looked up.

"This is the God's honest truth. I used my dad's first name cos he'd passed away and had never been in any trouble. The ABH on the woman in the pub was years ago, and I only pushed her but she fell and cut her head on a table. Marie doesn't know about it, and I didn't want her to be hurt by the police lies about the ABH, like my parents were. I never did anything wrong . . . I've been stitched up, and you can't make me admit to something that I haven't done."

"Tell me what a cab driver was doing up a tree in London Fields in the middle of the night?"

Allard pointed to Jane. "She made that up . . . you even said yourself that she didn't see me. I felt ill, so I parked my cab and went for a walk. She approached me and asked if I wanted sex. She started screaming and then you lot turned up and kicked the shit out of me, for nothing."

"Fine, you keep on lying . . . but your clothing and the stocking mask have gone to forensics and will be checked to see if any of the fibers on them match those recovered from the clothing of the other indecent assault victims . . . and the young girl who was raped."

"I want to make a phone call, I want to speak with a solicitor!" Allard's voice was raw and edgy.

Annoyed that Allard wouldn't break, Moran ordered him to be taken back down to the cells. Two uniform officers came to escort him, and as he walked out he turned and stared at Jane.

"Why are you doing this to me? Why are you lying?" Allard had a pitiful expression on his face, as his dark eyes held hers for a moment, then he turned away as he was escorted out of Moran's office. Jane asked if she really was going to be the one to tell Allard's wife what happened. Moran sighed and said that if Allard had confessed she would have been, but as he hadn't been broken yet, Moran would tell Allard's wife and when she had a meltdown Jane could talk to her while they searched the house. He also remarked that he wouldn't be surprised if the wife had been knocked about and, as so often happens in domestic violence cases, she was probably too scared to report it and was in self-denial.

Jane wondered why, during the interview, Moran never asked Allard any direct questions about the rape of the teenage girl. She approached the question from a more discreet angle.

"If you'll be questioning Allard in more detail about the rape, sir, could I sit in again?"

"We'll see. I was hoping he'd confess to the indecent assaults, then I could use the similar facts in each case to press him further about the rape, and maybe even charge him with it. Though it would be a bit of a wing and a prayer if it got to trial."

Moran instructed Jane to type up the report of the interview, after which she was to accompany him and Edwards on the search of Allard's home.

CHAPTER FOUR

Jane struck the typewriter keys angrily as she typed up her report recording Allard's refusal to admit his assault against her. Her stomach rumbled as she hadn't had time for lunch, and the lack of sleep the previous night was catching up with her, but as she detailed Allard's accusation that she was the one lying, she didn't feel so tired anymore. Instead she couldn't wait to go on the search to his house and prove he was guilty of the crimes he wouldn't admit. Jane stood up and was just rolling the report out of the typewriter when DI Moran and DC Edwards stopped by the incident room. Moran gestured to her.

"Get your coat, Tennison, we've got a search warrant for Allard's house. That's the good news. The bad news is that it's quite a trek to bloody Walthamstow."

Before Jane could reply Moran and Edwards had continued down the corridor. Jane looked longingly at the sandwich and cup of coffee on her desk. She was ravenous, so she grabbed the sandwich in one hand, and her hat and coat in the other. As Harris passed the doorway, he looked in.

"You'd better not think about eating that in the patrol car, Tennison . . ."

Jane sighed and hurriedly took a few large bites of her sandwich before putting the remainder of it back on the plate on her desk, and rushing out to the yard to join Moran and Edwards.

The Allards' home in Walthamstow was a three-bedroom semi-detached house. It had a rather neglected front garden, which appeared to be the norm in that street. Moran parked the car and got out, followed by Jane, Edwards and the SOCO. Moran banged on the front door, which was answered by a petite, attractive Asian woman.

"I'm DI Moran, are you Marie Allard?"

"Yes, I am." The woman looked frightened. "Oh my God! Has something happened to Peter? He not come home and I been worried sick . . ."

Moran interrupted, saying that her husband had been arrested and that he had a warrant to search the premises. He handed her a copy of the warrant as he pushed the door open and walked in, followed by the three others.

The inside of the premises was well kept, with the usual children's toys scattered about. The hall had parquet flooring, with a floral printed runner that continued up the stairs. The banisters were painted white and large framed pictures of the Allard children hung on the white walls. The children, aged eight and five, were out in the garden playing with an older woman. Marie pointed to the living room and asked them to go in. Moran went first, followed by Jane. Edwards and the SOCO remained in the hall. The room had a distinct oriental influence, with bamboo furniture, various fake potted plants, and a print of Vladimir Tretchikoff's "Chinese Girl." There was a pale green rug, and on the windowsill in the corner was a gaudy statue of the Virgin Mary standing next to a cheap vase containing a velvet rose. Moran asked Marie to sit down.

He didn't waste time and explained that her husband had been arrested for a number of sexual assaults and rape. Marie couldn't believe what she was hearing, shaking her head in disbelief.

"Do you understand English, Mrs. Allard? You're Filipino, aren't you?"

Marie looked affronted at Moran's questions and replied curtly.

"Yes, course I understand you . . . I already spoken to you. I just in shock. My husband is gentle man and never hurt me or my children."

Moran pointed to Jane and told Marie that her "gentle" husband had attacked and molested WPC Tennison, threatened to cut her throat with a knife and punched her in the face. Marie looked shocked. She couldn't believe what she was hearing and kept repeating, "No . . . you wrong, you wrong . . . it not true." Moran continued and told her that if he hadn't been stopped he would have raped WPC Tennison as, it was suspected, he had done on a previous occasion to a teenage girl.

Marie was shaking uncontrollably. Her dark curly hair had a low fringe and she kept touching her forehead and tugging at a stray curl. She looked at Jane, her eyes welling up with tears, as if wanting her to say it wasn't true.

Jane was surprised by Moran's directness toward Marie. It was as if he'd had enough of being messed around by Peter Allard and was determined to get to the truth, by whatever means necessary.

Jane touched her cut lip and spoke softly. "It is true, Mrs. Allard. He did this to me, and he had a knife in his possession. I believed at the time that he would have raped me, but for my colleagues' intervention."

Marie was clearly in a state of shock and started to cry. At that moment the children rushed in, stopping when they saw their mother. Marie tried to smile and assured them that she was fine and had just had a bit of bad news.

"I'm sorry, children, come here." Hilda Allard followed the children into the room. Seeing Marie's distress she, like her daughter-in-law, immediately thought something had happened to her son, Peter. Moran was as blunt with her as he had been with Marie. He explained that he would need to search the house, including the children's bedroom, and it would be best if their gran took them out for a walk. Hilda flatly refused and insisted that she wanted to be with her daughter-in-law. She was quite overweight with tight permed gray hair and big raw hands.

Marie was struggling to control her emotions, but took a deep breath and turned to her mother-in-law.

"It OK, Hilda, I be OK . . . Maybe it best if you take children to your place, and I call you later."

Hilda was hesitant but eventually agreed. After removing her apron and collecting her handbag she left the house with the children. Moran waited until the front door closed behind them before asking Marie, in a softer tone than before, if her husband had ever abused her. Marie shook her head, her wide dark eyes blinking rapidly.

"No! Never! We been married for ten years . . ." Moran sat beside Marie and kept his voice quiet.

"Is it all right if I call you Marie?" She nodded and he continued.

"Women who are abused, or frightened of their husbands, are often in denial and say nothing because of fear of further violence. Your husband committed a violent sexual assault last night, and similarly other assaults he is suspected of, as well as a rape. These were all committed late in the evening, between ten and midnight. Were you never concerned about what Peter was doing out late at night?"

"He drive a cab and always work evening shifts, some time until early hours. Then he can be with the children in the day. I only worried this morning when he not come home."

Moran glanced at Jane and, turning back to Marie, asked if she had a normal, healthy, sexual relationship with her husband. Marie looked offended and shook her head.

"My sex life not to do with you."

Moran shrugged his shoulders. "Well, it can't have been that great if he had to go out and attack other women."

Marie became tight lipped and continued to tug at her hair, winding the strands through her fingers in an almost obsessive manner. Moran got up from the sofa, walked over to Jane and stood with his back to Marie. Leaning forward, in a hushed voice, he said to her, "I think she's hiding something . . . I want you to stay with her and see if you can get her to open up. I'll go and search upstairs with Edwards and the SOCO."

"Yes, sir."

She felt that Moran had been a bit harsh on Marie as she may have been totally unaware of what her husband was like outside his home life. It seemed unlikely to Jane, by the state Marie was in, that she would deliberately portray a loving family façade to protect her husband. When the others had left the room Jane sat down beside her, saying softly that the news must be an awful shock for her and asking if she would like a cup of tea or coffee. Marie shook her head, and without looking at Jane asked if her husband really had attacked her.

Jane hesitated before answering.

"Yes, he did . . . but my split lip happened while he was trying to escape, so it may have been accidental . . ."

"I can't believe it! He never been violent toward me . . . never in all our time together. We've known each other since we were teenagers."

"So are you saying that your husband has never hit you?"

"Never! I keep telling you, he is very gentle, kind, man. And he take care of us, here in our nice house."

"Do you own this house?"

"No, we rent it. We been here five years. Before that we had very nice house in Maidstone."

"I'm so sorry but I need to ask you some embarrassing questions about your sex life."

Marie began to frantically twist the curl on her forehead between her fingers. Without looking at Jane she asked if their discussion was confidential and just between the two of them.

"Yes, Marie, it is completely confidential."

Jane felt bad knowing that she would later have to report whatever Marie told her to DI Moran.

Marie took a deep breath, stopped nervously twisting her hair and looked at Jane.

"He always been gentle in bed, and even though we not have sex recently, he never been pushy or forced himself on me. He would never do that . . . he always very thoughtful, even now when . . ." She stopped and Jane sensed she was holding back about something.

"What did you mean when you said you hadn't had sex recently?" Jane asked gently.

Marie continued, saying that it had been about six months. She had an ovarian cyst, which made sex very painful, and she was waiting for an operation on the NHS.

Jane sympathized.

"I am so sorry, Marie. I had an aunt with the same problem, and I remember she said it was extremely painful. So if you couldn't have sexual intercourse in the normal way, did you try any other methods?"

Marie blushed and bowed her head, deeply embarrassed as she continued explaining that although they couldn't have full sex she regularly pleasured her husband with masturbation and oral sex.

"He want me to try anal sex but it hurt too much, so he stopped and he never ask again. You see what I mean about him being kind and gentle?"

"And you were never suspicious when he was out late at night?"

"No, never. He sometimes call me three or four times to make sure I am OK."

"Thank you for your honesty, Marie."

Marie seemed relieved to have discussed such personal matters, and was calmer now. "Please, tell me what my husband has done? I can't believe it."

"I'm afraid I can't go into the details of the investigation."

"Please . . . I need to know, to try and make sense . . . Why you here? Why you searching my home?"

"All I can tell you, Marie, is that your husband is adamant he didn't commit any indecent assaults or rape . . . but he did attack me."

Marie looked perplexed. "If he didn't do them, then why he attack you?"

"I don't know . . . only he can answer that. You need to ask him yourself, Marie. They might let you speak to him if you visit the station later. Here's my contact information at the station—please call me if you have any questions or want to tell me anything else."

Jane scribbled her details onto a clean page in her notebook, which she then tore out and gave to Marie.

As Marie put the folded note into her pocket DI Moran walked back into the room. "We've searched yours and the children's bedrooms, but why is the third bedroom locked?"

"My husband uses it as a gym, he didn't want the children going there and hurting themselves on the equipment."

"Do you have the key?"

"I don't know where he keeps it."

"Isn't that a bit strange? That your husband wouldn't tell you where the key was?"

"I don't know, not really." Marie shrugged.

Moran looked at her hard, then left the room to go back upstairs.

Jane noticed that Marie had become very tense, her hands clenched at her side. Suddenly there was a loud crashing sound from upstairs as the officers kicked open the locked door. Marie was on her feet in an instant, running up the stairs and shouting at them to stop ruining her house. Jane followed to try to calm her down. The bedroom door had partially come away from its hinges and the lock lay on the floor among splinters of wood.

Inside the small room was a five-foot-high thick wooden pole with bits of rounded twelve-inch wooden handles sticking out of it. Two rectangular leather bags of sand were screwed into the wall and hanging above them was a collection of martial arts swords, and two wooden sticks connected at one end by a short chain. On another wall were pictures of Bruce Lee and other martial arts posters from the film *Enter the Dragon*.

DC Edwards was looking around the room.

"What the fuck is all this?" He pointed to the wooden figure in the middle of the room.

The SOCO grinned. "That's a Wing Chun dummy, for practicing martial arts. Some of the indentation marks on it are from a knife. The wooden things on a chain are nunchucks, and the sand bags are for karate punching."

Moran and Edwards looked at each other, bemused.

"You into all this martial arts crap then?" Moran asked.

The SOCO shrugged. "Not really . . . I just like watching martial arts films. If your man uses this sort of gear a lot, then his hands and feet are lethal weapons."

Moran looked at Marie who was hovering in the doorway.

"Does he spend much time in here?"

She nodded, saying that her husband practiced martial arts and used the equipment regularly.

"He a keep fit fanatic, and he not even drink."

Moran looked inside the wardrobe. There was a small travel suitcase on a shelf. He pulled it down and found that it was locked. He turned to Marie.

"I don't suppose you know where the key to this is either?"

Before she could answer he grabbed one of the large knives from the wall and cut the material on top of the case open, ripping it back to expose the contents.

Inside the travel case were a number of pornographic magazines, together with a clear plastic bag containing a quantity of pills. Concealed in the middle of the magazines were two folding pocket knives. Moran hadn't seen this type of knife before, and looked at Edwards while he held them up. The SOCO interjected.

"They're called balisongs, guv, originating from the Philippines and used in martial arts. I'd guess the pills are steroids of some sort. They're not illegal, though, a lot of body builders use them and—"

Moran interrupted him. "Yes, I know what steroids are, thank you . . . they also affect a man's sex drive and make them violent. All makes sense as far as our suspect is concerned."

Edwards picked up one of the magazines and flicked through it, hastily dropping it back in the case.

"Ugh, some of the pages are stuck together!"

Moran had seen enough and instructed the SOCO to bag up the weapons and suitcase with its contents as evidence. He looked at Jane and, not caring that Marie was still within earshot, asked about their discussion about her sex life. Marie looked forlornly at Jane, hoping that she wouldn't reveal details about the private conversation they'd had. Moran had put Jane on the spot, and she hesitated, looking at Marie as he became impatient for an answer.

"Come on, out with it!" Jane tapped Moran's elbow.

"Sir, could I possibly have a word with you in private?"

"What?"

"Marie is incredibly shy, but she has admitted that they have been unable to have sexual intercourse for some time."

Moran looked quizzically at Jane.

"For Chrissakes, Tennison! She's going to be cross-examined in court if she gives evidence for the defense. If she can't tell me about it, you tell me."

Jane looked at Marie regretfully, sad that she was having to breach her confidence so openly.

She went on to tell Moran about Marie's ovarian cyst, how she pleasured her husband, and that he'd asked her for anal sex. Moran gestured toward one of the hardcore magazines entitled *Anal Pleasures* and, holding it up sarcastically, said that it was obvious where her husband got that idea from. An embarrassed and tearful Marie looked at Jane with disgust, saying that if they'd finished searching they could get out of her house. By now Moran had really lost his patience and held up more of the magazines in front of her.

"You see the sort of filth that your husband likes to look at and wank over, Mrs. Allard . . . just because you can't satisfy him? He takes these pills and gets so worked up he prowls the streets in a mask then molests and rapes defenseless young women. I find it hard to believe you didn't suspect something was wrong."

Marie began sobbing and demanded that they get out of the house.

"I not want you here anymore . . . You bad people . . . You been in my children's bedroom."

In the car Moran was jubilant at what they had uncovered. Although circumstantial, the porn magazines and the steroid pills were all good enough evidence to show Allard's state of mind and propensity to commit sexual assaults. Jane was quiet and Moran asked her what the problem was.

"I'm sorry but I just felt for Mrs. Allard. In effect she is an innocent victim. I mean, maybe at one time her husband was a good man."

"Grow up! That's utter bollocks! There have probably been more sexual assaults carried out by him in and around London that we don't know about. Indecent assault wasn't enough for him so he went on to rape, and if we hadn't caught him when we did there would have been more rapes and probably a murder committed by him as well. Mrs. Allard's state of mind is not your problem. Her husband brought this on himself and if she at any point suspected something was amiss she should have told someone. Like that tough-looking mother-in-law . . . judging by the size of her hands I wouldn't be surprised if she could give someone a walloping."

It was nearly 4 p.m. when they returned to the station.

"You both head up to the canteen and get something to eat while you write up your notes. I'll join you after I've booked in the property we seized from Allard's house," DI Moran instructed DC Edwards and Jane.

Sergeant Harris was at his desk in the front office and on seeing Moran he mentioned, "Allard has been asking to speak with a solicitor."

"I want to do a further interview first, before getting a solicitor involved," Moran replied as they walked together through to the charge room.

"But now we know Allard's identity and address he should legally be allowed to consult with a solicitor," Harris pushed.

"I know the rules, Sergeant Harris, but with the evidence I found at Allard's house, and what his wife told us, I reckon I can get him to confess to all the indecent assaults . . . and the rape. A solicitor is just going to tell him to say nothing."

"I'll stick my neck out if you think you can get him to roll over. I'll mark up on his sheet that he hasn't requested a solicitor. He's allowed one phone call so let me tell him that after the search of his house his wife was in a hell of a state and he should phone her. You never know, it might work in your favor and get him to finally tell the truth."

Moran was on a high so he told Harris to go ahead, as after what he'd said to Allard's wife she probably thought her precious husband was now the scum of the earth. He also hoped that her emotional distress would make Allard feel at his lowest ebb, and that would make it easier to break him during an interview.

Moran put the small traveling case down on the charge room table, opened it up and showed Harris the pornographic magazines, balisong knives and the tablets. Harris picked up a magazine and flicked through it, pausing here and there to take a good look. Moran asked Harris if he'd mind listing the property as he wanted to get some food in his stomach before the second interview with Allard. Harris nodded and asked how Tennison was. Moran shrugged.

"She needs to toughen up a bit."

Surprised by Moran's comment Harris remarked, "Jane must have thought she was going to be raped, though."

"No, not about that . . . she was terrific last night. But her attitude with Mrs. Allard . . . she was a bit soft and kind of pussy-footed around with the woman. I think she needs to be tougher in those kind of situations and not get emotionally involved."

"You know Tennison has expressed an interest in joining the CID, but I don't think she's ready for it yet. What do you think?" Harris asked.

"In some ways I agree. She's obviously not afraid of the rough end of the job, but investigative-wise she's got a lot to learn yet, which could make her a liability in certain situations."

Harris didn't need to say anything. He knew what Moran meant by "certain situations" and finding missing evidence if and when necessary. Moran went up to the canteen, leaving Harris checking over the items from the suitcase. It was quite a lengthy process as he was spending time studying the porno magazines, and paying even more attention to the fitness and body building magazines.

DS Lawrence had called from the lab to say that they had found fibers from the suspect's clothes on two of the indecent assault victims, but nothing, as yet, connecting him to the rape. Moran, accompanied by Jane, got ready to re-interview Allard. Harris informed them that Allard had phoned his wife and had spoken with her for at least ten minutes, and appeared to be quite distressed both during and after the call. Harris had tried to listen in but it was difficult as he was booking in a noisy drunk who kept singing "Underneath the Arches" at the top of his voice. However, Harris said that he thought Allard may have confessed to his wife, and most surprisingly he hadn't asked for a solicitor after the call.

Moran booked out the property seized from the martial arts room for the interview. A clearly subdued Allard was brought up from the cells and taken to Moran's office.

Moran opened the interview by getting right to the point. "Have you changed your mind and decided to finally tell the truth and admit these assaults?"

"Why were you so horrible to my wife?"

"You've no one but yourself to blame for this situation. If you had admitted the offenses before we went to your house then things may have been different," Moran calmly responded.

The suitcase was then placed on the desk in front of Allard.

"Do the porn magazines and the two martial arts knives belong to you?"

"Yeah. I like to keep fit by training at Wing Chun. I use the balisong knives and nunchucks on the wooden dummy I have in the spare room."

Moran glanced at Jane as she made notes.

"Thing is, Peter, that doesn't explain the hardcore porn magazines," Moran said in an amiable way, which surprised Jane after his approach and attitude in the first interview and at the house during the search.

"I bought them from a sex shop in Soho."

"For masturbating?"

Allard looked embarrassed and said nothing.

"OK, Peter, I understand that you're embarrassed, but I'll take that as a 'yes.' What can you tell me about these pills . . . are they steroids?"

Allard nodded.

"Tell me, did you feel an even greater sexual urge when you took them, as opposed to looking at the porn?"

"I took them because they helped me train longer and harder, and gave me greater muscle definition, all right? It's not illegal to buy them."

"Maybe not, but we know about the problems with your sex life at home. Listen, Peter, I can understand how frustrated you must have felt . . . all pent up and in need of sex . . . it must have really pissed you off not getting sex from your wife?"

Allard tightened his lips, clenched his teeth and took a deep breath.

"None of this is her fault, none of it. She didn't know what I was doing and just thought I was out working nights in the cab."

"Did you tell her what you'd done when you called her on the phone earlier?"

Allard slowly lowered his head, then replied that his wife had told him to tell the truth.

Moran nodded. "She's right, Peter, because it will be better for you in the long run. So take your time and go slowly . . . WPC Tennison will be writing down your confessions."

Allard kept his head lowered, eyes to the ground, as he explained that he had tried to cope with his wife being unable to have full sex with him. He even appeared to be embarrassed when he said that they had found ways round it.

Moran tapped the desk. "I know—she told us she'd give you a hand or a blow job instead . . . but I'm more interested in the women you forced yourself on."

Jane saw Allard tighten his hands into fists. He appeared sickened at the way Moran had spoken about his wife, and Jane watched with interest as Allard took deep breaths to calm himself down, breathing in through his nose and holding it before releasing it through his mouth with a slight hissing sound.

"OK . . . it started because I wanted to stop the feeling of anger . . . my frustration . . . understand? I paid prostitutes for sex in the back of the cab. Anyway, one night this tart ripped me off by snatching my money bag and running off. You know, I honest to God despised myself for what I was doing, but this slag angered me so much. I mean, she got away with a whole day's takings, and I'd done two runs to Heathrow Airport. So I decided I'd take what I wanted from prostitutes without paying, as they would be unlikely to tell the police. I would park my cab near known prostitute haunts, dress up in dark clothes and watch them. When one walked away from a group, or her pimp, I reckoned she was probably going home and I would follow. I'd put on the stocking mask, grab them from behind and feel their tits while I touched my dick."

"It turned you on and you masturbated."

Allard nodded and Moran looked over at Jane to see if she was keeping up with taking down the details. She continued writing for a moment before giving him a small nod to continue. Moran leaned back in his chair. He spoke in a very matter-of-fact tone.

"Well, Peter, seems you underestimated the two prostitutes who came forward to report you. And two of your other victims were not on the game, they were just young women innocently walking home after an enjoyable night out or, as in the case of your arrest, a WPC acting as a decoy. You following me, Peter? Because, apart from WPC Tennison, you have destroyed those women's lives and they're now afraid to leave their homes."

Allard looked shocked and tried to explain that from the way they were dressed he thought that they were all prostitutes.

"Well, you were wrong. So how about you start helping me out by giving me full details of your attacks? That means I need you to describe the victims and where and when the attacks occurred."

Allard started talking. It transpired that there had been two other attacks the police didn't even know about. Moran tapped the desk with his pencil as if mulling over everything he had just heard.

"OK, I notice that you haven't admitted exactly what you did to these women."

Allard shook his head. He took another long deep breath before he said quietly that he felt ashamed and found the details difficult to talk about.

Moran leaned closer to Allard. "OK, Peter, I can understand you have feelings of guilt, who wouldn't, but see how much better you feel after telling the truth about what you did?"

Allard nodded.

"And I can also understand that it must be even harder for you to admit to rape. I took a statement from the young victim . . . it was harrowing, even for me, so don't make her relive the whole thing in court. Tell me the truth . . . tell me exactly what happened, in your own words."

Allard looked Moran in the eye then slowly turned to face Jane. For the first time she noticed that without that flare of anger in his face, Allard was exceptionally good-looking. His thick hair was well cut, he had high cheekbones with wide apart, deep set, dark brown eyes, and when he lowered them in a submissive manner he had long, thick eyelashes.

"I have never raped anyone and I am so sorry for what I did to you . . . I honestly never meant to hurt you. I was just trying to get away . . . please believe me. I am truly sorry."

Jane jumped as Moran suddenly banged the flat of his hand down on the desk.

"You scared the shit out of her! If she hadn't resisted and we weren't there you would have raped her, wouldn't you?"

Allard looked shocked.

"No . . . No! I swear before God, I never raped any of the women! That was never on my mind. I only touched them and masturbated."

"Indecent assault wasn't enough for you . . . you wanted more. You needed full sex to satisfy your urges and the only way you'd get that is by raping a young girl."

"No . . . No, you're wrong, I—"

"Then why did you have a flick knife on you? The exact same type of knife that the teenage rape victim described seeing?"

Allard began twisting uncomfortably in the chair.

"Please! . . . I didn't commit any rapes! You *know* I wasn't carrying a knife. I've never carried a knife, not even in my cab." He nodded toward Jane. "I only told her and the others I was carrying one so they wouldn't scream!"

Moran accused him of being a liar. But Allard was adamant, claiming that he only ever committed the indecent assaults and he would plead guilty to those in court.

"You think we're stupid? You're only admitting the assaults as the lesser of two evils . . . Right? *Right?*"

Allard looked pleadingly at Jane.

"Honest, I wasn't carrying a knife . . . I was never going to rape you . . . I've never raped anyone!"

"Bullshit! You couldn't have consensual sex with your wife, anal or otherwise, so the only way you could eventually satisfy your needs was to commit a rape."

Allard refused to answer. Moran accused him again. Allard still said nothing.

"You think I don't know steroids make a man sexually violent, and that you're remaining silent because of your guilt about committing rape? She was seventeen the same day you raped her, and she's now so traumatized she won't leave her home."

Allard said nothing as he sat up straight. Moran paused, looked him in the eye and nodded, as if he'd just realized something.

"You also don't want to admit to the rape because of your wife. You think she'll accept the indecent assaults because they are in some way her fault, but raping a teenage girl, she won't accept that. Well, even if you don't confess, believe me, I will make sure she comes to realize it was you and sees you for the animal that you really are."

Allard looked helplessly at Jane.

"Why don't you tell him the truth? I might have said I had a knife, but I didn't . . . that was only to frighten you. I thought you were someone else. Why are you lying? You know I've been set up with the flick knife, because he wants to charge me with a rape I didn't commit."

Jane didn't know whether to believe Allard or not. There was something about his desperate pleas that made her feel uneasy about the whole situation. Moran picked up his desk phone, called the duty desk and asked for a uniform PC to be sent up to his office. He then told Allard that they would conclude the interview for now as he had further inquiries to make. Jane partially held up the pen in her hand as she had a question she wanted to ask. Irritated, Moran repeated that the interview was over.

Feeling frustrated, Jane went to the CID office, where DC Edwards was sitting at his desk writing.

"Where is everyone?" she asked.

"They're in the pub celebrating one of the detectives' birthdays. As soon as I've finished these notes on the search of Allard's house I'm joining them, if you want to come?"

"DI Moran is with DCS Metcalf and he wants you to prepare the charges against Allard for all the indecent assaults."

Edwards looked annoyed and mumbled something about having enough bloody work to do already and missing out on the booze-up.

"I have to do the CRO, but could give you a hand as well if you need it?"

"I have to go downstairs and get some blank charge sheets and the Guide to the Wording of Police Charges for an indecent assault and assault on a police officer," Edwards said as he walked toward the door.

Jane shouted across the room, "Moran said the list of the victims' names was on his desk."

Edwards raised his hand to acknowledge he'd heard her as he left the room.

Jane thought she'd be helpful and get the list from Moran's office. She looked on his desk and to one side in a plastic desk tray she saw the list on top of a thick file. She picked up the list and noticed the file underneath had "DI Moran" and "Indecent Assaults" written on it. She was curious, picked up the file, placed it on the desk in front of her, sat down and started to flick through the victims' statements. It quickly struck Jane that not one of the six victims mentioned actually seeing a knife, but in all of the cases the suspect had worn a stocking mask and said "I've got a knife so don't scream!" Jane remembered Allard saying something similar, but couldn't quite recall his exact words.

She was about to replace the file when she saw another file with Moran's name on it marked "Lamb Lane Rape" in the plastic desk tray. She knew that Lamb Lane was only a stone's throw away from London Fields where she was attacked and, opening the file, she took out the victim's statement and started to read the salient points. The suspect had grabbed the victim from behind and held a flick knife to her throat and said, "If you scream or struggle I'll cut your neck." Again she believed this was similar to what had been said to her by Allard. Jane read on. The rape victim stated that when the man had been on top of her and had penetrated her she noticed he had bad body odor and that his breath smelt of alcohol. Jane recalled Marie saying that her husband didn't drink and she also remembered the sweet smell of aftershave when Allard had grabbed her from behind. However, what really struck Jane was that in the rape victim's statement the assailant was wearing a black balaclava with eye holes, not a stocking pulled down over his face.

She heard someone in the CID office and quickly put the rape statement back. She picked up both files from the desk to put them back in the tray, but in her haste she dropped them.

"What are you doing?"

She looked up and saw DC Edwards staring at her. "I, er, was trying to find the list of victims and just picked up some files when I heard your voice . . . It startled me and I dropped them."

Edwards helped her pick up the statements, which she put back in the case files. He noticed DI Moran's name on the Indecent Assaults file and asked Jane if she'd been lumbered with writing the report. Jane nervously shook her head, saying that she was just interested in reading the victims' statements. Edwards sensed from her tone and demeanor that something was wrong, even more so when he noticed that she'd also dropped the rape file.

"Did you ask Moran if you could look through these files?"

Jane knew it wasn't worth lying. "No, but I didn't really know much about any of the cases so I was just having a quick read of the statements."

"Listen, Jane, one thing you don't do is go snooping through a senior officer's files. If Moran found out, you'd never get in the CID, in fact you wouldn't even be allowed to cross the threshold into the main office again!"

"Are you going to tell him?" Jane asked, looking worried.

Edwards hesitated at first, then reassured Jane that she could trust him to keep quiet, but he sensed something else was making her nervous and asked her what it was.

Jane explained that no one had seen a knife in any of the indecent assaults, and in every attack the suspect wore a stocking mask, but in the rape he wore a balaclava. She was about to continue when Edwards interrupted.

"So what? It's a form of mask, just like the stocking Allard wore. Moran is way more experienced than the two of us, and if he thinks all the attacks and the rape are linked then he has good reason. He can't just ignore Allard as a possible suspect, can he?"

"No, I appreciate that, but the attacker in the rape held a knife to the victim's throat and said 'If you scream or struggle I'll cut your neck—'"

Again Edwards interrupted. "Yeah, exactly like Allard said to you, Jane. So let's just agree to differ and get on with what DI Moran told us to do."

"It's not what he said to me . . . and there are other glaring differences between last night's assault on me and the rape."

Edwards looked at her. She had her CID pocket book in her hand.

"Allard said to me, and this is word for word . . ." Jane looked at her pocket book. "'I've got a knife . . . so keep your mouth shut, you fucking thieving whore, or I'll cut your throat wide open this time,' but he didn't even hold a knife to my throat."

"For Chrissakes, Jane, apart from a word or two it's the same . . . so just drop it."

"The rape victim also said her attacker smelt of BO. Allard was so close to me that I could smell his aftershave."

"So? He could have been sweating like a pig after stuffing himself with steroids, for all we know."

Again she referred to her pocket book. "Allard said in the interview, 'I paid prostitutes for sex in the back of the cab.

Anyway, one night this tart ripped me off by snatching my money bag and running off.' "

"It's called motive, Jane, he's telling you why he committed his crimes. No, I'm wrong . . . he's actually trying to blame prostitutes for the fact he became a pervert. He also attacked women who weren't prostitutes!"

Edwards was losing his patience.

"But he thought they were . . . just like he did with me. In fact, I think it's possible he thought I was the same prostitute who stole money from him, that's why he said 'thieving whore.' It was personal . . . maybe he wasn't going to rape me, maybe he was going to drag me behind the Lido so he could beat me up."

"Oh, and that makes it all right, does it? That means Allard's not so bad after all?"

Jane persisted. "I'm not saying that . . ."

"Then what are you saying?"

Jane took a deep breath and sighed. "I think Moran planted a knife on Allard because he was already convinced the person committing the indecent assaults and the rape were one and the same . . . And I don't know what to do about it."

"Now you really are losing it, Jane, accusing a DI of planting evidence."

She looked at Edwards and could tell he had doubts. "So you're saying that senior officers aren't dishonest?"

"Come on, Jane, what would the point be in the guvnor planting a knife? It doesn't take the case much further as there's no other evidence that Allard committed the rape. He isn't even charging him with the rape, so where's your fit-up theory then?"

Jane looked confused. "He isn't?"

"Well, he only said to prepare the charges for the indecent assaults and the one on you, didn't he?"

"Well, he might charge him later."

"Why? He knows that if he did the Solicitors' Department will read through the statements and see the inconsistencies between the indecent assaults and the rape."

"I don't understand."

"Jane, there's no way they would run a trial with no positive identification and only the knife as evidence. So take my advice and let it drop."

"But it's not right . . ."

"If you say anything to DI Moran, or anyone else for that matter, then you can forget ever making detective."

"Are you being serious?"

"Yes, I am. You'll become persona non grata . . . no one will ever trust you, or work with you. Look at the way we all had to cover for Bradfield's screw-up—even you."

"My God, Brian! Bradfield died! What we're discussing here is whether someone planted evidence, or not."

"Someone? Someone . . . ? Nick Moran can be an arsehole, but he's got a number of Commissioners' commendations and is well respected. Apart from anything else I'll get dragged into something that might get blown out of all proportion. I've only been a DC for three years and I'm not prepared to screw up my career."

"I understand your predicament, and under the circumstances I'll let it rest." She walked out, unable to discuss it further as Edwards obviously didn't want to continue.

As Jane walked along the corridor toward the ladies' locker room DCS Metcalf was heading toward her wearing a smart suit and tie. Jane saluted and said, "All correct, sir," which was the normal address to senior officers. Metcalf smiled and informed her that "All correct" is fine to a detective and that the salute was for senior officers in uniform.

"It's just force of habit," Jane replied.

"DI Moran has been updating me on your arrest of Allard and how well you coped under extreme pressure. I'm impressed, congratulations on an excellent job."

"Thank you," said Jane. "Could I possibly have a word about my future career and becoming a detective?"

Metcalf looked at his watch. "I saw the result of your final probationer's exam—your marks were excellent and top of the class. As it happens, after speaking with DI Moran I was going to have a chat with you about your future, but I have an appointment to go to right now. What shift are you on tomorrow?"

"I'm on my CID attachment and not sure whether I'll be on a late or early shift."

"I see. I'm out all afternoon and won't be coming back to the station."

"I could come in early? In my own time if necessary?"

Metcalf agreed. "See me in my office at 10 a.m."

Feeling exhilarated by his compliments, Jane went into the ladies' and then returned to the CID office. DC Edwards was at his desk writing up the charges. He raised his finger and pointed to DI Moran's office and mouthed, "He's in there." She quickly grabbed a CRO 74 from the file cabinet and after putting some carbon paper between the sheets placed it in a typewriter. She opened her pocket book and started to fill out all of Allard's details and circumstances of arrest to be placed on criminal records at Scotland Yard.

"Has one of you two been going through my files? The statements are out of order."

Jane looked up and saw a stern-faced Moran standing in his office doorway holding up the Indecent Assaults file. She looked at Edwards and knew that she had to tell him it was her, but she was so nervous she couldn't instantly think of a valid reason. As she turned back to Moran, Edwards suddenly spoke up.

"Sorry, sir, I was looking through the file and dropped it by mistake. I didn't realize I'd put things back in the wrong order."

"What were you looking through them for?"

"I couldn't read one of the victims' names on your list and I just wanted to double-check it against the statement for the charge sheet."

"Well, next time ask me . . . I don't like people rummaging around on my desk."

"Sorry, sir, it won't happen again," Edwards said.

Jane mouthed "Thank you" to Edwards as Sergeant Harris walked in.

"Allard's wife has rung to ask if she can visit him," Harris announced.

Moran shrugged. "She can, but not until tomorrow morning as we have to formally charge, fingerprint and photograph him this evening."

"OK, I'll ring her back and inform her."

Having completed the criminal records form, Jane was tired and decided to go back to the section house rather than go for a drink. It was only a ten-minute bus ride and she always stood on the footplate ready to hop off at her stop. As the bus traveled down the road she noticed a tall, statuesque girl pushing a pram with a toddler in it. The girl was dark skinned, and had long dark hair that hid most of her face. What caught Jane's interest was that she was wearing a pale blue rabbit fur coat, identical to the one she had worn as a decoy. She shuddered as she recalled what had happened to her at the hands of Peter Allard. It really sunk home that she could have been seriously assaulted, to the point of Grievous Bodily Harm, if it hadn't been for Moran and Edwards.

CHAPTER FIVE

Jane walked into Hackney Police Station at 9:30 a.m., just as Marie Allard was coming out from reception. Jane realized that she must have visited her husband. Marie looked awful, as if she was in a world of her own. Jane called out her name but Marie carried on walking until Jane caught up with her.

"Marie, how are you doing?"

Marie suddenly broke down in tears. "I was prepared to stand by him for what he done, even though it was bad and wrong, but I could never forgive him for rape."

"I understand. But although your husband initially lied about the assaults, he has always denied the rape and he isn't being charged with it."

Marie stepped back angrily. "What you talking about . . . he admitting it."

Jane was shocked, instantly feeling that she had been stupid to have believed Allard's lies and doubt Moran's integrity.

"I'm so sorry . . . you must feel as if your world has been torn apart. Did he confess to you just now, during your visit?"

"No, I not seen him. He was taken to the Magistrates' Court before I got there."

Jane was confused. "How do you know he confessed?"

Marie was in floods of tears. "That detective inspector who came to the house, he saw me just now in the station. He say Peter been charged with the rape and indecent assaults and he be remanded in custody at the court to stand trial."

Jane was now even more shocked. "He confessed to DI Moran?"

"Yes, in an interview last night. I not believe it at first, but Moran show me Peter's signed confession and I see his signature."

Jane didn't know what to say to Marie. She had genuinely believed that Peter Allard was innocent of the rape, but to hear that he had made a signed confession made her feel naïve and foolish for what she had said to DC Edwards about Moran planting the knife.

Jane told Marie that she had to go to work, and hurried into the station. She went straight to the CID office to speak with DI Moran. There were a few detectives at their own desks, but Moran's office was empty. Jane went over to Edwards's desk and spoke to him in a low voice.

"Where's Moran?"

"He's gone to the Magistrates' Court with Allard, to object to bail."

Flustered, Jane took a deep breath.

"Is it true that Allard signed a confession?"

Edwards nodded. He had a raging headache as he'd drunk too much at the birthday bash the previous evening.

"I can't believe Allard signed a confession . . . were you present?"

Edwards could see some of the other detectives looking at them both.

"Not here, Jane," he whispered. "I'll meet you downstairs in five minutes."

Jane waited impatiently for him in the locker room, tidying herself up in preparation for her meeting with Metcalf. She looked at her watch. There was only ten minutes left before she was due to be in his office.

DC Edwards walked in and shut the door.

"I'm sorry for what I said yesterday, Brian, but I really thought Allard was telling the truth about not being involved in the rape. What did he say? I mean, why did he suddenly confess?"

"I don't know—I wasn't present at the confession as I'd already gone to the pub."

"Did Moran say anything to you at the pub?"

"He didn't come to the pub, but he was all cock-a-hoop about it first thing this morning. He said he'd charged Allard with the indecent assaults and was fingerprinting him when he suddenly broke down and made a signed confession. Moran couldn't believe it himself."

There was something about his tone of voice that didn't sit right with Jane.

"So, Moran was alone in the fingerprint room with Allard when he confessed?"

Edwards nodded.

"Should Moran have had someone else present when he wrote down the actual confession?"

"There's no fixed rule about needing two people present, it's just advisable to counter any allegations of it being false," Edwards explained.

Jane hesitated before she spoke. "You're not convinced about the confession, are you? Do you think we should take it further . . . speak with Metcalf maybe? I'm seeing him in a minute about joining the department—"

Edwards was quick to interject.

"No, I don't . . . definitely not. If you raise any queries regarding Allard being fitted up by DI Moran, the first thing you'll be asked for is proof . . . and the fact is you don't have any. It's his word against yours, and you won't win."

"Come on, Brian, you know DI Moran obviously decided Allard was guilty of the rape as soon as we arrested him. When Allard lied about what happened with me Moran decided his course of action and planted the knife. The more Allard lied, the more it played into his hands . . . he'll probably claim that Allard's emotional stress with his wife made him break down and confess—"

"For Chrissakes, Jane, wake up and get real! You've got more to lose than gain here. Why ruin your career for a piece of shit like Allard? He split your lip, he terrified the life out of you and other helpless women whose lives he's ruined, not to mention not giving a damn about his wife's feelings. He'll get a long stretch, whatever happens . . . and to be frank he'll get what he deserves."

Jane shook her head. "For a crime he may not have committed . . ."

"Listen to me, Jane, neither of us knows the truth, but if he's signed a confession he's screwed. We both know he lied at the start about his arrest and who he really was . . . Allard did himself no favors, so you and I don't owe him anything. Lemme tell you, there have been plenty of people like the guv who look upon a fit-up as what is called 'noble cause justice.' You might think they have a warped sense of loyalty to the job in bending the rules and making up confessions or fabricating evidence if they are convinced someone is guilty. I don't . . . I really don't, because if the ends justify the means, that's a success. If you want to be part of CID you'd better get used to it and learn to turn a blind eye fast."

Jane took a deep breath and looked at him in disbelief as he turned to leave.

"Wait a minute . . . I can't believe what you're saying! That's not justice, it's corruption, whatever way you look at it."

Edwards ran his fingers through his hair and sighed as his cheeks flushed.

"That's the big dilemma, Jane. But with no proof there's no case . . . so there's nothing you can say, no matter how bad you feel about it. You need to learn quickly who the bent cops are and try to avoid working with them. If they try to get you involved in something dodgy, just say no and walk away. But don't ever say anything to anyone else because everyone will think you're a snitch and ostracize you."

Jane shook her head. "I'd be hated because I told the truth about a dishonest police officer? That can't be right."

Edwards sighed; his head was really throbbing now. "No one said it was right, Jane, it's just the way it is. It's how you define the word 'corrupt,' and in my eyes Moran isn't corrupt. He doesn't take backhanders or steal from drug dealers."

"Really? Well, do you think Moran might have assaulted or threatened Allard to get him to sign a false confession? Is that what you define as 'noble'?"

"For Chrissakes, Jane, no way . . . He might have come off second best in the fingerprint room, or in a cell alone, with a bloke like Allard who has karate skills and is a martial arts expert."

"There's no need to be sarcastic, Brian . . . Whatever you say, I don't believe Allard would have knowingly signed a false confession if he was innocent."

He was losing his patience. "It's Moran's word against Allard's, and we can't be sure of the truth either way. I'm on your side, Jane, but I'm not stupid enough to shout about it. So let's just forget we ever had this conversation, OK? After what you did the other night you've already got one foot in the door of the department . . . don't fuck it all up now. Go and see Metcalf and reap the rewards, and we'll do the lab form for the steroids when you've finished."

Edwards walked out of the locker room. Jane waited a few moments as the implications of their discussion sank in. This was some learning curve. She looked in the mirror and put some foundation over the bruise above her cut lip, powdered her swollen cheek then headed out of the locker room for her meeting with Metcalf.

Jane knocked on the door. "Ah, Jane." Metcalf invited her in, gesturing to her to sit down. "I hear you've had good news and that Allard has admitted the rape?"

"Yes, sir," Jane replied against her will.

"Excellent. When this case appears at the Old Bailey the judge will no doubt commend you. You'll also be put forward for a Commissioner's Commendation for your part in the arrest of a very dangerous man."

Jane sat bolt upright on the hard-backed chair. "I'm sure that the trial will be very interesting. Do you think Allard will actually plead guilty?"

Metcalf laughed. "Given he has confessed his crimes and signed a statement to that effect, he'd be mad to go for a not guilty claim and risk a much longer sentence." He smiled coldly. "Anyway, let's talk about your future, Tennison . . . Tell me, where do you see yourself in three or five years' time?"

"I'd like to think I'd be a detective, sir."

He gave her an icy stare. "Are you sure that's what you want? It may not be the best career path for you at this time."

Jane was taken aback by Metcalf's attitude. He had promised he would recommend her for the CID after DCI Bradfield's death.

"Excuse me, sir, can I ask if DI Moran or Sergeant Harris have said anything to you about me joining the CID?"

"No . . . why do you ask? Is there a problem between you and them?"

Jane blushed. "No, sir. I had told them I'd like to join the department and I just wondered if they had spoken to you favorably, or otherwise, about me."

"Detective Moran said you did a good job on the Allard arrest, and Sergeant Harris has never mentioned you . . . but I try to avoid conversations with him as he usually has something to moan about."

He gave a short bark.

"Could I ask why you think the CID may be the wrong career path for me?"

Metcalf formed a church steeple with his fingers, and leaned his elbows on the desk.

"I'm not saying that being a detective isn't right, but it may not be the right choice in the long term. There is always the possibility of a more rewarding opportunity."

"What would that opportunity be, sir?"

"Well, if you sit the sergeant's promotion exam and got a mark in the nineties you would automatically be considered for the Special Course."

"I see . . . but Sergeant Harris has already said he wouldn't recommend me to sit the exam yet."

Metcalf glanced away, staring at a small stain high on the wall behind her.

"Well, Jane, I would recommend you for accelerated promotion, whereby you could be a uniform sergeant within three years and an inspector within five."

Jane paused for thought. She then said quietly, "It's very tempting to have a go at accelerated promotion, but I think first I'd like to make detective, work in the CID and maybe sit the exam later."

"But you could still apply for the CID even if you pass the promotion exam," Metcalf pointed out. "You might find it worth studying to sit the exam in January next year, then apply for the CID once you've passed."

Again Jane took time to think about it. "Could I become a detective and then sit the exam after a year or two in the CID?" she asked politely.

She could tell that Metcalf was now becoming a trifle impatient as he drummed his fingertips on the edge of the desk.

"If you pass the exam, as a detective, you would be required to work in uniform for one year before you could return as a detective sergeant."

Jane bit down on her bottom lip. One side of her mouth was still scarred where Allard had struck her but she kept tight control and audaciously reminded Metcalf of their previous conversation after Bradfield's death. Metcalf's cheeks turned pink. It was hard to determine if it was from anger, or whether he had forgotten that conversation.

Eventually he said very quietly, "I'm a man of my word and if that's what you want then I'll recommend you for the next CID interview board in about a month's time. But I'm only able to recommend you, and passing the board is entirely down to how you perform on the day in front of the panel." Metcalf peered at her and his tone became brisk. "Do your homework and brush up on CID procedure." He stood up to signal that their meeting was over and Jane saluted him.

"I wish you'd stop doing that, Tennison . . . a handshake will suffice."

"Thank you very much, sir, I will remember that."

Standing ramrod straight she walked out, very pleased with herself, and reckoned she had handled the meeting well.

Jane went straight to the property store to book out the steroids recovered from Allard's address. PC Doig, the property officer, was a pleasant, rotund old soul who originated from Glasgow. He had a strong Scottish accent that, even after twenty-five years in London, was often hard to understand. He was badly injured after being hit by a car in the line of duty and had spent the last four years assigned to desk duties in the "dungeon," as officers referred to the basement property store.

"Hello, wee Jane, how ye doin'? I heard you pulled a real belter the other night, arrestin' that rotten bastard Allard for rape. That's a nasty cut he gave your lip."

"Thanks, Dougal, but it wasn't just me who made the arrest."

"You're a canny lass that's fer sure. Now, what're you aboot?"

"The bag of tablets in the Allard case, please."

"Aye, did ye see them magazines he had? I could nae believe the dirty pictures in 'em when I had a wee gander." He walked off down the aisle of high shelving to look for the property.

Jane tried not to laugh at his remark about the magazines, as he'd obviously had a good "gander."

"Right, here ye are. I need yer ta sign in the book here. Are they going ta the lab?"

"Yes," Jane said.

PC Doig put the bag of tablets down on the desk and opened up the property book. He pulled a pen out of his pocket and handed it to Jane, asking her to fill out each section with the date, property exhibit number, case name and description of the property. The page was nearly full and as she filled out each section she couldn't help but notice the entries above the one she was making. The dates went back three days and she was surprised that nowhere among the entries for withdrawal or deposit was there a blue rabbit fur coat. Moran's name was there but only relating to the deposit of the Allard property. She flicked back a few pages to double-check, but still found no entry for the coat. Jane distinctly remembered Moran saying the fur coat was evidence in a "handling" case and asking her to leave it on a chair in his office as he needed to put it back in the property store.

"The fur coat I used for the decoy operation . . . I was just wondering if it was returned to the store, as it was evidence in a case?"

"What fur coat? I've nay had any fur coats in here. If I did, believe me I'd be wearin' it . . . it's that damn cold doon here."

"It was blue rabbit fur, and waist length."

"Nope, d'nay what yer talkin' aboot, Janey . . . If it was ta do with an overnight prisoner then it may never have got doon here, and could ha been locked in the charge room cabinet."

The word "prisoner" sparked a memory in Jane's mind. It was DC Edwards telling her that Moran had gone downstairs to put the fur jacket back in the property store, and release a prisoner he had in on suspicion of dishonest handling. Then Sergeant Harris had told her that DI Moran released his other prisoner the same night she arrested Allard.

She filled out the rest of the details about the steroids in the property book. Why had Moran lied to her about the rabbit fur coat? It just didn't make sense . . . unless there was something he wanted to hide. She thanked PC Doig for his help.

Jane went straight to the charge room to look through the prisoner arrest and release records for the twenty-four-hour period before and after Allard's arrest. She was thankful there was no one there, other than a cleaner. She went over to the bookshelf, removed the Prisoner book and sat down at the charge room desk to look through it. It didn't take long. Early in the morning on the day of the decoy operation, DI Moran had arrested a Mary Kelly, aged twenty-nine, unemployed, and of no fixed abode. Jane's eyes opened wide when she read that Kelly was arrested on suspicion of handling stolen goods and Moran had released her, without charge, in the early hours of the morning . . . after Peter Allard was arrested. The Prisoner book didn't say what the "stolen goods" were, but Jane knew it would be recorded on Mary Kelly's arrest sheet, which would be kept in date order in a large binder, along with all the prisoners kept in custody at Hackney. As she was about to replace the Prisoner book the charge room door opened and Sergeant Harris appeared.

"What are you up to, Tennison?"

She'd already prepared an answer in anticipation that someone might walk in on her, and pointed to the bag of steroids on the table.

"I've got to fill out a lab form regarding those tablets and I needed the time we booked Allard in. I forgot to put it in my notes and couldn't remember," she said and then stood up, replaced the Prisoner book on the shelf and quickly left the room before Harris could say anything. She was annoyed that she was unable to see what property was logged against Mary Kelly's arrest record, but was almost certain it had to be the blue rabbit fur coat. She'd try to sneak back later to have a look, but the more Jane uncovered the more she felt something was seriously wrong.

She thought about the woman she had seen on the way back to the section house the previous evening. The tall, dusky skinned, statuesque girl who was wearing a pale blue rabbit fur coat. Jane wondered if she was Mary Kelly, but the reality was it could have just been a coincidence and she didn't get a good look at the woman's face so she doubted she would recognize her again. Jane also knew that as Mary Kelly was released without charge no fingerprints or photograph would have been taken, but she might have a criminal record for previous offenses. An idea occurred to her and she decided to seek out PC Donaldson.

PC Donaldson, the station collator, was one of the oldest and longest-serving officers at Hackney. He was overweight with ruddy cheeks and a thatch of white hair. He was perched on a stool in front of his desk reading a newspaper, his chipped mug of coffee beside him. There were other chairs in the room but he found them uncomfortable because of his bad back and preferred the stool as it kept him more upright. The room was crammed with filing cabinets, large and small, containing files and card indexes on every known criminal and persons of interest in Hackney. The basement room had strip lights and only one window, which was so high up it was dirty and cobwebbed, and had obviously never been opened.

"Morning, Tennison," he said with a warm smile.

Jane had become very fond of Donaldson. He was always pleasant and helpful and she stood smiling as she watched his wide bum splay over the edges of the stool. His police issue trousers hung a few inches above his ankles and revealed his thick crepe-soled black polished shoes.

"I just wanted to check out someone's name with you."

Donaldson eased himself down from his stool. "No problem . . . the name is?"

"Mary Kelly."

"I know that name . . ."

Jane looked pleased. "Do you? What do you know about her?"

Donaldson paused as he looked through the female index cards under the name "Kelly." He turned to Jane.

"That's strange, there's no Mary Kelly in here . . ."

"If someone is arrested, but not charged, their details and reason for arrest should still be filled out on a form and submitted to you?"

"Yes, but sometimes officers forget or can't be bothered."

Jane became worried. Could Moran have deliberately failed to submit, or have even destroyed, Mary Kelly's collator's card?

Donaldson suddenly clicked his fingers. "Got it! Mary Jane Kelly, she was his last victim."

Jane looked excited. "Whose last victim? Did someone assault Mary?"

Donaldson looked at her as if she was a bit dim. "No, Mary Jane Kelly was Jack the Ripper's last victim . . . that's why the name was familiar. I've read every book on that crime and watched an old movie about him . . . still shockin' all these years later. She was a prostitute addicted to rot-gut gin . . ."

Jane felt deflated, but suddenly thought of a long shot on the back of what Donaldson had said. "Do you keep records of women arrested for prostitution?"

Donaldson smiled. "Yes I do, but there's so many . . . and they use and share a multitude of different names. Some of them could fill a phone book! It's hard to remember who's who, so I put together a photograph album of them all."

He went to a cabinet and took out a large photo album filled with pages of various women, of all ages and skin colors. "As you can see, each one is numbered and I have a corresponding index card or file for each number. I keep the main index card under the name they gave when first arrested and charged."

Jane sighed. She'd only seen the woman in the rabbit fur coat briefly, and from a side-on view. Nevertheless, nothing ventured, nothing gained. She sat at the spare table and started to flick through the pages, each of which had nine photographs. Donaldson sat back up on his stool and continued to read his newspaper.

Although Jane was frustrated and growing impatient she took her time. After ten minutes she was halfway through the album without seeing anyone she even remotely recognized. It didn't help that all the pictures were black and white and taken from chest height. It was another five minutes before a picture caught her attention. It wasn't the dusky faced girl herself, but the coat she was wearing. Jane was almost certain it was the same fur coat she had been given to wear as a decoy, and if it was she wanted to know why and who it belonged to.

"This one here, number three hundred and twenty-six . . . I think this might be her."

Donaldson leaned over his desk to a small notebook that had "TOMS" written on the front of it. He licked his finger and started to turn over the pages.

"Ah ha, here it is . . . Janet Brown! You ever seen her? She's the dizzy blonde who does impressions on *Who Do You Do*. She's really good, and very funny."

Jane was lost. She didn't have a clue why Donaldson suddenly wanted to talk about TV impressionists. He went over to one of the female index filing trays, pulled it open and after a second or two pulled out an envelope containing some index cards. He placed it on the table in front of Jane and removed the cards.

"Number three hundred and twenty-six is Janet Brown, but not the impressionist . . . First arrest for soliciting eight years ago, CRO number D72/261." He flicked the card over. "Aliases Lily, Sugar Susie, Jane, Angie . . . to name but a few." He stopped reading out the list of aliases and ran his finger down the page.

"Looks like she's never used the name Mary Kelly before, and come to think of it I can't recall a Tom who has. I remember seeing the Ripper crime scene pictures of Mary Kelly in the Black Museum at the Yard . . . her body was horribly mutilated."

Jane felt ill at ease. The more she found out about Moran's involvement in the arrest of the so-called Mary Kelly, the more suspicious she became. She had nothing concrete to go on, but she was determined to dig deeper. Donaldson picked up Brown's mug shot and tapped it.

"This may not be the girl you're looking for . . . as I said, many of them share and use the same names. The best way to confirm someone's identity is through their fingerprints, as they can be matched to the first sets ever taken on their CRO file at the Yard."

Jane already knew about fingerprints. It was as if Donaldson had forgotten that she had nearly two years' service, but she didn't want to offend him so just thanked him for the information. She was eager to read Janet Brown's cards and concentrated on what was in front of her.

Janet was five feet eight inches tall and weighed 125 pounds. To Jane this indicated she must be a slender woman. Her date of birth was February 20th, 1945, making her twenty-nine. Jane looked at the scrap of paper she had made notes on about Mary Kelly's arrest. The date of birth was the same. The most recent mug shot of Janet was five months old, having been sent over from West End Central Police Station after she was arrested by a local PC for prostitution in Soho. The picture surprised Jane because she was exceptionally beautiful, with dark skin, dark hair, wide almond shaped eyes, a small neat nose and wide dark lips, which were probably accentuated with lipstick. There was a sullenness to her expression, and the hand that held up the card had long painted nails.

Janet's last arrest, in 1972, was for loitering for prostitution in London Fields. It then dawned on her that DC Edwards had said DI Moran used to be on the Clubs and Vice Unit. She looked up at Donaldson.

"Is Clubs and Vice based at Scotland Yard?"

"No, they work out of West End Central. Why?"

"Nothing, I just wondered if they might know of Janet Brown." But the truth was she was wondering if there was a connection between Moran and Janet Brown from his time with Clubs and Vice.

Jane sighed. Everything seemed to be going from bad to worse. She noticed that Janet had never served a prison sentence, which she thought was strange due to the number of arrests she had had for soliciting. Jane questioned Donaldson about it, and he shrugged.

"Could be a soft magistrate, or it's possible she's a snout for someone on the Vice Squad and trades details of pimps and johns to avoid prison. If she appeared in court and a good word is put in by the Vice officer she'd probably just get a fine. Paying it off just means turning a few more tricks in one night."

"Sounds like a vicious circle," Jane remarked.

Donaldson put his arm on her shoulder. "Will you keep your eye on the shop for me while I nip up to the canteen for a couple of sausage rolls and a coffee?"

Jane nodded and gave Donaldson a warm smile. No sooner had he left the room than he popped his head back round the door.

"Do you want anything?"

"No, thank you."

He smiled and jokingly said, "And no sneaking any of my index cards out the room . . . you know it's against the rules."

Jane grabbed the memo pad from Donaldson's desk and started to make shorthand notes from Janet Brown's cards. One of the cards gave some details of her background. It stated that she was born in King's Cross, her mother was English and father an American GI. She had lived in America for part of her life, then returned to London after her mother had died. Jane wished the card had more details about Janet Brown's life, but she knew that it was normal for only a brief family history to be recorded on a CRO file. What was of interest was the fact that Janet Brown gave her address, when last arrested in Soho, as 86 Graham Road, Hackney.

Having recorded as much as she could on the memo pad Jane ripped off the pages she'd written on, folded them up and put them in her handbag. She gathered up the cards to put them back in the envelope and on opening it saw a copy of an Incident Report Book, which was used by uniform officers, and had been filled out by PC 489 Grant, who was based at Hackney, but on a different relief to Jane. The IRB was about a "Serious Assault" on August 23, 1974. She also recalled having read the teenager's statement saying that her rape had occurred on the 23rd, but had not been reported until two days later when she had an emotional breakdown in front of her mother. To Jane it seemed obvious that the same man may have attacked Janet Brown and the teenager. She couldn't understand how, or why, DI Moran had missed the connection. Jane opened the IRB and started to read it.

On 8.23.74 I was night duty patrol covering 5 beat. Just after midnight I received a radio call about a drunk woman outside the basement flat of 58 Navarino Road. I attended the scene and the woman had a severely bruised face and what appeared to be a knife wound to her neck and chest. She was semiconscious and did not smell of alcohol. I also noticed that her clothes were in disarray and there was a handbag on the floor next to her. She was wearing a blue fur coat, white top, miniskirt and long boots.

I asked her what happened but she was incoherent and in a state of shock. I called an ambulance and accompanied her to the Homerton Hospital. She said nothing during the journey. I looked in the handbag to try and identify the woman and found a letter addressed to Miss J. Brown of 86 Graham Road.

At the hospital she was treated immediately in the emergency area and sedated, thus I was unable to get any information from her. I contacted the Night Duty CID and informed them of a possible GBH/Rape, and that the attending doctor said no one would be able to speak to her until the following morning.

CID said they would make an entry in their Night Duty Occurrence Book for the DI to see in the morning, and also asked me to make out a crime report sheet on my return to the station. (Major Crime 1324 refers.)

I left the hospital and returned to Hackney where I checked the collator's index cards and found a record for a Janet Brown, who from the mug shot was the same woman I escorted to the hospital.

Lifting the mug shot up Jane found two more black and white photographs. One looked as if it had been taken around the same time as the mug shot, but the other photograph was more recent and shocked her. Janet had severe bruises around her eyes and one of them was bulging like a ping pong ball. Her lips were swollen and split. It was very obvious that she had suffered a severe beating. Checking over the dates and times of the various arrests for soliciting there was a brief mention of the assault stating that J. Brown had come into the station to report it, but had later withdrawn the complaint and refused to press charges. She was unable to give a description of the assailant.

Listed on the crime sheet was a memo from DI Moran stating that the victim refused to substantiate the allegation and had said the injuries were as a result of a fall. "No crime" was then underlined.

Jane couldn't believe what she'd just read. She was now convinced that Janet Brown, Mary Kelly and J. Brown were the same woman. Moran must be hiding something, not just from her, but from everyone else in the station. Navarino Road, where the woman was found, was just a stone's throw from the north end of London Fields.

Jane was now certain she had been wearing Janet Brown's rabbit fur coat on the night she was assaulted. She could find no mention of whether or not she was an informer. Even if she was, all informants were usually registered under a false name and a record kept under lock and key in a cabinet by the DCI.

Donaldson returned and Jane handed him the index cards.

"She took a severe beating."

"Yep, I noticed that . . . But you know these girls risk that happening. A lot of them are out soliciting to pay for their drugs. You arrest them, and in the worst cases they do time in Holloway Prison, but then they get out and go straight back to work. They have these scum pimps who they pay for so-called protection, but a lot of the time it's those creeps who knock them around."

"Do you think Janet has a pimp?"

"I don't know, sweetheart, maybe . . . Some of them work out of flats over in Mayfair. That's where the top brass work nowadays. They get customers from the Dorchester Hotel, and some of them even have the cheek to dress up fancy and go into the bars."

"Do you think Janet could work in Mayfair?"

He shook his head and said he doubted it as she was a darkie. Jane was eager to leave and thanked Donaldson again. As she opened the door she turned back.

"You know, I think you're one of the best officers here in Hackney . . . You're always so helpful, and I really appreciate it."

"Well, thank you, Tennison . . . nice to know I'm appreciated. But I just do my job. I'll be retired soon. I loved being a copper out on the beat . . . gets lonely down here. After I got wounded I reckoned I'd be back in civvies, but luckily I was allocated this position."

"Wounded?"

"Yep, got shot by one of the Krays' gang . . . big shootout."

Jane looked horrified and Donaldson laughed.

"Na, not really . . . tripped over a drainpipe and broke me hip!"

Later that day, before she was officially on duty, Jane came across DI Moran in the CID office, his Cuban-heeled boots up on the desk, leaning back in his chair and looking at the topless model on page three of *The Sun*. He was wearing a rather snazzy suit and a colorful tie. DC Edwards was typing at his desk and looked over at her. He almost gave her a warning glance, as he nodded his head toward Moran. Jane knew that Allard had been taken into the Magistrates' Court and bail had been denied but she still asked, rather tentatively, "How did it go this morning? Good news about the confession, sir . . ."

"Yeah, yeah . . . I was about to go off duty last night when I was told Allard wanted to speak to me. Next thing I knew he started pouring his heart out about the rape and admitted that he wore a balaclava because his wife said something about some tights of hers going missing."

He stood up, tossing the newspaper to one side.

Jane nodded. Although Moran sounded perfectly plausible she was still dubious and asked what Allard had done with the balaclava. Moran didn't flinch.

"He said he threw it in a rubbish bin after the rape."

He glanced at his watch.

"Listen, I'm busy and can't stop and chat all day . . . Allard is not the only case I have to deal with. But thanks for all your help and for making the arrest. By the way, Allard also signed the notes you took during the interview after the search and you'll need to countersign them sometime . . . you'll find them on my desk."

Jane smiled as he hurried past her, and she went into his office to look over his desk. There were numerous files so she had to search through everything to find the notes. Just as she was beginning to sift through them, Sergeant Harris barged into the main room.

"Good, you're here . . . take over the front desk, Tennison. I've got a drunk down in the cells who's creating havoc. You know Allard was remanded in custody and his defense solicitor has requested an 'old style' committal, which'll be heard next week. Have you signed the notes from DI Moran?"

"I haven't finished working on them yet."

"I just need you to sign what's there."

Jane came out of Moran's office. She leaned on a desk and flicked quickly through the documents until she saw the note slip requesting her signature. She signed it and passed it over to Harris. He took it and jerked his head for her to get to the front desk.

Jane hurried out as Harris organized the papers and Moran walked back in with a cup of coffee.

"You get her to sign them?"

"Yeah, here you go."

Harris handed them to Moran, and left. There was a tense atmosphere in the room as Edwards glanced over, not missing anything that had just taken place, but he quickly returned to typing.

"You got a problem, Brian?"

"No, guv."

"Good, because we don't have one and we are going to get that piece of karate shit put away for a long stretch."

"I hope Jane will be able to handle being questioned in court . . . It'll be her first time and some of these barristers are lethal."

Moran walked into his office, kicking the door open wider with his foot.

"Give me a break . . . he's going to plead guilty for a string of assaults as well as the rape. We have his confession, so she might not even be called to the witness box."

Edwards said nothing as Moran's door slammed shut. He hoped it would run that smoothly. He jerked his tie loose and his collar button came off and rolled onto the floor. He knew that if Tennison was called to give evidence he would be too, and just the thought of it brought him out in a sweat.

CHAPTER SIX

A week later, Jane paced nervously up and down the police officers' waiting room at Old Street Magistrates' Court, going over
her notes on the arrest and interviews of Peter Allard. She had
given evidence at the Magistrates' Court during her probation,
but they had only been minor offenses for shoplifting, criminal damage and drunk and disorderly where her evidence was
straightforward and the defense solicitor asked only a few questions in cross examination. Giving evidence at Crown Court
was a different matter.

On his first appearance at court earlier in the week Allard,
he offered a plea of guilty to the indecent assault charges and
assault on a police officer. However, when he was told about his
client's initial denial concerning the rape charge and the alleged
confession, Allard's solicitor had requested an old-style committal on the rape alone. On hearing the evidence the magistrate
would decide if the case should be committed to the Old Bailey
for trial by jury.

DC Edwards sat quietly, biting his fingernails, while DI
Moran read *The Sun* and drank tea from a polystyrene cup.

"It's not as if you're gripping the rail at the big house, so
bloody well sit down and stop worrying, Tennison," Moran
said sternly, then, licking his finger, flicked over to page three
as usual and commented on the breasts of Jilly Johnson.

Jane sat down next to DC Edwards and spoke quietly. "What's
he mean by gripping the rail?"

"Giving evidence at the Old Bailey under a hostile defense
barrister," DC Edwards replied.

"Allard's got a barrister representing him today, hasn't he?"
Jane asked apprehensively.

"Yes, a QC, and by all accounts he's a bit of an ogre who likes to attack police officers in the witness box."

DI Moran closed his newspaper and threw it down on the table next to him.

"Would you two shut up! The magistrate will have read your statements and you'll be cross-examined by Allard's counsel, that's all . . . it's no big deal." He looked at Edwards. "What are you doing? Trying to put the fear of God in her? Allard made the confession to me, so I'm the one who'll get all the flack, not you!"

"I was just trying to prepare her, sir."

"Oh shut up, Edwards."

Moran looked at Jane.

"You'll be fine . . . Just stay calm and answer yes or no, three bags full, sir . . . all right?"

At that moment the door to the waiting room opened and the court usher stuck her head round the door.

"Right, your case is under way in Court One."

Jane jumped up, brushed her uniform down and headed toward the door.

"Where are you going?" the usher asked.

"To sit in court," Jane replied, somewhat confused by the question.

"I'm sorry but DI Moran is on first. You have to wait in here and not discuss the case with your colleague. I will come and get you when it's your turn to give evidence."

Moran sighed as he stood up.

"She's fairly new to all this. You can sit in after you've given your evidence, Tennison, but not while another officer is giving evidence—otherwise you'd know the questions that were put to me and the answers I gave, which kind of goes against the course of justice."

That's rich coming from you, Jane thought to herself, as Moran left the room.

After the usher closed the door Edwards looked at Jane with a worried expression.

"Moran wants me to say I saw him search Allard at the scene of the arrest. He's adamant he had the flick knife on him—"

Jane shook her head as she interrupted Edwards. "But we both know you didn't see him search Allard, and neither of us saw the knife until Moran produced it out of thin air in the charge room."

"Yeah, but if the confession wasn't genuine then why would Allard even sign it? Allard could just be trying to muddy the waters and Moran could be telling the truth. Maybe we're wrong."

"Who are you trying to convince, me or yourself? I agree it's strange that Allard should sign a confession if it was false, but for all we know Moran could have threatened him about his wife and kids, or tricked him somehow . . . who knows? There's no way I'm fabricating evidence and saying that I saw Allard searched at the scene, and neither should you. Like Moran just said, he's the one who will take the flack . . . besides it's his career on the line, not ours, if he's lying."

"You're right, Jane, and at the end of the day the magistrate will decide if there is enough evidence to commit for trial."

"Which is unlikely when you look at the facts of the rape compared to the indecent assaults. I took another look at the rape victim's statement and the way he smelt of body odor and . . ."

Edwards stood up and moved toward the door.

"Where are you going?"

"I need the loo again," Edwards said, as he hurried out of the room. Jane shouted after him to get her a coffee then continued reading over her notes. She was now feeling more nervous than before everything he had just said.

When Edwards returned fifteen minutes later he looked pale, almost as if he'd been sick. Jane suspected he had, though she didn't ask. She stood up and moved toward the door.

"You need a pee as well?"

"No, I asked you to get me a coffee. Do you want one?"

"Sorry, I forgot. I'd better not have one in case I'm called next."

Jane went into the cell area of the court and asked the custody sergeant if she could get a coffee. He smiled and told her to help herself, but to leave five pence in the small metal tin next to the kettle. She took her time as she didn't want to get into a deliberation about the case with DC Edwards, so she had a quick chat with a PC whom she recognized from the section house. As she returned to the officers' waiting room with her coffee she crossed the entrance hall of the courts and saw Marie Allard coming out of Court One in floods of tears.

"Are you all right, Marie?" Jane asked, as she approached her out of concern.

Marie slowly looked up at Jane with a mixture of contempt and loathing in her eyes.

"You all in this pack of lies together, aren't you? You don't care about the truth. My husband admitted the indecent assaults, but he never confessed to rape, did he?"

Jane felt apprehensive. She didn't really know what to say, but she was upset by the state Marie was in.

"I don't know, Marie . . . I wasn't present when DI Moran took the confession."

"I just sat in there and listened to him lie. Peter deserve whatever he get for assaulting those poor women, but not to go to prison for years for something he not do."

"It may not come to that, Marie. The magistrate could decide there's not enough evidence to send your husband for trial."

"And if he go to trial, what happen then? Will you stand up for him and tell truth?"

Jane didn't know what to say and regretted ever approaching Marie Allard. The courtroom door opened and the usher looked surprised to see Jane.

"What do you think you're doing, officer?" she asked.

"I was just asking Mrs. Allard if she was all right, as she looked very upset."

"Well, you should not be speaking to the defendant's wife—it is totally inappropriate. Now please return to the officers' waiting room and tell DC Edwards he has been called to give evidence."

Jane felt distressed that she had made such a stupid error. She had been genuinely concerned about Marie Allard, but resigned herself that what was done was done and there was nothing untoward in her approach. As she entered the waiting room she told DC Edwards that he'd been called. Jane looked at him.

"Brian, there's something you need to know."

"What? What's happened? Tell me quickly, before I go in there."

"I just got told off for speaking with Marie Allard . . . she was in an awful state."

"You what? How could you be so stupid? She might get called by the defense as a witness."

"I don't think so. She was sitting in court listening to Moran give his evidence so she can't be a witness."

"Of course she can—the magistrate may have allowed her to sit in as she could be giving evidence on her husband's character."

"But I thought—"

"Well, you thought wrong. For Christ's sake, what did you say to her?" Edwards began to ask, as the waiting room door opened and the usher stood there with a frown.

"I hope you two are not discussing the case, especially not Officer Tennison's inappropriate conversation with Mrs. Allard?"

"No," Edwards replied, as he sheepishly left the room.

Jane spent the next half-hour worrying about what she may now be asked and what to say when she was called. A part of her considered that maybe it would be some form of justice if her actions caused the rape case against Allard to be thrown out, but it could also be the end of any ambitions she had of ever joining the CID. It was over half an hour later before the usher came and collected Jane. As she walked into the court she could see Peter Allard looking forlorn in the dock, as did his wife who was now sitting in the public area. DI Moran and DC Edwards were seated in the corner of the room. Edwards looked nervous and avoided eye contact with Jane, whereas Moran had a smug grin on his face as if the case was going his way. As Jane entered the witness box the usher handed her a Bible and a card with the oath written on it. Jane raised the Bible in her right hand, looked over at Moran and read the oath.

"I swear by Almighty God that the evidence I shall give shall be the truth, the whole truth and nothing but the truth. Jane Tennison WPC 517 attached to Hackney Police Station."

Allard's barrister stood up. "I am Anthony Nichols QC and represent Mr. Allard. May I say, officer, you read the oath with some conviction."

"Thank you, sir," Jane replied, glad that he had appreciated it in the manner she intended.

"May I ask, though, why you directed it toward DI Moran and not the magistrate as is normal practice when an officer takes the oath?"

Realizing her mistake Jane looked at the magistrate. "Sorry, sir, it was remiss of me."

The magistrate smiled. "That's all right, officer. Please continue, Mr. Nichols."

"Well, let's hope it was a faux pas, officer, as opposed to an inference toward the truthfulness of evidence that we have heard from DI Moran today."

Nichols was in his late forties, with fading red hair carefully combed over to hide its thinning. He wore a pinstripe suit and blue cotton shirt with a white collar.

"My client wishes to express his deep regret about the indecent assault, not only on you but the other women, and that splitting your lip with his elbow during the arrest had not in any way been deliberate. However, he pleads guilty to that offense as, although it had been reckless behavior, it nevertheless constituted an assault on a police officer."

Jane said nothing in reply to the barrister's remarks. Nichols flicked over a page in his notes, which were laid out on the table in front of him.

"My only question to you about the arrest of Mr. Allard is whether or not at any time he had possession of a knife?"

"He said he'd got a knife."

"Yes, but did you *see* one, officer?"

"Sorry, no . . . not until I was at the station."

"Did you physically search him at the station?"

"No, DI Moran did."

"And you saw him find the flick knife on Mr. Allard at this point?"

"No, I was in the police surgeon's room treating my cut lip."

"Where was DC Edwards at this time?"

"I assume he was in the charge room with DI Moran."

"Well, you assume wrong. According to the evidence he just gave he was in fact looking for the duty sergeant to come and book the prisoner in."

"I wasn't aware of that."

"Were you aware that DI Moran searched Mr. Allard at the time of his arrest and allegedly found the flick knife in his possession?"

"No, I only knew when DI Moran produced the knife from his own pocket in the charge room that he said he found it on the defendant."

Nichols was about to continue when the magistrate interrupted.

"Is there any point in pursuing this line of questioning? DC Edwards has told you he saw DI Moran search the defendant at the scene and put something in his own pocket, but being dark he could not say what it was. It's reasonable to assume it was the flick knife. DI Moran has stated that, because WPC Tennison was in such a distressed state having just been savagely attacked by your client, he decided it was best not to mention, or show her, the knife, until they had returned to the station."

"It is relevant, sir, because I believe that DI Moran left the charge room on the pretext of needing the toilet so he could get the flick knife to plant on Mr. Allard in his first step toward falsely implicating him in the rape."

"Well, DC Edwards has said that he never saw DI Moran leave the charge room, and although he went to get the custody sergeant he was certain the DI would never leave a prisoner alone, particularly for such serious offenses."

"Well, my client is adamant that DI Moran left the room briefly and I would argue that DC Edwards is lying."

The magistrate frowned.

"And the officers argue that your client is lying, Mr. Nichols, but it is a matter for me to decide who is telling the truth or not. So please move on with your questioning of WPC Tennison."

Jane couldn't believe what she had just heard and now understood why Edwards had avoided eye contact with her, and Moran had looked so smug when she entered the courtroom. She was nervously anticipating Mr. Nichols asking if she thought Edwards was lying and Moran had planted the knife but was surprised when, as advised by the magistrate, he changed his line of questioning.

Nichols flicked over to another page of his notes and spoke in a begrudging tone.

"Moving on as requested. Now, WPC Tennison, you were present during two interviews that DI Moran conducted with Mr. Allard?"

"Yes."

"And would you accept that in the first interview he lied in essence because he was worried about what his wife would think of him?"

"Yes, and I think that was why he gave us false details about who he really was."

"And in the second interview he admitted his crimes. Apart from the rape, that is?"

"Yes, that is correct."

"And you contemporaneously recorded the interviews on the correct forms."

"Yes, I did."

"Did you ask Mr. Allard to read and sign the interview notes?"

"After the first interview DI Moran asked him to and he did, but after the second interview I didn't personally because—"

"A confession to a number of indecent assaults and a denial to a violent rape, yet you didn't follow one of the basic principles of the Judges' Rules concerning the interrogation of a suspect?"

"I had to take Allard back down to the cells and he was asking to make a phone call and to contact a solicitor—"

"A solicitor he never got, yet was entitled to speak with under the Judges' Rules. Tell me, WPC Tennison, do you even know what the Judges' Rules are?"

"Yes, we had to learn them at training school—"

"Well, they obviously didn't sink in where you're concerned, did they?"

Jane felt embarrassed and flustered. Although her experience in court was limited she knew Nichols was playing mind games with her.

"It was remiss of me not to, and at the time I should have said something, but DI Moran was in charge of the case and didn't mention the signing of the notes until later."

"When did you sign the notes of the second interview?"

"The following morning."

"And when did DI Moran and my client sign them?"

"I don't know, but as I recall their signatures were already on each page when I signed them."

"Were you present when the alleged confession was made to, and recorded by, DI Moran?"

"No."

"Have you taken part in a conspiracy with your colleagues to frame an innocent man with a crime he did not commit?"

"No, I have not," Jane replied strongly, resenting his accusation.

"Do you think DI Moran has fabricated evidence and been supported in his lies by DC Edwards?"

Jane had no choice but to pause and think how she should best answer the question. She now knew that Brian Edwards had lied to the court, yet in some ways she sympathized with him and realized it was probably down to the fear of being ostracized by his colleagues. As for Moran, she knew deep down he had lied and looking up she could see the expression on his face. It was then that Jane wanted to shout out at the top of her voice "Moran is a liar," but she couldn't do it. She couldn't ruin her own career on a gut feeling with no evidence.

"I'm surprised the question is something you have to think about, officer, as the answer should be a simple yes or no," Nichols said with arrogance, pushing her for a reply.

"Sorry, I was upset by your insinuation that I or my colleagues were in any way dishonest. So the answer to your question is *no*."

"Do you know Marie Allard?"

"Yes."

"And have spoken with her on three occasions, I believe?"

The magistrate stopped taking notes and looked up at Mr. Nichols.

"According to the papers I have read, WPC Tennison only met Marie Allard when she went to search the house."

Nichols now informed the magistrate that on the morning of Peter Allard's first court appearance Jane spoke briefly with Marie outside the police station and then again at court this morning. The magistrate looked perturbed and asked Jane what the conversation was about. Before Jane could answer, Nichols informed him that Mrs. Allard said WPC Tennison innocently asked how she was, and after expressing her concerns about the evidence against Mr. Allard, WPC Tennison had said that the magistrate might decide there was not enough evidence to send the rape charge for trial.

The magistrate gave Jane a stern look before continuing. "And what makes you think that, officer?"

Again, Nichols added fuel to the fire with a haughty smile. "Exactly what I was wondering, sir, and may I also add that at the meeting outside the station WPC Tennison seemed surprised and somewhat shocked when Mrs. Allard informed her that her husband had allegedly confessed to DI Moran."

Jane looked crestfallen. She knew Nichols had belittled her and her evidence, yet in other ways she knew she'd dug a hole for herself. Now she wished it would open further and swallow her up so she could get away from what was becoming an intimidating and uncomfortable experience. Jane knew that, after her earlier answer about DI Moran and DC Edwards, she had to avoid intimating they had lied, even if it meant dropping herself further in the mire. She took a deep breath before continuing.

"I read all the indecent assault victims' statements and compared them with my own experience at the hands of the defendant. It seems to me that his actions, accent and words used differed from those carried out in the rape. The flick knife was actually seen and physically used in the rape and the assailant wore a balaclava, as opposed to a stocking mask like the defendant did when arrested by me."

Mr. Nichols nodded. "Very astute, officer, and apart from the false confession, an argument I was going to put forward as to why there is not a prima facie case or evidence to commit Mr. Allard to the Old Bailey for trial."

The magistrate did not look best pleased with either Jane or Mr. Nichols. Jane could sense that no matter what Mr. Nichols said, or even if she herself had stated that she believed Moran had fabricated the evidence, there was no way the case was not going to be committed for trial.

The magistrate removed his glasses and put them down on the desk.

"I have read the police report, as well as all the victims' statements, the defendant's interviews and his confession. At first Allard lied about the attack on WPC Tennison, then he lied about who he was and where he lived, facts he has since admitted. Once faced with insurmountable evidence, and the knowledge that his wife knew of his crimes regarding the indecent assaults, he capitulated and admitted his guilt. But he still denied the more serious crime of rape. It seems to me that there is always the possibility that his guilt eventually weighed so heavy that he did indeed confess to the rape. I see no reason why he would sign a false confession. However, that said, it is for a jury to determine guilt or innocence and from the evidence I have heard and reviewed so far the rape charge will be committed to the Old Bailey for trial."

Nichols did not look pleased and asked if he could bring one further thing to the magistrate's attention.

"If you must, Mr. Nichols, but I fail to see what you can add to change my mind."

Nichols now asked the usher to hand Jane a photocopy of the original second interview and said he wanted her to look at the bottom of each page and confirm that she had signed each and every page. As Jane flicked through the document the magistrate asked Nichols what the purpose of the exercise was, as the defendant was not challenging anything asked or said in either of the interviews contemporaneously recorded by WPC Tennison. Nichols asked him to bear with him for a couple more minutes.

As Jane looked through the interview she noticed that there were two pages that did not bear her signature. She was about to flick back when Nichols spoke.

"Is there a problem, officer?"

Jane looked glum as she put the notes down on the witness box. "I don't appear to have signed two pages of the interview, yet DI Moran and Mr. Allard have. It may have been an error on my behalf."

"Oh, don't worry about that. I don't suspect you of anything untoward. We all make mistakes when we are in a rush and not concentrating. Do you have a pen?"

"Yes," Jane replied, wondering what was going on in Nichols's mind.

"I know the interview is a photocopy of the original, but would you mind quickly signing the two pages for my benefit, just so everything is tickety-boo for my file?"

Jane got out her pen, flicked through to the pages that were unsigned, duly wrote her name and number and held out the papers to the usher to return to Mr. Nichols.

"Please double-check the pages you just signed."

Jane was puzzled. "I know I just signed them and you saw me do it, so why?"

"Read the two pages you just inadvertently signed," Nichols said pointedly.

Jane now turned to the two pages, put the others to one side and couldn't believe what she started to read. It was the alleged confession made by Peter Allard written by DI Moran.

Nichols picked up on her expression of amazement.

"You see how easy it is to be tricked into signing something when you are confused and flustered, as was Peter Allard when DI Moran asked him to sign what he believed was the record of the second interview. Like DI Moran did, I simply slipped the confession into the middle of the bundle and you, in all innocence, signed the confession as if you were guilty of a crime you never committed."

Jane felt awful but now realized that Nichols was probably right and DI Moran had indeed tricked Peter Allard into signing the false confession by slipping it into the bundle and then removing it before she signed the record of the interview. She looked up at Moran but he didn't bat an eyelid, and Mr. Nichols, having made his point to the magistrate, sat down.

The magistrate didn't look impressed and cleared his throat.

"You have made your point by using WPC Tennison as a scapegoat, Mr. Nichols. However, I am still of the opinion that the charge of rape will be committed to the Old Bailey for trial. I also accept that your client has pleaded to the indecent assaults and assault on a police officer, for which I can sentence him today. In my opinion, the penalties of imprisonment in this court are inadequate with regard to the seriousness of the offenses. Therefore, I will commit him for sentencing in custody at the higher court by the presiding judge on completion of the rape trial."

Peter Allard jumped up in the dock, pleaded his innocence and shouted that he had been tricked by DI Moran. The magistrate told him to sit down and be quiet, but he wouldn't desist and now Marie Allard joined in by shouting that the officers were all liars. It became so unruly that the magistrate ordered Allard to be taken to the cells and his wife removed from the courtroom. When this was done the magistrate stood up, said the case was over and that all parties could leave, then he left the room by his personal side entrance.

As Jane stepped out of the witness box she looked at Moran and Edwards with disgust and let them leave the room before her.

Jane picked up her police hat from the waiting room. There was no sign of Moran or Edwards. She stepped into the street and was relieved to see that Marie Allard wasn't there. As she stood at the bus stop an unmarked CID car pulled up and Moran leaned out of the passenger window.

"You want a lift back to the station?"

"No, I'll make my own way."

"Please yourself," he replied in a dour tone. "You did all right in there, Allard's barrister thought he was bloody Perry Mason." Moran waved his arm for DC Edwards to drive off.

Marie was making the children's breakfast of cereal and scrambled eggs on toast. The kettle was on and the toast was under the grill. She had already called them twice and could hear them running noisily from room to room. The "nice house" was in complete disarray, with cupboards and drawers open everywhere.

"Breakfast! Come to the table NOW!" she shouted, as she went out of the kitchen into the hall. Her son ran out from the sitting room, followed by her daughter. The little girl had a red velvet rose clipped into her hair. It was the treasured rose from the vase next to the statue of the Virgin Mary.

Marie snatched it from the child's hair, screeching, "You know never to touch that . . . you very, very naughty girl, and you get punished."

"Punished like Susie Luna," her son said gleefully.

Marie was shocked and looked so frightened that he felt guilty.

"Sorry, Mama . . ."

"Sit down at the table. Do as I say right *now*, both of you."

Marie went into the sitting room. She crossed herself and kissed her crucifix, and tried to calm herself down. How did her son know that name? What made him say it? The fear gripped her again. She was about to replace the rose in the vase next to the Virgin Mary, but instead she tore it to shreds, stuffing the frail leaves and velvet petals into her apron pocket.

Marie went back into the kitchen to finish preparing the children's breakfast. They sat very quietly watching her as she frantically whisked the eggs in a bowl, spilling some on the counter. The toast was now burning under the grill, and the kettle was whistling loudly. Then the phone started ringing shrilly in the hall, making her physically jump. She turned the kettle off and grabbed the toast from under the grill, almost throwing it onto the table.

"You put on butter," she said to the children. The phone carried on ringing as Marie hurried to answer it.

"Hello?"

She heard nothing but silence. Puzzled, Marie asked again, "Hello? Hello—who is this?"

Irritated by the silence, she was about to hang up when a voice crooning the words of a familiar Rolling Stones song began to come through the phone. Marie froze as the voice got louder and louder.

"Who is this?" Marie asked again. But the voice didn't stop, now almost screaming the words to "Angie" down the line.

"What you want?" Marie was crying now, shaking, her hand gripping the phone, unable to put it down.

The singing stopped abruptly and a hoarse voice answered.

"Five hundred pounds in used notes. If you report this call, I got the evidence to put your husband away for rape. I'll call again in two days."

Marie heard the line go dead. The receiver felt like a heavy weight in her hand as she slowly replaced it. She stood rooted with fear in the hallway. She didn't know what to do.

CHAPTER SEVEN

Jane looked out of the window; the leaves were falling now and the warmth of September had long gone and an autumn chill was in the air. She was sitting nervously in a small anteroom at Scotland Yard, wearing full uniform. While a PA was working busily at a nearby desk, Jane took a final look at some small note cards she had written. A male uniform officer came out of the interview room in a state of distress. Pulling off his clip-on police tie he kicked at a chair, and Jane, now even more nervous, got up to go in, but the PA told her to wait and said that she would be called when they were ready.

Over the PA's intercom Jane heard a gruff male voice asking for WPC Tennison to be sent in. She stood up and smoothed out her uniform, picking off some fluff from her jacket. She took a deep breath and entered the room.

Three men, a Commander, a Detective Chief Superintendent and a DCI, sat behind a long table. Jane was invited to take a seat opposite them and the Commander, who was sitting between the two other officers, flipped open a file with her name on it. "WPC Tennison, we know your name, would you be kind enough to tell us who will be interviewing you today?"

Jane looked puzzled as there were no name cards. However, she'd done her research and knew the three senior officers' names. She looked at each of them as she gave their names.

"You'd be surprised how many people don't do their homework and get it wrong, like the last officer."

Next the Commander asked why she thought she should be made detective. Jane swallowed. "During my time in uniform I feel I have proved myself capable through hard work and tenacity."

The DCI asked, "Have you any registered informants?"

"No, sir, I reacted on anonymous information. I did some research before obtaining a search warrant which resulted in the discovery of a quantity of stolen goods."

She was then asked what the goods were and sheepishly replied they were clothes from Woolworths, but it was an organized gang of women shoplifters who were selling the goods on a market stall.

"Hardly the crime of the century," said the DCI. "Well, I expected to hear something a bit more interesting and worthy of someone who wants to become a Met detective."

"I recently acted as a decoy and subsequently arrested a man who was wanted for a series of indecent assaults on women, as well as a rape."

"Did he indecently assault you?" the Commander asked.

"Yes," Jane replied, blushing and wondering if they already knew about the case.

"What exactly did he do?" the Superintendent asked. It felt as if he was reveling in Jane's obvious embarrassment.

"He touched me, sir . . ."

He smirked. "How did he touch you? Was it a quick squeeze or a full-on grope?"

"He grabbed me from behind, and he groped my breast. Then he tried to drag me to a darkened area by the Lido. When I attempted to break away from him he hit me in the mouth with his elbow, splitting my lip. I thought he was going to rape me, sir."

The Commander looked at her file and then glanced up at her, tapping the page with his finger.

"It states here that the suspect alleged that in actual fact you assaulted him?"

Jane was tight-lipped as she informed them that the suspect attacked her first and that she had defended herself.

The Commander turned over another page, again tapping it with his forefinger.

"According to this report it says that you hit him across the head with a truncheon, also delivering a well-aimed kick to his groin?"

One of the other two men sitting at the table winced, saying that he didn't know women carried truncheons. Jane was becoming very tense.

"I borrowed one from a colleague and had it tucked up my coat sleeve."

They smiled.

"Forward thinking and good planning—well done. No doubt he deserved a good whack across the head."

The Detective Chief Superintendent asked, "Has he been convicted?"

"The magistrate committed him for sentencing in custody at the higher court on completion of the rape trial."

He turned to another page, and whispered to his colleagues.

The DCI picked up the report, and took over the questioning. He remarked that Jane had previously been interviewed by A10 department over an allegation that a DS Gibbs had assaulted a drug dealer and had stolen his money.

Jane was very defensive, but maintained her control, as she explained, "The drug dealer withdrew the allegation and DS Gibbs has been reinstated to duty."

The Commander pointed out that this didn't mean it hadn't happened. He took the report back and flicked to yet another page. It seemed like an age before he looked up again.

"You were interviewed by A10 a second time over a botched bank raid, during which an explosion occurred and a DCI Bradfield and WPC Morgan were both killed?"

Jane became very subdued. "I was the officer who initiated the investigation when I recognized the main suspect's voice from an audio tape." It was very difficult to ascertain what all three men were thinking. They whispered to one another, and passed the reports back and forth, reading and turning pages.

The Commander then quoted from DCS Metcalf's report, which said that Jane had stuck to her guns about the suspect and although the investigation had ended in tragedy she was above reproach and had acted in a professional manner at all times. He was recommending her for the rank of detective. She felt the blood rushing to her cheeks. Metcalf had done as he had promised after all. The Commander added, "The final decision, however, rests with us. Please wait outside."

Jane stood up, gave a slight nod, and walked out. As she closed the door behind her, her legs felt like jelly. She sat back down in the chair outside the interview room.

The PA looked up. "You're the final candidate, how did it go?" she asked sympathetically.

Jane frowned. "Not too well."

"Well, don't look so worried. There's another board for detective in a year's time."

Jane sank back in her seat, convinced she had failed. The intercom buzzed and she was called back into the interview room again. She stood in front of the panel trying to hide the shake in her legs.

The Commander spoke. "It has been a tough decision and we are not all in agreement. The CID in London only has a handful of women within their ranks and you have been recommended by DCS Metcalf, a highly respected and astute senior officer. However, you're still young in service compared to so many of the other candidates, and there are only a limited number of vacancies to be filled . . ." He paused before asking Jane for her warrant card, which she handed to him. He took it, smiled, and handed her back a new one. When she looked at it she saw the words "Detective Constable Tennison."

The panel congratulated her and told her that as from Monday she would be posted to Bow Street Police Station CID. She was to report there at 10 a.m. to meet her new DCI. Jane's legs still felt very wobbly as she left, this time not with trepidation but with sheer excitement. She was so happy that she wanted to shout the news out to the world, and dance down the wide staircase.

After her interview, lightheaded with relief, she'd headed to Oxford Street and decided to treat herself to some clothes before going to see her parents to tell them the good news. That Friday evening Jane stood at the familiar front door, still wearing her uniform under a new raincoat. She had a bag of new clothes in one hand and a bottle of champagne in the other. She didn't use her key as she wanted to give her parents a surprise. She couldn't wait to tell them the good news. Mrs. Tennison opened the front door and, seeing the bottle of champagne, she clapped her hands before Jane could say a word.

"Oh! Pam didn't tell me she'd spoken to you!"

Jane was confused.

"About what?" she asked, as she dropped the shopping bags in the hallway and took off her raincoat.

Her mother rushed into the living room to announce that Jane had arrived with a bottle of champagne. Jane followed her mother into the room, holding her new warrant card in one hand and the champagne bottle in the other.

"I'm really excited about this! . . . Look at my new—"

Pam grabbed the bottle, grinning, as Mrs. Tennison said, "So are we! It's such wonderful news, isn't it?"

"How did you know?" Jane asked.

"Pam told us, of course! We're absolutely thrilled! I'll get some champagne glasses so we can all celebrate."

"How did she know I'd passed the interview board?" Jane asked, somewhat confused. There was a stunned silence in the room.

"I'll be starting at Bow Street Police Station on Monday."

"Oh . . . we thought you'd come to celebrate Pam's wonderful news."

"What news?" Jane asked.

"She's pregnant, so you'll soon be an auntie."

Mrs. Tennison went into the kitchen and opened the cupboards looking for champagne glasses. Almost as if it was an afterthought she asked, "Will you still be in uniform at Bow Street?"

Jane patiently explained that she was now a member of the plain-clothed CID and that she'd been made detective. She proudly held up her new warrant card. Mrs. Tennison glanced at it and then handed it back.

"I think it's safer in uniform, dear, after what happened to those detectives in the bank explosion."

Pam now joined them.

"I would think that central London isn't a very safe place, what with that bank explosion. And now you're really going to have to take care of yourself as you'll have responsibilities as an auntie. If you agree we both want to have you as Godmother."

Mrs. Tennison very obviously didn't want to talk about Jane's work and told her father to get a tray for the glasses and open the bottle of champagne so that they could celebrate Pam's pregnancy.

Jane felt totally deflated. It was as if her news was trivial in comparison. She tried to put on a brave face, smiling and then toasting Pam with her champagne. Mrs. Tennison asked Jane if she would be moving back home.

"Not at present."

"How will you get to and from Bow Street?"

Jane said that she hadn't had time to look at the best route yet. Mr. Tennison opened a drawer in the kitchen and took out an *A—Z.*

"Right, always best to be prepared . . . let's have a look. You can get the Central Line to Holborn, then change onto the Piccadilly Line for one stop to Covent Garden, then walk through Covent Garden to Bow Street."

It was unbelievable. Suddenly everyone was concentrating on the route for her to get to her new job.

Mrs. Tennison was quick to point out that the Bakerloo Line from Maida Vale was just down the road and went directly to Charing Cross. Bow Street was only a short walk from there. So Jane should move back home.

Mr. Tennison changed the subject. Pam, who always liked being in the spotlight and had just snatched it from Jane with her news about being pregnant, began asking everyone to list the names they all liked best for either a boy or a girl. Jane sipped the rather tepid champagne and glanced at her father. He raised his glass to her.

"Congratulations, my darling . . . You must be very proud, as am I. You're going to be Detective Jane Tennison . . . good girl, shows they must think a lot of you."

"Thank you, Daddy, I am very proud."

"I know, if Pam has a girl let's call her Jane!"

"Oh no!" Pam objected. "Plain Jane? No. I think she should be called Tiffany."

"You don't want to call a baby girl after a lampshade!" Jane's mother said, horrified.

"A Tiffany shade, Mother, is of great value."

As usual Jane saw her sister dominating the conversation and stealing her limelight. "What about Victoria?" She might as well add her own two pennies worth, she thought, smiling as she sipped her champagne.

CHAPTER EIGHT

Jane looked around at the flushed faces of her colleagues. They were squashed into the saloon bar of the Warburton Arms, which was full of people celebrating the weekend. She'd just finished her last shift at Hackney before starting at Bow Street on Monday and was heading out of the station door when Harris accosted her. "Didn't think we'd let you leave without saying goodbye, did you, love?" Blushing, Jane had been escorted to the pub across the road and now all the team were there. They had passed an envelope around to fund an open bar, with Ron the landlord monitoring the cash flow. He had provided sandwiches, sausage rolls and packets of crisps on the counter, alongside bottles of red and white wine. Everyone congratulated Jane and wished her well, especially DI Moran who had obviously been drinking more than his fair share. His tie was pulled loose under his open shirt collar, and he had one arm around DC Edwards's shoulders, who was also looking rather drunk.

"Well, you're going to be up against it at Bow Street, Tennison . . . everything is on high alert after the IRA bomb in Guildford today. You better be careful in the West End too, with it being close to Covent Garden Market, where you get a lot of scum, and drop-ins from any of the Met officers going to the courts. Who's the DCI there?"

Jane shrugged her shoulders. "I'm not sure, sir."

"Well, it's always good to have a change of scenery, but it depends on who's the guv, you know . . . You can get a lot of flack. If you want my advice, and you can take it or leave it, but . . ."

He used two fingers to point to his eyes, and then directed them to Jane's.

"Keep your eyes open, listen and learn, and above all . . . remember . . ." Moran seemed to lose track of what he was saying, as Edwards propped him up.

"Just remember . . . keep your nose clean, right, Brian?"

"Yes, guv."

Jane had drunk more of Ron's lukewarm white wine than usual. Sergeant Harris was also getting into the swing of it and insisted on passing Jane a drink and taking over the conversation. He clinked her glass so hard it almost shattered.

"Congratulashuns!" he slurred, downing his entire glass and placing it back on the bar. "So you'll be stationed at Bow Street . . . Here's something I bet you didn't know . . . Sherlock Holmes wrote about the station in his story 'The Man with the Harelip' . . . no, that's not right . . . it was 'The Man with the *Twisted* Lip' . . . I don't usually come to these dos but I felt on this occasion I should as, I have to admit, I'm proud of you, Tennison . . . You've handled yourself very well under extreme circumshtances . . . Have another drink . . ."

"No, thank you, I'm fine." Jane held up her still half full glass.

"Yes, you are fine, but you know, we've all been marked . . . every one of us . . . doesn't matter how long ago, it's inside . . . and you come in here like always and you see youngsters like you moving on, but they're like ghosts . . . You keep expecting to see Kath Morgan with her G and T putting money in the juke box, and Len Bradfield over at the billiard table slapping a fiver down . . . he was a bloody useless player."

Harris picked up another glass of wine.

"Sorry . . . don't want to put a dampener on things . . . like I said, it was some time ago now, and I don't usually make an appearance at these leaving drinks . . . They're mostly just an excuse for everyone to get pissed . . . have you got a drink?"

"I'm all right, Sarge. I'm glad to have this opportunity to thank you for all your help while I've been here."

He cocked his head to one side, then he suddenly leaned forward and gave her a dry kiss on her cheek.

"Maybe I know more than you ever realized . . . you handled yourself well, considering how close you were to Bradfield."

Jane flushed and was suddenly eager to leave, not wanting to discuss her relationship.

Harris said quietly, "We all have secrets, some best kept that way. I have one that I've never let be known."

Jane couldn't help herself. "You, Sergeant?"

"Yes, but you keep this to yourself. I'm part of a ballroom formation team, and we've got a good chance of being in the finals at Blackpool . . . Old Time waltz is my specialty."

Jane was completely taken aback as he gave her a sweeping gesture with his arm and stumbled backward, bumping into Edwards. Moran suddenly stepped in beside Jane and reached for a glass of wine. He had a lit cigarette in his mouth and leaned closer to her, keeping his voice low.

"We'll get a few more drinks down him and if the right music's on the juke box he dances, and we all have a good laugh! He never remembers in the morning . . . when he's had too much to drink he always gives away his ballroom dancing secret."

Moran gave Jane a lopsided smile but his expression was serious.

"Everyone has secrets, don't they, Jane?"

Jane was uneasy, not about the increasingly drunk Harris, but about the way in which Moran had looked at her when he had said "everyone has secrets." Did they all know about her relationship with Bradfield, her secret? Did they make derogatory remarks about it and gossip about her being a one-night stand after he had sent her off the case? Jane was blushing profusely and just wanted to leave.

"So, we're going to have a snooker game and get down to some serious drinking . . . are you up for it?" Moran asked.

"Actually, I think I should just go back to the section house and get a good night's sleep."

Jane turned to put her glass on the bar and thank Ron. The envelope funds had now all been spent, and the plates of food were empty. Pints of beer were being lined up and numerous officers from the station were crowding the bar.

"I'll walk you over there. It's late, and this is a dodgy area at night."

Moran held her elbow and guided her through the crowds. As they reached the pub's double doors Jane insisted that she was more than capable of walking back by herself. Moran pushed one door open and leaned in toward her.

"I just want to straighten something out. You seemed a bit tense after the court hearing . . . is anything bothering you? If it is, just spit it out so we can clear the air. Do you have a problem, Tennison?" Moran cocked his head to one side, exhaling a lung-ful of cigarette smoke. Jane hesitated, then shook her head. She didn't feel that this was either the time or place to discuss her reservations, and Moran was too close for comfort. He appeared to have sobered up and his deep, piercing eyes were making her feel nervous.

"No, sir . . . no problem."

"Good. I have masses of cases coming in, but we'll be seeing each other when the Allard trial kicks off. In the meantime I'll give your thanks to everyone."

She gave him a small smile, doubting whether anyone would have actually missed her leaving the pub. The festive atmosphere inside had become rather raucous.

"Goodbye then, Tennison, and good luck . . . Detective Constable . . ."

"Thank you, sir."

Jane walked down the pavement to cross over the road to the section house. When she turned back to the pub Moran was still watching her. He tossed his cigarette butt onto the ground and stamped it out with the heel of his Cuban boot. Perhaps he was aware of her infatuation with Bradfield, and maybe even knew that she had slept with him. But it didn't really matter now; she was moving on and away from Hackney.

CHAPTER NINE

Jane had spent Sunday tidying her room, changing the bed linen and generally preparing for her new job at Bow Street. She had meant to allow herself plenty of time on Monday morning but her alarm didn't go off. She dressed hurriedly, glad that she had taken the time to lay out her new suit and blouse the previous night, and was on her way within fifteen minutes.

Remembering her father's instructions, she took the Underground to Covent Garden, which was just a short walk from Bow Street. She passed the Royal Opera House, with its beautiful white pillars and marble steps, having picked up her pace to cut across from the big fruit and vegetable market. The wonderful heady scent from the huge array of flower stalls was enough to lift anyone's senses, but Jane was just intent on reaching Bow Street Station as quickly as possible as delays on the Underground meant she was running late.

As she waited to cross the busy road she looked at the station building. It didn't remind her of Hackney, but it was of the same era—the heavy station doors with the iron blue lamp above them. No wonder Conan Doyle used it in his story—it looked like a very intimidating Victorian building.

Jane hurried in through the main entrance. Inside it was a similar layout to her old station. There was the reception desk with the wooden counter, and a flap that could be lifted to allow officers to pass in and out, and very worn red leather chairs lined one wall.

The desk sergeant was terse and suggested that, as she was late, she should go directly to be introduced to her DCI and wouldn't have time to be shown around. He didn't introduce himself, or give her the chance to ask if she could use the ladies' cloakroom to tidy herself up. Instead he banged up the counter flap and gestured for her to follow him. He strode ahead through the annex room, and then along a stone tiled corridor. Jane struggled to keep up as she desperately tried to tuck stray strands of hair back into place and make herself presentable. She was still carrying her raincoat and shoulder bag as they climbed a small flight of stone stairs onto the first-floor landing. Numerous offices led off the corridor and she could hear the sound of telephones ringing and the officers manning the comms room radioing out to the patrol cars. She might be in the glamorous West End now but the inside of a police station remained the same wherever you were. The familiarity was reassuring and Jane was comforted by the faded, yellowing walls and the vast array of posters. They reached the DCI's office and the duty sergeant turned to face her. Jane asked if he could just give her a moment to tidy her hair but he seemed totally uninterested. He held out his hand for her raincoat as he knocked on the DCI's door.

"I don't usually do this . . . show you to his office. But you're late and . . . There's a WDC Jane Tennison to see you, sir."

Jane glanced at the plaque on the door: "DCI P SHEPHERD."

"Come in." The voice was quiet and authoritative.

Jane entered the DCI's office. She was surprised to find that Shepherd was a diminutive and unassuming man. He was about five foot eight with a very pallid complexion and an unlined, boyish face. He had thick wavy hair that was parted to one side, with short sideburns, giving him an even more youthful appearance. His desk and walls were adorned with pictures of his wife and teenaged kids, with not one police photo, badge or crest. Before he could say a word there was another knock on the door and the sergeant ushered in DI Spencer Gibbs.

Shepherd introduced the two of them to one another. Jane was surprised that Gibbs barely reacted as he explained to the

DCI that they already knew each other from Hackney. She was shocked by his gaunt appearance and slightly offended by his refusal to look at her. They both drew up chairs to sit in front of Shepherd's desk.

"Jane, I am sure you know that after a long period of sick leave, followed by light duties at NSY, Gibbs was recently promoted to DI and sent here to Bow Street. I am obviously aware that you must have both had a very emotional period after the explosion that killed DCI Len Bradfield and WPC Kath Morgan. However, I feel sure that, although the experience will have left an indelible scar, it was more than eighteen months ago. Time is a great healer and I trust that you can now both concentrate on your future here at Bow Street and that working together will not be a problem."

Jane noticed Gibbs tense up at the mention of the explosion, and saw him grip the side of the chair seat with both hands. It was still very raw for them both and Jane, unlike Gibbs, had remained at Hackney where the two of them had been based at the time of the incident. In many ways she agreed with what Shepherd had said about time being a great healer, but she knew instinctively that perhaps she had coped far better than Gibbs.

After a brief talk about what DCI Shepherd expected, and how he encouraged his officers to be a team and always share information, he asked DI Gibbs to show Jane to the CID office and introduce her to the CID clerk, Edith, who would allocate her a desk. Jane and Gibbs both replaced their chairs, shook the DCI's hand and left his office.

As soon as the door closed behind them Gibbs gave Jane a sidelong glance, gesturing for her to follow him. He was even thinner than she remembered and his hair still stood up like a wire brush. He was wearing a smart suit with a thin tie, a fashionable small-collared shirt, with the cuffs a bit short over his skinny wrists and long tapering fingers. He was also wearing rather smart shoes with tassels and moved like a dancer as if he was about to spin round to face her on his heels.

"How's your rock band?"

"We broke up." He changed the subject. "You look very smart and ready for business."

"Thank you . . . you look very dapper yourself."

"Dapper?"

"I like your shoes."

He looked down at his feet, and then back up at her.

"I ordered this suit from Mannie Charles . . . d'you remember him?"

"Not really."

"He was the tailor who was selling all the hooky suits to the CID. We all ordered them, and found out later they were nicked from Horne Brothers' warehouse and the labels were switched. We'd all got them made to measure and paid up front . . . he delivered them after . . ."

Gibbs turned away, pulling at the knot in his tie.

"Kath Morgan had one made, and the guv . . . he'd wanted this flashy lining, with six buttons on the breast . . . old Sergeant Harris took it cos he was the only man as tall as Len. I didn't know what to do with it, and Harris said, you know the way he was, 'I'll have that,' and it was still in the plastic wrapping. Anyway, I reckon when he saw the striped silk lining he knew he'd never wear it . . ."

Gibbs turned on his heels before Jane could reply. She followed him as he headed down the corridor and a few uniform officers passed them. Jane asked him how he was, but he ignored her. She continued speaking.

"I understand how you must feel about Bradfield and Kath . . . I think everyone has found it really difficult."

Gibbs came to an abrupt stop and spun to face her.

"No, you don't know how I feel . . . It just threw me a bit to see you. I've got to go. The ladies' locker room is straight ahead and the CID room, DCI's and DI's rooms are all on this floor. See you later."

Gibbs strode off, then paused to turn back.

"The duty sergeant, Eric Fuller, is a bit of a pompous prat and just like old Sergeant Harris—but a foot shorter!"

Jane found her way to the ladies' locker room. She was surprised at the number of lockers that had been allocated. There were obviously more female staff members than there had been at Hackney Station. She took the key from locker 12, placed her handbag inside, and hung her jacket on the relevant hook. She then quickly tidied up her hair and made her way to the CID office.

The door was halfway along the corridor, and the room itself was far larger than the cramped and dated office at Hackney. Not that this office had any modern equipment, but it was much lighter and the desks were newer. She remembered the embarrassing incidents when she had snagged her stockings on the wooden desks at Hackney, and hoped she wouldn't be doing the same in this office.

The two clerical women on the far side of the room were busily typing reports. The matriarch of the office was a very solid, stout woman with small round spectacles and had her gray hair in a tight bun. She rose to her feet, removed her spectacles and in a very loud voice asked, "Are you WDC Jane Tennison?"

"Yes," Jane replied nervously.

"I am Edith Pickard, a former policewoman. I never liked being thrown in at the deep end with integration . . . I preferred the specialist role in the women's force, which I've now worked in for many years. I was very disillusioned as I was only ever given a day's warning that I was to be assigned to full shift duties with the men."

Jane was puzzled as to why Edith needed to tell her all of this.

"I am very pleased to meet you." Jane extended her hand.

Edith gripped her hand and shook it vigorously.

"I've allocated you a desk at the back. You'll be the only WDC here at Bow Street. We have twelve male detectives and two detective sergeants."

Jane made her way toward the empty desk, which had a rather dilapidated-looking office chair with one wheel missing. There was a wilting pot plant on the desk.

Edith patted the sleeve of her mauve jumper.

"I've always had a tinge of regret that I left the force, and I have to admit that I am a tad jealous that such a young girl has been assigned to us . . . But I'm sure we will get along very well. The two ladies on the far side are Gillian Thomas and Irene Marsden, both diligent and hard-working clerks. With a DCI like Shepherd we all have to keep on our toes. Right, let me explain the functioning of the office and the shifts. The CID duty book is kept in that drawer, and the crime book in that drawer."

Jane looked up as a figure appeared in the doorway. Edith glanced over.

"Good morning, sir. I was just introducing young Jane Tennison here to the workings of our office, and how you like to keep it very ship-shape."

DCI Shepherd gave her a wan smile.

"I don't know what I would do without your more than capable hands, Edith."

Shepherd turned to Jane and asked if she had seen DI Gibbs as he was not in his office or in the canteen. Jane recalled Gibbs's abrupt departure and suspected he'd left the station but she didn't want to get him into trouble. "Sorry, sir, he said he needed to go."

Shepherd put his hands on his hips.

"Bugger it . . . Edith, are there any other detectives about? I've had uniform officers calling in a suspicious death at a flat in Aldwych."

"I'm so sorry, sir, but we have two court sessions today and the other officers are dealing with investigations."

Shepherd was clearly irritated by everyone's absence, and was annoyed that he would have to attend himself when he was so busy with paperwork and reports. He looked at Jane.

"Tennison, leave a message on Gibbs's desk telling him to be at the scene as soon as he returns."

He walked briskly out of the office. Edith handed Jane her official notebook and two sharpened pencils.

Jane said softly, "I wish he'd asked me to attend . . ."

"Good heavens, it's only your first day! You've got a lot to learn . . . he's not going to entrust you with a sus death yet."

Just as Jane was wondering if she should have asked DCI Shepherd whether she could accompany him, he popped his head back into the room and said, "You haven't got time to chat, Tennison . . . Grab your coat and get a move on!"

Edith pursed her lips. Obviously she had been mistaken and this new WDC knew how to get ahead. It hadn't been like that in her day, not that she would ever think of returning to uniform. She'd had enough; and it was only a suspicious death, so hardly anything to get excited about.

It was a short walk from Bow Street Station to the flat in Aldwych. Shepherd walked briskly, with Jane keeping up beside him, as he spoke about his wife and children, and how in his book "family always comes first." Jane nodded, getting an impression of her new DCI as a family man—a hard thing to be in the police force, what with the long, irregular hours and the frequent after-hours get-togethers in the pub.

They arrived at a four-story building split into flats. The PC at the front door stated that a Barry Dawson, aged twenty-six, had returned home from work earlier that morning to find his wife Shirley, twenty-three, dead in the bath while his baby daughter was sleeping in the playpen.

"Where is he now?" Shepherd asked impatiently.

"Mr. Dawson is in a highly distressed state, sir. Both he and the child are currently with the next-door neighbor in the basement flat. The police doctor arrived to pronounce 'life extinct' and is already upstairs. He requested the attendance of the laboratory liaison sergeant but he was busy dealing with another scene, sir, so we've been waiting for backup. There's also a dog, sir, in a cage. We haven't let it out as we're not sure what to do with it—he's a bit nasty."

DCI Shepherd looked at his watch and told the PC that he would like to speak with Mr. Dawson, but first he wanted to view the scene and talk to the doctor. As they stood outside the flat the DCI said, "Tennison, don't touch or disturb anything."

He put his hands in his coat pockets and lifted them up toward Jane, somewhat reminiscent of a flasher, demonstrating his method of allaying the urge to touch anything at the crime scene. Jane took a pair of thin leather driving gloves out of her handbag and put them on.

They proceeded together up to the top floor, passing a pay-phone mounted on the wall. On the top-floor landing there was a collapsible Maclaren pushchair leaning up against the wall. The front door was open and they went inside into the narrow hallway. There was a double bedroom to the left, a single spare room beside it, a bathroom on the right, and a living room, kitchen and dining area ahead. No lights were on apart from inside the bathroom. Shepherd tapped on the open bathroom door and walked in, followed by Jane. The doctor, dictated by procedure, was crouching down by the bath feeling for a pulse on the victim's left hand. She was motionless and face up in the bath, her eyes wide open, as if frozen in time and staring into space. Her long, thick dark hair floated around her head in the scarlet blood-stained water. The tap end of the bath had a blood smear down it. A dressing gown was on the floor next to the bath. DCI Shepherd introduced Jane to Dr. Henry, who gave her a noncommittal glance as she took out her notebook.

Dr. Henry lifted the victim's head out of the water, then let her head go, and it sank slowly down into the water. Suddenly a few bubbles escaped from her mouth and nose. Jane gasped.

"She's breathing!"

Dr. Henry laughed and explained that the bubbles were just some trapped air in the chest, which had been released by him moving her. It was difficult for Jane to take everything in. The small bathroom was full of various shampoos, medications and creams, numerous baby lotions and a bucket of dirty nappies. There was a towel rack holding some grubby towels, and the lino floor was stained and marked as if it had been laid many years ago. The washbasin was cracked with a dirty rim around it, and on the edge of it stood a plastic cup containing toothbrushes and a tube of toothpaste.

"Right, your victim—she may have had an underlying heart condition that caused her to fall, but doubtful at her young age. From the injury to the forehead it looks like she slipped in the bath and fell forward and may have knocked herself out and subsequently drowned. The wound is not that deep and there is a blood smear on the main tap but she could have bled freely from it. The water is cold so most likely she was originally taking a bath sometime in the early morning."

"So nothing suspicious?" DCI asked, as he looked at his watch.

"Not that I can see," the doctor replied, and started to fill out a form, adding that the water on the floor had probably come from the splash overflow when she slipped and banged her head.

Leaving the doctor to complete his forms, Jane and DCI Shepherd moved out of the bathroom and went toward the bedroom. Shepherd glanced into the room from the doorway. The curtains were closed, the bed unmade and the room smelt musty. It was very scruffy and untidy. There was a baby's cot near the bed with filthy sheets, and piles of dirty clothes were strewn around the floor. Shepherd could see nothing untoward. Nor was there anything in the second small box room. It looked as if the occupants were starting to redecorate, but it was full of odd bits and pieces of furniture.

They moved on to the living room, which contained a baby's playpen scattered with toys, and a high chair with a full bowl of food, a spoon and a baby's bottle of milk that looked untouched. A three-bar electric fire was burning bright orange and nearby was a laden clothes horse. Beside it stood an ironing board with an unplugged iron and a blouse draped over it, ready to be pressed.

Through an archway Jane noticed an old dark velvet sofa and a worn armchair. Off to one side was the kitchen area with a sink and a draining board stacked with dirty pans and crockery. Old-fashioned cupboards lined the wall around the cooker and fridge, and the floor had a threadbare carpet with large gaps showing the floorboards beneath. Behind the sofa was a dog in a small cage which began leaping up and down, snarling and growling as Jane approached. Jane froze as it leaped toward her, trying to get through the bars. The DCI pointed out that the sofa was covered in white dog hairs so it was obvious that the dog must have usually been free to roam around the flat.

"Don't let it out—that's a bull terrier. We'll have to get the owner to come in and sort it out . . . they can sometimes be very aggressive."

Shepherd looked at his watch again.

"We're just treating this as a non-suspicious accidental death."

"Should I get the uniform PC to radio the station and see if a lab liaison sergeant is now available, sir?"

DCI Shepherd glanced at her as if she was stupid.

"What for? There's no forced entry, no signs of a disturbance . . . totally non-suspicious. And you heard the Doc say that it's accidental?"

Jane hesitated.

"Yes, I know, sir . . . Should I get a photographer to the scene?"

Shepherd ignored her. He was obviously eager to leave and went to the open front door shouting down to the PC to radio the station and ask them to see if a SOCO was now available to take some snaps of the body.

"Snaps?" Jane thought, appalled. She felt that his manner was incredibly uncaring and insensitive, considering that the victim's husband might be able to hear him shouting.

Shepherd turned back to Jane and told her he would return to the station and call the coroner's officer to let him know about the death.

"The coroner's officer will arrange for undertakers to attend and remove the body to Westminster mortuary. Tennison, you take a statement from the husband. It doesn't have to be here and now, but we'll need it for the coroner's report."

He turned and walked out before Jane could ask any further questions, leaving her unsure about exactly what to do next.

She returned to the bathroom and the doctor handed her his scene examination report. Jane noticed a rolled up bath slip mat by the washbasin, next to a child's potty, and remarked to Dr. Henry how tragic it was that they had a slip mat and hadn't used it. He was as eager to leave as Shepherd, and pointed out that the mat was probably for the child. Jane hovered as he closed his medical case, and tentatively asked what she should do.

"The coroner's officer will sort everything and advise you accordingly. Now, I have to dash, my dear—I've got a prisoner to examine at West End Central."

It was a very eerie feeling for Jane to be alone with the dead body in the bath. She still couldn't get over the young woman's eyes, curious as to why they were open, staring at her as if crying out for help in the last moments of death as she drowned. The dog was still barking in its cage and Jane was relieved when DI Gibbs walked into the bathroom, despite him smelling like a brewery.

He held up the note she had left and anxiously asked what she had told the DCI.

"That you'd had to go out."

"OK, thanks . . . So what's going on here?"

Jane told him what Dr. Henry had said and that the DCI had gone back to the station, instructing her to treat the death as non-suspicious and complete a report for the coroner.

Gibbs moved past Jane and crouched down to examine the dead woman.

"I'll bet any money on it that the DCI has no intention of going back to the station. He got the PC downstairs to radio in and inform the coroner's officer of the details. He finds excuses to slip away so he can get home to his wife and kids. He doesn't socialize or drink much either. His nickname is 'Timex' because he's always looking at his watch!"

Jane smiled, glad of him being with her. Gibbs sat back on his heels and took a closer look at the victim's face.

"I hate it when they have their eyes open like this . . . freaks me out. Did the Doc say how long she'd been dead?"

"No, all he said was that she must have got into the bath early this morning as the water's cold. She slipped forward, I think, and hit her forehead and he said she might have knocked herself out and then fallen back into the water."

"So what's he saying . . . ? She steps into the bath, slips forward, smacks her forehead against the middle tap? Funny . . . I would think that if she fell forward she would be face down in the bath. Unless she was standing up when she fell and hit her head, then recoiled backward?"

Gibbs dipped his fingers into the water, then reached up to the towel rail to dry them.

"Ughhh, these are soaking wet . . . that's odd . . . Did the husband say he used them to mop up the water at all?"

"I haven't spoken to him yet. The wound might have bled so she was still alive when she fell in the bath," Jane said, gesturing with her hand toward the body.

Gibbs sighed and looked around the dirty bathroom. The PC from downstairs appeared, and shouted toward them from the open front door. The dog started barking hysterically again.

"There's still no photographer available. The coroner's officer has been informed and undertakers should be here in about an hour. I'm supposed to be off duty at 3 p.m. and the station has radioed asking if they want another PC to relieve me here at the premises."

Gibbs walked out of the bathroom. "I'll authorize you four hours of overtime, even if you only end up doing two."

"Thank you very much, sir. The neighbor has contacted Dawson's mother and she's on her way over from Rotherhithe in a cab."

Gibbs turned to Jane. "The victim's husband is a Barry Dawson. His wife's name is Shirley," she told him, glancing at her notebook.

"OK, well, I should be getting back to the station."

"I'm unsure what to do at the scene, Spence. I mean, do I just stay here and wait for someone to come and help me?"

"Draw a sketch plan of the bathroom scene in your notebook. As we can't get hold of a photographer, take as much detail as you think they'll need."

The dog started barking again and Gibbs went into the sitting room. She saw him bending down to the cage and shouted for him not to open it. The dog went berserk again, hurling his body at the cage bars.

"Do you think I should call the dog section to take it to Battersea?" Jane asked.

"No, Dawson can take the vicious thing with him to his mother's, it can't stay here. We don't know if it's been fed or how long it's been caged up."

He walked back into the living room and stood with his arms folded. He glanced around the room, and then crossed over to some shelves where there was a stereo system alongside a ringed record holder. He thumbed through the albums and pulled one out.

"Jim Morrison . . . The Doors . . . Well, at least he's got good taste in music, which is more than can be said for the state of this dump . . . This was Bradfield's favorite band."

Jane watched as he carefully replaced the album into the record holder and quickly changed the subject.

"Do you want to speak to the victim's husband?" Jane asked.

"No I don't, unless he wants to say something. If so, it's your job and you need to gain experience in dealing with these kinds of situation."

"I'd be grateful if you came with me, Spence." Jane didn't want to make a mistake on her first case.

Gibbs cocked his head to one side and grinned.

"OK, where is he?"

"With Mr. Cook, the next-door neighbor."

Jane and Gibbs left the same officer manning the front door of the house and went next door. The neighbor, a retired bus driver, lived in the basement with his invalid wife. When Gibbs knocked Jane could hear a baby crying. Mr. Arnold Cook opened the door. He had so far been very accommodating but from the expression on his face he was now clearly eager for everyone to leave.

"My wife is very frail and I need to get her lunch. They're in the front room, and the baby has done nothing but cry. Barry is distressed . . . such a terrible thing."

"Thank you very much, sir. I'm Detective Inspector Gibbs and this is WDC Tennison. If we could just have a few words with Mr. Dawson I'm sure we can be out of your way quickly."

Mr. Cook led them to the sitting room doorway. His wife was in a wheelchair in the hall by their open kitchen door.

"Are they still here, Arnold? I can hear the baby crying . . . have you given them a cup of tea?"

"Yes, love, now you go back into the kitchen."

"You'll have to push me . . . I can't turn this chair."

Mr. Cook waved his hands for Gibbs and Jane to go into the sitting room as he tended to his wife.

Barry Dawson had long, mousy blond hair tied in a pony-tail, with blue eyes that were set wide apart. He had a very fit physique and was rocking his baby daughter in his arms. The little girl was clearly distressed, and was red faced from crying. She kept calling out "Mama" between screams and was probably also hungry. Jane gave the baby a sympathetic smile.

Dawson paced up and down trying to soothe her, then stopped by a tea tray with a plate of biscuits. He picked one up and gave it to the little girl who eagerly grasped it in her tiny hand and started sucking at it.

As the baby was now placated, Gibbs and Jane introduced themselves and gave their condolences.

"I believe you found your wife, Mr. Dawson, is that right?"

Dawson gritted his teeth and looked as though he was about to break down, but took several deep breaths to calm himself.

"Sorry . . . I'm so sorry. She needs changing, and my wife . . . Oh God! I can't believe this has happened . . ."

"It's all right, sir . . . it can't be easy for you. We'll try and get this over with as quickly as possible. When you found her, was she lying back in the bath, not face down?"

"When I opened the door she was lying there in the bath, facing upward . . . And dear God, her eyes were wide open . . ." he sobbed.

It took a short while longer before he was able to compose himself enough to give them a clear statement of what had happened. As he did so the little girl fell asleep in his arms and Jane began to take some cursory notes in her pocket book.

Barry Dawson stated that he was a porter at St. Thomas' Hospital. He had been on an early shift and said that when he had left their flat in the morning his wife hadn't been feeling well, and had recently been complaining of headaches and dizzy spells. Barry had tried phoning the communal phone in their building a number of times in the morning to see how she was, but there had been no answer. He said that he usually always called at around 10 a.m. to check that she had taken the dog out for a walk. Desperately worried about her and the child, Barry had asked his boss to let him leave at around 11 a.m. and on returning home he had found his wife's body in the bath. In a state of shock, and not knowing what to do, he had run to his neighbor, Mr. Cook, who had dialed 999.

Jane held up her pencil.

"Excuse me, Mr. Dawson . . . Could I just verify the timings? You called home at 10 a.m., but there was no reply?"

"He just said that, Tennison," Gibbs interjected.

At that moment the doorbell rang and on answering it Mr. Cook returned to say that a Mrs. Dawson was at the front door.

"Oh thank God, it's my mum . . . MUM!"

Mr. Cook stepped back from the sitting room door as Rita Dawson hurried into the room. She was very overweight, and only five foot two, with badly dyed red hair. She was wearing a floral midi skirt with open sandals and white socks.

"Oh Jesus, God . . . I can't believe this . . ."

There was an outburst of grief between them. The child started crying and Mrs. Dawson took her from her son's arms.

"Oh you poor little soul . . . she's sopping wet, Barry! Have you fed her? She must be hungry."

Rita calmed and soothed the child, who stopped crying when she was given another biscuit to suck on. Rita asked what had happened as Barry slumped into the winged-back chair, holding his head in his hands.

"Dear God, Ma . . . I found Shirley . . . She was in the bath . . . I kept on ringing her and when I got no answer I came home from work." He broke down in tears again.

Jane explained what the police doctor had said and also advised them that she needed to get a statement from Barry. He was becoming more and more upset, repeating over and over that he shouldn't have gone to work knowing she wasn't well.

"What are you talking about? What's going on? . . . I don't understand what you're talking about," Rita said.

"It's my fault, Mum . . . it's all my fault . . ." Barry replied.

Jane quietly explained that there had been a tragic accident and that it wasn't Mr. Dawson's fault.

"But I will need to take a full statement from you, Mr. Dawson," Jane explained.

"Do I have to do it now?"

Jane was sympathetic and said that he didn't have to do it straight away, but then Gibbs stood up.

"It would be helpful if you could do it now, sir, so that we have all the facts written down."

"Listen, I think poor Barry has been through enough at the moment and needs to be with his daughter. They should both come home with me," Mrs. Dawson said, suddenly protective of her son and grandchild.

Gibbs glanced at Jane and shrugged, saying that tomorrow or the next day would do.

"I need to get some clothes . . . but I can't face going into the flat again," Barry replied.

Rita comforted him. "I'll stay with you, darlin', but I've got to get some of my granddaughter's possessions too . . . She needs nappies, pajamas, and some of her toys, her bottles . . . I need her pushchair . . ."

Gibbs, by now becoming rather frazzled, instructed Jane to accompany them to the flat and mentioned his concerns about the dog.

"What's the matter with the dog? He's not got out, has he? Is he lost?" Mrs. Dawson said.

Jane quickly replied, "No, he's in the flat. It's just that he was getting very agitated, growling and snapping at us in his cage."

"Well, it's no wonder with all the comings and goings . . . It's not in his nature to be vicious, he's usually a softie, even with strangers. He's probably hungry and wondering what's going on as he's been locked in his cage all day."

Something about Mrs. Dawson's reply jarred with Jane, then she realized that Mrs. Dawson seemed more concerned about the dog and had hardly reacted to the fact that her daughter-in-law had been found dead in the bath.

By the time they had been let out of the basement by Mr. Cook and had returned to the Dawsons' flat the little girl was screaming again. Mrs. Dawson tried to calm her, jiggling her up and down in her arms. Jane found the noise wearing, making it hard for her to think.

They headed up the stairs, with Barry lagging behind. Mrs. Dawson displayed a toughness about her as she firmly told her son that whatever he was feeling he had to help get everything sorted to take over to her place. They all went into the flat and Gibbs quickly closed the bathroom door. Mrs. Dawson fetched a large, scruffy suitcase and collected her granddaughter's belongings. She instructed Barry to pick up some dog food and gather whatever clothes he needed.

Jane and Gibbs stood to one side.

"She's a tough broad, isn't she?" he said quietly.

Jane nodded. "Yes . . . But I think right now they're both in shock. They're sort of acting on automatic pilot."

Gibbs ran his hands through his hair. "Yeah, tell me about it . . ."

Mrs. Dawson picked up feeding bottles and nappies, and threw a few baby toys into the suitcase. She did everything while the little girl was balanced on her hip. Barry handed a few of his own personal items to his mother to add into the open case on the bed. He crossed over to the dog's cage. The dog had not barked once since they had returned and was now cowering in the cage, shaking. Jane noticed that in Barry's presence he seemed completely submissive, his tail between his legs. "See, I told you he's a softie," Mrs. Dawson said, sticking a rather dirty dummy into the child's mouth.

"Go and shut the case, love, and ask them to get us a ride home. I'll start going down with the pushchair."

Barry clipped a lead onto the dog's collar and went into the bedroom to get the suitcase.

Jane offered to help but Mrs. Dawson shook her head and then looked slowly around the flat.

"You know, she was a shockingly lazy girl . . . young, you see, never done housework, and to be honest I've not really taken it all in, but she was a good mother . . . God knows how it happened."

"She may have fallen while she was getting into the bath, and hit her head."

"Terrible thing is, I was supposed to come by early this morning. I had a problem with my washing machine and had to wait in for an engineer to fix it. Shocking to think that if I'd been here I would've found her."

"Do you have a set of house keys, Mrs. Dawson?"

"Yes, but I was going to babysit . . . I often come by and help out when I'm not workin'. I take Heidi to the local playground and walk the dog."

Barry closed the suitcase and, with the dog following on the lead, he went out of the bedroom and handed Jane his wife's key to lock the door behind them. Jane asked him if he could come into the station the following afternoon to make a statement. Mrs. Dawson was still by the open front door.

"Have you told them at work yet, Barry? You'd better, because you're in no fit state to go in."

Barry replied that he hadn't told them yet, and had only come home because he was worried when Shirley hadn't answered the phone. He seemed to be in a daze, standing with the suitcase in one hand and the cowering dog on the lead in the other. Gibbs told them he could take them over to Rotherhithe, but told Barry that he needed to make sure the dog was kept on a lead in the back of the car.

As they headed down the stairs Gibbs turned to Jane.

"Listen, I'm going to go straight home after I've dropped them off."

"What? . . . Am I going to be left here on my own then?"

"You'll be all right. Just call it a day once the body's been taken to the mortuary by the undertakers. I'll see you in the morning and we can go over what you should put in your report for the coroner."

Jane stood uncertainly in the doorway for a while, then decided she would make a few inquiries with the other tenants. She went outside to find the uniform officer who was still standing patiently in the street by the main entrance to the building, which was one of a substantial row of Victorian houses divided into large high-ceilinged flats.

"Look, I'm going to see the tenants, but call me if the undertakers arrive, OK?"

"Will do," said the PC, hoping he wouldn't have to wait much longer. Now he'd had the promise of overtime regardless, he was keen to head back to the station.

Jane knocked on the door of the ground-floor flat but, as she'd expected, there was no reply. She had already been told that the couple left for work early and she just wanted to make sure. She was about to walk up to the first-floor flat when Mr. Cook appeared at the front door.

"Is everything all right?"

Jane nodded and he stepped further inside the hall.

"The people in that flat won't be back until after six."

"Do you know their names?"

"Yes, Mr. and Mrs. Johnson. But I only know them to say hello to . . . nice couple . . . they work in the City."

"Do you know who lives in the first-floor flat?"

"Nobody, it's empty. You'd have to contact the landlord. I think he's going to do it up because the previous tenants moved out a good few weeks ago. Same as the basement, it's empty and full of old furniture."

"Thank you very much. Do you know how long Mr. and Mrs. Dawson have lived in the top flat?"

"Why, do you think something's not quite right?" he asked.

"No . . . obviously there has been a tragic incident, but I need some family background details to give to the Coroner's Office."

Mr. Cook explained that they had moved in about a year ago and seemed a nice couple. He said that he got on quite well with them, but they didn't really socialize as such.

"My wife is wheelchair bound and I'm her main carer. I'm always very busy, so I don't really know them all that well."

"When was the last time you saw her?"

"My wife?"

"No, Mr. Cook, Shirley Dawson."

"Well, not today, obviously. To be honest I can't remember if I saw her yesterday, but she did walk the dog regularly. Then today Barry banged on our door in a dreadful state, rambling incoherently that something had happened to his wife. I told him to stay at my place while I went up to their flat, and when I opened the bathroom door I saw Shirley in the bath. I was going to check for a pulse on her neck, but when I put my hand in the bath I could feel that the water was cold and it was obvious she was dead. So I thought it best not to touch her. I found little Heidi sleeping in the playpen in the living room."

"So their daughter was in the flat?"

"Yes, I picked Heidi up and took her downstairs so that I could call the police. Barry was in a terrible state and he said that he had tried to call his wife. It was a regular thing he did, you know. Like I said, she would walk the dog of a morning. Barry works at St. Thomas' and Shirley stayed at home to mind the child, so when I got back to my place I called 999 . . ."

Jane continued making notes, then hesitated. She found it strange that Barry hadn't dialed 999 himself, or picked up his daughter before going to Mr. Cook's flat. She also underlined the note she had made that Mr. Cook said he opened the bathroom door.

"The bathroom door was closed when you went into the flat, Mr. Cook?"

"Yes."

"Thank you very much, you have been very helpful. Do you recall the landlord's name?"

"No, he's not my landlord. All I know is that he's a nasty piece of work, and a real cheapskate. He owns the head lease and charges heavy money for doin' maintenance work . . . but as you can see it's not that clean on the stairs and landings, and the gutters are all in bad shape."

"Thank you, Mr. Cook."

Jane went back upstairs to the Dawsons' flat and half closed the front door behind her. She checked her watch and wondered how long she would have to wait for the undertakers. She thought about making herself a cup of tea but didn't think she should, and the filthy sink full of dirty cups was not very appealing. She looked around the room and opened her notebook to write about the state of the flat. She flicked back and forth, looking at what she had written when questioning Mr. Cook. Something else struck her as being unusual. The high chair tray had a bowl of cereal and a bottle of milk that looked untouched on it, but when Mr. Cook had entered the Dawsons' flat to check on Shirley he said he found the baby asleep in the playpen. Jane wondered if Shirley had run a bath for herself, prepared the child's breakfast and then at some point later decided to have a bath, leaving Heidi in her playpen.

As Jane sat on the edge of the dog-haired sofa she noticed a camera partly hidden behind a cushion. It was a little Kodak 126 Instamatic. The reel had twenty-four photos but only five had been used. She hesitated, then decided that rather than making detailed notes and drawings of the flat she would use the camera to record the scene. She felt certain that Barry Dawson wouldn't mind her using it.

Jane started in the bathroom. She lifted up the dressing gown left beside the bath, and hung it on the back of the bathroom door. Under it was a pair of panties and a bra. She placed them on the same hook as the dressing gown. Using the camera she then took two photographs of the deceased. She felt queasy looking at the dead woman's eyes wide open, and backed out of the bathroom deciding to use up the rest of the film on the other rooms.

The PC from downstairs appeared and asked how much longer she was going to be. Jane explained that she was waiting for the undertakers and when they arrived he could go.

"I'm sorry, you've been here a long time. I don't know your name."

"Arthur Miller, Detective."

Jane smiled. "Very auspicious name, if you have literary ambitions."

He shook his head, obviously not having a clue what she was talking about.

"Runs in my family. Father was Alfred, my grandfather was Albert—all of us are AM. Used to get some laughs just using our initials, and my sister was called Pamela, PM." He chuckled, then hitched up his trousers.

"Truth is I need to use a bathroom . . . I've been on duty since ten this morning."

"I don't think you can use this bathroom, but I'm sure Mr. Cook in the basement flat next door will oblige as he's been very helpful."

"Thanks . . . If I go there now, I'll come straight back."

"Yes, that's fine."

PC Miller left Jane finishing the reel of photographs, but there was still no sign of the undertakers. She was about to go and use the communal payphone to check back with the station when Miller returned and said he was now back on duty at the front door. He stood staring at her as Jane remained by the open bathroom door, then sighed and joined her, looking into the bathroom.

"How do you intend to get the body out of the bath?"

"Well, I don't . . . The undertakers will do that."

"No they won't, because that's not their job, if you don't mind me saying so. It's your role and you have to bag and tag as you're dealing with the scene. The undertakers will take the body to the mortuary, but in all my years I know they won't move a body. They really are 'more'n my job's worths.' But far be it from me to tell you what you should do."

Miller turned to walk off. Jane was so unsure of herself that she touched his arm as he went.

"Please don't go . . . I mean, I really don't know what I should do. I've never been in this situation before."

"Well, I can send out for a body sheet, and bring it up to you. But I'd say that first up you should pull the plug out of the bath."

"Right, yes. I'll do that. How long will you be before you bring up a body sheet? Or could I just use one of the sheets from the flat?"

"No, you'd better wait. It's got to be plastic. I'll radio in for one to be brought over. Would you like a cup of tea?"

"I'd love one . . . but I don't think we should use the kitchen, besides which it's not very clean."

"Mr. Cook's bringing me one over. Nice chap, letting me use their toilet. His wife's crippled, you know, and he's her main carer."

"Yes, I know. I would really love a cup of tea."

She heard him thudding back down the stairs and went into the bathroom. She looked at the bath and noticed that the plug chain was broken and not connected to the overflow waste pipe. There were no blood stains anywhere around the lip of the bath, only the still visible smear on the tap. She had no choice other than to remove her jacket, take off her leather gloves, roll up her sleeve and stick her hand in the cold blood-stained water to pull out the plug. The victim's legs were either side of her hand

and she closed her eyes as she felt for the chain and gave it a jerk. The stained water gurgled and then began to seep down the plug hole.

Jane was sitting on a chair in the living room writing up her notes when Miller came back. He was carrying a large white plastic sheet under one arm and two cups of tea.

"Thank you so much." She took the tea and sipped. It was very sweet, very strong and not particularly warm but she drank it all before placing it down on the coffee table. Miller waited, then helped her unfold the wide plastic sheet, which was the size of a small double bed.

"Right, let's have a look at her and work out the best way to get her out."

They stood side by side at the bath tub. The body was wrinkled from being in the water for so long, her long wet thick hair dripping around her shoulders.

"Well, good thing is she looks a bit underweight. First, lift her hands above her head and I'll get her feet. On the count of three we'll lift her body up and over the bath rim and onto the sheet."

Jane asked Miller if he'd got any rubber gloves. He shook his head. It didn't seem to bother him but it made Jane feel very queasy.

"I'm going to the kitchen to see if there are any washing-up gloves to wear."

Miller shrugged and waited, his hands on his hips.

Jane returned, saying that she couldn't find any.

"Right, we've got no choice. On the count of three . . . one . . . two . . . lift her arms up, and three."

Jane used her bare hands to lift the body. The arms were slippery and cold and on the first attempt Jane lost her grip and toppled forward. Miller was holding on to Shirley's feet and ankles.

"A dead body is always heavier than you think, even when it's a petite female. Right, let's go again. One . . . two . . . three, lift."

They managed to lift the body onto the sheet.

"Now put her arms at the side of her body, wrap the sheet over and twist and tape the ends, so you end up with what looks like a big Christmas cracker."

Miller left Jane to finish wrapping up the ends as he went back on duty. Jane waited impatiently for the undertakers to arrive.

Several hours later, feeling tired and emotionally drained, Jane left the mortuary having booked in the body and been told to prepare a report for the coroner. As she left through the rear yard, she saw DS Paul Lawrence, the lab liaison sergeant, outside smoking with a cup of tea. She didn't approach him immediately, wanting a few moments to prepare herself as her heart beat rapidly. She had this reaction almost every time she saw him, since he had been the one to tell her that neither Kath nor Bradfield had survived the explosion.

Lawrence glanced up and saw her. He took in the strained look on her face.

"Hi there . . . Are you coping all right?"

"I'm fine, thank you. Please don't give me the spaniel eyes."

"Sorry?"

"I've moved on, Paul, and I really don't want to talk about what happened," she said sharply.

"Um, spaniels have brown eyes . . . mine are blue. I was told you got a thrashing from some bastard when you were acting as a decoy?"

"Oh, sorry . . . yes. I'm sort of recovered from that. I thought you were referring to what happened at Hackney."

"I doubt if any of us will ever be able to fully recover from that nightmare. You know what Sergeant Harris always says?

'They were marked,' and you either come through to the other side of it, or you lose it." Seeing her stricken face he changed the subject.

"I heard you were at the scene of an accidental death as well? Never pleasant . . . I think I'm due to do a forensic search at the victim's flat. I've been dealing with a PM from a homosexual murder in Knightsbridge. I'm getting sick and tired of being shuffled from one station to the next, and spending hours in the lab. What are you doing here?"

"I brought the body in with the undertakers. PC May, who was on duty, was really rather unpleasant and abrupt . . . He told me that I needed to type up a sudden death report. I also need to get a reel of film developed at the chemist, with photos of the scene on it."

Lawrence looked puzzled and asked why she was taking scene pictures to the chemists and not the lab. Jane explained that there had been no photographer available at the death scene, so she'd used a camera she found at the flat. Lawrence laughed.

"Listen, when I'm finished at the mortuary I'll be walking back over Lambeth Bridge to the Met lab so I'll take the film to the photographic branch for development."

"Oh, thank you." Jane handed him the roll of film.

"I'll contact you at Bow Street when they're ready."

"I'm sorry if I sounded rude earlier. I didn't mean to. I've been on this case all day and I'm exhausted. Do you think I could make out the report first thing in the morning? DS Gibbs said he would walk me through it, but he's gone off duty."

Lawrence shrugged. He finished his tea, dropped his cigarette end into the dregs and threw the polystyrene cup into the bin.

"Look out for Gibbs. He took Bradfield's death badly . . . Had a bit of a meltdown. His attachment at Bow Street, and working under DCI Shepherd, will be very different for him. Shepherd's a 'go by the rules' and 'get off home' time watcher. He won't tolerate Gibbs's old ways."

Jane smiled and nodded, as Lawrence patted her arm.

"Good to see you, Jane. As you were on the non-suspicious death and I've just been called back to do a forensic search, I presume that it's conclusive?"

"Well, I'm not too sure exactly what the next step is. Her husband, Barry Dawson, mentioned that she had been very anxious and had been feeling unwell."

"Did you find any medication at the flat?"

"No, I didn't."

"Well, you should maybe check that out. If you like I can be over there tomorrow, when I have some free time."

"I'd appreciate that, thank you."

As he walked off Jane felt relieved that Lawrence would be at the flat the next day. Right now she just wanted to get back to her room at the section house and have a long bath. She needed to cleanse herself from the grime and the terrible smells in the Dawsons' flat, as well as the experience of having to lift the body out of the bath. She looked at the bloody water stains on the cuffs of her shirt and shuddered. She thought of the body and changed her mind—she'd have a shower instead.

Marie Allard had just put her children to bed and was making herself an omelet and a cup of tea when the phone rang. Her heart started racing every time the phone rang at this hour. She knew it would not be her mother-in-law and, as she had arranged with her husband that he would call from prison midmorning, after the children had been taken to school, she knew it couldn't be him either.

Marie went into the hall toward the ringing phone. She slowly picked up the receiver and took deep breaths as she heard the coins drop and knew who the caller was.

"Hello?" she said, nervously.

It was the same horrible sing-song voice again, coming through the receiver quietly at first. Marie began to shake as the voice got louder.

"Angie, Angie . . ."

"Leave me alone! I paid you . . . I did what you asked . . . just leave me alone!"

"Can't do that. I want another five hundred. Unless you want him to be put away for rape. Same procedure . . . get off the bus, put the envelope into the rubbish bin and get on the next bus. Need it by Tuesday . . . you got the time to get the money."

Marie was in tears as the caller hung up. She replaced the receiver, then ran into the kitchen as she remembered she had left the pan with the butter on the gas ring ready to cook her omelet. It was burned and smoking and she hurled it into the sink. She couldn't eat anything now, and felt the bile come up from her stomach as she retched. Since Peter's arrest she had lost a lot of weight, and she had been unable to sleep. She knew deep down that she had to tell someone what was going on but she was scared. She was even afraid to mention it to Peter when he called. He always sounded so depressed and often broke down weeping because he missed the children. He constantly told her how much he loved her, and how sorry he was for all the distress he was putting her through. He protested that he was innocent and had been fitted up by the police. He also told her repeatedly that she must not blame herself, and her inability to be intimate, for his behavior. It did, stupidly, make her feel that it was her fault. As they only ever had a few minutes for each call she hadn't told him about this "Angie" person and the blackmail, but she knew she would have to soon as she couldn't cope anymore. The constant questioning in her mind never stopped. She did blame herself and the guilt was consuming her.

Her mother-in-law had succeeded in finding a driver to rent Peter's cab and give her a cut of his takings, so there was some money coming in. But paying off this "Angie" was eating into their savings. Sitting in her immaculate kitchen, filled with the smell of burnt butter, Marie didn't even have the energy to wash the pan. She closed her eyes, telling herself over and over that she should go to the police. She had to tell someone, but what if this "Angie" did have evidence to prove Peter had committed a rape? She doubted that she would be able to cope or face the consequences.

Marie went upstairs, checked that the children were sleeping and then undressed and cleaned her teeth.

She hadn't washed her hair or worn makeup for days. She crawled into bed and curled up into a ball. But she couldn't sleep as all she could hear playing over and over in her mind was that raucous voice screaming, "Angie, Angie, Angie, Angie . . ."

CHAPTER TEN

Jane arrived at Bow Street, refreshed and on time but feeling slightly nervous. She had to write up a coroner's report, which she had never done before, and she was worried she would make a mistake. On entering the building she found Gibbs coming out of his office carrying a cup of coffee. He was very obviously in need of a shave and a clean shirt, and Jane was unsure whether he had come into work early, or if he had in fact been there all night. Gibbs beamed at her.

"Morning, Tennison! I see you have replaced the official uniform with something a little more glamorous . . . the navy suit and crisp white shirt suit you well."

"Thank you. I've got to do a coroner's report and I could really do with a bit of guidance."

He made a point of looking at his watch.

". . . if you have the time?" Jane added.

"For you, WDC Tennison, I always have time."

Jane couldn't tell if Gibbs was being serious or sarcastic. However, he took her through exactly what was required. They recorded the date the body was found, Monday, October 7th, and that it had been reported by the victim's husband, Barry Dawson. They also recorded the doctor's notes and as she typed up the report Gibbs sat on the edge of her desk, making sure everything had been done properly.

"You've got to make two copies: one for the coroner and one for records. Then get it over there ASAP as they'll want to do the PM at the mortuary. Although as far as I can make out it's all done and dusted."

Edith marched in, looking as though she was in a foul temper.

Gibbs opened his arms wide and grinned at her.

"Good God, Edith, you grow more lovely every day!"

"And you look as if you've had another night on the tiles. Go and have a shave before DCI Shepherd sees you looking like that."

Gibbs laughed and walked out.

Edith thumped her briefcase down on the desk, opened it up and took out her sandwiches and flask.

"Is everything all right, Edith?" Jane asked.

"No, it is not. I've had problems with my mother. The carer was late . . . She's such a dope of a girl, but Mother can't be left on her own as she has dementia. It's very difficult making sure she doesn't wander off. I have had to put child gates at the top of the stairs as she's very adept at sneaking out of the house, often only in her nightdress. One time she was stark naked!"

"That sounds very stressful. Has she been suffering for a long time?"

Edith muttered, "Too long."

Jane handed Edith the copies of her report and folded the top sheet into an envelope to take it over to the Coroner's Office.

"I'm just going up to the canteen for breakfast—can I get you a cup of tea, Edith?"

"No, thank you, I bring my own," said Edith, indicating the Thermos. "I like to get everything sorted before the others get here."

Jane nodded then she hurried out, losing her bearings slightly before heading up the stone stairs to the third floor. As it was still early she didn't have to queue, so she picked up a tray and got a plate of scrambled eggs with bacon and toast, and a cup of coffee. As she turned to make her way toward the rows of Formica-topped tables she saw Gibbs sitting at the far side, finishing his breakfast.

"Do you mind if I join you, Spence?" she asked, and he shrugged.

Jane sat down opposite him and noticed that most of his eggs and bacon were untouched as he lit a cigarette and pushed the plate away.

"I just spoke to DS Lawrence . . . he said he wasn't too happy about some of the photographs from the Dawsons' flat. He said he was going over there, and asked if you could leave the keys with the duty sergeant so that he can collect them," Spence said, putting the lighter back in his pocket.

"I don't mind going over there to meet him."

"Fine, but when you've finished with him go and find out when they're doing the PM on Dawson's wife."

"Are you going to take a statement from him?" Jane asked.

"If you want to do it, go ahead. We might as well get the case closed, and move on to something else."

Jane started to eat her scrambled eggs and felt the table shaking from Gibbs's foot constantly twitching beneath it. He looked around the canteen, then back at Jane as she pushed her unfinished plate aside. The toast was soggy and the eggs were overdone.

"Shall I also check out St. Thomas' Hospital, where Barry Dawson works?"

"Why?" Gibbs snapped.

She shrugged. "It's just that he said he left work because his wife didn't answer the phone and he was concerned, so he came home . . ."

"Well, I doubt you'll need to go there if it's a non-sus death. Any reason to think he was lying?"

"There were a few things at his flat that didn't quite add up. For example, the little girl's high chair had her drinking bottle and bowl of cereal on it, untouched. Yet the neighbor who found Mrs. Dawson said the baby was sleeping in her playpen."

Gibbs leaned on his elbows. "So?"

"Well, if Barry Dawson found his wife in the bath when he got home, why didn't he call 999 instead of going to a neighbor? And why didn't he pick up his daughter?"

"Come on . . . He finds his wife dead in the bath, freaks out and runs next door. The guy was totally emotionally drained, and if his daughter was asleep why wake her up? Listen, Jane, if you don't mind me saying so, don't start digging around trying to find something untoward. The Doc confirmed accidental non-suspicious death."

Gibbs pushed his chair back.

"I'm going to get a shave . . . beady-eyed Edith doesn't miss a trick. A word of warning about her: you start nosing around about a case that's not your business—that's out of order. She's known as 'Cop Out' because she left the force to be chained to a typewriter. And she's all over DCI Shepherd like a rash."

Jane didn't reply as he walked out of the canteen. He was obviously impatient to get on to another case. She finished her coffee and carried her dirty dishes to the counter, tipping her cutlery into the tub of soapy water.

At the Coroner's Office she was told that, as yet, no PM had been organized for that morning. Jane decided she would go to the mother-in-law's address in Rotherhithe to get a statement from Barry Dawson as she needed details regarding the time he had returned home and found his wife.

She also wanted to ask a few more personal questions regarding his relationship with Shirley, to see if there was anything that gave further indication of exactly how the "accident" had occurred. Something didn't feel quite right, whatever Spencer said.

Jane gave the details of her whereabouts to the duty sergeant, then caught a bus. It was almost ten o'clock when she arrived at 15 Allcott Road. It was a rather rundown area with council houses that had small, mostly paved, front gardens strewn with bicycles, and motorbikes parked up alongside the rubbish bins. Number 15 had a chipped blue door with an empty milk crate standing next to the doormat.

Jane rang the bell and waited. There was the sound of a dog barking loudly, which Jane presumed was the one taken from the Dawsons' flat. Rita opened the front door, still wearing a dressing gown and slippers, and holding the dog back by its collar. She pursed her lips in irritation on seeing Jane.

"I've only just fed Heidi . . . She's been crabby all night long and has had me up and down. But come on in and I'll get Barry down . . . he's still in bed. Down, Buster, good dog."

Mrs. Dawson restrained the dog as Jane nervously followed her inside into an immaculate, lino-covered hallway with flowery wallpaper. Mrs. Dawson gestured toward a door leading into a lounge.

"Go on in, and he'll be with you. I'll put Buster out in the back yard. Do you want a cup of anything?"

"No, thank you."

"What's your name, dear, I've forgotten?"

"I'm WDC Jane Tennison."

Mrs. Dawson nodded and closed the door. The room was spotless, with a large, overstuffed sofa and chairs and a coffee table in front of a big fake coal electric fire. On the mantelpiece were numerous photographs of the little girl, Heidi, and a few wedding pictures of Barry and Shirley. Jane sat on the comfortable easy chair and opened her notebook, waiting for Barry. She heard Mrs. Dawson calling him, and the dog started barking again. Then there was the sound of someone hurrying down the stairs.

"Did you call the hospital? I don't want you losing your job."

"Yes, I've called them. Can I have a cup of tea, Mum?"

"I'll bring one in for you. I'm not going into the school today so I'll give Heidi a bath."

"Thanks, Mum."

Jane turned to the door as Barry walked in. He was wearing a clean pressed denim shirt and jeans with loafer shoes but no socks. It was obvious that he had just bathed as his wet hair was combed back from his face and he smelt of some kind of lemon soap. Jane stood up and Barry shook her hand.

"Sorry to keep you waiting . . . I didn't get much sleep. I don't know what I would do without Mum."

Jane sat back down and Barry stood for a moment, deciding where he should sit, then went over and sat in the center of the sofa.

"I heard your mother saying she wasn't going into school—is she a teacher?"

"No, she's a cleaner at the local primary school, and does the kids' lunches as well. She's always worked, even when my dad was alive. He passed away a few years ago. He was a hard grafter and ran a small garage repair yard, and Mum sold it on to his partner. She could have moved out from here but all her friends are local, and if it wasn't for her we'd never have been able to get the deposit for our flat. She also helps out with the mortgage."

"Oh, so you own the top-floor flat?"

"Yes. The one below us was rented, then the landlord got rid of the tenants and now he's doing it up to sell it. The couple on the ground floor also own theirs."

"What about the basement?"

"That's just full of junk and I think he's going to do that up as well. He manages the property and he's supposed to keep the communal areas painted and carpeted but hasn't done anything since we moved in despite charging us maintenance. The roof has problems as well, but he's a typical shark landlord."

Jane made a few notes, more interested in putting Barry at his ease as he constantly kept looking over at the photographs, then turned back to face her.

"My mum only works part time, doing the lunches, and she can probably take Heidi with her. I don't know what I'd do without her . . . She's going to see about a local nursery school that takes them at Heidi's age. Shirley was going to start looking into it . . ." Barry turned away, close to tears.

"This shouldn't take too long, Mr. Dawson. I just need to have a clear time frame of exactly what happened yesterday. I'm sorry if it distresses you, but if you could give me the details of when exactly you left for work . . ."

"Six o'clock in the morning. I was on early shift. We do alternate two weeks, of days and then nights."

Jane jotted in her notebook, while Barry continued. "I was quite busy up to around my break time, then I went into the canteen for breakfast."

"What time was that?"

"Oh, it'd be about seven thirty. Then at ten o'clock I went to use the payphone in the casualty department. It was a regular thing I did . . . call home to see if Shirley was OK. Usually she would be waiting with Buster and Heidi to go out for a walk. Anyway, I rang, but got no reply. I remember I had to ask one of the other porters for some change, so it might have been a bit after ten when I called. As I got no answer I stood around awhile, then I started to get worried."

"Why was that?"

"Well, she hadn't answered and the night before she'd not been feeling very well. She used to get these sort of anxiety feelings, which was why I always made sure I called her. I started to get worried. I'm not sure how many times I tried the number. You see, she was still in bed when I left for work, and so I really got concerned."

Jane waited. Barry clasped and unclasped his hands, then gave a long sigh.

"I left the hospital and got the bus home. I'm not sure of the exact time but I let myself in and called out to her, but got no reply. Heidi was in her playpen fast asleep, so I went into the bedroom and then . . ." He bowed his head as his eyes filled with tears.

"I went into the bathroom and I found her . . ." he sniffed, trying to control himself. "I'm sorry, but I still can't really take it all in. It all seems like a blur, you know . . . running next door and getting the old bloke to go and see Shirley . . . He went over and the next minute he's got Heidi and he's calling 999."

"Why didn't you call the police yourself?"

"I don't know . . . I don't know . . . it was seeing her in the bath . . . Oh God! If only I'd come home earlier, you know, not waited, because she really wasn't herself the night before. Maybe I shouldn't have gone into work . . . I just keep on asking myself these questions, over and over . . . what if . . . what if . . . ?"

"Did Shirley suffer from depression?"

He looked up and gave a small shrug. "Not really, it was just that she would get very anxious."

"Was she on any medication?"

"No, just took something from over the counter at Boots."

"Did she see a doctor about her anxiety?"

"No. We have a local GP, but I don't think she'd been to see him recently."

The door opened and Mrs. Dawson walked in carrying a mug of tea and a tea towel. She crossed over to a small coffee table and lifted it up to put it beside her son. Then she picked up a magazine to place down on the polished surface and put down his mug.

"Are you all right, son?"

Barry's face crumpled and he stood up, saying that he needed to go to the bathroom.

"Excuse me," he said to Jane and left the room.

"He's taken it very badly . . . done nothing but cry. I mean, for all her faults he loved Shirley. He was a good husband and dotes on Heidi."

Mrs. Dawson picked up one of the wedding photographs and, with almost a compulsive need to clean, wiped the glass and frame.

"She was lovely looking, but oh dear . . . shocking at keeping the flat clean. I was always going over there to give it a good vacuum and dust. I've even taken home bags of washing for Heidi and Barry. I was there one time and she was ironing his best shirt. I told her that wasn't the best way to iron, that you should always start on the sleeves, then the two sides and lastly the back. Then use a spray starch for the cuffs and the collar. Shirley says to me that it was a waste of time as who sees all of the shirt when you wear a jacket. Lazy she was, but he didn't mind. Not even when it was more takeaway than anything cooked."

"So did this create friction between you and your daughter-in-law?"

"Oh no, she was a lovely girl . . . just not used to looking after the flat. To be honest, Barry was always about to do some redecorating, but working such long hours he never really got around to it. Shirley never had a mother to teach her anythin' domestic . . . well, she obviously had one but she was placed in foster care when she was Heidi's age . . . she was shoved from pillar to post until she was in her teens . . . that's how they met."

"I'm sorry . . . how did they meet?"

"One of my best friends, Norma, is a foster carer. God knows how many kids she's looked after in her lifetime. She's a bit too old to take on any more kids now . . . But she brought Shirley around here a few times, and they got on well, and the next thing he's got engaged to her."

Jane remained silent as Mrs. Dawson picked up one framed photograph after another, dusted it and replaced it in exactly the same position. She then turned to look toward the door and moved closer, lowering her voice.

"You know, one time there was a bit of a rumor that Heidi wasn't his—Shirley was a few weeks gone when they married, you see—but he wouldn't have it. Worships that little girl, and she's got his blond hair and blue eyes. Shirley was . . . well, we never really knew anything about her background, but she was not all white."

"So was there someone else Shirley was seeing?"

"Now listen to me . . . don't go adding two and two and making it five. It was just a rumor. Shirley was engaged to Barry at eighteen and there was never anybody else since they were married. She might have been a bit jealous and that made her anxious, but Barry never messed around. He loved her and I've been out of line saying anything against her. The way I like to keep everything spick and span was the way his dad used to like it. He always said he could eat his dinner off my kitchen floor."

Barry walked in and she immediately straightened up.

"What you been saying, Mum?"

"Nothing . . . I was just saying how your dad liked the house immaculate. He'd come in from work and straight into the bath for a scrub up, because being a mechanic he wore greasy overalls and had filthy hands."

"I don't think this is the time to go into that, Mum. He's been gone a long time and you know how grateful I am, and always will be, for what he did for me and Shirley."

Mrs. Dawson realized she had said too much and gestured to his mug of tea.

"Don't let that go cold, Barry."

Jane watched as he ushered his mother out of the room, closing the door behind her.

"She's always had a few things against Shirley, me marrying her for one. She reckoned she was too young, but she paid for the wedding, her frock and everything. Shirley had no family and had been in foster care for most of her life, but I never wanted anyone else."

Jane watched him as he stared at his wedding photographs. He was close to tears, and Jane stood up, closed her notebook and picked up her handbag.

"I'll type this up and then you'll be asked to sign the hand-written copy. I have to inform you that you will be required to make a formal identification at the mortuary."

"What? I don't understand . . ."

"I'm afraid it's necessary. Maybe you could ask your mother to accompany you? Or she could make the identification herself?"

"But I've already seen her. I really don't want to do this . . . I can't . . . I mean, I don't want to have to see her again!"

"I can make a call from here and order a car to take you to the mortuary. Or if you agree I can make an appointment for later this afternoon, and meet you there? May I use the telephone to arrange it?"

Jane was shown into the hall and used the telephone on a small table to call the Coroner's Office.

She was relieved when Barry agreed to make his own way to the mortuary and said he could be there at two o'clock. He was obviously distressed but said that he needed his mother to stay at home to look after Heidi. As he went upstairs to get ready, Mrs. Dawson came into the hall.

"Let me show you out, dear. He's taken this very badly . . . I keep on thinking that if I hadn't had trouble with my washing machine, I'd have been there, and I would have found her instead of poor Barry."

"Yes, you said you were going to babysit . . . ?"

"That's right . . . but my washing machine went on the blink so I had to wait for the engineer. Shirley had a hair appointment so I was going to their flat to look after Heidi. She used to get her hair straightened, because it was so curly. I was relieved,

I can tell you, when Heidi was born and had Barry's blond hair. It's impossible to get a comb through those curls . . . I know because some of the kids at the school need a special type of Afro comb."

Jane tried to steer her back onto the subject.

"I'm sorry, Mrs. Dawson, I'm just trying to piece together the time frame. So, you were going to go to your son's flat on the morning that Shirley was found in the bath?"

"Yes . . . I did try to call her, you know, to let her know I wouldn't be coming, but she didn't answer the phone."

"What time was that, Mrs. Dawson?"

Rita hesitated, then shrugged.

"Well, it would've been early . . . like a quarter to nine . . . but like I said, the phone rang and rang. Maybe she didn't hear it because she was running a bath . . . but I wasn't that worried."

"Why not?"

"Well, if I didn't turn up she would've taken Heidi to the salon with her . . . to Pearls and Curls, over in Brick Lane by the market."

"Did Barry know you were going to be at the flat?"

"Yes—like I said, I often go over there to give Shirley a hand—"

She suddenly stopped and took a sharp intake of breath.

"Oh God! . . . I can't believe she's never going to be there again!"

After comforting her Jane thanked Rita and went to the front door to leave. As the door closed behind her she took out her notebook and jotted down some notes, including the name of the hair salon. Something didn't quite add up.

Jane went back to the station to type up the statement ready for Barry to sign when they met at the mortuary. Edith was in the incident room and told Jane that DS Lawrence had called and wanted to speak to her regarding some photographs. There were a number of detectives working in the room at the various desks. The two clerks were busy as there had been a spate of break-ins and a complaint from market holders about being threatened.

Edith was carrying an overflowing ashtray across to the waste bin. Pulling a face in disgust she emptied out the cigarette butts into the bin.

"The DCI wanted to see you as well. There's been a pickpocket incident on a female tourist in Soho—the perp is slashing handbag straps with a razor. DCI wants you to go to the Marquee Club on Wardour Street to interview the manager about it."

Sighing, Jane checked her watch and grabbed her coat.

Jane was sitting on a bar stool taking notes from a young barman with a Newcastle accent. The nightclub was being vacuumed and the dingy bar was filled with dirty glasses and bags of empty beer bottles being removed to the bins.

"So are you aware of anyone inside the club being robbed?"

"No, but I only work on certain days of the week . . . I mostly do clearing up in the mornings, and different staff come in for night work."

"Do you know what time they will be coming on duty?"

"No, you'll have to ask the manager as he lists the staff. But he's not here right now."

Jane took down what few details she could report and left the club, walking back down Wardour Street. She passed a seedy strip club called "Dolls House," with a heavy-set bouncer standing outside, his arms folded across his huge chest. There were afternoon and lunchtime shows advertised outside: "Live Girls, Live Dancers, Live Girls, Live Dancers," flashed the neon signs. Loud music was thudding from the narrow entrance that was concealed with cheap plastic curtains.

As Jane stepped off the pavement into the road to avoid the bouncer, a woman came out of the club. Jane stopped and stared. The woman was wearing the same, or similar, blue rabbit fur coat that Jane had worn when she had acted as a decoy. She looked at the woman's face, certain it was the same woman she had seen in the photographs, the woman who had been pushing the baby stroller. But before Jane could even contemplate approaching her the woman hailed a taxi and climbed inside, passing within feet of Jane.

"See ya later, Angie!" the bouncer yelled. Jane was confused for a moment, then she recalled the list of aliases on the charge sheet and knew it had to be Janet Brown, aka Angie, who had been held at Hackney Station. She watched the taxi disappear then walked back to the strip club as the bouncer ushered in the nervous punters. There were various sexy photographs of the strippers in provocative poses displayed in a cracked glass cabinet.

Jane looked over the photographs and noticed a semi-nude shot of the woman. The bouncer swished through the plastic curtains and confronted her.

"Live girls, you want to see live girls, darlin'?"

Jane turned away abruptly and could hear him laughing.

"Takes all sorts, love! . . . Live girls, dancing jig jiggy."

Jane caught the bus back and finished her half-eaten sandwich. She had so many things to think about. Having to show Barry Dawson the body of his wife, detail the so-called bag snatcher, and yet uppermost in her mind was the woman called Angie. There was something that kept on niggling her about her arrest. The photographs of her beaten face, and why Jane had been asked to wear her coat the night she had been assaulted. Lastly she thought about the forthcoming trial of Peter Allard. There was no confirmed date but she knew it would be announced soon and she wasn't looking forward to it.

Jane sighed. "Why do you care?" she muttered to herself. After what he had subjected her to, she felt angry with herself for wasting time thinking about him. She had loathed being grilled by his defense council and she knew the interrogation was likely to be worse at the trial. But what really worried her was the fact she was certain Moran had planted the knife and lied about the confession. She wondered if Moran had also lied about Janet Brown, or Angie; and why he had her rabbit fur coat?

Jane opened her notebook and jotted down a reminder to contact old Donaldson from Hackney Collator's Office. She knew he would have the home address of Janet Brown because she remembered seeing it on the charge sheet. She couldn't recall it offhand but just for her own peace of mind she wanted to have an off-the-record meeting with the woman in the blue rabbit fur coat.

CHAPTER ELEVEN

The prison visiting room was jam-packed, and the noise was deafening. Uniformed prison officers patrolled between the small tables allocated for the visitors. As most of the prisoners were on remand waiting for their trial, they allowed children to accompany the visitors.

Marie Allard sat anxiously opposite her husband. She had made an effort with her appearance and had washed her hair and put on some makeup, but she still looked gaunt and unwell. Peter was also bothered by the din. He was clearly very tense and kept on twisting his head, complaining that his neck hurt and they wouldn't give him anything for the pain.

"They took away what I brought in at reception . . . your mum has sent in a package," Marie said, unsure how to broach the subject of the blackmail.

Wanting to put it off as long as possible, she discussed the kids and Peter was adamant that they should not be brought in to see him. After what felt like an interminably long time he leaned forward and looked directly into her eyes.

"Are you all right?"

"I'm OK. Your mum is handling rent from taxi and we also getting a cut of the fares."

"I know that, she told me that when she came in. And you've got our savings if there's any major funds you need for the house. The mortgage is being paid direct from the account. You're not sick, are you?"

"No, no . . . but I need to tell you something . . ." She was close to tears. "I not know what to do . . ."

"Do about what?"

Marie took a deep breath. "I got a phone call . . . I not know if it man or woman . . . they sing words, at first quiet then shouting. I don't know what to do . . . they scream out someone's name . . ."

"What?"

"On the phone. I get scared to pick up the phone again in case it them. You know someone called Andy?"

"Who?"

"It's maybe a woman . . . strange accent . . . like some kind of song, over and over . . . then in horrid voice saying she know something about you."

Peter straightened up in the chair.

"I dunno anyone called Andy. Are you sure you heard it right?"

"Maybe Andy, or Angie . . . I don't know."

"Angie? Was it Angie?"

"Yes, maybe . . . you know a woman with that name?"

Peter clenched his fist and shook his head as Marie took out a handkerchief and blew her nose.

"She say she got evidence against you for that rape charge and that she could have you put away for long time."

"What? Are you crazy? You know I was fitted up by the cops! I never signed that confession, it was a lie! I swear before God I am telling you the truth, Marie."

"She want more money . . ."

"What?"

"I said she want more money. Please don't shout at me! I paid her five hundred so she not go to police."

"Christ Almighty! You already paid her? Are you out of your mind? Just repeat exactly what this bitch is saying to you, because this is blackmail! You know that, don't you? It's bloody blackmail!"

"I know what it is, Peter, but she keep saying she has evidence that she can prove you done the rape. I very worried . . . I paid her first time, but she call me again and want another five hundred."

Peter held his head in his hands. He knew who it could be, but he wasn't about to tell Marie. He looked over at the officers, then turned back to his wife.

"Go from the beginning, Marie, because I'm not quite understanding what this is all about."

Bit by bit Marie told him everything. She recounted how she had been instructed to take the money wrapped in a newspaper and put it into a bin by the 73 bus stop on Park Lane. She was crying when she said that she had done exactly as she had been asked, then took the next bus that came so she never saw who collected the money.

Peter kept on rubbing at his neck, then running his hands through his hair. He was sweating and obviously very agitated. Seeing his wife crying and being unable to calm her made it worse.

"Should I go to police?" Marie looked at her husband. He was still in good shape despite his complaints about the food being pigswill.

"Listen, I would lay money that it's that bent fucking officer who stitched me up. I don't know anyone called Angie, I swear on my kids' lives I don't . . . I mean, five hundred quid is a hell of a lot of money . . . it's more'n a month's takings for God's sake, and it's blackmail . . . it's bloody blackmail!"

"She want me to do same as I did before, on Tuesday. Tell me what to do, Peter. I not know what to do." He took a deep breath.

"Right, my worries are that if this bitch is trying it on then you need to contact the cops. But then part of me is freaking out because I am innocent, Marie, and I'm banged up in here until I can prove it at the trial. I didn't rape anyone, and that woman is lying because there is no evidence against me. But if she's workin' with that bent DI Moran they could screw me over . . . so maybe try and find out who she is, and do what she wants."

"You mean pay her again? But I should go to police?"

"Listen to me, OK? Yeah, go to the police but, and listen good, if you find a connection with this bitch and it's to Moran then the case against me will be slung out of court, understand me? You need to find out if there is a connection, sweetheart, that's all I'm saying."

"I not know, Peter, I so nervous about doing it again . . ."

"You're going to have to do it, Marie. If you do I can get that false confession thrown out. This is what you do—make it look like you get back on the bus. You have to find out who she is, because it's all a pack of lies."

"I not understand. You mean, I leave money like before, but not get on bus? Please don't lie to me, Peter . . . if you know who she is then why would she say these things?"

Peter became increasingly agitated as Marie started crying again. He leaned closer and patted the table with the flat of his hand.

"Money . . . that's obvious, isn't it? But we need to find out exactly what they're doing."

Marie wouldn't meet his eyes, refusing to look up.

"Look at me . . . we can get through this. We've talked about what I did, Marie, you know why I did those stupid assaults. I mean, it was me being frustrated because we couldn't have sex. I'm disgusted at myself and you know I love you more than anything else in the world. I love my kids and I want to make it up to you. I never raped anyone . . . it was just me grabbing their tits, feeling them up. It was dumb and stupid and I am so ashamed because of how it's turned out. I want to get out of here. My defense lawyer is really positive the case against me will be thrown out, and after the time spent in here I'll be released straight away."

Marie nodded, but she was still frightened and unable to look at him.

"So what you want me to do?"

"Pay her . . . find out who the hell she is, because it's all bullshit. I'm innocent and I'm scared they're trying it all on and using you. There's no evidence connecting me to that rape, because I didn't do it!"

"What if it has to do with Susie Luna?"

Allard sighed deeply and leaned back, shaking his head.

"Don't even think of that . . . it was over a long time ago. This is what is important, and I'm depending on you. Don't you dare tell Mum about this blackmailing bitch. I don't want her worried. You know what she's like, so just keep this between us until we know if this bent detective is behind it."

The clanging bell rang loudly to indicate that visiting time was over. Marie agreed to drop the money again and said goodbye, watching as her husband was led away. She tried to smile when he glanced back at her but when she left the prison her head was throbbing so much she thought she was going to faint. She felt sick and couldn't stop herself from breaking down in tears. By the time she got home she was shaking. She had only just taken her coat off when the phone rang. Her hand shook even more as she picked it up.

"Hello, Marie? It's me." It was her mother-in-law. "I rang earlier to find out how Peter was. Did you take the food parcel in?"

"Yes, Hilda, I did."

"Are you all right? You sound very down, dear."

"That prison always give me big headache. Peter was OK . . . he still waiting for the date of trial."

"Taking their bloody time. Listen, I was goin' to pop over as I have some cash for you from the bloke using Peter's taxi. It's not a lot but he pays the rent regular into the account."

"Can you pick up kids from school?"

"All right, love, I can do that. So I'll come by later then, all right?"

"Thank you, Hilda."

Marie replaced the receiver and sat down on the stairs, her head in her hands. She started crying because deep down she had thought Peter would tell her to report the blackmail to the police. She was trying to accept his reason for her not doing so, that it was the police officer who lied about his confession. She had to force herself to trust her husband but she couldn't silence the nagging doubt that he'd known who Angie was.

Eventually Marie went into the kitchen to prepare the children's tea. She made an effort to clean up the kitchen, set the table and had made boiled eggs with toasted soldiers ready, when the front door opened.

"We're home, love!" Mrs. Dawson called from the hallway. She took off the children's coats and hung them up on the hooks along with all the other outdoor clothes.

"Tea's on table. No need to get them changed, they can do it later."

"OK, go on in, the pair of you."

Hilda hung up her own coat as Marie ushered the children into the kitchen. They sat down obediently as she poured two glasses of milk and told them they could have ice-cream after their eggs. Hilda walked in and gave a cursory glance at the table.

"Shall I take their heads off for you? Then you can dip the soldiers in. I always like eggs for breakfast, but never mind. Just tap the top of the egg—you don't want to eat bits of shell now, do you?"

Marie said quietly that they could do that themselves and she would go and run them a bath.

She sat on the edge of the bath, making sure the water was not too hot and poured in some Matey bubble bath to make it smell nice, watching as the bath filled with bubbles. She took two towels from the airing cupboard and rested them on the heated towel rail. She could hear Hilda downstairs organizing the children while they finished their tea. Eventually they went into their bedroom and took off their school clothes, putting on their dressing gowns in preparation for their bath.

Marie let Hilda take over in the bathroom and collected clothing to put in the washing machine, having already laid out clean shirts and underwear for the following morning.

Returning to the kitchen she saw the dirty dishes piled up on the draining board, and by the time she had washed and cleaned up the mess left on the table, she could hear the shouts and yells from upstairs. They wanted to watch TV but Marie didn't want them coming down so she went to the stairs and called up.

"Do your homework, then I'll read story."

It was a while before Hilda joined her in the kitchen, carrying in her handbag.

"What's all that wood hammered across Peter's games room for?"

"Police damaged door, and I not want the children going in there. He has knives in there, and he always keep it locked."

"Bloody disgusting. Did the coppers take anything away?"

"Yes."

"Fitting him up they are . . . I dunno how, but we'll get through this, Marie. The kids're washed and clean and playing, but it's earlier than usual. Maybe let them come down and see a bit of TV before bedtime?"

"I still got headache. After you go I read to them. You want cup of tea?"

"I'll do it, love."

"I already made a pot, yes or no?"

"Yes, I'll have a cuppa while we go over the accounts. The bloke that's renting out Peter's taxi is paying in weekly with a cut of his takings and I'm putting it into your joint bank account. But I want you to see how much you can depend on coming in."

Hilda opened her bag, took out a small notebook and an envelope of cash.

"If you give it to me I can put it in the account myself."

"Whatever . . . it's just what Peter told me to do as I know exactly how much we should be getting in. Not that I don't trust the bloke but I've asked that he details all the fares. He's getting a good price to rent the taxi and he's using our Peter's ID, which is not exactly legal as all taxi drivers are supposed to have done their knowledge tests."

"I know, I know . . ." Marie put down a mug of tea in front of Hilda and opened a packet of biscuits.

"Are you all right?" Hilda asked, spooning in sugar and stirring her tea.

Marie sat down opposite her mother-in-law.

"I mean, if there is anything you don't understand you should tell me because being Filipino I'm sometimes not sure if you do."

"I been here since I was thirteen years old . . . of course I understand and I very capable of doing our accounts."

"No need to get snappy with me, dear. Don't think I don't understand the strain you must be going through, but so am I and I've got Cherrie, who's a constant worry. She's not to be told . . . she wouldn't understand anyway but she keeps on asking when Peter's coming round. He's such a good son, and takes such good care of Cherrie. He always has done, ever since we knew she wasn't right. But it's a heavy weight on my shoulders because I have to take her back and forth to the mental care home. I always think she was the reason their dad left, and going through the divorce was a terrible time."

Marie sighed. She had heard the story so many times before, but she didn't have the strength to interrupt so she just sat there nodding "I never thought I'd get through it, but after he died we had the taxi and he'd only just started paying it off. So it was virtually new for Peter to take over and he made it a good business, working all hours. He's a good provider, and I know if anything, God forbid, was ever to happen to me he'd take over caring for Cherrie. He's a good man."

"Shall I count money?" Marie said, unable to listen to her mother-in-law's repetitive conversation.

"You've got to be positive, Marie. I can see you're not looking your best. Have they given you a date for the operation?"

Marie was counting out the bank notes from the envelope.

"Not yet."

Hilda drained her mug of tea and placed it carefully back down on the table.

"He told me all about it. I'm not laying any blame on you, love, but my son is a handsome man and you know what they say—if they're not getting it at home they'll stray, that's what this is all about. I know Peter. He was always one for the ladies and when he was a teenager they were all after him. He could have had his pick, I can tell you."

Marie glanced up as she made a note of the amount on the back of the envelope. She knew her mother-in-law had never approved of her or, for that matter, really liked her. It had been difficult to handle. Even when her children were born Hilda made disparaging remarks about them looking oriental. Eventually she had grown to admire their silky dark hair, as Peter had similar coloring. Now she never admitted ever saying anything untoward, but Marie had heard Peter giving his mother a severe talking to, even threatening that if she didn't appreciate his love for Marie then she would not be allowed to see her grandchildren.

"One hundred and twenty pounds." Marie tucked the money into the envelope.

"And you got all his savings to pay out for the mortgage. And you know if you ever do get short, which I doubt, I've got a few quid and also the benefits for Cherrie."

Marie could not even think about telling Hilda about the phone calls, and just wanted her to leave.

"Did you give Peter the food parcel?"

"I told you, yes."

"I'll visit him tomorrow. And you said there's still no news about the date for the trial?"

"No."

"It's disgusting. He's innocent and it's breaking my heart because I know my son. I hope you keep a positive attitude. I think you should take the kids in to see him as it's tearing him up being away from them."

"I not want to do that."

"Why not?"

Marie picked up her mug and rinsed it in the sink.

"I not think they should see him in prison."

"Remand, Marie, he's not in prison, he's on remand."

"It's still prison. I already get sick when I take them to school and pick them up because the other mothers stare at me. It's been in the newspapers, Hilda . . . they too young to understand why their dad is away. I not taking them to those awful visiting sections."

"Listen to me, your husband is a good father and a good son. If any of those bitches say anything, or give you nasty looks, you tell 'em to piss off and mind their own business. If you don't stand up for him like I'm doing, how do you think he will feel?"

Marie gave up. She didn't have the energy to argue, and, thankfully, Hilda looked at her watch as she had to collect Cherrie.

"I have to go. I can come by again tomorrow."

Marie followed Hilda into the hall as she got her coat. She opened the front door and stood patiently waiting.

"Call me tomorrow and I can be here to make their tea."

"I call you."

Hilda hesitated then leaned close and gave a dry kiss to Marie's cheek.

"Put the money in the bank."

"Yes, I will."

"Tarra, love."

Marie closed the front door and slipped the chain lock on. She looked over to the stairs where her children were standing side by side on the top step.

"When's Daddy coming home?"

Marie went up the stairs and took her son Kim by the hand. "You have to be a big boy because you are eight years old and Mummy needs you to be very well behaved."

Leann, Marie's little girl, put her arms around her mother's neck. "I am a very good girl and I always look after you, Mummy."

Marie kissed her. "Yes, sweetheart."

"I'm five years old."

"You're my big girl."

"So when is Daddy coming home?" Kim repeated.

Marie answered abruptly, "I don't know . . . I don't know. And please don't ask me again."

"Has he been naughty?"

Marie's eyes filled with tears. "Yes, and you know when you are naughty you have to be punished."

CHAPTER TWELVE

An old Victorian archway covered the rather majestic entrance into the stone cobbled yard of the mortuary, where the mortuary vans and ambulances were parked. The reception area was housed in a modern extension, and was accessed through two large glass doors. Inside, the floor was covered with blue linoleum and there was a small reception desk, which was invariably empty as they were always short-staffed and there was never an employee to work behind it.

A row of straight-backed chairs lined one wall and the overhead lights gave the reception area a yellowish hue. Although the reception was some distance from the rooms used for postmortems and the chill section where the bodies were kept, a faint smell of disinfectant permeated the area. The smell became much stronger along the corridors.

Jane had arrived five minutes late and Barry Dawson was already in the reception sitting on one of the hard-backed chairs. He was obviously nervous and as soon as she passed through the double glassed entry door, he rose to his feet. Jane gave him a friendly smile of encouragement. Having now been to the mortuary on numerous occasions she was familiar with the routine, but she had never previously handled a viewing alone.

"I just have to check if there is an assistant mortician available."

"Do I wait here?"

"Yes please, Mr. Dawson. Have a seat and I will come straight out."

Barry sat back down, hunching his shoulders. One knee jerked as he kept his eyes on the door through which Jane had entered.

It took longer than she had said as there was no assistant around, but eventually it was organized and the numbered drawer 312 listed and checked as holding the body of Shirley Dawson. Jane opened the door and gestured for Barry to join her. He hurried toward her and Jane again gave him a nod of encouragement as she let him pass her before closing the door behind them.

Barry was standing ramrod straight as Jane explained quietly that he just had to confirm his wife's identity. They would usually have taken the body into the small chapel next to the mortuary, but due to staff shortages they would have to see Shirley in the chill room. The assistant slid open drawer 312. The body was covered with a white shroud, which was slowly eased back. Shirley's eyes were closed, her hair had been combed neatly away from her face and, apart from the stitched wound in the center of her forehead, it was as if she was sleeping. Barry looked down. He ran his fingers on his right hand over his lips, swallowed and Jane could hear his sharp intake of breath.

"Is this your wife, Shirley Dawson?" Jane asked quietly.

"Yes . . . yes, it's Shirley."

Jane gave a small nod to the assistant who covered Shirley's face and slid back the drawer. Barry remained standing and she had to gently take his arm and guide him out of the room. Back in the reception area he started to cry.

"They will be doing a post-mortem this afternoon, Mr. Dawson, and—"

"I need to go to the flat to get things for Heidi. Can I go back there?" She was surprised by his question.

"I'll contact you as soon as we have clearance."

He nodded and wiped the tears on his face with the back of his hand. He was obviously deeply distressed.

"Would you like me to get you a taxi?"

"No . . . no, I need to get some fresh air, walk for a while. I can't quite cope at the moment."

Barry left and she saw him hurrying down the road, only then remembering that she should have told him about using the camera she had found in his flat. She was disinclined to hurry after him so instead she turned in the opposite direction to make her way to the Dawsons' flat to meet up with DS Lawrence.

Jane had become more resilient since her initiation in the morgue with DCI Bradfield. She had been at the identification of the murder victim Julie Ann Collins. Nevertheless, it could not be described as easy and she completely understood why Barry Dawson had been so distraught. By the time she got to the Dawsons' flat it was almost four o'clock. She buzzed the entry bell for the top flat. The lock clicked back loudly as she entered the hall and made her way up the stairs. The front door to the flat was wide open and as she stepped through the entrance there was the flash of a camera.

"Hi . . . it's only me," she said, as Lawrence turned and smiled.

He had long, thick blond hair with a center parting. It often fell forward so he had a habit of continually running his fingers through his hair to keep it off his face. Lawrence was always well dressed, but was rather old-fashioned in comparison to many of the Met police. He wore cord trousers and cotton shirts, with a tweed jacket that had leather elbow pads. He often had a woolen tie drawn down to the second button of his shirt. Jane had also noticed that his brown brogues were always rather scuffed, but despite his traditional appearance he had a very youthful manner.

"I expected you earlier . . . I had to get the keys from the duty sergeant as Gibbs said they would be left there for me. I've been taking some decent photographs. I picked up the ones you took with the Kodak but they're not that clear." He indicated a brown envelope left on the small coffee table as he packed his camera away.

"I've done a good check over the place, and if it's OK with you I'll be getting back to the station."

Jane was sifting through the photographs. As Lawrence had pointed out, they weren't good quality.

"This one I took of the dressing gown on the bathroom floor," she said, holding up the photo.

"What about it?"

"Well, it's just odd . . . if you were taking a bath and wearing the dressing gown, that would come off first, then the underwear. But the knickers and bra were folded underneath it."

Lawrence glanced at the photo. "Well, it's on a hook in the bathroom now."

"Yes, I did that."

He cocked his head to one side. "Shouldn't do that . . . I mean, not that I think there's anything suspicious. Maybe that's just the way she undressed."

Lawrence stood beside her as she thumbed through the rest of the photographs until she reached one with a woman turning toward the camera.

"Is that the victim?" he asked, and Jane shook her head.

"No, I don't know who she is. There were a few photographs already on the roll of film . . . same woman again . . . and another one."

Lawrence leaned closer as she fanned out the three photographs. They all seemed to have been taken as if the woman was unaware of being photographed.

"Maybe a friend? But it's odd that the woman is never looking into the camera and seems unaware she's being photographed. Mind you, I've seen a lot stranger . . . and some pornographic ones that beggar belief . . ."

"Did you really mean it when you said you were becoming fed up with working as a forensic liaison?"

"Yes. We're always strapped for finances and there's a lot of new scientific experiments coming on board. I'm finding it more and more frustrating because I spend most of my life checking fingerprints or, like today, looking over a crime scene that basically isn't one. I've applied to work with CID but the reality is forensic sections are deemed more important, and probably they are. It's just frustrating because I'd like to become more involved in the investigations instead of being stuck in a lab twenty-four-hours a day."

Surprised at his outburst, Jane asked, "But what you do is becoming more and more vital to investigations, isn't it?"

"Yes, I know . . . but try telling that to DI Moran . . . even DCI Shepherd isn't that encouraging. You know, the only person who really drew me in, and encouraged me, was Len Bradfield. After what happened to him I sort of allowed myself to get buried in the lab. Part of that was because of the guilt, and I still feel it."

"Guilt?"

"Yes. I had the chance to stop him going ahead with the operation. I knew early on that he was taking risks, but he persuaded me . . . he even had me on the team. I've never felt such adrenalin . . . Facing the outcome has been hard because I keep on thinking that if I had intervened he might still be alive."

Lawrence smiled sadly, running his fingers through his hair as Jane replied.

"But you can't blame yourself, Paul. If you do, then how do you think I feel? If I hadn't recognized that voice on the tape, if I hadn't identified the bank robber and his family, the operation would never have taken place."

He touched her shoulder. "Do you really believe that?"

"Yes. I don't dwell on it, I can't . . . but it took me a long time to get over the awful feeling of guilt." Jane thought about the way her heart would suddenly beat rapidly, and her breath quicken. How reminders, even seeing Lawrence today, brought back the feeling of helplessness and panic that she'd had to teach herself to control.

"You are very young, and were just a probationary officer then. I think both Spence and I carry the responsibility within us because of our positions . . . it rears up when you least expect it. All I really want to do now is get onto an investigation and prove myself capable of handling it."

There was a moment of embarrassed silence, as if he felt he had disclosed too much of himself, and he gave another sad smile.

"Sorry . . . didn't mean to lay that on you, Jane. Can you lock up and organize getting the key back to Mr. Dawson?"

"Yes, of course."

Lawrence left as Jane put the photographs and negatives into her bag. She felt depressed, but at the same time pleased that he had confided in her as she had always liked him. Now even more so. She checked the time and realized she would soon be off duty, so might as well return to the section house. As she locked the front door and headed down the stairs the door of the flat below opened and a thick-set, swarthy man wearing a fawn donkey jacket gestured toward her.

"Are you anything to do with the flat above? Only I need to check something out in their bathroom."

Jane introduced herself and explained that there had been a tragic incident and that Mrs. Dawson had been found dead.

"What?"

"Mrs. Dawson had an accident and—"

"Is their bath water running?"

She found it extraordinary that he showed no reaction whatsoever and said sharply that she was certain the bath water was turned off.

"Well, it might be turned off now but you come and take a look at this. I don't have a key to the Dawsons' flat because they own the place but I might need to put in a claim for water damage."

Jane followed the objectionable man into the flat, which was stripped down to the floorboards with ladders and tins of paint lined up in the entrance hall.

"I'm having the place refurbished and redecorated but this is really bad damage."

"I'm sorry, I didn't get your name?"

"Eric de Silva. I own this place, plus the head lease of the entire property. Come on through here."

Jane dutifully followed him into the bathroom, which was directly below the Dawsons' bathroom.

He pointed up to the ceiling. "Look at that. This was only painted a week ago."

The ceiling was wet and a pinkish water mark covered one side of the wall. He then pointed at the floor.

"See, it's dripped down the wall onto the floor. That's water damage. Their mains water tap needs to be turned off in case this is from their water tank as it's directly above this bathroom."

Jane agreed but refused to hand over the keys to him. She couldn't wait to get away from him and returned upstairs saying she would double-check that all the taps were turned off.

The bath taps were off, and the kitchen taps likewise. She located the water tank and mains tap in the airing cupboard and made sure these were also turned off. Returning to the bathroom she stood in the doorway. Something didn't make sense. The water marks in the flat below were obviously recent, and when she checked the water level rim still obvious in the bath it was in no way reaching the overflow or top of the bath. The pinkish color of the water down in the flat below could be caused by the blood from Shirley's head wound. But when her body was found there was no way the bath had overflowed. Jane had pulled out the plug so she knew exactly what level the water had been.

Bending down she could see that part of the board surrounding the bath was quite loose, and when she gave it a hard tug a section moved back easily. Jane jerked and pulled again and this time the old cheap tile came away. Leaning it against her legs she could see that there were pools of water still beneath the bath. The corking was sodden and wet. She propped the board back and decided that she needed to speak with de Silva again. She hurried down the stairs but the flat door was locked and there was no answer when she knocked. She went back upstairs to get her handbag and was about to leave when she saw the tea mug left on a side table. It had been brought in for her by the duty officer, from the next-door neighbor, when she was first there. She picked up the mug to return it, locking the door behind her.

Jane headed down to the basement flat and rang the doorbell. Mr. Cook opened the door. Jane explained she was returning the mug.

"Who is it?"

"It's the policewoman, love. Come on in, the wife's on sentry duty." He laughed, opening the door wider and gesturing with his hand for Jane to follow him.

"I really have to get back to the station."

"Be nice if you gave her an update on what happened next door."

"Yes of course, you were very helpful, Mr. Cook," Jane said, as she went into their sitting room. His wife was in her wheelchair positioned by their basement window. This was the room where Barry had been with the baby and his mother.

Mrs. Cook wheeled herself round to be able to face Jane, and indicated for her to sit on the sofa.

"Make us a cuppa, will you love?"

Her husband nodded and walked out. Jane perched on the edge of the sofa and gave Mrs. Cook a few details about the incident, and explained that they were waiting for a post-mortem report but it appears to have been a tragic accident.

"Shockin' . . . I had spent ages in the kitchen cos poor Barry was in here in a terrible state. Then he had the baby with him howlin' . . . give me a headache. Mind you, it was more action than I seen for years. That poor girl, drownin' like that."

"Did you know her well?"

"No, just to give a wave. I sit by the window . . . not that I can see that much, bein' in the basement. But I always saw her with the dog of a morning. Sometimes she'd bend down and give me a smile."

"She went out regularly in the morning, didn't she?"

"Yes, always about ten o'clockish, baby in the pushchair . . . pretty little thing . . . tragic now, havin' no mother. But he's a good lad."

"How well did you know Barry?"

"Not well. He's come in a few times, but they were just a young couple. He always said if we ever needed him he'd be over, but my husband takes care of everything."

Mr. Cook walked in with a tea tray and a packet of ginger biscuits.

"I really can't stay, but thank you." Jane half rose, wanting to leave.

"Did you tell her about the door?"

Mrs. Cook waved her hand. "No, I hadn't got around to it. Being in the basement we can hear it, you know, if any of the tenants next door buzz their door open. What they do is ring the bell for who they're seein' and they can buzz the front door open from their flat."

Jane had used it and Lawrence had opened the door for her. Mr. Cook came back in with a teapot.

"I don't know if she did go in but I heard the buzz. What time did I say it was?"

Jane was becoming impatient and looked at Mr. Cook.

"She's talking about the morning, you know, when Barry found the poor girl."

"That's right . . . I was sitting here having my morning cup of tea, in me dressing gown. I can tell if there's any post for us or if the paper boy's delivered, but it was about eight, was it?"

Mr. Cook poured the tea, and held up the milk jug. Jane smiled, thanking him.

"So, at eight o'clock . . ."

"Yes, or maybe a bit earlier. First, there was the woman, up and down, up and down . . . you can hear quite clearly down here . . . you know, footsteps on the pavement outside, click, click, click . . ."

"I'm sorry, I don't quite follow. You saw a woman outside?"

"That's right. She went back and forth, and then I heard the clunk from next door . . . you know, like I said, as if someone had let her in."

"Can you describe this woman?"

"No, love. Look for yourself, I can only see the feet and up to the knees."

"You are sure it was a woman?"

"Yes, dear . . . men don't go wearin' high-heeled black patent leather shoes now, do they?"

Jane smiled but the shoes caught her interest. "Was there anything else you noticed about the shoes? Were they unusual in any way?"

"Expensive I'd say, pointed at the front and with very high heels . . . maybe four or five inches."

"Thank you, Mrs. Cook, you've been very helpful. Just to make sure I've got it right . . . you saw this woman pacing up and down, then you heard the buzzer from next door, and it was around eight o'clock on the morning that Shirley was found . . ."

"Yes, dear, that's right . . . I don't know if it means anything."

Jane smiled politely and thanked the couple again for their hospitality. As it was already after 6 p.m. she didn't return to the station but went back to the section house. In her room she spent time compiling her notes before getting an early night. As she reflected on her findings, the Cooks' information about the mystery caller and the water-stained ceiling, she knew it wouldn't make her popular but tomorrow morning she would discuss her concerns with DCI Shepherd.

CHAPTER THIRTEEN

Jane was eager to share her thoughts with DI Gibbs but he wasn't in his office, or in the canteen, so she took her coffee and toast back to the incident room. She had just sat down at her desk to type up her report when Paul Lawrence walked in carrying notes for Edith to pass on about another case he was working on.

"Can I have a quick word, Paul?" Jane asked.

He looked at his watch, then smiled. "Sure, but make it fast as I've got a date with some blood tests."

Jane gave him a brief rundown about the water marks in the flat below the Dawsons', and then told him about the neighbor hearing the door release buzzer allowing someone to enter. She also explained that the owners of the ground-floor flat had left for work, and the middle flat was empty, so she believed it was possibly Shirley who let the woman in. As she was describing the black patent leather stiletto shoes seen by Mrs. Cook from the basement window, DCI Shepherd walked in and interrupted.

"I just spoke with PC May at the mortuary. Pathologist agreed with me and Doc Henry. He concluded that the Shirley Dawson case was accidental death by drowning. There was water in her lungs and stomach, and the injury to her head was consistent with a fall in the bath."

Lawrence looked at the DCI. "It might not be that straightforward, sir. Tennison has raised a couple of things that she thinks are out of place. I'd like to visit the scene with her."

"What things?"

"Just some inconsistencies. Tennison was at the victim's flat yesterday and there appears to be water damage to the flat below the Dawsons'—"

The DCI interrupted. "Well, obviously the bath water splashed about and overflowed after she'd slipped and cut her head open."

"There's also the possibility the victim may have had a female visitor that morning," Jane said.

"How do you know that?" the DCI asked, looking annoyed.

"I spoke with a neighbor, sir, Mrs. Cook. She saw a woman who she believes rang the doorbell at the flats, and then she heard the buzzer for the door latch go . . . I believe the woman was let in by Shirley Dawson—"

"Hang on, Tennison, just stop right there. The neighbor saw a woman yet only 'believes' she rang the doorbell and went in . . . What nonsense is that?"

Jane explained the circumstances of Mrs. Cook being in a wheelchair, and being able to see people's feet from her basement flat.

"They were very expensive-looking patent leather shoes, with pointed toes and a high stiletto heel, and . . ."

The DCI raised his eyes to the ceiling and shook his head. Even Lawrence looked at Jane rather surprised by what she'd just said, though he didn't doubt it was true.

Shepherd smiled at Jane and quietly said, "So our new WDC wants to challenge my opinion, the police doctor's opinion and the wisdom of a pathologist in favor of a woman in a wheelchair who saw a pair of patent leather shoes?"

"Well, I do question it, sir . . ."

"Do you really, Tennison? It's been classified as non-suspicious and PC May has informed the coroner of that fact. Now, get out there and start investigating that pickpocket with the razor before he does some real harm to anyone who tries to stop him."

Jane wanted to add that she also wasn't happy with Barry Dawson's behavior, but Lawrence looked at her and surreptitiously shook his head for her to keep quiet.

"Who was the pathologist that carried out the examination, sir?" Lawrence asked.

DCI Shepherd looked at him sternly, but Lawrence was quick to give his reason for the question.

"Tennison will need his name for her report."

"That new chap, who's just come down from Leeds . . ."

"Dr. Forrest," Lawrence said. The DCI nodded and then left the room. Jane sighed and lifted up her hands.

"Honestly, it's as if I am not allowed to have an opinion!"

"Forrest's an old boy who's self-opinionated and lazy. Rumor has it he screwed up a few jobs in Leeds by misdiagnosis and only applied for the job down here cos he was under pressure to hang up his medical bag and retire."

"Could we get someone else to look at Shirley Dawson's body?"

"I doubt it . . . besides, it's not protocol. Prof Martin is head of the Pathology department. He and Forrest are drinking buddies. You'll need something more to persuade the coroner to give the go-ahead for a second PM."

"Will you help me, Paul? I just have a feeling something is wrong, but I don't know enough about forensics and dead bodies . . ."

Lawrence shook his head.

"But why not? You told me yesterday that you wanted to have a more central role in investigation—this could be your opportunity. Please, Paul, I have such a strong gut feeling about this."

"Gut feelings are not a bad thing, as you already know from when you recognized the bank robber's voice. But you need to find hard evidence to prove them. I'm in the lab all morning, but after lunch let's meet at the Dawsons' flat and we'll go over it inch by inch together. If we find anything solid to go on I'll approach another pathologist I know for advice and an off-the-record second opinion. In the meantime, why don't you make some inquiries about Barry Dawson at the hospital? See if his statement about what time he left the hospital and returned home matches with his work records."

Jane nodded. "Thank you, I'll call you."

Lawrence left Jane alone in the CID room. She was halfway through reading the autopsy report when Edith arrived for work. She was in a very tetchy mood again as her mother was continuing to be difficult.

Not wanting to be drawn into a long discussion about what Edith's mother had got up to in the night, Jane left the autopsy report on her desk to finish later and said, "Edith, I'm going over to St. Thomas' Hospital to check a few details out."

Edith rolled some fresh paper into her typewriter.

"On whose authority? I've got you down for making further inquiries about this bag slasher . . . is DI Gibbs going with you?"

"No, he's not in yet."

Edith looked at her watch. "That man is skating on thin ice. He is supposed to be working on the bag slasher case. Well, go along to St. Thomas' and I'll tell Gibbs when he deigns to come in."

"It's still very early," Jane said, hoping she hadn't got DI Gibbs in trouble.

"Early birds, my dear, catch the worms. Right, let me go over this autopsy report and hopefully that's one case sorted."

Jane was at St. Thomas' Hospital by eight thirty. She went straight to the porters' rest room in the basement. It was a very untidy, smelly room with old wing-backed chairs, worn carpet and overflowing bins. There were food plates from the canteen left on a low table, with full ashtrays and old newspapers littered around. The off duty night porter was resting in one of the moth-eaten chairs, as the morning shift came on ready to work.

Jane was able to check that Barry Dawson was on duty and had arrived on time that day as usual. However, nobody could recall seeing him after he clocked on at six forty-five and it was suggested that Jane go up to one of the wards on the second floor as the porter, a Mario Goncalves, was handling patients scheduled for theater and he had been on duty the same morning.

Jane made her way toward the nurses' bay to ask if Mario Goncalves was available to have a quick chat. The nurses were drinking tea and one was at an open cabinet selecting medication to put into rows of small containers with name tags. Jane introduced herself. They were very pleasant and offered her a cup of tea, explaining that Mario was taking a patient to the X-ray unit but was expected back any moment. Jane declined the offer of tea and stood beside the small horseshoe desk. On one wall there was a large cork noticeboard with time schedules, postcards and patients' room numbers pinned to it. There were also menus, a diet sheet listing special needs, and numerous photographs of nurses' outings and birthday parties, plus a few thank-you cards.

Jane checked her watch. She had to constantly step aside as one nurse after another came into the bay or left. She glanced back at the cork board for something to do, and one photograph caught her attention. It looked as if it was some kind of celebration party, and she recognized one of the girls in the photo as the nurse selecting the medications. But there was a redhead standing behind her and Jane moved closer for a better look.

"Excuse me?" Jane looked at the nurse who was locking up the medication cupboard.

"In this photograph . . . who is that red-headed girl standing behind you?"

"That's Katrina. It was a drinks do for the new nurse."

"Does Katrina work here?"

"She did, but she left about eight or nine days ago. She wasn't happy and didn't get along with us. There was a bit of a situation."

"Could I ask you what it was?"

The nurse wheeled her trolley out from the bay. "Not entirely sure . . . not my business really. Can you excuse me?"

Jane had to step aside, and turned to one of the other nurses. "Why did Katrina leave?"

There were hooded looks between her and her colleagues. Jane explained that she was making inquiries regarding a police investigation and would be grateful if they could answer her question. A plump nurse stepped forward and introduced herself as the Ward Sister.

"Her name is Katrina Harcourt. Basically she was not up to a very professional standard as she had been working with some temping agency before she came here. In fact, she wasn't here for that long . . . no more than eight or nine months."

Jane opened her bag and took out the envelope of photographs she had developed from the reel of film. She selected the black and white photograph of the woman caught on camera.

"This is her, isn't it?"

"Yes, she had really auburn hair. Very pretty . . . but like I said, we all have a job to do here and she wasn't very well liked."

"Do you have an address for her?"

The nurse was becoming rather irritated by Jane as the phone kept on ringing and they were preparing to go on the wards. They were able to give Jane the last address they had for Katrina, which was the nurses' accommodation close to the hospital, then Mario appeared with a wheelchair. He was very affable and good-looking, and stacked the wheelchair into the annex before he joined her in the corridor. They sat on some hard-backed chairs as Jane introduced herself and asked him about the morning of Shirley's death.

Mario said that everyone was very sad for Barry as he had not, as yet, returned to work but had called in explaining his reasons.

Mario was able to confirm that Barry had eaten breakfast as usual in the canteen that day. Then he recalled that later that morning he had been in the A&E corridor when Barry had asked him for some change to use the payphone.

"It was about ten thirty. He had been calling for some time and asked me for change as he said he couldn't get through. He was very agitated."

"Did he say why?"

"Yeah, he said he was trying to call his wife, but wasn't getting any reply. So he had called his mother, but he was very concerned. I gave him some change, but I had an emergency to attend so I didn't see him again."

"Did you know a nurse called Katrina Harcourt?"

Mario appeared evasive, and shrugged his shoulders.

"Yeah, she worked here on Ward C . . . but I wouldn't say I knew her."

"Did Barry know her?"

"Like I just said, she used to work here so we all get to know each other. She left under a bit of a cloud, but that's all I know."

Jane thanked Mario, then went up to the canteen to double-check if any of the serving ladies recalled seeing Barry having breakfast that morning. It was rather a pointless inquiry as they all remembered seeing Barry at breakfast every day if he was on the morning shift, as he was a regular, but none of them could confirm categorically seeing him that particular day.

The row of houses was quite run-down and they were mostly divided up into bedsits. Gassiot House, the address she had been given, was at the end of the row. Jane rang the bell for number

12. She was about to turn away when the front door was opened by a woman carrying a mop and bucket.

"Do you know if anyone is in number twelve?" Jane said as she showed her ID.

"I don't, love. I just clean the landings and hallways, but not the rooms."

"Do you mind if I go and check."

"No, go ahead—it's on the second landing."

Jane moved up the wide staircase. The threadbare carpet had bald patches and the wide polished oak banister rail was obviously from a more affluent period when the property was perhaps privately owned. It appeared that every room had now been made into bedsits. There were bathrooms on each floor and the ceiling was cracked and peeling in places.

Number 12 was at the end of the corridor. Jane knocked, waited, then tried again. There was no response. She was about to try one more time when the door opened.

"Yeah?"

"I'm so sorry to disturb you—"

"Listen, I've not had time to clear up . . . you're early." The girl was wearing flannelette pajamas and had tousled hair, with a sleeping mask around her neck. She swung the door open and gestured for Jane to come in.

"I'm on nights . . . this is really inconvenient."

Jane stepped into the shambolic room, which had the curtains drawn shut and two single beds on either side. The unmade bed had sheets and blankets piled up on it, with cardboard boxes on the floor beside it. Hanging on the back of the door was a nurse's uniform and cape.

"I would like to introduce myself, as I think you may be confused." Jane took out her warrant card and held it up. "I am Detective Constable Jane Tennison. I'm making inquiries about Katrina Harcourt."

"What?"

"I'm sorry, what is your name?"

"Brenda March. I thought you were here to take up the other bed. Katrina doesn't live here anymore, and she's cleaned out all her stuff."

Brenda sat on her bed and switched on a bedside lamp. The untidy room was quite large, with a chest of drawers covered in makeup and perfume bottles. There was a huge free-standing wardrobe with the doors open and a jumble of clothes spilling out, and a dirty laundry bag dumped beside it. On a side table was an electric kettle with bottles of milk, tins of coffee and tea bags, and packets of biscuits. Chipped mugs were lined up alongside a saucer with used teaspoons.

"I am sorry to inconvenience you but I just need to ask a few questions about Katrina."

"As I said, she doesn't live here anymore and there's another nurse moving in today. I am going to tidy up, but she left her side in a mess. I didn't get in until after my shift and I'm really knackered. Katrina paid up until the end of the week, so I've had the place to myself."

Jane glanced further around the room. There was a wash-basin with dirty towels on a rail, and a broken mirror above it.

"How well did you know Katrina?"

Brenda shrugged and got up to open the cheap curtains.

"Well, she slept here, but I wouldn't say I knew her that well. We were often on different shifts so she'd be sleeping when I was working. But she was OK. What's this about?"

"I'm just making inquiries and would like to talk to her. Do you have a forwarding address for her?"

"No, she left in quite a hurry. Said she didn't get on with the new Ward Sister and was fed up, so she packed her stuff. In fact, I wasn't here. I think she has parents in Brighton."

"Do you know Barry Dawson?"

"Yes, he's a porter at the hospital. I was told that his wife had died . . . is that what this is about?"

"Did Katrina know him?"

"I suppose so. I mean, it's a big hospital but you do eventually get to know most of the staff."

"What can you tell me about Katrina?"

"Like I just said, I didn't really know her. I mean, we weren't friends. Sometimes we'd have a drink in the pub after work with everyone. She was very attractive, very stylish, but she was quite edgy cos she knew the other nurses didn't really get along with her. They didn't reckon she pulled her weight and wasn't as professional because she had mostly worked in care homes before. She didn't take to all the rules and regulations you have to adhere to when you're in a hospital like St. Thomas'. Apparently she was often late and complained a lot."

"Did she have a boyfriend?"

Brenda frowned. "I think she had someone, but I dunno who. She was quite secretive about whoever it was. You know, if it was a doctor the gossip goes round like wildfire. Everyone always thinks that nurses go after the doctors. She used to get all dressed up and she had some nice clothes."

"So you think she was having an affair with someone from the hospital?"

"Well, I did think it might be a doctor or one of the surgeons, but I never saw her with any of them outside the hospital. Whoever it was gave her a necklace . . . oh yes, and a nice ring . . . she showed me the ring, it was a garnet but not that extravagant."

"So when she showed you the ring what did she say?"

Brenda sighed. "She didn't actually show it to me . . . it was on her bedside table and being a bit nosey when I was here I took a look at it. There was a card with a heart on it as well. Look, I don't know what all this is really about. She was very unpleasant when I asked her if it was an engagement ring, because I was obviously letting her know I'd seen it. She had a temper on her and was telling me to mind my own business. I just let her rant on at me because I had been nosey. She sort of apologized for being so nasty to me and then she told me that the reason she was so upset was because of a previous engagement she had and whoever it was broke her heart."

"To someone from the hospital?"

"No, she said it was a while ago. She was preparing her wedding, had a designer dress, bridesmaids and everything arranged by her parents and he must have dumped her . . . she became very upset and said she didn't want to talk about it anymore because she had virtually had a nervous breakdown about it."

"Did she mention to you who it was? Maybe gave you his name?"

"No, just that he was a doctor and that he had hurt her deeply. And he cost her family so much money as they couldn't get the deposit back from the venue they'd booked for the reception."

"That must have been awful for her."

"I suppose it was, and that was why she was so secretive about who she was seeing. She did tell me something else . . ." Brenda chuckled.

"What else?"

"Well, she said that she took a pair of scissors and cut her wedding dress to shreds. It was a bit freaky because she started to laugh, you know, as if it was funny . . . but obviously it wasn't. Anyway, it was shortly after that that she left and we never discussed it again."

Jane smiled and thanked Brenda, apologizing for waking her. She was unsure just what she had gained from the interview; however, she did now know that Barry Dawson's statement about when he had left the hospital was confirmed by Mario Goncalves.

On the bus back to the station Jane went over her notes and jotted down the timing of Katrina leaving the hospital and bedsit. This would have been a week before Shirley Dawson drowned. She was uncertain about the connection, it just made her wonder why there were three photographs of Katrina Harcourt on the roll of film from the Dawsons' camera.

Jane used a payphone to call DS Lawrence at the lab. She agreed to meet up with him at the station so they could walk to the Dawsons' flat. It was almost midday when they set off and Jane gave Lawrence the details about her visit to the hospital and her questioning of Brenda March. He listened attentively and then asked if Jane could be on the wrong track, as from what he had gathered Barry appeared to be very distressed about his wife's death.

"Yes, he was . . . but I have a suspicion that perhaps he could be the man having an affair with Katrina. There is also the possibility that it was Katrina who had been outside their flat on the morning Shirley died."

"All this from the photographs we developed?"

"Yes, it was Katrina. Even though the photos were black and white I recognized her from a photograph at the hospital. She has red hair."

"Well, Mrs. Cook only saw a woman's feet so that's going to be hard to prove. Also we can't be one hundred percent certain she went into the Dawsons' flat. We also don't have her fingerprints on record, so that can't help us."

Climbing up the stairs to the flat, they discovered the front door was ajar. Lawrence indicated to Jane to be silent as he moved in front of her and entered the hall. They could see no one, but the sound of hammering drew them toward the bathroom.

Barry Dawson was on his knees hammering the bath panel into place. He had a bag of tools with screwdrivers and heavier hammers beside him. Lawrence knocked on the door and Barry turned round in shock.

"Mr. Dawson, I am Detective Sergeant Lawrence and you already know WDC Tennison. Can you explain exactly what you are doing here?"

Barry stood up, his face flushed. "I was repairing the bath panel, putting it back into place. I have every right to be here . . . it's my flat and I need more clothes for myself and Heidi. Perhaps you could tell me what *you* are doing here?"

"OK, Mr. Dawson, you can get what you need but then you must leave. We'll contact you as soon as you are allowed access. We're just having a once-over to be totally satisfied. I am a forensic officer and I have been asked by the coroner to examine the flat."

"I haven't finished."

"Just leave it as it is, Mr. Dawson. WDC Tennison will accompany you to get the items you need."

Barry didn't take long. He used an old holdall, taking clothes for his daughter and a few items for himself, and said that he would be returning to work the following day. Jane watched him silently, and when he was ready to leave she walked him to the front door.

"One more thing, Mr. Dawson. I have to apologize as I used your camera while I was here, to photograph the bathroom." Jane gestured to the small Kodak camera she had left on the coffee table.

"That's not mine. I've never seen it before."

"Oh, well, we'll reimburse you for the reel of film I used. There were some photographs that had already been taken on it."

Jane went to her bag and took out the envelope containing the images. She selected the three black and white photographs of Katrina and handed them to him. She watched closely as he glanced at them, but he showed no reaction and appeared to be unperturbed.

"I don't know who this is. I don't want them."

He tore up the photographs, tossed them onto the table next to the camera and left the flat carrying the holdall. Lawrence came out from the bathroom.

"Well, it's still sodden beneath the bath, and the tide mark is clearly shown. I used the screwdriver Mr. Dawson was using—come and have a look."

Lawrence leaned over the bath and indicated with the screwdriver that the waste pipe was blocked. He felt it wasn't a recent blockage but was a build-up of hairs and thick soap that had congealed.

"No water could have leaked down below this way—it had to have come from the bath being overfilled."

"I know the water level was not high because I pulled the plug out, and as you can see from the blood-stained rim it was nowhere near overflowing."

"Might have happened when she fell backward and the level rose."

She watched as he tested the small residue of blood still on the central tap, and then looked around.

"No other blood drops. This is the only congealed blood at the scene, so it's likely that when she hit her head, she subsequently fell backward and slid under the water, drowning."

"Was she standing up when she hit her head?"

He frowned, then shrugged. Jane watched as he took samples of the blockage and then photographed the bath.

"Barry said he didn't own the camera and when he was shown the photographs of Katrina he denied knowing her, and then tore them up."

"Well, that's interesting . . . but you still have the negatives?"

"Yes."

"OK . . . now, get into the bath. I need you to show me something."

"What?"

He laughed. "Just want to test something. I remember when we first met, at the autopsy of that murdered girl, and old Professor Martin asked you to get on the floor as he wanted to demonstrate how he thought the victim had been beaten. He asked you to put up your arm as if protecting your body from the blows . . ."

"Don't remind me! I was so embarrassed because I thought he wanted me to lie on the floor. I smelt of Dettol for days afterward, it was all over my uniform."

Lawrence smiled at the memory.

"Right, step into the bath. There was no mat, right, so take off your shoes and in you get."

He held her hand as she stepped into the bath.

"Now, we are presuming the water was turned off and the bath was filled. So, did she step in and find that it was boiling hot, leaned toward the taps, slipped and cracked her head? Just try it."

In her stocking feet Jane leaned toward the central tap. She pretended to hit her head, and then leaned back.

"It would be more likely that she would end up forward, on her knees?"

He nodded, then took Jane's hand to help her out.

"But if she really cracked her head hard she could have lost her balance and been unconscious, falling back into the water," he said.

Jane put on her shoes and followed him out of the bathroom.

"OK, let me have a good look over the place and take some more photographs."

Jane was fascinated by how carefully Lawrence moved around the flat. The high chair was still in place and the food remained on the tray. He examined the playpen, then stood at the ironing board. Near to that was a clothes horse with a few items ready to be ironed, with a water spray and some starch in a basket.

The iron was on its side, not placed into the section at the end of the board. Lawrence examined the iron very closely, running his finger along the rim. He took close-up pictures of the iron and Jane smiled as he had a habit of muttering to himself. The iron had been recently cleaned. He looked around to see if there was a rag or something that had been used to wipe it because it had a faint smell of Dettol. He then replaced the iron and checked the flex, bending down to the socket on the wall beside it.

"This is interesting . . . it looks to me as if the plug was wrenched out of the socket because the wires are not only frayed, which could be a result of frequent use, but two of the wires are disconnected so the iron would not be usable. And it could give you an electric shock if you tried to use it."

He stood up with his hands on his hips.

"OK, I don't like this. Blouse on the ironing board ready to be pressed . . . baby's food on the high chair tray . . . next-door neighbor hears the front door buzzer after she has seen a woman pacing up and down outside the basement . . ."

"That was at eight o'clock," Jane said.

"Right. But we know Barry was calling the payphone on the landing at the hospital trying to reach Shirley at ten or ten thirty, but received no answer. He leaves the hospital and arrives home at eleven to find his wife dead in the bath."

"One more thing," Jane added. "His mother said she was going to be here at the flat but didn't turn up because she was waiting for an engineer. Barry said he made a call to his mother so he would know she was not here with Shirley as arranged. A witness said he appeared to be very anxious and subsequently left the hospital. But surely if he also knew his wife was going to have a hair appointment why was he so anxious that she didn't answer the phone?"

Lawrence checked his watch.

"OK, I am going to pull in a favor and see if I can get a more experienced pathologist to get over to the mortuary and check Shirley's body. I'm going to have to move fast before it's released for burial because I need to know whether her head injury is in fact totally consistent with the fall in the bath."

Jane could feel the tension mounting.

"I keep thinking about Barry's reaction to the camera. He said he didn't know Katrina, but he had to know her from the hospital."

Lawrence replied, "Maybe he didn't own the camera. What if it belonged to Shirley? Taking a long shot, what if she had used it to take the photographs of Katrina as she had found out Barry was having an affair with her?"

"Brenda said she had a mystery boyfriend from the hospital," Jane interjected.

"So, what we have is a possible motive . . ." Lawrence continued. "A love affair, right? She confronted Barry and they had an argument. On the other hand, it could all be inconclusive."

"I honestly don't think he killed her," Jane said, biting her lip.

"Or perhaps they were in it together," Lawrence continued. "You need to trace this Katrina and find out if she was involved with Barry. Dig up whatever you can on her, but until we have more we keep this just between ourselves and don't inform DCI Shepherd. We need to prove that this was not accidental death, but murder."

"I'll go back to the station," Jane said, collecting her bag.

Lawrence grinned. "Well, I'm going to have do a bit of schmoozing to get old Professor Martin on board. He may be a pain in the arse but he's top notch . . . when he's sober."

Jane laughed. She had met "old Prof Martin" numerous times since she had first met Lawrence. She had learned that alongside his drinking and cigar smoking, his jovial and loud bellowing voice was often a cover as he was a very knowledgeable and dedicated man.

Lawrence held open the front door for her as they left.

"We might be in luck. I doubt the coroner will release the body for the undertakers' embalming before the funeral on Monday . . . let's hope not."

They split up outside the Dawsons' flat and Jane walked the few yards to pass the basement next door. She was going to continue but paused and bent down, looking through the railings. Mrs. Cook was sitting in her wheelchair knitting, but she looked up as if she had heard her footsteps. Jane gave a small wave and Mrs. Cook smiled and waved back. Jane was satisfied that Mrs. Cook was possibly right about the high-heeled footsteps. She was beginning to feel very confident that this was going to be her first murder case with the new station.

CHAPTER FOURTEEN

Jane completed her notes on the inquiries at St. Thomas' Hospital and what she and Lawrence had determined from their visit to the Dawsons' flat. It was five-thirty and, after checking any messages and details that had been listed for her to oversee, she had nothing left to do. There was a report file disclosing that there had been further bag snatches in Wardour Street and one report from the Marquee Club that there had been a theft of a woman's handbag, but there was no point going now; better to wait until later as she might catch the manager. She had a few words with the duty sergeant before leaving, then decided that to fill the time she'd do a catch-up at Hackney to see if there had been any developments or if a trial date had been set for Peter Allard.

It felt strange returning to her old stamping ground. DI Moran ran the CID at Hackney very differently to the way DCI Bradfield had done and the atmosphere felt a little strained, even more so when she entered the CID office. DC Brian Edwards was wearing an overcoat and had cotton wool stuck in one ear, with a streaming nose. He looked up when Jane knocked on the door.

"Hi there," Jane said.

Edwards sneezed loudly.

"Stay well away from me—I'm contaminated. I've had this bloody cold for two days. As you can see, everyone has scarpered out of the office."

"Why don't you go home?"

"The guv's asked me to do all this checking into old cases, and wants to see if I can get a result before Allard's trial."

"So we haven't got a date yet?"

"Nope . . . But it can't be far off. I've found out that five years ago Allard used to rent a property in Maidstone, worked as a bus driver, then returned to London after his father died and took over his taxi."

"What's this got to do with his trial?" Jane asked.

Edwards became hesitant, blowing his nose. "Moran's concerned that there might be questions about the confession . . . He reckons the pattern of Allard's assaults, and the attack on you, means that there could have been more in his past."

"Have you found anything that might be connected?"

"Give me a break—have you any idea how many sexual assaults take place in these areas . . . Hackney, Peckham, Walthamstow? I haven't even started on Maidstone yet because that'll be a different force. And you know how protective forces are about their own information."

Edwards sneezed loudly again.

"Bless you!" Jane said. "Is DI Moran in his office?"

"No. He went out to buy a christening present for DC Ashton's new baby."

Surprised by Moran's enthusiasm for gift buying, Jane thanked Edwards and went out of the CID office, heading down to the Collator's Office in the basement. On the way she popped into the ladies' locker room, giving an affectionate tap to the "LADIES ONLY" sign on the door. Kath's legacy was still intact. As she came out five minutes later she bumped straight into DI Moran, who was carrying an enormous donkey-shaped piñata.

"Good evening, Tennison. I can only presume you're here for the celebration drinks for DC Ashton's baby girl?"

"No, sir. Actually I just came in to see if we had a trial date for Peter Allard."

"No, we haven't. Those wankers at the court are taking their bloody time, as usual. The boys will be surprised to see you."

"If you don't mind me saying so, sir, I don't think a donkey piñata is a particularly appropriate present for a newborn baby?"

Moran chuckled loudly.

"No . . . no, Tennison. We fill it with shillings wrapped in pound notes, and we all take turns in hitting it with a truncheon, but not too hard . . . then hopefully it will be Ashton who smashes it open and collects the loot."

"That's a very innovative idea, sir. Whoever thought of that?" Jane replied, clearly thinking that it wasn't innovative at all.

Moran beamed in response. "I did! And for the baby I've got this . . ."

He delved into his coat pocket and pulled out a small pink teddy bear.

"So, are you coming over to the Warburton to have a drink with us?" he asked.

"Thank you, sir."

As Moran walked away with the huge piñata tucked under his arm he turned back to Jane.

"I'll let you have the first crack at the donkey!"

Jane watched Moran as he went down the corridor, looking rather ridiculous. She had just had the perfect opportunity to discuss with him her concerns about the blue rabbit fur coat, and couldn't really understand why she hadn't done so. But if she spoke to the collator it would probably iron out her queries.

Donaldson was getting ready to go home and seemed surprised to see her.

"How is it at Bow Street?"

"Fine. Rather quiet actually. I was dropping in to see if a trial date had been set for Peter Allard."

Donaldson shrugged and Jane hesitated before asking him if she could take a look at Janet Brown's file and record sheet. He looked at his watch and seemed ill at ease.

"It's nothing important, just for personal reasons."

She watched him go to a filing cabinet and waited as he sifted through the drawer and then slowly closed it.

"Not here."

"I don't understand."

Donaldson picked up his coat from a hook behind the door, and folded it over his arm.

"I didn't think files were allowed to be removed from the Collator's Office," Jane said, as Donaldson picked up an old battered briefcase left beside his desk.

"I can't help you, but sometimes one of the detectives might come in. Now, I need to lock up and get home."

Jane sensed he was being evasive and was certain he was lying, but she didn't want to question him any further as he was getting impatient for her to leave. She had always found Donaldson to be very helpful in the past and she was disappointed.

She had a light supper in the canteen upstairs and could see the ostracized Brian Edwards sitting in a corner by himself, sneezing loudly. He looked terrible and everyone else was clearly avoiding him. On the next table the young DC Ashton joined a few other officers. He was carrying a tray with shepherd's pie and a syrup sponge and custard, and was surprised to see her.

"Have you been assigned back here again?"

"No, I just couldn't resist the food. I hear congratulations are in order, and that you're a father now."

"Yeah, it was a bit of a surprise—not exactly a shotgun wedding, but sooner than we'd planned. Are you coming over to the Warburton later? Moran's organized it."

"Yes, looking forward to it."

After applying some lipstick and tidying herself up in the ladies' locker room, Jane made her way over to the Warburton Arms.

The usual array of sausage rolls, cheese and ham sandwiches and obligatory packets of crisps were being laid out on the bar counter by Ron. DC Donaldson was unloading beer from two crates, and placing the bottles beside the food. Jane wondered if this was the reason he had been in such a hurry to leave the Collator's Office. She was still confused as to why the file on Janet Brown was missing. Jane crossed over to Donaldson as he poured a beer for himself.

"All these beers are on the house, and we've got three bottles of white and three red . . . what's your fancy, Jane?"

"I'll have a glass of white, please."

"Well, go and get the bottle opened, and ask Ron for some ice."

At that moment the double doors to the pub banged open. Moran led the team in, still holding the donkey piñata. He shouted at Ron.

"Ron, we need to get this thing hung up!"

Ron looked at him in total bewilderment.

"What the hell is that?"

"It's a piñata. It's full of cash and we're going to take it in turns to hit it with a truncheon, and whoever smashes it open gets the contents!"

"Well, you're not hanging that pissatto, or whatever it is, in the main bar. You can take it into the snooker room and hang it up from one of the lights in there. But if anyone damages the table or the lights, you'll be paying for it."

The celebration for Ashton's baby was beginning to spiral out of control. Everyone was eager to attack the piñata, but Moran was refusing to allow a truncheon near it until they had consumed all the drinks he had provided. He kept on repeating, to one officer after another, "Don't bloody hit it hard . . . this is for Ashton. He's broke, and he needs to get all the cash inside."

At one point he even put his arm around Jane and repeated his warning to her. "I know you can throw a good whack with a truncheon because of Allard. But just tap it."

Jane smiled. "Yes, sir, I'll just tap it."

"Good. I asked Spence to come over as he knew DC Ashton before he got hitched—poor sod—said he was on an assignment at the Marquee Club. Haw haw! If his band are playing they'll empty the place."

At that point there was a very loud cheer as the team were impatient for the "smash and grab." By this time DC Ashton, who had obviously had more than his fair share of free drinks, was wearing a white hat with a bobble on top. Hanging around his neck was a huge sugared dummy that one of the other officers had bought from the market fair.

"Quiet, everybody!" Moran yelled. "As everyone knows, we've all chipped in for the amazing contents of our donkey. And the first person to attempt to smash it open is DC Donaldson."

Yet again Moran, now clearly inebriated, whispered loudly, "Don't hit it too hard!"

This encouraged everyone to cheer, in unison, "Tap, tap, tap . . . Tap, tap, tap . . ."

As each officer used their truncheons one after the other, Moran encouraged Jane to use his truncheon to attempt to break it open. Jane was terrified that she might hit it too hard.

As she raised Moran's truncheon DC Edwards yelled, "Go on, Tennison, hit it like you hit that rapist!"

Jane had a momentary flashback of how she had struck Peter Allard and almost unintentionally she drew her right hand back and walloped the donkey, which by now had a very bedraggled leg and tail. She had meant to aim for the head, but accidentally hit the belly. There was a massive "Whoooaaa" as a large split appeared. Jane was mortified that the contents were about to come spilling out, as Moran yelled, "Give the truncheon to the new Daddy!"

Jane quickly passed the truncheon to Ashton. There was a loud cheer of encouragement as he took a full swing and hit the target dead center. The donkey burst open, and instead of the usual array of sweets out fell all the cash contributed by his colleagues.

Jane felt quite emotional as she watched the young detective, almost in tears, as he realized how much everyone had given to support him.

It was now coming up to ten o'clock and the party was beginning to wind down. Jane thought she would take the opportunity to go to the Marquee Club as so far she had only been able to question a member of staff in the daytime. Moran noticed that she was getting ready to leave.

"Are you off now, Jane? You got me quite worried there, when you took that swing at the donkey. I thought you were going to bust it wide open!"

Jane couldn't work Moran out. One moment he seemed so affable and obviously well liked, and was clearly a very generous man. But there was just something else that she couldn't quite put her finger on, and she wasn't sure that she could entirely trust him. As she turned away Moran took her elbow and leaned in close.

"I hear you were asking Donaldson about a missing file? Take my advice, Tennison—don't meddle, or ever question anything I've done . . . I'll always get to hear about it. Trust me, we're going to put Allard away for a long time."

Jane was about to think of something to say, but he turned away, the opportunity gone. She saw him go to Donaldson and say something in his ear; both of them turned to look at Jane as she left the pub. Jane took a bus to Regent Street and walked along Oxford Street, looking into the lit-up windows of all the big stores. She wasn't that interested in fashion and crossed over Oxford Street toward Wardour Street. There were groups of young teenagers standing smoking outside the Marquee Club. There were posters for music groups pinned up outside, and the big crowds had not yet arrived to see the main band playing that evening.

Jane showed her warrant card to gain entrance and walked down the stairs into the club and bar area. It was busier than she had anticipated and there was a band tuning up on the small stage. She felt and looked out of place and was beginning to think she shouldn't have even considered being there on her own. She was relieved to see DI Spencer Gibbs sitting on a stool at the bar. He looked very disheveled and was wearing tight leather trousers and a stained T-shirt under a dirty denim jacket.

"Hey there."

Jane moved closer and was shocked when he turned toward her and appeared to be very drunk.

"I was just going to do a bit of a catch-up and ask about the report—"

She didn't have the chance to finish as he lurched forward off his stool and made a grab for her arm.

"Let's go . . ." he slurred, and gripped her elbow tightly, maneuvering her roughly through a group of drinkers. Jane didn't argue as Gibbs was really pushing her forward and up the stairs, his hand deep into her back as they passed lines of clubbers coming down the stairs. When they got outside she turned on him.

"There was no need to do that."

Gibbs straightened up, took hold of her arm again and hurried her along the street.

"What's the matter with you?" she said, dragging her arm free.

"I'll tell you what's the matter with me, Tennison . . . I'm down there acting as a piss artist and you come in sticking out like a sore thumb with copper written all over you."

"What?"

"I'm doing undercover, trying to track down the bastard that uses a razor to cut the straps of women's handbags. He should have had a go at yours . . . it's a police issue shoulder bag! What the hell were you doing, and who told you to work the club tonight?"

"I meant to get a new bag," she replied sheepishly, not mentioning that she had showed her warrant card to get in.

"Terrific."

"I'm sorry, I just saw that there had been further reports . . ."

"Christ," he muttered, and then looked up and down the road. "You want a coffee? I can't go back in for a while now."

Jane nodded and they headed back into Oxford Street, then left into Poland Street and left again into D'Arblay Street to a small cappuccino bar. It was rather seedy with a shelf counter and high stools, and Jane sat with her back to a wall, unseen from the wide window onto the street. Gibbs bought two cappuccinos and joined her. He opened three packs of brown sugar, heaping them onto the froth in his cup, then used a spoon to stir it before tapping it against the saucer.

"We reckon whoever is nicking all the gear might move up a notch and use his razor on one of the chicks' faces, as reports are coming in that the attacks are getting nastier. He's probably a junkie needing money fast cos he's now working the clubs as well as out on the street, but he's an amateur. We got professional pickpockets around here, some work in gangs—like the South Americans."

Jane sipped the frothy coffee, and apologized again.

"Listen, I won't say anything about this tonight, Jane, but you need to sharpen up and get into line. You're in CID now and you don't go batting solo. Do you think I would stay in a club on my own? I've got two other guys outside bloody backing me up."

"I'm sorry. I was just at a loose end. I went over to Hackney to see if there was any update on the rape case but they are still waiting for a trial date."

"What rape case?"

"It's just an old case, pretty straightforward."

Gibbs lit a cigarette, and inhaled deeply. He gave a brief glance around, took out a hip flask, unscrewed the cap and tipped a measure into his half-full cup.

"Can I tell you something?" Jane asked quietly.

"Sure."

"I don't know if you know this, but I was used as a decoy. And, well, I've just got this feeling that something's not quite adding up and I'm not sure what to do about it. I wore a blue rabbit fur coat that belonged to a prostitute called Janet Brown."

Jane continued telling him about seeing Janet Brown's file in the Collator's Office, and that it had subsequently disappeared. She went on to describe how she had seen her exit one of the strip clubs the last time she had been in Wardour Street, but she didn't get the opportunity to talk to her. Gibbs didn't look at her as she explained about her concerns regarding the knife and the signed confession Peter Allard had made, and how tough it had been in court.

"I don't know if he did the rape he is accused of."

Gibbs turned and looked at her, shaking his head. "Wait . . . wait, I'm trying to follow you, darlin', but you get attacked and smacked in the mouth by this guy, who has admitted the sexual assaults?"

"Yes, but not the rape."

"Did he also admit to the assault on you?"

"Eventually, yes he did, and when it happened he said that he was holding a knife to my throat, and I managed to kick him off me. Then DI Moran and DC Edwards arrested him. He swore that he didn't mean to attack me and I got his elbow in my mouth, which caused my lip to split and bleed. But he maintained that it was only because he was trying to escape arrest."

Gibbs gave a sarcastic laugh.

"I didn't see the knife, and then DI Moran produced it as evidence, and next the signed confession."

"What the hell is your problem, Jane?"

"It's just that a few things don't add up . . . I mean, do you think Moran would plant evidence?"

"What?"

"For the rape?"

Gibbs leaned back. "Do you give a shit? Or, more to the point, do you care?"

"Yes I do, because the rape will be a far longer sentence and if he is innocent—"

"Innocent? Christ, Jane, are you out of your mind? What the hell are you doing wasting time even contemplating whether there was any kind of subversive activity? Did he or didn't he have a knife—it's just bullshitting and I hope the bastard goes away for as long as possible. I would say that is Moran's only interest. He's a good cop, and a tough one who worked Clubs and Vice for years. Moran's sticking his neck out as he said he found the knife and didn't involve any other officers. And if you don't mind me saying so, you've only just got your foot into the CID, so mind your business."

Jane looked away as Gibbs took out his hip flask again and emptied the contents into the remainder of his coffee.

"I hear you've been seeing a lot of Paul Lawrence. What's he doing?"

"Well, he was very supportive when I queried the non-suspicious death."

"Oh, you queried it, did you? Well, aren't you just a busy know-all? Let me give you another word of warning—don't go behind DCI Shepherd's back either. He has a mean streak: although he might appear to be a quiet, affable type, he's got a steel core and he goes by the book. If you start encouraging Paul Lawrence to work outside his forensic duties—"

Jane interrupted. "I haven't done that!"

"That's not what I've heard. You've got him working on this non-sus death as a possible murder because of evidence you are digging up. Let me tell you, you dig up anything and you give it to the team . . . that includes me."

"I just haven't discussed certain things because Paul said we needed further evidence . . ."

"We? We needed further evidence? Listen to yourself! And what's Paul Lawrence 'Forensic Detective' investigating on your say so?"

"It's not my 'say so.' He just agreed with me."

"Jesus Christ, Jane! Haven't you listened to anything I've been telling you? You have to stop this and not drag Paul into something that could get him into deep trouble."

"Well, for your information I am not 'dragging' him anywhere. Maybe you don't know as much about him as you think you do. In reality he is fed up with forensic science and spending most of his time in a laboratory checking out fingerprints and toxicology reports. He's told me he wants to become a more integral part of the CID."

"Did he also tell you about how he's been coping?"

Jane looked confused. "I don't understand."

"Lawrence almost had a nervous breakdown, although I don't know if you can ever really have an 'almost' breakdown . . . Unlike me, he stayed on at Hackney after Bradfield and Kath died. I got out, and I got help. Lawrence didn't. So let me tell you, behind that floppy hair of his and his tweed suit, Mr. Affability has been tormenting himself—"

Jane interrupted him, becoming very defensive. "He's talked about that to me, that he's apportioned some of the blame to himself about what happened. I think every one of us has felt guilty in some way."

"Guilty? I don't feel guilty. I was having the best time of my life. I've never known such an adrenalin buzz . . . there's nothing like catching blaggers red-handed, and this wasn't for a couple of Rolex watches, this was big time. So I've never felt any guilt. I had the horror. I heard Len say to Kath what a great moment it was. I saw the way she looked up at him . . . she was so proud, and he was as steady as a rock. Then . . . boom . . . they were gone. I had their blood and brains splattered all over me. I'm not guilty, Jane, I'm damaged."

Gibbs stopped himself, knocked back his coffee, his legs jumping again. He stood up. "OK, I'm out of here. I'm going back to the club to do the job I've been ordered to do. Why don't you get off home?"

Jane gave a rueful smile and thanked him for the coffee. "I'll finish my drink first, Spence." She watched him leave from the window of the café. He didn't look back at her but headed along the street toward Wardour Street. She wasn't bothered about finishing the cold cappuccino, she just didn't want to walk with him. She waited until he was out of sight then left the café, and walked down Wardour Street in the opposite direction to Gibbs toward Shaftesbury Avenue.

As she walked south she passed numerous lowlife and bouncers standing outside seedy strip clubs with thudding music. The street was filling up with clubbers, mainly groups of young guys drinking from beer cans and laughing loudly. Jane kept to the edge of the pavement and only glanced toward the club she had seen Janet Brown leave. The same muscle-bound thuggish bouncer was bellowing out "Live girls," but after her dressing down from Gibbs Jane had no intention of even attempting to see if Janet Brown was working there.

Blinking arrows pointed to a side turning leading to Berwick Street, and opposite were two strip clubs. It was déjà vu because hurrying out from one of them was Janet Brown, wearing the rabbit fur coat. Jane had to wait for the traffic to move before she could cross the road and hurry toward her. She saw her with a young boy who was getting out of a taxi. Janet handed the boy something and then to Jane's disappointment got into the taxi before she even got close. The boy was still standing outside the dirty plastic strip curtains at the open doorway to "Sexy Slave Dancers."

He was wearing filthy jeans, worn gym shoes and an over-sized man's jacket, and he had short dirty red hair surrounding a grimy face. The closer Jane got to him it became clear he was even younger than she had thought.

"Excuse me, can I talk to you for a second?"

"What-d-ya-want?" he said through gapped teeth.

"I need to talk to the woman I just saw you with, in the blue fur coat."

"She gone to work." He turned as if to walk away.

"Is it a club?"

He glared at Jane. "What you want to know fer?"

"Please . . . I really need to talk to her."

"You're fuckin' filth, aintcha? Well, piss off."

He did a duck to pass Jane and she caught his sleeve.

"Just a minute . . ."

He was too fast and was off, heading in the direction of Berwick Street. During the day this was filled with market stalls, but at night there were numerous sleazy strip clubs, doors opening up for the rooms above and the call girls were out in force. Jane followed and was able to see the boy entering one of the small stores selling girlie magazines. A sign was stuck to the dirty window, saying "ADULT LITERATURE." Inside were racks of glossy porn magazines with just a counter, shelves and a till. On one shelf there were what purported to be 8mm Disney films, but in reality the boxes contained hardcore porn imported from Amsterdam.

There was a red lightbulb making the dingy shopfront glow with a reddish tinge. A woman was stacking books and shoving them into piles beneath the counter. She had bleached blonde hair and two glittering clips either side of her head. Her face was plastered with thick makeup and outlines over the edge of her lips in a bright orange red. As Jane walked in the woman stuck out her chest. She wore a tight knitted sweater with crochet flowers.

"Yes, love? If you're after the lesbian section it's on the shelf behind you."

She smelt of powerful, sickly sweet perfume. Jane showed her warrant card, which didn't seem to faze the woman at all.

"Listen, we paid out this week, darlin', so don't try it on with me. I got a lot of work to do and I am not interested in havin' the female touch, if you know what I mean."

"I just wanted to ask that young boy something. I'm not here for any other reason."

"I don't know him . . . never saw anyone comin' in." She lit a cigarette.

"I just saw him walk in," Jane said firmly.

"Well, maybe he just walked out the back way. I dunno . . . I'm busy, love, doing the inventory."

"What's through there?"

"Just a back room for the storage. But, lovey, if you want to start snoopin' around in here you'll need a warrant. Like I said, we paid up."

Two girls walked in and passed directly behind Jane, entering the door she had seen the red-haired boy go through. The blonde woman ignored Jane as she continued checking over paperbacks and stacking them below the counter.

"I would just like to talk to the boy, please."

Unseen by Jane, the blonde pressed a bell beneath the counter. Next minute banging into the small shop via the same door came a pot-bellied man wearing a black suede fringed cowboy jacket, with a silver cowboy buckle over his expansive waist and baggy green cords.

"What's goin' on?" he said angrily.

"She just walked in, Stevie. Shows me her warrant card and wants to go out back to talk to Ginger."

"What the fuck do you want, darlin', because we already have an arrangement and we don't like Old Bill standing in full view of the effin' winder."

"I just want to have a few words with the boy I saw coming in here. I am not here for any other reason. This lady here denied seeing him when I saw him walking in."

"What you want with Ginger?"

"I don't think that is any of your business. Now, if he is here please could I talk to him?"

Jane was losing patience but at the same time becoming very unnerved by Stevie's attitude.

"He works for the girls and would have gone out the back way. Now, you just piss off, all right?"

"I'm sorry but he looked about twelve years old . . . What exactly do you mean that he works here?"

Stevie hitched up his trousers and gestured to the blonde to leave.

"He's just earnin' a few quid, darlin' . . . the strippers don't like leavin' their gear unattended in the clubs' dressin' rooms when they're on the stage, so they pay him and he makes sure nothin' gets nicked."

Jane was shocked but stood her ground.

"I really don't want to come back. I just want to have a few words with him here, or outside your shop. It's about someone I need to contact."

Two more girls walked in and it was obvious by the way they were dressed they were on the game. They smiled at Stevie and went into the back room. Stevie hesitated, then followed them.

He bellowed, "Oi Ginger, come outta there . . . now, before you get me angry."

The same ginger-haired boy slunk out and Stevie gripped him by his neck, pushing him toward Jane.

"I dunno what you been up to but this copper wants to talk to you. Now get outta here wiv her, and if it's thievin' I'll have ya knocked to hell an' back."

The boy was not afraid of the muscle head man, instead he shrugged him away and looked at Jane.

"What you want?"

"Get the hell outta the shop . . . go on, move it!" Stevie jerked his thumb toward the door.

Jane went outside with the boy, who didn't seem at all bothered by her presence. He leaned against a wall near the shop entrance.

"I don't want to get you into trouble, Ginger, but I saw you getting out of a taxi, then a woman wearing a blue rabbit fur coat got inside."

"I don't remember."

"I saw you not ten minutes ago. Now, I need to know where she was going."

"No fuckin' idea . . . She works the clubs, that's all I know. She taxi hops, goin' to any amount of strip clubs round here, or maybe goin' home."

"Do you know her address?"

"No."

"What's her name?"

"You pick one . . . they all use different ones. I think it's Janine, but don't quote me. That's show business, ain't it."

"How old are you?"

"Twenty-one."

Jane sighed and tried another tack. "Look, you are only young and shouldn't even be out here at this hour, never mind working the clubs as Stevie told me."

"Yeah, well, I got a sick mother wiv lung cancer and no dad . . . I gotta earn a crust for me sisters. All I do is just look out for their belongings and they give us a few coppers."

"I don't want to report you to the social services, Ginger, so please tell me where you think I might be able to contact that woman."

"She might have gone over to the nightclub in Swallow Street. I swear by Almighty God that's all I know . . . ! Give us a break, darlin', I don't want Stevie and the old lady givin' me a hard time."

Jane sighed and shook her head.

"All right, thank you."

He gave her a cheeky, gap-toothed smile. "Any time, sweetheart . . . take it easy."

Jane walked off, contemplated heading over to Swallow Street, which was a narrow lane off Piccadilly Circus leading into Regent Street. But remembering Gibbs's warning about working alone, she caught the late bus back to the section house.

Over the last few days, Jane had been inundated with a number of petty crimes connected to the major upheaval with the proposed move of the Covent Garden market to southwest London. As she had the entire weekend off, she decided that she would see her parents. She was looking forward to the safe normality of her home after her week in the murky world of strip clubs and prostitution.

Jane had made thorough notes about her encounter in the adult bookshop, which she was sure was also a brothel, and would check everything out the following Monday. It had been such a revelation being in that seedy part of London, and she was concerned about the references to CID being paid off to turn a blind eye.

When Jane arrived at the flat it was, unusually, her father who answered the door and ushered her in, indicating for her to be quiet.

"What's wrong, Dad?"

Mr. Tennison shut the door. "Your mother's in with Pam . . . it's not good news . . . she's very distressed. When she got here she was crying her eyes out."

"What's happened?"

Mrs. Tennison came out into the corridor.

"Jane . . . I didn't expect you. You never called, did you?"

"No, Mum. I've got the day off. Is everything all right?"

"No . . . Did you tell her, Daddy?"

"No, she's only just arrived."

"Mum, what's happened?"

Mrs. Tennison gestured for Jane to follow her into the lounge.

"Pam has had a miscarriage. She started feeling poorly and then had terrible stomach cramps. She went into the toilet and . . ."

"Has she been to the hospital?"

"Yes. Tony took her to the emergency ward at St. Mary's but they confirmed it. Nothing they could do. Are you going to stay for lunch?"

"Yes, if it's not too much trouble?"

"No, I'm doing a pork roast. You go on into our bedroom and talk to Pam."

Pam was lying down with a wet flannel folded on her forehead. Jane sat beside her.

"I am so sorry, Pam . . . Mum's just told me."

Pam slowly removed the face cloth. Her face was puffy and she was red eyed from crying.

"It happened when I went to the toilet . . . such terrible pains, and then . . ."

"Did they tell you why it happened?"

"No, Tony said it was because of being on my feet all day at the salon, but this very nice doctor said that pregnant women can work up to eight and a half months so it wasn't because of me working. But I won't go back just yet."

"No, you should just rest."

"I started getting all the baby things. I didn't choose pink or blue because we didn't know if it was a boy or a girl," Pam said as she began to cry.

Mrs. Tennison walked in carrying a mug of tea for Jane. "Here you are, Jane dear. Would you like another cup before lunch, Pam?"

"Yes please, Mum."

Mrs. Tennison walked out and closed the door silently behind her.

"It won't be the end, Pam . . . I'm sure you'll get pregnant again."

"I know, I know . . . that's what the doctors said. But it won't be for a while, because I have to give my body time to heal."

"Yes, I know, the body is very resilient."

"I know that. I'm on my feet all day. You have no idea how long it takes to do a perm. And I've wondered if it is the smell of doing a perm that's caused the miscarriage. It's very pungent, you know.

"I had this client who was really very objectionable. Complained that the rubber of the rollers smelt. I said to her, 'Well, if you think they smell bad, you should go to another salon.' Well, she didn't like that. And then as she was leaving she wanted to book in a second appointment. I said to her, 'I might not be here in three months' time.' Because that's how long you have to wait before you can do a perm again. Well, she got very upset and apologized to me for being rude. And then I said, 'I'm pregnant, that's why I won't be here.'" Pam's face crumpled.

Jane patted her hand. "Don't upset yourself."

"Well, I am upset. I'm not pregnant, am I?"

It was a difficult couple of hours before they eventually left the bedroom and went to have lunch. Mrs. Tennison had set the small table in the living room, as she liked to keep the dining room for formal occasions. The pork had already been carved and there were roast potatoes, carrots, spinach and gravy.

"Have you got any apple sauce, Mother?" Pam asked.

Mrs. Tennison jumped up.

"Of course, darling, of course we have . . . it's apple and mint jelly, is that all right, Pam?"

"I'd prefer just apple sauce, but never mind . . ."

Jane noticed that, as distraught as her sister was, Pam still managed to pile the food onto her plate.

Mrs. Tennison said that she'd made an apple pie, but she was out of custard so they were going to have it with Wall's ice-cream instead.

Jane reached over and patted her mother's hand. "That sounds lovely, Mum."

Mrs. Tennison smiled.

"So, let's talk about something different . . . Jane, why don't you tell us what you've been doing this week? We haven't seen you since you started your new job. Are there any other female officers working at the station?"

"I am actually the only female detective . . . but I do have a wonderful mentor, Edith, who runs the main office." Jane exaggerated to reassure her mother. "She used to be a police-woman so she knows all the ropes, and she has a lot to deal with because her mother sadly suffers from dementia."

Pam pushed her empty plate to one side, and leaned her elbows on the table.

"Well, that's worrying, having the only other policewoman suffering from dementia."

"No, Pam, Edith doesn't have dementia—her mother does. Sometimes she escapes from the house, and once poor Edith found her wandering naked in the street!"

The doorbell prevented her having to continue her description of Edith. Mrs. Tennison started clearing the lunch plates as Pam's husband, Tony, came into the living room.

"Would you like some apple pie and ice-cream, Tony?" Mrs. Tennison asked him.

"That would be lovely, thank you."

Tony pulled up a chair to sit beside Pam.

"How are you feeling, my darling?"

Pam picked up her napkin and used it as a handkerchief, blowing her nose.

"It comes over me in waves, Tony, the grief . . . I'm finding it very hard to deal with. One minute I was wondering what maternity dress to put on, and the next I was on the toilet . . ."

Tony patted her hand.

"I know, darling, it's terrible, just terrible, but we have to be strong."

Jane looked at her rather overweight brother-in-law as he too started to weep.

"I am so sorry, Tony . . . it's very sad, and we all feel deeply for your loss."

"Could I just have the apple pie without the ice-cream, please?" Tony asked, as Mrs. Tennison placed the apple pie on the table.

By the time they both left Jane just wanted to go back to the section house and really didn't feel in the mood to discuss her work. It wasn't until she was about to leave that her father asked if everything was all right at Bow Street.

"Everything's fine, Dad. I really like being in plain clothes with the CID."

"Anything interesting?"

"Not really . . . I'm just a fledgling detective so I'm not assigned to anything important." She gently placed her hand to touch his lips, whispering, "I'm all right, Daddy."

Jane didn't mention being used as a decoy, the fact that she had been assaulted, or that she was now working on her first possible murder inquiry. She never even broached the subject of the strip clubs or young Ginger working with the strippers. It wasn't that she didn't want to, but her life was so different to Pam's and she understood that they had lost their first grandchild and that was all they were really interested in for the moment.

After Jane had left the Tennison flat, her father had made a pot of tea for her mother and they had sat down beside each other on the sofa.

"I thought she looked well," Mr. Tennison said.

"She didn't, poor girl . . . but it's hardly surprising. Mind you, she's still young so they've got many more years to keep trying."

"I meant Jane . . ."

"Oh, yes . . . I was going to say to her that she should call more often and not just turn up without letting us know. It was lucky I was doing a pork roast so we had plenty of food."

Mr. Tennison stood up, saying that he would start on the washing up.

"Thank you, dear. I noticed Jane didn't offer to help . . . but that's her, never very domestic really, was she?"

Mr. Tennison turned on the hot water and began to scrape off the grease from the baking tray. He looked over the array of pans and dirty dishes as his wife sat cupping her hands round her tea. He squirted in the washing-up liquid and used the plastic bowl to soak the dishes. It took him almost half an hour, balancing the plates on the draining board before moving on to scrub the baking trays he had left to soak. Mrs. Tennison was still sitting staring into space, her tea cup empty, when he went in to take it from her.

"Are you all right, darling?"

Mrs. Tennison seemed to be miles away and was almost startled when he took the cup from her hands.

"I had a scare, do you remember, with Michael? I went to bed for two weeks, and didn't dare put my feet on the ground in case I had a miscarriage. But it was all right, and then I had Jane and then Pam so I'm sure she'll get pregnant again. But she should give up work at the salon . . . she spends too many hours standing."

Mr. Tennison patted her head gently, knowing what she was really thinking about. Their first-born son, Michael, was only two when he had drowned in the neighbor's pond. They had both buried their grief tightly beneath the surface, but when it rose the pain was excruciating. He returned to the sink to dry the plates as he recalled Jane running toward him, her arms outstretched with Michael's small worn teddy bear in one hand.

Mr. Tennison was ashamed about what had happened. After Michael's tragic drowning he had hidden his son's favorite toy in his desk drawer. Jane had somehow found it, even though he had given strict instructions that the room he used as a home office was out of bounds, as it was "where Daddy worked." He had wrapped the small teddy bear in tissue paper and tucked it into the bottom drawer of his desk, along with a silver napkin ring and one of Michael's small slippers. Jane had always been inquisitive and had discovered his secret mementos. She had gleefully run toward her father to share her discovery with him, and he had slapped her very hard and had scolded her for being so naughty and going into his office.

The young Jane had been shocked as she had never been physically reprimanded so severely. Mr. Tennison recalled the way her blue eyes had glared at him, as she recoiled. In a very grown-up manner she had said, "I didn't mean to upset you, but you shouldn't be nasty to me. I thought you would like to hold Michael's teddy bear and I was just happy that I found him."

Mr. Tennison had been left speechless, and had been unable for some time to go to her and apologize. He had tried to explain why he had reacted in such an awful way but Jane had just walked away from him. As young as she was it had been a considerable time before she forgave him. When she did she simply climbed up onto his knee one night and put her hand gently over his lips.

"It's all right, Daddy."

That had been the way she had said goodbye to him at the door earlier, her blue eyes holding his and touching his lips as she had done all those years ago as a child. Mr. Tennison wondered if everything was all right with her work. He felt guilty that neither he nor his wife had asked how her new job was going.

Mrs. Tennison remained sitting by herself as he finished the dishes, drying them all and placing them back into the cupboards. He wiped all the kitchen surfaces.

"All ship-shape, dear," he said brightly, and she turned and smiled.

"Thank you, dear."

CHAPTER FIFTEEN

Marie sat on the end seat of the lower deck of the number 73 bus. She'd been lucky to get a seat, as the bus was packed full of Saturday shoppers. She had the thick envelope containing the money on her lap, wrapped inside an old newspaper. When the bus stopped by The Grosvenor House Hotel in Park Lane she got off and watched as the bus drew away, just as she had done previously. As she had been instructed, Marie placed the parcel of money into the litter bin attached to the bus stop. She had to dig it in among dirty cartons and used bus tickets before she was able to make sure it wasn't too visible. She then got onto the next bus as soon as it drew up.

Marie remained on the foot stand, holding on to the bar, as the bus moved slowly down Park Lane. A few moments later her heart was pounding as she jumped from the moving bus. She had to gasp for breath as she hurried back toward the litter bin where she had left the money. Marie moved along the pavement close to the buildings in the hope she would not be seen, but she could clearly see the 73 bus stop and the litter bin. She kept on edging closer, just as Peter had instructed her to do, in the hope of catching the woman red-handed and being able to confront her.

A scruffy red-haired boy was running toward Marie. He then stopped and with his back to her rummaged in the bin. Marie watched as he took out the wrapped envelope and tossed the newspaper covering aside, running back up Park Lane toward Marble Arch. Marie hurried after him and saw him turn into Green Street, then he disappeared from her sight for a moment.

As she rounded the corner Marie could see the boy up ahead, approaching a taxi with its engine ticking over and the passenger door open. The boy dived inside and the door slammed shut as the taxi moved off. Marie closed her eyes, wanting to weep with frustration as she reluctantly turned back toward Park Lane.

Inside the taxi Janet Brown hugged the envelope close to her chest and held a ten pound note up between her fingers.

"Good work, Ginger . . . here you go, as promised."

He reached out to take it, but Janet held it away from him.

"You gotta keep your mouth shut about this and not tell a soul. If you do, I'll find out and you'll get a whippin'."

"I won't tell no one."

"OK . . . You get this tenner for now. There'll be more for you to do but you got to keep your mouth shut."

She dangled the note in front of him and Ginger snatched it, kissing it with glee.

"I luv ya! Can yer drop me off at Carnaby Street? Gonna get a new pair o' shoes."

It was a short cab ride from Green Street to North Audley Street, then round the top of Grosvenor Square onto Brook Street. The taxi crossed Regent Street onto Great Marlborough Street, where Ginger got out. Janet watched him run past the big posh store Liberty, heading toward Carnaby Street. She had another look inside the envelope, then leaned back and smiled.

"Easy money."

She started humming to herself. "Angie, Angie . . ."

It was early on Sunday morning and DS Lawrence and Professor Martin's qualified assistant, who had been working alongside him on numerous cases, were walking into the mortuary. Angus McLean knew how to deal with the garrulous pathologist. He admired him and had learned a vast amount while working with him. Angus also knew that he was earmarked to take over when the old boy retired, which would be in the not too distant future. Angus was rake thin with horn-rimmed glasses. He had come from working-class roots but his sharp intellect and diligence had brought him to Martin's attention. He had been very hesitant about agreeing to meet with Lawrence and was worried that Professor Martin would not approve.

DS Lawrence had been equally reluctant to ask for the favor, but repeatedly said that he just wanted a second opinion and told Angus that he was not required to do anything unethical. They were given access to the chill section at the mortuary by an assistant mortician, whom Lawrence reassured by saying that he was welcome to remain with them as it was just going to be a quick appraisal of the non-suspicious death notice. The body had not yet been released for burial, so there was nothing untoward about the visit.

Angus looked at Lawrence. "OK, let me take a look at her."

Jane stripped her bed and put fresh sheets on, leaving the used ones in the laundry bag for the cleaners to collect the following day. She then went to the laundry room and did her washing and ironing. Back in her room she hung up her pressed shirt and put her clean underwear in the drawer, gave her shoes a quick polish, and then made her way out to pick up a newspaper.

She was surprised to see DS Lawrence entering the building. He hurried toward her and asked if he could have a few words as he needed to give her an update. They went into the quiet room and although the TV set was on the room was empty.

"I've just come from the mortuary, and want to talk a few things over with you. First you need to understand that when you have a non-suspicious death it is not unusual that a detailed PM is not required. It's not exactly cutting corners, but it's not as in-depth as for a suspicious murder."

"Yes, you discussed this before."

"Right, but if there had been a very detailed PM it would entail the removal of the scalp and the face being lifted, to check the frontal wound.

"I am not inferring that there was anything incorrect about the report. But if the assumption was that the blow to her forehead from the taps was not that heavy or deep but enough to maybe render the victim unconscious, I would have taken steps to ensure there was no other head wound."

"How do you mean?"

"She had very thick hair. There was a considerable amount of blood in the bath water, which makes it obvious that she was alive in the water as she continued bleeding. Her hair was still wet when her body was brought into the mortuary and dried by the time the PM took place."

"Are you saying that there could have been another wound?"

"Possibly. But this would only have been discovered if the victim's head was shaved. Again, I am not saying that the PM was fast-tracked, as this is often the case when you have a coroner's report stating that it was a non-suspicious death."

Jane cocked her head to one side. "It would be interesting to find out, but we don't have much time as the family have been given clearance for the burial. Do you think you have enough evidence to get a second PM done?"

Lawrence ran his hands through his hair.

"No, we don't have enough evidence . . . Also I don't want to get my friend in any trouble as his information was off the record and Professor Martin probably won't be happy. If anyone could prove another PM should be done it would be the old boy himself."

"So what do you suggest we do?"

Lawrence was becoming increasingly concerned. "Our problem is this: if we believe Barry Dawson was involved then we would have to prove that he did have time to get out of the hospital, kill his wife and then return to work to make the phone calls to give himself an alibi."

Jane could feel Lawrence's hesitancy, and was unsure what to say to him. He continued.

"Also, we have to consider the possibility that someone else killed Shirley Dawson, and if so who and for what reason?"

"Well, maybe it could have been the woman who visited her? Or, if she was having an affair, could there be another suspect? I mean, if we believe that Shirley buzzed someone in, it's likely that she knew them."

"Yes, but if it was Barry he would have had his own front door key."

Jane sighed. They were getting nowhere and had nothing to support their possible motives. Lawrence stood up and Jane sensed what was coming.

"I have to tread very carefully, Jane . . . if I am wrong, if we both are, then this could really get us into deep water. I think we should just call it quits because I am not prepared to jeopardize my career and be put back in uniform."

"Is Dawson back at work at the hospital?" Jane asked.

Lawrence shrugged. Using the page on which he had sketched Shirley's head to demonstrate the wounds he jotted down his phone number and address.

"I don't know. Why don't you sleep on it? If you think of anything then call me, but I'm not going any further with this. I'm sorry . . ."

Jane smiled, hiding her disappointment. "Yes, maybe you're right."

They walked out together and she headed up the stairs to her room.

She sat on her bed and stared at the sketch and was about to toss it into the waste bin. She had been so excited as she had been the one to instigate the possibility that Shirley Dawson was a murder victim. She knew DS Lawrence had been of the same opinion but he had now decided against trying to prove it. The small sketch had no face but if she closed her eyes she could see Shirley, her eyes wide open, her hair floating in the bloody bath water. Jane recalled what it had felt like to lift her lifeless body out of the bath and wrap her in the plastic sheet.

She had made up her mind. Even if Paul Lawrence wanted to walk away, she could not. It was not a question of proving that she was right but of wanting justice for Shirley Dawson.

It took over an hour for her to get to St. Thomas' Hospital and she went directly to the porter's room. She was told that, due to his recent absence from the wards, Barry Dawson was on a weekend shift and was working in the A&E department. Jane made her way to A&E and eventually spotted Barry Dawson pushing an empty wheelchair from a curtained booth.

"Mr. Dawson . . ."

Barry turned, surprised to see her. Jane walked beside him and asked if they could talk privately. Barry hesitated before checking the time and saying that he would be on a tea break in ten minutes and could join her in the small coffee bar attached to the department.

It was a good fifteen minutes before he showed up. The coffee bar was closed and the shutters were pulled down to the counter. Barry sat down in a chair opposite her and apologized for keeping her waiting, explaining that it had taken a while to get a patient up to a ward.

Jane had her notebook open and thanked him for agreeing to see her, explaining that she simply wanted to double-check a few things with him. She discussed his alibi and how he had called home to talk to Shirley as he had been concerned about her.

"That's right. As I told you, she had said that she wasn't feeling well. We had this arrangement that I called her at the same time every morning when I was on early shift. When she didn't answer I was worried, so I called my mother because she was going over to the flat to look after Heidi. But my mother said she had to wait in for an engineer to fix her washing machine. So I tried Shirley again, but still got no answer. That's when I decided to go home."

Jane nodded and jotted down what he had said.

"So, did you need permission to leave the hospital?"

"By rights, yes . . . but I had a break coming up so I just left."

"So what time exactly did you get to your flat?"

"About eleven to eleven thirty. Then I found her in the bath and went to the neighbors to call for help."

"Why didn't you use the payphone on the landing at your flat?"

"I was in a terrible state . . . I wasn't thinking straight."

"Can you describe exactly what happened after your visit to the neighbor?"

"I've told you all this . . . I don't understand why you're asking me to tell you all over again."

"Just to make sure the report is correct and that your statement can be verified, Mr. Dawson."

"I went next door. Mr. Cook said he would go up and see Shirley and he brought Heidi back as she was crying, although when I left she had been sleeping in her playpen. We called the police and an ambulance, and then my mother came . . ."

"When you went home and found Shirley in the bath, did you touch her? Move her at all? Even feel her pulse to see if she was alive?"

"No . . . no . . . I knew she was dead. I didn't need to touch her, I knew it. I work here, so I know the signs. I was in complete shock."

Jane closed her notebook.

"Thank you. That all seems to tally up. And there was no one else in your flat, is that correct?"

He leaned back in his seat.

"No, I let myself in and the bathroom door was open. I called out for Shirley and then went in and found her."

Jane put the lid on her pen. Having watched numerous interrogations by now, she gave the appearance of being satisfied with Barry's statements. He pushed his chair back, presuming the meeting was over.

"Just one more thing, Mr. Dawson . . . I showed you the photographs of this woman."

Jane slid the pictures of the woman whom Barry had previously denied knowing toward him. He had ripped them up but was unaware that Jane had the negatives and had made copies, which were now being laid down, facing toward him, on the table.

"We now know that these are photographs of Katrina Harcourt."

Barry turned away; his knee was jerking.

"We are also aware that Katrina worked here at St. Thomas'. It's therefore a bit confusing for us to find photographs of her on a reel of film taken from a camera that was in your flat. You also denied that the camera belonged to you. So can you explain why you have three photographs of Katrina Harcourt?"

Barry was becoming agitated.

"If you didn't take these photographs, and say that the camera didn't belong to you, could it have been your wife's? Is it possible that she took the pictures?"

He shrugged.

"If you look at the photographs, Mr. Dawson, they appear to have been taken when Miss Harcourt was not aware of being photographed. Would Shirley have any reason to want to take pictures of Katrina?"

"I don't know."

"Mr. Dawson, I think you need to start being honest with me. I've spoken to Brenda, who shared a room with Katrina, and she said that Katrina was having an affair with someone. It was quite a heated relationship and had been going on for some time."

He turned away and sighed. "All right . . . I'm sorry, I was sort of freaked out. The truth is . . . I was seeing her."

"Did Shirley find out?"

"No . . . no, she did not. I had finished with Katrina . . . it was just a stupid fling, and I regretted it. I told Katrina I didn't want to see her again and then she left the hospital."

"Just a fling? But you bought her a ring, didn't you?" Jane was flying by her shirt tail because she had no proof that Barry had purchased a ring, let alone given it to Katrina, but she recalled what Brenda had said and decided to see if she could get a reaction from him.

"You know, Barry, I am really trying to piece this all together, but some of it just doesn't make sense. You deny that you own the camera, and at first you refused to admit that you identified Katrina in the photographs."

"Yes . . . yes, I did."

"Why did you lie about it?"

"I was just trying to cover up the fact that maybe Shirley had found out after all . . . But I swear to God, she never said anything to me. Now I'll never be able to explain because she's dead . . ."

"So Barry, you now admit that you were having an affair with Katrina? To me it sounds like more than just a fling, because you bought her a ring, didn't you?"

"OK, yes, I did . . . but it was to sort of finish the situation, you know, say it was over and that I loved my wife and didn't want to lose her or Heidi."

"I see. And Katrina just accepted the end of the affair, did she?"

"Yes. She decided to leave the hospital and get a job elsewhere."

"Mr. Dawson, I don't want to sound rude . . . I've not only seen these photographs of Katrina, but I've also seen a photograph of her in the nurses' bay. She's a very attractive woman. According to Brenda, the girl she shared a room with, she always dressed very beautifully, was rather sophisticated, and I am sure would not like the description of your relationship being 'just a fling.'"

"Yes, she was very beautiful, and classy with it, and I have to admit that to begin with I was amazed that she would even be interested in someone like me. Then I found out that she put herself about a bit . . . I wasn't the only one."

"Can you give me the name of anyone else at the hospital that she was seeing?" Jane asked.

"No, I can't! She had her own private life that was nothing to do with me. To be honest I had wanted to end it much sooner, but she could get aggressive and told me that I would be very sorry if I broke up with her, and that there would be serious consequences. All the lies I've told were to cover up my shame about betraying Shirley . . . I was petrified that Katrina was going to report me to the hospital. I was never serious about us—as I just said, it was a stupid affair. She put it about and there were plenty of others having sex with her."

"And you're certain Shirley didn't find out? I mean, if this camera doesn't belong to you and was found in your flat, the photographs must have been taken by Shirley. Was she going to confront you?"

"No! I told you, she didn't know . . . But maybe she had found out and that's why she was so anxious lately . . ."

"I see. So when you say Shirley wasn't feeling well when you left for work, was it perhaps because, as you've just suggested, she was very anxious because she had found out? And that was why you were so worried when she didn't answer the phone for your usual call?"

"Yes . . . yes, I admit that now . . . that's why I was so concerned."

"I don't quite understand this, Barry. You knew that your mother was going to babysit Heidi that day because Shirley had a hair appointment in the morning?"

Barry was sweating and was clearly feeling very uncomfortable.

"Yes, but my mother wasn't answering the phone there either. So then I called my mother at her house, and she told me that she hadn't been able to babysit because there was something wrong with her washing machine."

"So, on previous occasions when Shirley had a hair appointment did she ever take Heidi with her? Your mother wasn't concerned when she tried to contact Shirley and didn't get an answer—she presumed that your wife had taken your daughter with her to the hair salon."

Barry was visibly flustered.

"Listen, you're making this stuff up. I'm not going to answer any more of your questions."

He pushed his chair back so hard that it toppled over. He picked it up, slamming it back down, then leaned toward Jane.

"You've got no right."

Barry walked away, his hands clenched into fists. Jane picked up the photographs and slipped them back into her notebook. If she had any suspicions before that Barry Dawson had played some part in the death of his wife, she was now even more concerned. It was imperative for her to find Katrina Harcourt.

Jane didn't feel it was necessary to talk to Brenda again, but as she turned the corner in the corridor she bumped straight into her and decided it was too good an opportunity to miss. Brenda didn't recognize her, and Jane had to repeat her name and show her warrant card. "I'm so sorry. I've been on duty since the crack of dawn. The Ward Sister is off at her son's wedding, and we're down two nurses . . . it's been chaos here."

"I'm sorry to ask this of you, Brenda, but it is a police matter. I wonder if you could possibly retrieve Katrina Harcourt's records for me?"

Brenda sighed. "Well, you're in luck—I've got the Ward Sister's keys. Whether or not they'll still have Katrina's records on file is another story, but I'll have a look."

Jane waited patiently outside the small office for ten minutes until Brenda reappeared.

"Sorry I've taken so long, but I had to go through drawer after drawer in the filing cabinets . . . I can't let you take this away, but you can have a look at it here." Brenda handed Jane Katrina's file.

"If you want my opinion, either she falsified her CV, or the high demand for nurses enabled her to continue working via an agency. If you read that report she was totally ill-equipped to be on any hospital rota for supply nursing staff."

"Thank you very much for this, Brenda."

"I'll go and get a cup of tea while you read it, then I'll have to put it back in the filing cabinet. Here, hide it in this newspaper and don't tell anybody you've seen it."

After calling DS Lawrence, Jane left the hospital and hailed a taxi to take her to his home address. He lived in a small, out of the way mews near the Baker Street gates into Regent's Park. Number 17 Sussex Mews was tucked into a cobbled side turning in a row of well-kept houses with adjoining garages. Jane rang the bell and waited. After a moment Lawrence opened the door and gestured for her to follow him in through a small comfortable lounge. The furnishings were rather old-fashioned, with numerous antiques and framed paintings.

"Help yourself," he said, pointing to an open bottle of Chablis on a small table.

Jane folded her coat over a chair, and poured herself a small glass of wine. She had not anticipated that DS Lawrence would be living in such an affluent area, and took a good look around as she sipped her drink.

"Before you feel the need to ask, this place belongs to a relative. There's a demolition order for it to be pulled down within the next couple of years, to build a university college. Right, you can fill me in while I put the pasta on—I presume you're hungry?"

"Yes, I am. I didn't have any lunch. Thank you."

Jane followed him into a very small kitchen annex. As Lawrence prepared a pan of boiling water for the spaghetti, and opened a jar of Bolognese sauce, Jane gave him the details of her meeting with Barry Dawson. While she was speaking, he had taken out cutlery and napkins, and she had followed him back to the sitting room where he pulled out the leaf of a table leaning against the wall. He drew up two chairs, then returned to the kitchen to put the pasta into one pan and the sauce in to another.

"Katrina Harcourt was fired, she didn't leave of her own accord. She was late for duty three times and she was on the geriatric ward and never answered the patients' calls. She left poor old ladies desperate for bed pans . . . Apparently it was the second time they had caught her being abusive to elderly patients. I took a look at her CV—she's registered with various different nursing agencies, but had mostly been working in care homes."

Lawrence pulled out a chair for Jane and heaped far too much spaghetti and sauce into her bowl, but he was so fast that she didn't have time to stop him. He served himself and put the open bottle of wine between them on the table.

"Bon appetite . . . sorry, I don't have any parmesan." He topped up his wine glass and poured more for Jane.

She liked being with him. He was so relaxed and easy-going, and she noticed the way he tucked his napkin into his shirt collar before twirling his spaghetti round with a fork on his spoon. He ate and talked at the same time, apologizing for his lack of culinary expertise.

"How old is she?"

"Twenty-seven. According to her CV documents at the hospital, she's an only child, owns a Mini and has given her parents' home in Brighton, well, Hove to be precise, as her permanent address. According to Barry Dawson he was not the only person she was having sex with at St. Thomas'. He said she put it about and Brenda, the nurse she shared a room with, said she thought Katrina was maybe seeing a doctor at St. Thomas'. To be honest, I suppose having a scene with a porter is not in the same league."

"He's good-looking, isn't he?"

"Yes, he is, but not high enough up the pecking order. I got the feeling that Barry was a bit afraid of Katrina. We know she had previously been engaged to a doctor, had a wedding dress, bridesmaids and everything . . . but she was jilted at the altar. I think she set her sights on Barry Dawson . . ."

Lawrence continued ". . . And his wife found out . . . which explains those three photographs. So why did Barry become so agitated and anxious when he couldn't contact his wife, and knew that his mother was not going to be at his flat to babysit?"

"What if Shirley was already dead, and all he was doing was creating an alibi . . ."

"My God, Jane . . . so far this is just supposition and we've still got no hard evidence to get another PM. Dawson could arrange for Shirley's body to be removed for a funeral tomorrow, and I'm on duty in the morning."

"We have this afternoon so we could go and question Katrina Harcourt."

"But she might not be there," he said. "Hold on." He put in a call to ask the local CID to do a drive by and check if Katrina's Mini was parked outside the property address in Hove. When the call came back confirming it was, Lawrence looked up at Jane. "What do you think?"

"It's up to you, but I think as this is just supposition we should see if we can confirm our suspicions."

Lawrence was still unsure. He sighed. "We just have to be a bit careful because we're acting without any authority."

Marie checked the children were out playing in the back garden and went to lie down. She took two more aspirin for her headache. She climbed into bed. Even without Peter being at home she slept on the left side of the double bed as he always liked to be on the right. She lay back, closing her eyes, but she was too anxious to sleep. She had asked her mother-in-law to visit Peter and had lied that the children had been invited to a birthday party so she would have to go and buy a birthday present. Lies tumbled out one after the other because she was afraid to go and talk to him. She would have had to explain that, even though she had followed his instructions, she had only seen the young red-haired boy take the money and get into a taxi.

Marie was only just able to function, making the children their meals and washing and ironing. But any time she was alone she felt sick and sat in the kitchen crying. Afraid to answer the phone, she often let it ring and ring, scared of hearing that awful voice singing the same song over and over. She also hated speaking to her mother-in-law, who asked one question after another, telling her what a good man her son was and how lucky Marie was to have him. Even when Marie had called her about the prison visit she had constantly interrupted, eventually asking about the bank account and why she had withdrawn so much money. But Marie had said she would explain another time, and had put down the handset.

She was in a quandary as to what she should do. Then she decided that the one person who might be able to help her was that policewoman. It took a while for her to recall her name, and that she worked at Hackney Police Station. Marie thought of the note she had left and went downstairs into the hall. It was in a drawer of the hall table, by the telephone. Marie took it out and read the name, "Jane Tennison." Returning to bed she carried the note in her hand. She didn't know why but she felt comforted and decided that first thing in the morning, after the school run, she would come home and call her. Then the doubts surfaced again. Peter had warned her that the police officers had fitted him up, and that they could not be trusted. But even in her anxious state, Marie felt certain that the young woman might be able to give her some advice. She needed it because she had no one else to turn to.

CHAPTER SIXTEEN

Jane was waiting outside the small garage attached to the mews cottage as DS Lawrence drove out in a pale blue Austin-Healey Sprite sports car, the roof pulled down. He hopped out and opened the passenger door. He was wearing a Harris tweed cloth cap, and what looked like a thick dark green tweed shooting jacket. Jane got in and smiled saying that, like his mews house, she had not expected him to be driving a smart new sports car. He closed the garage doors and got into the driving seat.

"Well it's not exactly a smart new one, and to be honest with my long legs it's not that comfortable. But I like to drive out to the country on my days off and I got it at a very good price."

Jane wished she had worn a headscarf as the wind was blowing her hair loose from the hair grips. They drove through London to Croydon and onto the A23 Brighton Road. It was an hour and a half before they arrived on the outskirts of Brighton.

By the time they slowed down toward the town center Jane's initial impression that Lawrence was a careful driver had changed. He had put his foot down on the A23 dual carriageway and appeared intent on passing every vehicle, and her hair was now a tangled mess. Lawrence drove past the ornate Royal Pavilion, which looked very Arabian to Jane, with its bulbous domes, carved walls and beautiful gardens. They headed toward the seafront, the wonderful pier and fairground straight ahead. They passed the Aquarium on their left and, turning right, continued along the seafront, passing the Grand Hotel, and headed toward Hove. Lawrence pulled over to check a street map. By now it was almost four thirty and he passed Jane the map to double check their route. Jane studied the map as Lawrence drove at fifteen miles an hour.

"Second on the right," Jane said. Lawrence indicated and turned into the pleasant Hamilton Street, with well-kept gardens and freshly painted three-story houses. They passed a parked Mini outside number 34 and reversed into a space a few houses back. He got out to put the cover up as Jane searched in her bag for her hairbrush. She was on the pavement still trying to untangle her hair when he took his cap off and tossed it onto the front driving seat.

"Right, we work this nice and calmly. We're just making inquiries to check on Barry Dawson's movements on the day in question. Don't bring out the photographs until I give you the nod. Let's see how much she admits to and if she's going to co-operate."

Jane nodded, then hesitated. "Do I look all right, or still windswept?"

"You look fine." He stopped to run his fingers through his blond hair, and then walked up the path to the house with Jane following behind him.

There was a large potted plant at the door on a pristine black and white tiled step. The front door looked freshly painted and had a brass letterbox with a lion head door knocker. There was also a bell beside the door. Lawrence rang the doorbell and stepped back, waiting.

A pleasant-looking woman opened the door, wearing a pink house coat over a twinset and tweed skirt.

"Mrs. Harcourt?"

"Yes."

Lawrence showed his warrant card and introduced himself, saying that WDC Tennison was accompanying him and that they wished to talk to Katrina.

"My daughter . . . Yes, do please come in." She hesitated. "Is there something wrong?"

"No," he said charmingly. "We'd just like to talk to her, please."

"Do come in and I'll call Katrina. She was just making herself a coffee."

They were led into a very spacious front sitting room, filled with nice modern G Plan furniture, a large gas fire and decorated with flock wallpaper and a fur rug. There were numerous paintings, and copies of well-known artists hanging on the walls, and on top of a dresser were various family photographs.

Lawrence glanced at the photos and nodded at Tennison.

"Right house."

Jane turned to look at a line of silver framed photographs. There were two large ones of Katrina, one in tennis shorts with a racket and another standing wearing black riding boots and jodhpurs next to a white pony. But none of them looked very recent.

"Hello."

They turned as Katrina Harcourt walked in holding a mug of coffee. She was very attractive and slender, with an abundance of shoulder-length red curly hair. She had pale porcelain skin, which enhanced her green eyes. Her lashes were dark with thick mascara, and she appeared younger than they knew she was. However, she had a very mature and confident manner.

"Mother said that you're detectives?"

"Yes."

Lawrence introduced himself and Jane again. Katrina sat down on the edge of a thick cushioned sofa and crossed her slender legs. She was wearing fluffy slippers, and her legs were shapely and alabaster white. She was obviously a girl who stayed out of the sun despite the proximity to the beach.

"What is this about?"

"Do you know a Mr. Barry Dawson?"

"Yes, he's a porter at St. Thomas' Hospital."

"You worked there until recently?"

"Yes, that is correct."

"Were you aware that his wife recently drowned?"

"I think I heard about it."

"But you had already left St. Thomas' by then, isn't that right?"

"Ummm, yes . . ."

"So who told you about Barry's wife then?"

"Oh . . . I think my old roommate, Brenda, called me . . . it's very sad . . ."

Jane looked up. She knew Brenda hadn't said she'd been in touch.

"Did you know Shirley Dawson?"

"No."

"But you were well acquainted with her husband."

"Well, I'm not quite sure what you are inferring by saying I was well acquainted. I knew him as a porter and if he was on a wing I was working then I would obviously be aware of who he was."

"Well, we seem to have a different view because he has stated that you and he were having an affair, and that it had been going on for some time."

Lawrence glanced at Jane, who was writing in her notebook.

Katrina shrugged, sipping her coffee. "Well, that's porters for you. He has obviously exaggerated my being pleasant to him as something far more."

"So you are saying that you did not have a sexual relationship with Mr. Dawson?"

"If you need me to repeat it, then the answer is that I was not in any kind of relationship with him, and I am becoming rather confused as to why you are here."

Lawrence gave a small nod to indicate for Jane to continue the questioning.

Jane smiled. "It's just out of necessity really. You see, Mr. Dawson claims that you were having a sexual relationship. He says that it was nothing more than a cheap fling. According to him you were having various other sexual encounters, in fact he spoke about you in rather derogatory terms because he was not interested in having a long-term relationship with you."

"I don't believe this. Not that I give a shit because I have nothing whatsoever to do with him, and if he is saying those things about me then he's disgusting."

"So are you admitting that you and Mr. Dawson were having a sexual relationship?" Lawrence asked. Katrina glared at him.

"I am not admitting anything. I think you should leave . . . this is very upsetting."

"Did you know his wife Shirley?"

"No, I bloody did not! I've said this before . . . I just don't understand why you are here asking me these questions about my private business. If I did see Barry, then so what? Nothing is making sense to me . . . I mean, why are you here?"

"Because we have some questions that need to be answered regarding the death of Shirley Dawson. We have to check that everything her husband has told us is correct. Could you please tell me where you were on the seventh of October?"

Katrina closed her eyes.

"Seventh of October? . . . What day was that?"

"Monday."

"Oh yes . . . I was here. There's a new Arts Festival in Brighton and I went over there to see if any of the paintings interested me. We have a lot of artists in this area, and at one time I quite fancied the idea of running a gallery."

Lawrence turned and waited for Jane to finish making her notes before he continued.

"Am I correct in saying that Shirley Dawson found out that you and he were having a sexual relationship?"

"I'll tell you what is correct—he is a fucking liar! Firstly, he never told me he was married, or that he had a kid. Secondly, he came on to me and made me ridiculous promises until I found out the truth about him being married. I left my job at St. Thomas', which I was really enjoying, because I wanted nothing more to do with him and was disgusted that he had blatantly lied to me. I never met his wife."

Neither Jane nor Lawrence said anything for a moment. They remained silent and Katrina seemed unable to keep quiet. Her leg twitched as she kicked out with her slipper.

"I don't know what he's told you but I am now telling you the truth. I mean, it was virtually a one-night stand. I made a big mistake by trusting in what he told me. He said he owned his flat, that he would sell up and we would have money. I mean, please, he was promising me God knows what. I never had any intention of getting serious with him; he was just a porter for heaven's sake."

"Did you ever go to Mr. Dawson's flat?"

"No, I had no reason to go there."

"So, when you found out . . . ?" Lawrence said quietly.

"I finished with him, and left my job at the hospital."

In a quiet manner Lawrence told her that, contrary to her saying that it was her decision to leave St. Thomas', they had been informed that her contract had been terminated because of her unprofessional conduct. "That is total bullshit! It was my choice! They were always understaffed and we were constantly being asked to change shifts and work extra hours. I don't know who you are getting this information from but it isn't true."

"We also have information regarding your previous employment, Miss Harcourt, and that you had also been sacked from care homes for unprofessional conduct."

"Christ, if you think that washing dirty old women's shit off their bedclothes is professional. Dementia patients are never easy to deal with . . . I tried to be caring but I was never cut out to be ordered around by some vicious trumped-up Matron who didn't have the qualification to run any of the care homes I worked for. You give me any details you've got and I can qualify my reasons for leaving."

Jane stood up and asked if she could use the bathroom. Katrina told her there was a downstairs toilet further along the hall. Jane was becoming frustrated by their interview and felt that maybe Lawrence would be able to get more information on his own. They had not yet gained any further evidence or connection to the death of Shirley Dawson. Jane left the room and closed the door. She walked into the hall and at the end of the hallway she saw Mrs. Harcourt in the kitchen who, on seeing Jane, came out into the hall.

"Did Katrina offer you a tea or coffee?"

"No, but we're fine—thank you. You have a lovely house. It must be so nice living close to the beach."

"Yes, we retired here quite a few years ago now. My husband and I really enjoy bracing walks on the beach, and they have a very good theater in Brighton with some excellent productions."

"I'd love to see the rest of the house, Mrs. Harcourt . . . it's so beautifully furnished."

"Oh, let me show you around. When we moved there was a lot of work to do. My husband is a real one for putting up new wallpaper. He's very accomplished, and we like to have everything clean and fresh."

They went up the stairs. Mrs. Harcourt was so sweet and proud of her flock wallpaper, and new stair carpet.

"It must be nice to have your daughter home."

"Yes, she comes and goes but right now she's looking for a new position. So until she finds one we're happy she's here."

"I suppose there is a very good train service between here and London."

"Yes, but she has her own car, and she doesn't like to use the train when she needs to go to London for an interview, as they are always so crowded. She had a very important interview the other day and I had to put the alarm on to make sure she was up in time as she had to leave at the crack of dawn."

"Oh, can you remember what day that was, Mrs. Harcourt?"

"Yes I do, it was the seventh of October, because it was just two days after those awful IRA bombings in Guildford. She rang me from the petrol station on the roundabout by the A23, where my husband has an account, and she asked for permission to fill her car up because she'd left her purse at home."

"Do you recall what time that was?"

"Well, now you're asking me . . . I think it was before seven o'clock in the morning."

Jane was very complimentary as they toured the house. She was shown the master bedroom and then Mrs. Harcourt showed her Katrina's bedroom. It was a large room at the front of the house, with bay windows and fitted wardrobes.

"Oh good heavens, what a lovely room! Are those all fitted wardrobes?"

"Yes, we got a local carpenter in and he made them to my husband's specifications. He and Katrina are both very partic-ular about things."

Mrs. Harcourt opened one of the wardrobe doors, saying that Katrina liked her clothes to be color coordinated. Jane looked inside and glanced down at the shoe rack.

"She must never want to leave! I am so impressed . . . I wish I had a wardrobe this size."

Jane knew they had no search warrant, and spotting a pair of very high-heeled patent leather shoes was more than she could have anticipated finding.

As they were about to leave the bedroom Jane noticed on the dressing table a large framed photograph of Katrina in a wedding gown with a tiara and a beautiful long veil. She turned to Mrs. Harcourt.

"Oh, Katrina was married?"

Mrs. Harcourt picked up the photo. "Sadly the wedding never took place. Katrina ordered this gown from Ossie Clark—he's a very famous fashion designer—and the gown was satin chiffon Botticelli print. She had seen it in a fashion magazine and ordered it to be made especially. It was very expensive. Ossie Clark also designed her shoes and the bridesmaids' gowns."

"Good heavens, that must have cost a fortune."

Mrs. Harcourt replaced the photograph. "It did, believe you me. My husband couldn't afford it as he's retired. So Katrina foolishly took out a bank loan. She'd ordered cars and booked a reception at the Grand Hotel in Brighton. It was just awful because she ended up in debt."

"Is she still paying it off?" asked Jane.

"Yes, she's also paying for the lease on her car. I don't know how she manages it, because you don't get paid much as a nurse, do you?"

"Going to such lengths, a wedding gown and all the arrangements, must've been dreadful. Was it Katrina's decision not to go ahead with the wedding?"

Mrs. Harcourt hesitated and looked toward the doorway as if afraid she would be overheard. She lowered her voice. "No, it wasn't Katrina's decision, it was her fiancé's, although we had never met him. I don't even know if they were officially engaged, and to be honest I felt very concerned at the time because she'd only recently met him. He apparently just said he had no intention of getting married and didn't want to see her."

"That must have been dreadful."

"Yes, yes, it was." Mrs. Harcourt rubbed her hands. "It was humiliating. I never thought she'd recover and truthfully she had no one but herself to blame. And now she's still in debt, which is why she has to live at home with us. She has nowhere to go."

By the time Jane returned to the drawing room, Katrina was standing by the fireplace telling Lawrence that she had been almost suicidal when her engagement to a young doctor had fallen apart.

"I was devastated. I mean, it was a bolt out of the blue . . . one moment I was choosing my wedding dress and the next he had the audacity to call me and tell me it had been too much of a rush and he was undecided. Undecided? . . . I had booked the church and Mummy was organizing the reception! It gave me a total nervous breakdown."

Katrina hardly acknowledged that Jane had returned and was very tearful, acting as though she was a wronged woman. Jane picked up her notebook and jotted down "*Katrina in London October 7th —patent leather shoes in wardrobe*," before discreetly handing it to Lawrence.

Lawrence glanced down at Jane's note and wrote a quick message before handing the notebook back to her. He watched as Katrina sat down on the sofa, acting like the bewildered, jilted bride as she shook her head and sighed.

"So you have to understand that when Barry admitted to me he was married it felt as though it was all happening again. If you consider the lies I've been told and the promises I've been made I would never want to see his common little wife, let alone want to have anything to do with her. And I really don't care if she drowned. All I care about is that nobody is ever going to betray me again."

Lawrence stood up and quietly thanked Katrina for cooperating and for answering their questions.

"I am sorry if this has been distressing for you."

Jane stood uncertainly and joined him at the drawing room door. She thanked Katrina and then followed Lawrence out and into the hall. Mrs. Harcourt was in the kitchen, as

Lawrence smiled and said they would show themselves out. They didn't speak until they reached his parked car and got inside.

"Why didn't you let me show her the photographs?" Jane asked.

"It's called 'keeping your powder dry.' I guarantee we will be interviewing Miss Katrina Harcourt again, and this time with a search warrant. With what you discovered in her room I think we have enough leverage for me to talk to DCI Shepherd first thing in the morning."

Lawrence reversed in a three point turn before heading back toward the seafront.

"If it's OK with you, Jane, I think that I should talk to Shepherd alone. I don't want there to be any negative repercussions on you and how much you're investigating without his authority."

Jane stared out of the window.

"Do you really think we have enough evidence? I feel as though we should have questioned her further."

"Listen, you had confirmation from her mother that on the morning Shirley Dawson died, Katrina left Brighton early in the morning and drove to London. You also saw a pair of patent leather stilettos in her wardrobe. If we had continued to question her, or asked about the day she drove to London, or her shoes, all without a warrant, we could give her time to come up with an alibi, or get rid of the shoes. What we don't need is for her to hear any alarm bells ringing."

"Well, she certainly kept changing her story. One minute denying she was having a relationship with Barry Dawson, the next admitting it. But do we have a strong enough motive?"

"We do. It was when she said that Barry had promised to marry her, and told her he owned his flat. Plus, her mother said that she was in debt, so money is an incentive, and a motive to get rid of Shirley."

Jane sat quietly, taking on board everything Lawrence said. She still felt uncertain about whether Barry Dawson and Katrina were in on it together, or if Katrina had acted alone. As if reading her mind Lawrence turned toward her and smiled.

"I think they worked this together. If we can get that next-door neighbor to identify the shoes we can verify that at 8 a.m. on the day Shirley's body was found Katrina was there. It's a question of the time line. We are told Barry Dawson was seen at the hospital after 10 a.m. and there is a witness who is certain they saw him. But it could be that Barry came home earlier than he has stated, met up with Katrina, and both of them killed Shirley."

Jane remained silent. They drove back the way they had come, and she was thankful that this time the hood wasn't down.

"Can I just ask you something? At first Katrina was very scathing about Barry, being just a lowly porter. I mean, she is quite stunning, she's obviously well educated, and her mother was a sweetheart, proudly showing me all her husband's prowess with the décor and fitted wardrobes. It doesn't quite add up that she would go to such dreadful lengths to be a partner in crime with Barry, murdering his wife?"

Lawrence immediately replied that it was obvious to him. Katrina had recently been jilted at the altar and had been dismissed for her unprofessional conduct on several previous occasions. She was desperate, in debt, and had no job.

"Yes, I am aware of that. But do you think she would really be prepared to be a party to murder?"

"Yes, I do. I think she is a very dangerous woman with a psychopathic fury—did you hear what she said about the fact that she didn't care if Shirley Dawson had drowned, all she cared about was that nobody was ever going to betray her again, or stop her from getting what she wants? In this case it was Barry Dawson. If he wasn't a pawn then they planned it together. If I am successful in getting a more detailed PM, maybe we can prove it."

CHAPTER SEVENTEEN

Jane arrived at the station at eight-thirty the following morning and went straight to the incident room. DI Gibbs was already in his office, which struck her as unusual, and he glanced over at her as she checked for any instructions from the DCI. She presumed DCI Shepherd would already be re-interviewing the suspects. Gibbs was a mess and obviously very hungover if not still under the influence of alcohol.

"Is everything all right, Spence?"

"Can you get me a coffee, please, Jane?"

"Do you want the canteen brew, or for me to get a takeaway? There are lots of new coffee bars opening up around Covent Garden."

"I just want a fuckin' strong black coffee, Tennison, there's no need for you to schlepp out of the station, all right?"

Rolling her eyes, Jane went up to the canteen and, as requested, brought back as strong a mug of black coffee as she could get. Gibbs pulled a face when he tasted it, saying that she hadn't sugared it, and he went out to B Relief to use their sugar bag.

"I collared the bag slasher in broad daylight, right outside the big John Lewis . . . caught him about to rob a teenager. As I suspected, he's a junkie with a sheet as long as my arm."

"Congratulations!" Jane said, sitting at a desk.

"Message came in for you from the duty sergeant at Hackney. A woman, a Mrs. Allard, left her number for you to call her. I didn't tell DCI Shepherd that you were on a jaunt to Brighton with blondie yesterday . . . I hope you're not sleuthing around on something that you have no business working on."

Jane didn't have time to explain as DS Lawrence walked in but she made a note in her notebook, puzzled why Mrs. Allard was calling her.

"Morning, Spence, sorry I woke you up early. Now we need to talk to DCI Shepherd to get a second PM done. We're running out of time as Shirley Dawson's body is going to be released today for burial."

"So what exactly *have* you got?" Jane referred to her notebook.

"Barry Dawson was having an affair with Katrina Harcourt—she worked at the same hospital before she was dismissed. We believe that Shirley Dawson found out about their affair, and possibly followed them to take photographs of them together to confront him."

Gibbs scratched his head.

"Hang on, hang on. This isn't hard evidence, it's just supposition."

"We also have confirmation from Katrina Harcourt's mother that on the day Shirley Dawson's body was found, Katrina left Brighton at 6 a.m. and drove to London," Lawrence said impatiently.

Gibbs laughed.

"But you don't have any proof that she was actually at the Dawsons' flat? Even a parking ticket would be useful . . ."

"She has a pair of patent leather stiletto shoes that fit the description given by the neighbor, Mrs. Cook."

"Jane, she saw a pair of fucking shoes, not who was wearing them! Was there anything particularly unusual about the shoes?"

"No, they were just plain black patent leather shoes, with stiletto heels . . ."

". . . Like how many thousands of pairs sold in London? You would be laughed out of court if your main witness for the prosecution was a pair of bloody shoes!"

Lawrence sat on top of the desk beside Gibbs, running his hands through his blond hair.

"All right, what if I was to tell you that, on a purely gut feeling, Shirley Dawson was murdered? I've been concerned from day one about the position she was found in the bath tub, and there are other inconsistencies that Jane came up with from their flat. I think Shirley Dawson was murdered, and I think Katrina Harcourt had something to do with it."

There was a pause as Gibbs digested what he had just heard. He looked from Lawrence to Jane.

"And you have the same gut feeling, do you, Jane?"

"Yes, Spence, I do."

"And you reckon Barry Dawson is also in the frame for it? But he's got an alibi, hasn't he? He has witnesses who saw him making phone calls at the hospital?"

Jane was about to reply when Lawrence got up from the desk.

"I think we can break that alibi, but we have to have a second PM, and I'm going to need Shepherd to give us the go-ahead."

Again Gibbs hesitated, then walked back toward his office.

"OK . . . you'd better go and find him then."

DI Moran was feeling very impatient. He had been in to the Hackney incident room twice looking for DC Edwards. Eventually a clerk had arrived to start work and explained to Moran that Edwards had gone home early the previous night as he had a high temperature and his cold had turned into bronchitis. She went over to her in-tray, saying that she had a couple of memos that Edwards wanted her to pass on to him. Delving through the pile of paperwork she pulled out two sheets, clipped together.

"He's been making inquiries into any cases that had a similar MO to Peter Allard's, sir. I really felt that he should have gone home earlier—he didn't stop sneezing and was passing his germs all around the office. Anyway, just before he left he contacted the police division in Maidstone . . ."

"Maidstone? I told him to focus on local areas."

"Apparently that's where Peter Allard and his wife lived five years previously, sir, before he took over his father's taxi and came back to live in Walthamstow."

"Christ! You ask these young guys to do something simple . . . What the hell is he going that far back for?"

"I don't know, sir, you'll have to ask him. He's underlined the name 'Susie Luna,' but I've no idea what that means."

"I'll have to wait until he gets back. Meanwhile, I've got a situation—a woman's been pushed under a bus outside the Pembridge Estate. Can you ask DC Ashton to get a squad car—"

"Sorry, sir, but he's not in today," the clerk interrupted. "His new baby's got a very bad rash and his wife needs him to drive her to the doctor. You see, she's not breastfeeding, she's using formula milk and they often get an adverse reaction to that . . ."

Moran raised his eyebrows.

"See if you can get a plonk to drive me to the Pembridge then."

Jane was at her desk typing up a lengthy report on all the latest information she had gathered over the weekend. DS Lawrence had been in with DCI Shepherd for over half an hour. Edith was moaning about the stack of work she had to do, lodging the complaints that the market stallholders had passed to the station.

Lawrence rushed in and went over to Jane's desk.

"I've twisted DCI Shepherd's arm and he's given me the OK to get a second PM on Shirley Dawson. Prof Martin has agreed to come in after lunch. In the meantime, you'd better get over to the mortuary as Barry Dawson and his mother are due there to arrange the removal of the body for burial. I have some business to deal with in the lab, but I'll get over there as soon as I'm free. Just fend them off, and don't indicate that we are in anyway suspicious until Prof Martin has done his job. I'll take it up with the coroner. No matter what we think, we might just have to walk away . . . understand?"

Jane nodded and pulled out her typed report.

"DCI Shepherd wants your full report," Lawrence added, "and he wants it from every angle so don't miss anything out. Cover everything—he wasn't all that happy about that trip yesterday."

"I've just finished it, if you want to read it over?"

"Sorry, I don't have time, I'm needed at the lab." Lawrence hurried out and Jane stood up to take the report in to Shepherd. Gibbs appeared at his office doorway.

"What's going on, Tennison?"

"Oh, we've been given clearance for a second PM on Shirley Dawson."

Edith stopped typing and turned to stare at Jane.

"DS Lawrence instigated it, Edith, as he reckoned there were some discrepancies in the non-suspicious death report from the coroner. So he's organizing another inquiry."

"So what exactly is your involvement?"

"Well, I was on the scene, that's all." Jane hurried out.

Edith pursed her lips. "She needs taking down a peg or two . . . wasn't ever like that in my day, you know . . . straight from being a probationary officer into plain clothes. She's going to get a smack around the chops from DCI Shepherd—he was asking where she was earlier."

Ignoring Edith, his head pounding, Gibbs went over to the filing cabinet to pull out the reports on the Shirley Dawson case, then went into his office and shut the door.

By the time Jane arrived at the mortuary it was almost 2 p.m. Professor Martin hadn't arrived yet, and even when he did she knew it would take a considerable while before he could gain access to the body and begin the second post-mortem due to the paperwork. Barry Dawson was sitting in the reception with his mother. His daughter Heidi was asleep in her pushchair clutching a teddy bear.

"What's going on?" Barry demanded.

"I'm sorry . . . I have only just arrived," Jane replied quietly.

"We have been told that Shirley's body can't be released. We have organized for her to be taken to a funeral parlor as we are having her buried tomorrow morning."

"I'm sorry. I am not actually aware of what you are being told."

"Just what I said. I mean, you tell me what's going on."

"We have been informed that a second post-mortem has been requested and there was some suggestion that the first one was not as straightforward as it would seem."

Jane excused herself and said she would try to find out what was going on and would get back to them as soon as she could. Pushing open the door to the corridor she stopped as Mrs. Dawson called after her.

"This is bloody disgusting, you know," she said, pushing the little girl back and forth in her pushchair. "Barry's had to take another day off work, and we got family to organize. We get here only to be told that our funeral arrangements have got to be put on hold? You tell me, why?"

"If you just wait here I'll go and see what I can find out."

Jane hurried along the corridor and stepped back as a mortician assistant wheeled out a covered gurney from the chill room toward the autopsy section. Professor Dean Martin appeared, already wearing his rubber gown and black boots. Judging by the stains on his apron it was clear that he had already been at work. He gave a polite nod to Jane as he pushed open the doors to allow the gurney to pass in front of him, then the doors swung closed behind him. Jane was disinclined to ask permission to follow but stood waiting in the corridor until she felt it was time enough to return to reception. Barry Dawson had gone, leaving just his mother and the still sleeping Heidi.

"He's had to go to work . . . he's really distressed, and we need to get some answers. This is disgusting and there doesn't seem to be anyone I can ask."

Jane apologized and sat down beside her. She decided to take a risk in the hope that Mrs. Dawson might let something slip.

"Basically there seems to be some confusion about your son's statement. We now have information regarding a relationship he had with a woman called Katrina Harcourt."

"What? I've never bloody heard of her! This isn't right."

"I just need to double-check that I have your own statement correct, Mrs. Dawson. Could you please tell me exactly what happened on the morning your daughter-in-law was found at your son's flat?"

"I've told you! I was supposed to go and look after Heidi because Shirley had a hair appointment."

"Ah, I see. That's why you were going to babysit, because . . ."

"She was going to have her hair done at nine o'clock. But I couldn't go round there because my washing machine was faulty and I was waiting for the engineer to come. I've already told you this."

"Did you call Shirley to tell her that you wouldn't be able to babysit?"

"I rang the payphone in her house, but she never answered so I presumed she'd already gone out and had taken Heidi with her."

"What time did you call Shirley?"

Mrs. Dawson sighed.

"Be about a quarter to nine . . . but like I just said, she didn't answer so I presumed she had gone to have her hair done. I don't see why you want to know all this. She always asked me to look after Heidi if she was going out. And I presume that's why Barry got no reply either, when he called her."

"I am going to show you some photographs now, Mrs. Dawson. Could you tell me if you recognize this woman?"

Jane took out the three small black and white photographs of Katrina Harcourt and showed them to Mrs. Dawson, who shook her head. She sighed.

"Don't tell me that silly bugger was seeing another woman? I swear to God, he's unable to keep his ruddy dick in his pants! But he never mentioned nothin' to me about her, and he's been in a terrible state since Shirley died. So what difference does it make? He's always been a one for the girls, and I have to say that it's not easy for me neither as I got to look out for his daughter. He's got to go to work, and I mean he's still living at my place, and his dog . . . I don't know what he's gonna do when he moves back to his flat."

"Has he suggested selling the flat? I believe he owns it, doesn't he?"

"Yes, he does. He pays the mortgage, but his dad left him the money to make the down payment. Mind you, it needs a lot doing to it and the landlord is a nasty piece of work. Never does nothing about the communal areas. There used to be a general cleaner who'd collect their rubbish from the storage area by their flat and take it down to the basement. But since he got rid of her, Shirley's had to do it herself."

Mrs. Dawson rambled on, all the while pushing the buggy back and forth, until Heidi woke up and started crying. Mrs. Dawson was becoming more and more agitated now, standing as she rocked the pushchair. Jane discreetly glanced at her watch.

"You tell me what I should do, will you? I mean, we've arranged the funeral and now I don't know if it can go ahead. I just don't understand why there is this delay."

Jane stood up and once again checked her watch. She suggested that Mrs. Dawson return home and said that she would call her with an update as soon as she knew the details. Heidi was now howling loudly and Mrs. Dawson eventually agreed to take her home.

Relieved that she had gone, Jane sat waiting in reception. There was something about the cavernous, cold room that always had a faint smell of cleaning fluid and Dettol, which became stronger when you passed through the double doors into the chill rooms. The first time she had been in there was for the identification of murder victim Julie Ann Collins. She remembered how Julie Ann's father, after seeing his dead daughter, had become frighteningly enraged. Nothing had prepared her, after witnessing his overwhelming grief, for learning that he had instigated the brutal beating of his daughter. DS Lawrence appeared, having arrived via the back entrance.

"It's going to take a while . . . the old boy is being very methodical and won't be hurried. So far he has made no further conclusion and is ticking off the previous PM as all being acceptable. As soon as I get anything to the contrary I'll call you at the station."

Jane would have liked to have stayed but before she could argue, Lawrence left her to return to the postmortem. With nothing else to do, Jane headed back to Bow Street to wait for Professor Martin's PM report.

Marie Allard sat at the Formica-topped table in the visitors' section at Brixton Prison. The noise of the waiting families always gave her a headache. The children were mostly under five, so weren't at school like her own two. The babies screamed while the mothers and grandmothers shouted and tried to keep them from running between the tables. The male visitors always seemed much older than the prisoners they were visiting, with rough, worn faces. Many of them were rolling cigarettes and the

walls of the prison visiting room smelt stale and were yellowing from tobacco stains. The tin ashtrays were never emptied
and the officers walked up and down between the tables as they
waited for the loud clanging sound that heralded the prisoners'
entry into the visiting section.

Two wardens sat on high stools surveying the room and
making sure nothing illegal was passed across, or underneath,
the tables. Marie waited patiently, becoming more nervous as
the minutes ticked by. Then the buzzer sounded, the communi-
cation door was opened and a loud bell rang.

The hubbub of noise increased as the prisoners were led in,
and the men hurried to their allocated tables and loved ones.
Peter Allard wore creased and stained prison issue denims,
and was unshaven. He had always been so particular about
his clothes and his personal hygiene, with clean cut nails, and
shiny well-styled hair. Now he looked very pale, with deep cir-
cles beneath his eyes. As he pulled out the chair to sit opposite
Marie she could feel the weight of his depression.

"You all right?" he asked quietly.

"Not really . . . but I'm OK."

He looked down at his dirty fingernails, then glanced around
the room.

"So, did you sort it as I told you to do?"

Marie hesitated and then tightly clasped her hands.

"No, I never get another phone call. So I didn't do it."

He asked if she had got the money ready and Marie replied
that she had. One lie after another tumbled out. Part of her was
unsure why she was so afraid of admitting that all she had seen
was a young boy collecting the cash.

"I too scared to answer the phone, Peter," she admitted. "It's
such a lot of money, and with you in here."

"I called you last night . . . you know I got to wait in line to
use the payphone so I can't tell you exactly when I'll be calling,

but we get time around six o'clock . . . so pick up around then, as you know it'll be me."

"OK. You heard about a trial date yet?"

"No. Bastards are just keeping me here . . . I hope to God it's soon because I don't know how much longer I can last in this shit hole. You have no idea what it's like . . . a ping pong ball went missing and there was a big fight so we had to have a lockup for the entire day as punishment. As if being in this dump wasn't enough."

"The kids are fine, Peter."

"What did you buy then?"

"What?"

"Ma said you were taking them to a birthday party on Sunday."

"Oh yes, it was just a jigsaw puzzle."

Peter unclenched his hands and reached over to take hers. A passing warden snapped as he passed, "No contact, please."

Peter quickly withdrew his hand.

"Well, maybe that bent cop has got enough of my hard-earned dough and won't be blackmailing us for our savings."

From across the room a young thug stood up, shouting at the top of his voice, "The law sucks! Innocent until proved fuckin' guilty, my arse! It's a shit pile!"

Two officers removed the boy, who continued yelling and kicking out, leaving the two women at his table crying. Peter shook his head.

"That's true—I know it better'n anyone else . . . I'm innocent. You know it too, don't you? All I want is a fair trial so I can prove I was fitted up."

Marie felt ashamed that she was willing the bell to ring for the end of visiting time. She just wanted to go and collect the children from school. But for a further half-hour Peter repeated over and over that he was going to prove his innocence. At one point he was in tears, and Marie had never seen him in such a depressed state.

"I can't forgive myself for doing this to you, Marie, and to my kids. You know I love you and want to make it good when I get out. But I just get into a bad state, because it's so frustrating. I admitted what I did was wrong, but it wasn't serious, not like that other time . . . you know that, and you know why . . . but we'll be all right, as soon as I get out."

"Yes, of course we will."

The bell rang and Marie was free to go. But first she had to watch him being led out back into the prison section, as the door was bolted behind all the inmates. Once he was out of sight, Marie turned away. It was too late now, she'd lied to him. And what if there was another call from "Angie"? She was terrified there would be another demand, and the money in their savings account was running out.

At the mortuary Professor Martin peered through his half-moon spectacles at the right side of the victim's scalp. Using a fine spatula, he moved aside the thick curly hair, bent very close and sniffed. He then carefully parted a section of hair and turned to Lawrence.

"This is interesting. Can you see that a small section of hair looks frizzy? Not the section close to the face but just behind it? And if you lean in close you can just detect a slight smell of Dettol, but also burning. It's not strong, but then she was in the bath for some time. Can you see the strands are shorter here?"

Lawrence leaned in close and agreed. He watched as Prof Martin used sharp scissors to cut away the long thick strands and then, with the hair cropped, began to shave the complete right side of Shirley's scalp.

"Well, well . . . what have we here? I would say that this is what could have caused your victim to be unconscious, not the blow to her forehead. Can you see it?"

Lawrence looked at a strange V-shaped red mark, about three and a half inches in length. Prof Martin continued to peel back the face and remaining scalp hair to examine the skull.

"Easily missed, and I could be wrong . . . perhaps the victim was wearing a band of some kind that in part might have cushioned the blow from being that visible. And her hair was thick enough to hide the strange burnt section. But it is clear she was struck to the right side of her head."

Lawrence watched closely.

"The wound on her forehead is not the one that would have rendered her unconscious?" he asked quietly.

"No, it would probably have been caused by her falling forward and hitting the edge of the tap, as has been suggested, but having read the reports describing how her body was found, it doesn't quite add up. She should have been face down, not on her back."

"So you are saying that she was more than likely unconscious when she hit the tap with her head?"

"Yes, but in any case your victim was alive in the bath water, as her blood was still flowing out of her nostrils. I would say the young lady could have had a severe nosebleed from the blow."

Lawrence stepped back to allow Prof Martin to finish. His mind was reeling as he took in the consequences of this new information.

He was stunned.

By the time Lawrence returned to the station he was feeling exhilarated, and went straight to the incident room. Jane turned expectantly toward him as he came in and his triumphant expression told her all she needed to know. But a thrill still went through her when Lawrence said, "Our non-suspicious death is now very suspicious. Shirley Dawson was murdered."

CHAPTER EIGHTEEN

Two days later, after all the investigation she had instigated, Jane was very upset that DCI Shepherd excluded her from the inquiry. DI Gibbs and DS Lawrence were given the overall lead, with three other DCs who had been with Bow Street a lot longer than Jane. She had presumed that Shepherd would ask for her to be present and had even expected some acknowledgment from him when he had been asking Edith what DCs were available.

"Excuse me, sir, will you want me to discuss the report and my notes from my inquiries?" Jane asked.

He glanced toward her and then went back to looking over the lists of available officers, making suggestions of who he wanted for the briefing.

"As you will see, I have underlined sections that we will need to discuss, so please put them on my desk straight away," he told Edith.

Edith scurried out of the office and only after she had left did he turn his attention to Jane.

"Tennison, I think you have proved yourself to be very diligent. However, I have major issues with the fact that you have acted, or appear to have been acting, without authority. As you have only recently completed your probationary period and joined us here at Bow Street just over a week ago, I am warning you that I do not, and will not, have any detectives working without the full co-operation of the team. Your priority should have been to inform me of any new evidence or suspicions you acquired."

Shepherd walked out, leaving Jane shocked and confused.

Edith returned carrying a large stack of papers she had to check through and banged them down on her desk.

"My God, this has created a lot of extra work. Now I have to sort out what meetings he can be available for with all this new development."

"What exactly is going on in the board room?" Jane asked, watching as officers including Shepherd and Lawrence gathered round a large oval table in the room opposite.

"I am not privy to what their intentions are, dear, but this Shirley Dawson case is leaving the desk sergeant pulling out his hair."

Jane felt awful after the dressing down from Shepherd. As she was almost at the end of her shift she went into the ladies' locker room. She sat in a cubicle and, as much as she hated herself for doing so, she burst into tears. She was loath to admit it, but after a good cry she was feeling increasingly irritated that she had not been brought onto the case, after all the work she had done on it. She was also hurt that DS Lawrence had not intervened on her behalf. She collected her bag and jacket and left the station to return to the section house. She went to the laundry room and ironed a fresh shirt for the morning, then returned to her room. Sitting on the edge of her bed as she flicked through her notebook, she came across the message she had jotted down about Mrs. Allard calling Hackney Station, which had been forwarded on to the duty sergeant at Bow Street. She had not really given it much thought, having been so caught up with the Shirley Dawson situation. Glancing at her watch she saw that it was after seven. She hoped it wouldn't be too late to return Mrs. Allard's call.

Jane was also intrigued to find out what Mrs. Allard wanted, so she made her way down to the reception to use the payphone. It rang unanswered for a long time, and Jane double-checked that she was dialing the correct number. She replaced the receiver, waited five minutes and tried again but it still rang with no one picking up. She was about to go back upstairs to her room when DI Gibbs came hurrying through the reception doors.

"Ah! Just the person I was coming to see." He gestured toward her to join him.

"Come on, I'll buy you a drink over at the Warburton . . . Just want to have a bit of a chat."

"If it's to have a go at me I'm not interested."

Gibbs grinned. "I think you've had enough goes. I just need a moment of your valuable mind!"

She didn't bother fetching her coat as it was just a short walk across the road. Gibbs strode ahead of her, always seeming to have an excess of energy. Even though he was striding ahead he would half turn back toward her and then move forward; he was surprisingly elegant in his movements and had a natural rhythm. He shouldered the pub door, and held it open for her to pass him before he let it swing closed behind them. He ushered her to the bar and ordered a pint and a whisky chaser for himself. Jane asked for a dry white wine, which was never very dry and was usually rather tepid but Ron, the pub landlord, always dropped in a couple of ice cubes whether you asked him to or not.

Gibbs moved around the full pub to grab a small table in the corner, at the far end of the bar. He put his pint down and lit a cigarette, heaved in the smoke and then downed his whisky in one. Jane took an unenthusiastic sip of wine, waiting for him to explain why he wanted to talk to her. His right foot twitched as he picked up his pint and took a large gulp before he placed it back down onto the soggy beer mat.

"OK . . . I got to the meeting this afternoon halfway through as I was over at the Magistrates' Court with this bag snatcher. But I have to tell you that you've got a fan in DS Lawrence. He was very complimentary about your queries with the non-suspicious death. Shepherd was a bit tight-lipped and prissy about you being unethical et cetera, but he had to stand down a bit as it's now a murder inquiry. The old boy, Prof Martin, did a second PM and discovered an additional abrasion to the dead woman's head, right side on in an odd V shape. He's stated that this would have been the first blow. Anyway, I'm not here to go into that until we've done more of whom did what to whomever . . ."

Gibbs spoke very fast, his foot still twitching, and his eyes darting around the pub and snooker area.

"What did you want to talk to me about, Spence?"

"Well, I need you to explain how you got the information from the suspect—this girlfriend of the husband, Katrina Harcourt—and then how you saw the shoes that Dawson's neighbor gave a statement about, saying she didn't see the woman from above the knee."

Irritated, Jane replied, "There was nothing unethical about it. Katrina's mother invited me to see their home décor upstairs, and took me into Katrina's bedroom. She was very proud of her husband's DIY efforts and showed me the inside of Katrina's wardrobe with all the shoes. I didn't touch them."

"Don't get tetchy with me, I'm just looking out for you. When the judge hears that it wasn't exactly an eyeball witness who *only* saw a pair of legs and feet, it's going to be a tricky one, your Honor!"

"I'll tell you what was really interesting: Katrina Harcourt had a photographer to take glamorous pictures of her as a bride. She had the full wedding dress, veil, all designed by Ossie Clark, and because she was jilted it left her in debt up to her neck."

"I've heard of him. In fact, I bought a second-hand pair of snakeskin shoes designed by him."

Jane gave Gibbs a curious look before telling him exactly where she had seen Katrina's shoes, and relayed how she had asked Katrina's mother about her traveling to London on the day of the murder.

"Just need to check that you didn't mention anything about the coincidence, or say why you were interested in the patent leather high heels?"

"I just saw them because I was shown the inside of her wardrobe. They fit the exact description . . . five inch heels, pointed toes and black patent leather."

"Well, I shouldn't think they are going to be that useful . . . We might get you to parade up and down in them, but I doubt it. Anyway, we're going to Brighton with a search warrant and we have to get the local plods on our side. God forbid you should tread on anyone's patch . . . and it's imperative we don't give this Katrina any signals to do a runner."

"So is she a suspect?"

"Yeah, and DS Lawrence strongly believes they were in it together. But we're going to bring Barry Dawson in for questioning first thing in the morning. I could do without the schlepp out to Brighton, but you gotta do what you gotta do . . ."

"Was Professor Martin able to give a clearer time of death?"

Gibbs drained his pint.

"Nope . . . you know these pathologists, anywhere between eight and nine hours. I love it when they say possible nearest five hours or six. They won't ever allow themselves to be on the line."

"Well, we can put a time on it. If we take the neighbors' information, that they heard the buzzer go at eight o'clock, and we know there was no one in the basement, no one in the first or second floor flat, it would have had to have been Shirley."

"Yeah, I know that. Prof Martin said it was possible she'd been dead three hours. He also came out with the fact that the cut to her forehead was not that deep and would not necessarily have bloodied the water."

"But something did, because I saw it on the ceiling of the bathroom below," Jane interjected.

"The prof said it was a possibility that Shirley Dawson had a severe nosebleed, which could've been the outcome of her hitting her head on the tap. But due to her being in the water for however long she was, her lower nostrils were clear. He found a substantial clot up in the bridge of her nose. Apparently it was even harder with this victim because she was in the water and had drowned, but both PMs agree that she was unconscious, but still alive, in the bath, and Martin thinks that maybe she was held down."

Gibbs didn't ask Jane if she wanted another drink but pushed his chair back. His mood suddenly changed.

"He always used to sit over there, you know." He nodded toward a similar-sized table on the opposite side of the room.

"Most nights I'd find him eating one of those disgusting steak and kidney pies from the heated cabinet on the bar. He always said he was never going to eat another one, so when I saw him with a greasy sausage roll I said to him, 'Oh, not eatin' your usual crap then?' and he grins up at me and says, 'Some bastard ate the last one!'"

Jane could see the grief in Gibbs's face and knew he had yet to get over the death of DCI Bradfield. Struggling with her own feelings of loss, Jane didn't know what to say. But he quickly masked his sadness, turned back to her and thanked her for coming for a drink. He said he was going over to the snooker section to have a game, but he didn't wait for her reply as he moved away. Jane didn't even bother to finish her wine and left shortly after.

Jane clocked in for duty early at 7:15 the following morning. She was heading toward the incident room when DCI Shepherd approached her.

"Give me a minute in my office would you, Tennison?"

Feeling apprehensive, she popped her handbag in the drawer of her desk, picked up her notebook and hurried to the DCI's office. The door was open and he was sitting at his desk typing—he was very fast. He signaled to her to wait a moment as he finished and drew the paper out of the typewriter, removing the carbon and copy. He passed the top page over to Jane.

"I hope to have all these queries you noted confirmed before we begin the interrogations. It's imperative I have a firmed-up time line. I think perhaps I was a bit hard on you yesterday, but for obvious reasons. DS Lawrence was very complimentary about your investigative abilities, but learn from this, Tennison. Please attend the briefing meeting at 12:30 p.m. today, as a team of detectives have been working flat out."

Jane returned to the incident room and sat at her desk. Edith glanced over at her, then pushed her chair back.

"Do you mind if I say something, Jane? It was obvious yesterday that your nose was put out of joint. I am very aware of how much work you have been doing when you have been off duty, because I had to break down the reports for Shepherd."

Jane chewed her lip, not wanting to get into a discussion with Edith.

"You have to understand the pecking order, dear. DCI Shepherd accepted the non-suspicious death, so how do you think it looks when a young trainee who has only been here less than two weeks, and a female to boot, goes off and does her own investigation? And now they have confirmation that the first PM was not adequate and it is being investigated as a murder."

"I hear what you're saying, Edith . . ."

"Good. Make moves slowly, Jane, or they will have you back in uniform for insubordination. You were lucky you had DS Lawrence looking out for you."

"Thank you, Edith. Can I get you a coffee?"

"No, thank you, dear. But at the briefing just sit tight and listen. I've been there before you, Jane . . . they'll wipe the floor with you if you overstep the mark."

Jane gave Edith a rueful smile and went out to go to the canteen.

Jane arrived at the board room on the dot of 12:30, but already there was a team of detectives, some of their faces familiar to her, sitting around the table quietly discussing their notes. She was acknowledged but no one spoke to her as she sat down on one of the vacant chairs, hoping she hadn't taken anyone's seat. She placed her notebook down in front of her, along with two sharpened pencils.

The air was thick with tobacco smoke. Everyone fell silent as DCI Shepherd walked in and sat at the top end of the table, placing a thick folder in front of him. DS Lawrence was the last to arrive. He sat opposite Jane and was very intent on placing a large manila envelope on the table.

"Right, everyone . . . time is against us so let's run through everything as fast as possible before the interviews begin. Paul, what have you got for us?"

DS Lawrence laid out various black and white photographs on the table, showing the victim's head wounds and also the shaven head clearly showing the deep V indentation.

The photographs were passed around as Lawrence spoke.

"I am certain that this wound to the victim's head was the result of being hit exceptionally hard from the right side. The weapon, without doubt, is this . . ."

Lawrence pushed forward the photographs of the iron.

"As you can see, the iron was yanked out of the plug socket when the victim was attacked. Close-up pictures reveal the loose wires, and when tested the iron did not connect. As you can see from this photograph, the victim may have been standing up ironing, and there was a female's blouse on the ironing board."

Shepherd put up his hand to indicate that he wanted Lawrence to pause.

"We can conclude what the victim was doing before being struck, but as we are bringing in two suspects I need a clearer time frame of when this attack possibly took place."

"The neighbor Mrs. Cook, from the basement next door, is adamant that she saw a woman—but only from the knees down—wearing black patent leather high heels, pacing back and forth. Then she heard a very loud click, which indicated that someone, possibly Shirley Dawson, had pressed the entry release to open the front door."

"Time?" Shepherd asked briskly.

"It was between 8 a.m. and 8:15 a.m. This time was pinpointed by the paper delivery as the paperboy delivers at the same time every day, like clockwork according to his boss at the newsagent."

"Shirley Dawson had a hair appointment, not at 9 a.m. as we had first been told, but for 9:30 a.m. Her mother-in-law had agreed to babysit but due to her washing machine breaking down she could not be there. So she called the phone on the landing at the Dawsons' flat at a quarter to nine, but received no reply."

Shepherd flicked through his notes.

"Detective Summers, you were checking this out—what did you come up with?"

Detective Summers was a thin, balding man. He tapped his notebook.

"The hair salon, Pearls and Curls in Brick Lane, confirmed that they had Shirley's appointment booked in the diary for more than two weeks. Shirley was a regular customer: apparently she had exceptionally thick hair which had to be straightened and thinned. The salon say that they did not receive any call to say that Shirley was unable to keep the appointment. She had never missed any previous appointments."

Shepherd nodded as another detective held up his hand.

"I interviewed Mrs. Dawson yesterday evening and she confirmed that she had received a call from her son, Barry Dawson, at around 9 a.m. Mrs. Dawson was unable to confirm the exact time but the engineer had not shown up to repair her washing machine yet. Barry wanted to know why she was not at the flat as she was supposed to be babysitting. Barry told her that he had tried to call Shirley but had got no reply and Mrs. Dawson suggested that perhaps she had taken their daughter, Heidi, to the hair salon with her."

Shepherd was making notes, then looked up.

"Sir, I don't know if this is of interest but when I arrived at Mrs. Dawson's house she was out walking the dog and a friend was babysitting her granddaughter. She was quite elderly and her name was Norma Hall. She said she had been Shirley's foster carer, and that it was all very sad, particularly as Shirley had believed that this was going to be everything she had dreamed—"

"Is there a point to this?" Shepherd interrupted.

"Just that the last time Shirley had seen this foster carer she had been very depressed. Although they owned their flat and Barry paid the mortgage, he had done nothing to redecorate or refurbish it for them to resell and make a profit, which was the original intention, and he kept breaking his promises. She said that it was stressful having the dog to take care of, and having to carry the pushchair up and down the stairs. Even the rubbish had to be carried all the way downstairs into the basement and—"

"One second—is the basement used for bins?"

"No, sir, I checked first thing this morning and there's an old coal hole where all the tenants keep their bins. You gain access from the basement."

"Anyone checked these bins out?" Shepherd glanced round the table. "No? Let's do it then. I think we have a picture taken of a bucket with soiled nappies, yes? DS Lawrence, check out the bins. Can anyone tell me the value of the Dawsons' property?"

The same detective lifted his hand. "Yes, sir. The flat beneath them, which is being refurbished, is on the market for forty-five thousand pounds and the Dawsons' on the top floor is estimated at between thirty-five and thirty-eight thousand pounds. It's a good location."

"Good God! That's a lot of money," Shepherd muttered, then tapped the desk with the point of his sharpened pencil.

"If I could just continue, sir . . . I felt that I should talk to Norma Hall, the foster carer, again as she left when Mrs. Dawson returned. She has been taking kids into foster care for thirty years. She was not in the best of health but was very informative about Shirley, who was placed into her care when she was in her teens. She also said that it was via her that Barry Dawson had met Shirley. I was about to leave when Norma said something that seemed rather odd. When she had first found out about Shirley's death she went over to see Barry. She said that he was very emotional, crying and sobbing, but when she left the room he put on the television and seemed more interested in some football match . . . In fact, she said she heard him cheering and laughing."

Shepherd shrugged and looked around the table.

"I am hoping you have saved the best until last, DC Tomlinson?"

Jane looked across at the overweight detective who was stubbing out his cigarette.

"I re-questioned Mr. Goncalves, the hospital porter, as we have a statement from him and from Mr. Dawson regarding the calls made from the phone kiosk in the hospital corridor. You may recall that Barry Dawson said that he called home at 10 a.m., and on getting no reply became very worried as he claimed Shirley was not well and had been very depressed. He appeared to be very anxious and asked Mr. Goncalves for change, expressing his concerns over his wife's health and his need to call his mother again. He then claimed to leave the hospital and returned home to find his wife dead in the bath."

Tomlinson had everyone's attention as he explained tracking down the porter and then standing with him in the corridor and asking him if he could recall the exact timings. The porter said he was unsure and thought he had been told by Barry that he needed to leave as it was coming up to his break at 10 a.m. He said that he had given him some coppers and returned to the wing as he had a patient to take up to theater.

"I asked him to be very clear about exactly what he had heard. Did he hear the coins being returned as the call wasn't answered, or did he hear the call connect? He couldn't answer, but by my calculations Barry Dawson made one call to Shirley and got no reply. The next call was, he claimed, to his mother who was obviously not at his flat. Then there was a third call that the witness saw him ending when he returned to the corridor, and this time he said that Barry Dawson was very anxious. I was eventually able to get closer to the exact time because we went back to the theater records and it showed that Mr. Goncalves had brought the patient up into theater at five past ten, so adding on ten minutes to get back to the corridor he would have seen the agitated Barry Dawson much later than he had originally stated."

Jane noticed how Shepherd doodled on his notepad before looking around the room.

"I am just estimating this, sir, but going on the original time line from WDC Tennison, our victim Shirley Dawson could have been dead shortly after 8:30 a.m. I made some further inquiries and then spoke with another porter in their rest room at St. Thomas' and he checked over the old listings of on and off duty porters. He kept on referring to something being the 'Rose Cottage' duty and when I asked him what he meant he said that it was the porters' joke terminology for the mortuary."

Jane wrote this down and underlined it because she had never heard it mentioned before.

"Barry Dawson had a body to take to the mortuary at just after 8 a.m. When I went over there, a number of bodies were actually lined up, obviously covered over. Apparently there is often a delay or backlog . . . but Dawson delivered the body on time. So if we go by the time frame, he dropped off the body at 8 a.m. and was not seen again until after 10 a.m."

Everyone waited as Tomlinson lit a cigarette, drew on it deeply and then exhaled the smoke before he continued.

"Along with Detective Johnston, who was with me at the hospital, we checked out the mortuary. The main doors into the mortuary are directly across a courtyard into the hospital, and there is an exit door that opens straight onto the street."

At this point Johnston, a young, fresh-faced officer, took over.

"We decided that it would be possible for Dawson to take off his porter's jacket and leave the mortuary via the street exit without being seen. We then timed the journey from the mortuary to Dawson's address. If he got a taxi he could travel there in under half an hour. There are also a number of bus routes that he could have taken and that would add a good half-hour on to his journey. But it is possible that he could have returned to his flat, and been there at around 8:45 a.m."

Jane leaned forward, taking it all in. Her annoyance at not being involved was superseded by excitement. She was stunned by the amount of basic legwork the detectives had achieved, and by what they were suggesting.

Shepherd nodded his approval.

"Well done. I don't suppose you were able to find any witnesses who actually saw Dawson leave the mortuary?"

"No, sir, but at that time in the morning the hospital is very busy with breakfasts and patients waiting to go into theater for operations."

Again Shepherd tapped the page in front of him with the tip of his pencil.

"So, let's just walk through what we've got . . . Shirley is expecting mother-in-law to babysit. She prepares her little girl's food, then puts her in the playpen. She has a hair appointment for 9:30 a.m. and is maybe ironing the blouse she is going to wear. The doorbell goes, and this might even coincide with the phone ringing, but Shirley buzzes open the front door. It is possible that it was Katrina Harcourt, but Shirley is expecting her mother-in-law so she presses the door release. Shirley was already suspicious that her husband is having an affair, and has even taken photographs of this woman. Then there is a bitter argument—"

"Could I just interrupt here, sir?" It was Tomlinson again. "What I didn't mention was the fact that inside the porters' rest room there is a phone that connects to the wards. You can't make any outgoing calls as it's just intended for calling the porters for duties, and is an extension. If Katrina Harcourt worked as a nurse at the hospital she would be aware of the extension number and could actually call the hospital directly and ask to be put through to the porters' rest room."

"That's supposition, isn't it? Unless you have a witness who saw Dawson take a call in the rest room early that morning?"

"No luck, sir. But Dawson was there, and was on his way to the mortuary. It's possible that Katrina Harcourt could have contacted him there to tell him his wife was dead."

Shepherd rubbed his head and checked his watch. Lawrence pointed to the photographs of the iron and the wound to Shirley's head.

"Not dead but unconscious. We can conjecture what might have happened next . . . Barry returns and he and Katrina run a bath. Maybe Shirley started to come round, struggled, hit her head on the tap . . . they might even have held her down . . . It's imperative we find a time frame that confirms that the pair had liaised together."

"Of course it bloody is," Shepherd replied. "Did Barry and Katrina plan this murder? Or did Katrina, who may possibly have been wearing the patent leather high-heeled shoes and was maybe let into the flat by Shirley, become part of a spur of the moment attack? Because we have to be on firm ground to charge this duo."

Shepherd glanced at his watch. "Let's take a late lunch break, and be on standby for the interrogations this afternoon."

Jane returned to the incident room and flopped into her chair. She was exhausted and felt completely deflated. She knew that every one of the detectives had worked from the information that she had compiled, and she had received no credit for it. It was as if she hardly existed.

DS Lawrence appeared in the doorway and gave her a rueful smile.

"Well, that was impressive in there. I have to say, when old Shepherd gets to work he really shows his experience."

"And everything that I had reported was taken and used, but not one of them even looked in my direction."

"Get over it, Jane—they all worked their butts off."

"And I didn't? If it wasn't for me, Shirley Dawson would have been buried by now!"

Lawrence held up both hands in a gesture of peace.

"Look, I'm just on my way to the Dawsons' flat to check the rubbish bins . . . do you want to come along?"

"Why not? Give me the dirty work . . ."

Edith watched with narrowed eyes as Jane followed Lawrence out.

Jane sat in the passenger seat of the patrol car. Lawrence found a parking space a short distance from the Dawsons' building and together they moved down the basement steps, the old iron gate swinging back on its rusty hinges.

Lawrence wrenched open the wooden door into the old coal hole of the property. The bricks were coated in dusty cobwebs and the curved walled outbuilding had a grid in the ceiling that, in the old days, would have been opened and filled with coal for the fires in the house. Now it only contained four large lidded bins with flat numbers painted on each. They opened the bin labeled "Top Floor." It was empty but still had a very strong odor of moldy food and soiled nappies.

"Nothing here," Lawrence said, replacing the lid.

"Did you empty that bucket we saw in the bathroom?" Jane asked. "No."

"Well, maybe somebody else did . . ."

"Yes," he said tetchily, checking the other bins. Two of them contained a lot of paper bags and rubbish.

"Mrs. Dawson told me there used to be a person that cleaned the hallways, a sort of maintenance cleaner, who was hired by the landlord. But he'd got rid of her, so Shirley would have had to cart the rubbish down the stairs."

"What is the point to this, Jane?"

"It's the small trapdoor by the front door. You would put your bags of rubbish inside, lock it and the maintenance cleaner would collect them on certain days and take them down to the basement for you."

Jane sensed that she was irritating Lawrence, but couldn't really see why. As they still had the house keys they let themselves in and moved up the stairs to the top floor. They could see that the ground-floor flat had blocked in their trapdoor, and the same on the newly decorated second-floor flat. Workmen were inside painting, and from the amount of packing cases and boxes it looked as if a new kitchen and bathroom had been delivered.

They reached the top floor, and Lawrence sniffed. He bent down and slid the small bolt across the trapdoor to remove a dirty bag full of moldy food and soiled nappies. Without saying a word, he took the bag downstairs with Jane following quickly behind. Lawrence placed the stinking rubbish bag in the boot of the patrol car and they headed back to the station.

In the incident room Lawrence tipped the bag out onto a desk covered with newspapers. Ignoring Edith's protests, he began to pick through the rubbish. The stench was overwhelming. There were old milk cartons, clusters of rice and baby food, dirty disposable nappies, and even an old terry nappy had been thrown out. There were dog food tins and numerous soup and baked bean cans. Caught on the edge of a jagged tin lid was a small, folded, pale pink gingham headscarf. On one side of the scarf was a burnt V scorched into the cotton, with strands of dark hair attached.

Lawrence glanced at Jane and carefully used a pair of tongs to place the scarf into a paper bag. It was a very important find because it meant it had to have been removed from the victim by the person that struck Shirley across her head. The question was who had willfully murdered Shirley by placing her unconscious body in the bath?

DI Gibbs opened the door and instantly covered his nose.

"Christ . . . what is the stink in here?"

"Rubbish from the Dawsons' bins. How was Katrina?"

"She's being held in cell one. She's refused to have a solicitor and is creating merry hell."

He handed over the patent leather shoes in an evidence bag, and perched on the edge of the desk.

"You do know Katrina's mother has changed her statement regarding the day her daughter went to London? But we checked with the petrol station where the father holds an account—they verified that he authorized for her to fill the tank of her Mini on the seventh of October. We might be able to use this when we question her."

Lawrence reacted. "At the same time, we don't actually have a witness that saw her in London that day."

"I know. Are you in on the interrogation, Paul?"

Lawrence shook his head. "Nope, I'm down to be in when they question Barry Dawson. But I want to get this over to the lab to do a few checks."

DS Lawrence gestured to Jane. "Right, I've got everything I need . . . you can get rid of the rest of it." Before Jane could protest he'd already left.

Jane found it really extraordinary that both men seemed capable of not only talking across her but completely ignoring her presence. When they left the incident room Jane looked over to Edith.

"Am I invisible?" Jane asked tetchily.

"Yes, dear . . . that's why I'm doing clerical work. I got frozen out of any hope for promotion and this job will pay toward my pension. You can't change anything, as I have repeatedly told you. And you had better supply this incident room with some form of air freshener. That disgusting heap of rubbish should have been taken to the laboratory, not tipped out here. God forbid that DCI Shepherd should come in—it smells like a lavatory."

Jane began to wrap the newspaper around the remains of the rubbish as Edith continued speaking.

"Do you know why we put up with it? I'll tell you why . . . DCI Shepherd may have a rather pasty face, and thin twitchy fingers, but you underestimate him at your peril. I know he's had words with you, as have I, and I can tell that you're not exactly a happy bunny, but I'm not asking you to lick DCI Shepherd's boots . . . although there are some here that are more than happy to do so—"

She stopped abruptly as DCI Shepherd appeared in the doorway.

"I want you to sit in on the Katrina Harcourt interrogation, WDC Tennison. Fifteen minutes, my office."

Jane nodded, and waited for him to leave before she looked at Edith. She had two bright pink spots on her cheeks.

"Oh God, do you think he heard me?"

Jane, heading off to dispose of the rubbish, said "I don't think he heard you."

"Thank God. He's got the stealth of an ocelot."

CHAPTER NINETEEN

The door was ajar so Jane went into DCI Shepherd's office, knocking respectfully before she entered. Shepherd turned and nodded toward her as he carried on sifting through notes and statements. He checked his watch as she waited patiently, then instructed her to place a hard-backed chair up against the far wall. Sitting at his desk he motioned for her to put in place another chair directly in front of him.

"Right, you sit back there. I don't want you to be in her peripheral vision but I need to see you. If I nod my head toward you I want you to give a slight cough and I will make some kind of interaction with you . . . not sure what yet . . . I think it is going to take a lot of work to unnerve this lady."

"What . . . when I sit behind her?"

"Yes. I've used these tactics before—the interviewee just needs to be aware of someone behind them. It unsettles them, and by coughing you will distract her and give me the opportunity to choose my next line of questioning."

Jane was still unsure of what Shepherd's intentions were, but placed the chair for Katrina Harcourt as requested. She then went and sat at the far end of the room. DS Lawrence knocked and entered. He was carrying a large evidence bag containing the patent leather shoes.

"Put them on the desk," Shepherd said, and then asked how Katrina was behaving.

"Fairly quiet; she's not said anything and is refusing to have a solicitor present. She was more irritated than emotional in the car from Hove. She's sitting in the small interview room with DI Gibbs and had been given a cup of coffee and a cigarette when I last saw her."

"What about Barry Dawson?"

"He's in cell two, as it was empty. But he seems much more upset than Katrina. He asked us to call his mother, not a solicitor, as he wants her to know where he is."

"Thoughtful son . . ." Shepherd said, then checked his watch again.

"Right, let's have a go at her, shall we? If you get DI Gibbs to start on Mr. Dawson then we can swap over, all right?"

A few minutes later DS Lawrence came back into the office with Katrina Harcourt. She was wearing a tailored green linen suit and white blouse with high-heeled leather court shoes. Her flame red hair was loose and hung in natural curls to her shoulders. Jane took a good look. She had very pale skin and yet her eyes were enhanced by thick mascara lashes and dark gray-green eye shadow. She wore no jewelry.

Jane listened as Shepherd quietly went through the reason Katrina was being questioned, informing her again that she had the right to have a solicitor present if she wished. There was a brief moment when Katrina turned around to look directly at Jane. A flash of recognition registered on her face. She then sat straight-backed in the chair, facing ahead. She spoke in a very calm, clear voice and crossed her legs as if unconcerned about why she was being interviewed.

"I declined having a solicitor present because I have done nothing wrong. I would like to know why I have been subjected to having my poor parents' home searched and why I have been brought here for questioning with regard to Mr. Dawson's wife."

"You have been told that you are under arrest for murder, Miss Harcourt, but let's hope this unfortunate situation can be dealt with very expediently so that you can return home."

Jane noticed how charming Shepherd appeared, as if he was only interested in gaining Katrina's confidence and was on her side. He leaned back in his chair, smiling at her.

"Let's just go through the scenario, Miss Harcourt, because you have admitted quite freely that you do not want any representation. Is that correct?"

"Yes, simply because why would I need anyone to represent me when I have done nothing wrong? I have said from the outset that I have never met Barry Dawson's wife. I have also admitted, and I am not proud of this at all, that I did have a very brief affair with him because I was unaware that he was married, or that he had a young child. When I discovered this and found out that he had lied to me I ended the relationship immediately. I also left my place of work, since being there meant that I would obviously come into contact with him as we were both employed at the same hospital."

"That was very commendable of you." Shepherd casually glanced through the statements in front of him, then looked up.

"It must have been very distressing for you when your engagement to a doctor and hopes for future marriage were shattered, and the wedding never took place. Then to form a relationship with Mr. Dawson only to discover he had lied to you about his circumstances . . ."

Katrina shrugged her shoulders.

"Yes, but then I am too trusting . . . some would call me foolish."

"Oh, you seem to be a very intelligent woman to me. Nevertheless, you must have felt some degree of anger toward Mr. Dawson, perhaps even his wife?"

"I couldn't be angry with her as I never met her. As I said previously, as soon as I found out, although I was obviously hurt, I ended the relationship."

"I understand. Perhaps you could just clarify for me if this is you in this photograph?"

Shepherd held the three photographs that Jane had found on the film in the camera at the Dawsons' flat. He laid one down like a playing card and pushed it toward the edge of the desk so Katrina could clearly see it.

"Is this you, Miss Harcourt?"

She leaned forward and looked at the small black and white photograph.

"Yes."

"Where was this taken?"

She sat back in her chair and looked up to the ceiling.

"I don't recall."

"Take another look, Miss Harcourt."

She looked again, then prodded it with one finger.

"I think it might be in Regent's Park."

"What about this one?"

Shepherd placed down the second photograph.

"This is you again, isn't it?"

"Yes, I think it might be again . . . I mean, it is me, but it could have been in the park again."

"But you're not wearing the same coat?"

"I don't recall it being taken as it appears to have been taken when I was unaware."

"What about the third one, Miss Harcourt? Again you are wearing a different outfit. So it is quite possible these were taken on different days and at different times."

"If you say so."

"These were taken by Shirley Dawson. So it is clear that she was aware of you, and knew that you and her husband were having an affair."

"Maybe she was suspicious . . . I mean, he is obviously a liar. As I have said, I had no idea that he was married and had a daughter."

"So Shirley Dawson never approached you?"

"No, I never met her."

"Did you go to their flat?"

"No, I did not."

"So tell me, Miss Harcourt, how did you find out that Barry Dawson was not only married but also a father?"

"He told me."

"Yes, but was there some reason why he admitted to you that he had lied? Because it was quite serious, wasn't it? He had given you a ring?"

Jane could see Katrina's body tense as she swiveled in her chair and flicked back her long hair. Shepherd remained at ease, picking up the three photographs and stacking them together, tapping the edges of the desk. He appeared to be very calm, almost as if he was having a friendly conversation with the suspect rather than an interrogation. Jane found his demeanor interesting as she had never seen any of her other senior officers, particularly Moran, conducting an interview in such a relaxed manner.

"Did someone tell you that Barry was married, so you then brought it up with him? Or did he just come out with it and say 'Look here, this has got to end as I am a married man and have a family'?"

"I don't remember."

"You don't remember? Well, that's very strange. I mean, here we have photographs of you that were taken when you were unaware. One in the park, maybe two in the park . . . one you can't recall where you were . . . but you're wearing different coats. So these might have been meetings with Mr. Dawson, witnessed by his wife and taken as proof he was having an affair, do you agree with that?"

"It's possible, but if you are trying to get me to admit that she approached me or that I met up with her, then prove it. I never met her . . . I never went to their home."

"Did he promise to marry you, like your previous lover, the doctor?"

Shepherd glanced toward Jane and inclined his head slightly. Jane coughed and Katrina swiveled around to look at her. She said nothing, smirked and turned back again. DCI Shepherd changed the subject and raised his voice.

"You knew he owned his flat, which was worth a considerable amount of money, and believed he had every intention of selling it to finance your future together, especially as you were in debt due to losing a considerable amount of money paying for wedding photographs and bridal outfits that were never worn."

Jane could see Katrina crossing and uncrossing her legs as Shepherd continued, in his unnerving, quiet way, to put the pressure on.

"So when exactly did you find out it was all lies, that he had no intention of ever marrying you, that there was no future, and no intention of selling his home because he loved his wife?"

"I do not recall exactly how I found out, but when I did I confronted him and he admitted that he had lied and was ashamed."

"But you must have been angry. He was the second man to let you down, and this time he was, as you described, 'just a porter,' not even a qualified doctor."

"I wasn't angry, just upset that I had made the mistake of trusting him."

Shepherd glanced at Jane and again she gave a light cough. Katrina turned to glare at her.

"But you are known to have quite a volatile temper, aren't you? And you do skirt the truth, Miss Harcourt, because I am aware that you did not leave the hospital because of your emotional turmoil about discovering that Mr. Dawson had lied to you. Your contract was in actual fact terminated, and this had occurred numerous times before—you were accused of unprofessional conduct, specifically toward dementia patients at—"

Katrina stood up and Shepherd immediately gestured, calmly and quietly, for her to sit down again. Then he spoke quite sharply.

"Please, Miss Harcourt, remain seated. If you refuse I will have you removed from my office. You may disagree with accusations of unprofessional conduct but we do have them from your previous employers. I apologize if what I am saying is distressing but I am trying to ascertain exactly how Shirley Dawson died."

"If you can prove that I am lying then go ahead. I never met the woman and I was never at their flat. All I know is that she drowned in her bath."

"Could you please tell us exactly where you were on Monday the seventh of October?"

"This is absolutely ridiculous! I have already explained where I was—I was at home, and my mother can confirm it."

"On the contrary, Miss Harcourt. Your mother, when asked where you were on that date, recalled clearly that you had left home very early in the morning. And the reason that she remembered that you had gone to London was because you needed petrol for the journey, and asked permission to use your father's petrol account."

Katrina laughed.

"Listen to me . . . My mother is menopausal, she can't remember one day from the next. Surely it all makes sense that I had to use my father's account—I had no money on me and was therefore clearly not planning a long journey to London. I did come to London on a regular basis but I totally deny that I was anywhere near their flat on Monday the seventh of October. If you have a witness that saw me there then put me in an identity parade! I was not there, and have never been to Barry Dawson's flat . . . and *I never met his wife.*"

She sat back in her chair, folding her arms and smiling. Shepherd looked at Jane and yet again she made a soft coughing sound. This time Katrina not only turned to look at her but snapped, "You enjoying looking at my back, are you?"

Shepherd responded. "I'm sorry if she is unnerving you, Miss Harcourt. WDC Tennison, please come with me."

"She's not unnerving me," Katrina said, as Jane followed Shepherd out of the room.

He closed the door behind them and said to Jane, "Go over with me exactly what the neighbor told you about seeing the shoes. I'm not going to bring them up, but she's a hard nut to crack and I need to get her to admit to going to the Dawsons' flat."

Jane repeated that Mrs. Cook said she had seen whoever wore the shoes pacing back and forth on the pavement, and then heard the front door clicking open.

Shepherd nodded. "She's very confident about not being seen entering or, for that matter, leaving the flat. We have no evidence she was in there but I believe she was. I also think they are going to back each other's story up. You go and talk to DI Gibbs—ask him to leave Dawson alone and make out there is a breakthrough. Let's see if we can put the pressure on him, and I'll keep on going with her. Give it ten minutes, then return to my office and take up your seat. But pass me notes . . . scribble anything on them."

"Yes, sir."

Jane tapped on the glass panel of the interview room door. Gibbs looked up, told the officer to remain with Dawson and stepped out into the corridor to talk to Jane.

She told him, "So far DCI Shepherd has been unable to break Katrina Harcourt. She is insisting she didn't go anywhere near Dawson's flat, but he is certain they are both involved. He wants you to shake Dawson up and act as if Katrina is giving evidence that implicates him, to see if you can unnerve him."

"Terrific . . . he's not shown any break in his original statement, and keeps crying."

"Apparently he can bring on the tears. Katrina, in contrast, seems to be almost enjoying herself."

Gibbs nodded and was about to walk back into the interview room when Jane tapped his arm.

"Just a thought . . . all those calls he made from the hospital—if Barry knew his mother was going to be babysitting for Heidi but then couldn't come because she had to wait for the washing machine engineer, why did he become so anxious when Shirley didn't answer the phone? Logically it would make sense that she had taken Heidi to the hair salon with her, and he knew she had an appointment."

"I'm not following you."

"If we are going on the assumption that Barry was contacted by Katrina and left the hospital to meet her at his flat, they could have drowned Shirley in the bath . . . But they would have to leave before his mother turned up to babysit."

Gibbs ran his hands through his hair anxiously.

"But this is all supposition . . . We don't know if either of them were at the flat."

"I know we don't, Spence, but it is a possible scenario. I remember Rita Dawson saying to me that if she'd been on time she would have found Shirley . . . Do you understand, Spence? If Barry Dawson went back to the hospital to secure his alibi, he left his little girl Heidi all on her own."

"OK, OK . . . I'll give it a shot."

Jane made copious notes to hand to Shepherd as if there had been a development and returned to his office.

"Come in, WDC Tennison," Shepherd said curtly. Jane approached his desk and passed him the notes. Then, turning her back toward Katrina, she whispered, "Please read these, sir . . . it is very important."

Shepherd glanced down at her notes and showed no reaction at first. He seemed to be reading every line before a tense expression slowly formed.

"Excellent. Please take your seat, WDC Tennison."

"Yes, sir."

DI Gibbs took his time settling back in his chair. Dawson was chewing his lips.

"I am sure you know we are questioning Katrina Harcourt. There appear to be some discrepancies in the timing regarding the phone calls you made when trying to reach Shirley."

Dawson shrugged and said defensively that he had been worried because the last time he had seen his wife she had been very nervous, and it was a usual arrangement that he called to check on her at that time in the morning.

"What time did you leave home to start work at the hospital?"

"It was the early shift, so I left about six . . . six fifteen."

"You have admitted that you were worried about your wife, but did not actually attempt to call her until just after ten o'clock?"

"I was on duty so I couldn't call her before that time."

"But you did speak to your mother, and she told you that she was unable to babysit as she had a problem with her washing machine?"

"Yes."

"What time did you discover this?"

"I don't understand."

"It's very simple, Mr. Dawson . . . if you had been able to contact your mother and knew she was no longer able to babysit, why did you not call your wife until a considerable time later?"

"I was out of change."

"So, when eventually you did get the change to call your wife over an hour later, why did you become so alarmed . . . surely she'd gone to her hair appointment?"

"Because she didn't answer."

"But the logical response would surely have been that if your mother was no longer able to babysit, your wife would have taken your daughter with her to the hair salon?"

"I wasn't thinking that way."

"Why not?"

"I just wasn't . . . Shirley was not very well when I left."

"At six fifteen that morning?"

"Yes, so I went back home as soon as I could."

"Was your concern about your wife because she had found out about your affair with Katrina Harcourt?"

For the first time Barry was not quite so confident.

"No . . . that was not the reason."

"But she found out, didn't she?"

"Well, yes . . . but I had ended it all. I loved my wife and there was no question that we would divorce."

"Oh, so that had been a possibility, had it?"

"*No*! It was a stupid thing to have done, and I regretted it. It was just a one-night stand and it didn't mean anything to me."

"So Shirley just accepted that you had finished the affair? What about the photographs? When did she take the photographs of Katrina Harcourt?"

"Before . . . I mean, she suspected and took the pictures to confront me."

"Sorry, can we just go back on that? Are you admitting that you did in actual fact know about these photographs?"

"Yes, all right, yes, I did know, and Shirley told me that she'd seen me with a woman. She didn't know who she was, and I admitted to her that I had been very stupid, and that I regretted it and never wanted to hurt her."

"On the morning Shirley died what time did Katrina Harcourt call you at the hospital?"

Dawson pressed his body back into the chair and started shaking his head.

"I never received any call from her . . . as I keep on telling you, it was over between us. I have told you the truth! I called home and was worried about Shirley, so I left the hospital."

Gibbs felt as though he was getting nowhere, even with the scenario Jane had put forward. Basically they had no evidence to counteract Dawson's original statement.

DCI Shepherd was equally frustrated at going over the same ground. Katrina remained very controlled and uncooperative. She still insisted that she had never met Shirley Dawson and had never been to the Dawsons' flat.

"So you are admitting that you were having an affair with Barry Dawson, but you say that you have never visited his home?"

"Yes."

"How did you react when Barry told you that it was over between you?"

"How do you expect me to react? I was very hurt. I would say that has to be rather obvious. He made me promises and then confessed that he had lied."

"That he was not only married but had fathered a little girl?"

"Yes," Katrina almost hissed.

"And you just accepted that you had been treated as a casual sex partner, and that he had no intention of leaving his wife for you."

"That is pretty succinct . . . but what alternative did I have?"

"Divorce?"

"She wouldn't consider it."

Katrina knew as soon as she had said it that she had made a mistake and Shepherd was on to it. Jane listened intently, observing how he had cast his line and was now reeling it in.

"So you did discuss the possibility of Mr. Dawson divorcing his wife?"

Katrina was on edge for the first time, patting the hem of her pencil skirt as it rested on her knee.

"I think he might have suggested it . . . but I can't recall, because at the time I was shocked."

"So, Mr. Dawson suggested it but Shirley wouldn't agree? Then there would be the matter of custody of their daughter, and obviously if they were to contemplate a divorce then would Shirley agree to move out of their flat?"

Katrina was tight lipped.

"We never even discussed that as a possibility. This is really starting to be very tedious . . ."

"When you were let into Mr. Dawson's flat on Monday the seventh of October, did you confront Shirley regarding your relationship with her husband?"

Katrina had the audacity to laugh, shaking her head and threading her fingers through her long curls.

"This is preposterous! I was never in that flat, and I never met Shirley Dawson."

Shepherd looked over Katrina's shoulder at Jane. She could sense that he knew he had lost his catch, and for the first time he snapped angrily.

"What time did you call Mr. Dawson to tell him that you had struck his wife? Because that is what happened, isn't it, Miss Harcourt? You rang the doorbell and Shirley buzzed you inside the building."

Katrina lifted her eyes to the ceiling, laughing.

"I am giving you a way out to explain how it happened, Miss Harcourt, that it was never your intention to physically hurt Shirley Dawson," Shepherd shouted.

Katrina uncrossed her legs and leaned forward with a faint smile.

"I was never there, and you have no proof that I was."

CHAPTER TWENTY

Jane was in the CID office with DI Gibbs and DS Lawrence.

"Right now we have nothing to implicate either one of them," Gibbs said.

Jane replied, "Apart from the fact that one or other of them removed that headscarf, and put it into the rubbish bin after Shirley was hit with the red-hot iron."

Lawrence was fed up. "We know *who* was hit, Tennison, we don't know which one of them did it, and whether or not they were in it together. I've taken Katrina's fingerprints and I'll be back first thing tomorrow morning for another search of the Dawsons' flat."

Katrina Harcourt and Barry Dawson had been taken back to the cells pending further questioning on suspicion of murder. The duty sergeant was organizing meal trays to be taken to both the prisoners who had been kept separated and not allowed to see or speak to one another. DCI Shepherd had left, true to his usual time-keeping, in order to be at home with his family by 7 p.m.

"Barry could have left the hospital at 8:30 a.m., arrived home at—"

Gibbs interrupted.

"Please, Jane . . . 'could have' and 'might have' is not good enough . . . we have to find conclusive evidence to prove either one of them killed Shirley. Right now we can't prove it, and after this afternoon's questioning both of them will be lawyered up tomorrow."

"What if we don't find anything?" Jane asked.

"They'll walk . . ."

Lawrence headed out of the room, then paused.

"You both want a drink? I'm going over to the pub."

"Not for me, I need to be on my toes for the next round of questioning," Gibbs said, walking into his office.

"What about you, Jane?"

"No thanks, but could I come to the Dawsons' flat tomorrow?"

"Sure. I'll be there at 7:30 a.m. as I want to be back for the next round of interviews as well as Spencer, but I need a beer right now."

After Lawrence had left Jane typed up her report and filed it as the night duty staff took over. She was about to head out when, with a pang of guilt, she remembered Marie Allard. Jane took out her notebook and dialed the number she had tried to call the previous evening.

Marie jumped as she heard the phone ring. She was in her dressing gown after taking a long bath to calm herself, and the children were asleep. The sound of the phone made her shake. She walked slowly down the stairs, and in the semi-dark hallway the ivory-colored plastic phone looked ominous and threatening as it rang and rang. Marie was afraid to answer it in case it was that awful woman singing "Angie, Angie . . . ," the dreadful sound of the grating rasping voice. Or it might be her mother-in-law who was putting her nerves on edge with all her questions. She knew it couldn't be Peter as it was too late, and lights in the cells would already be out.

Marie reached the last step and stretched her hand out to pick up the receiver and answer.

Back in the CID office Jane replaced the receiver, having let it ring for ages. Perhaps it was too late to call. She made a mental note to herself to call earlier tomorrow. Marie held the receiver up to her ear and could only hear the dead tone vibrating as the call had been terminated. She started to cry and was soon sobbing uncontrollably. She was so afraid and didn't have anyone to turn to.

* * *

DI Moran was going out for a curry with some of his team at their favorite local Indian, the Star of India. It had been a busy day, arresting two thugs who were trying to get protection money from a local betting shop. They turned out to be rather sad figures, old-time gangsters, who were still reminiscing about the infamous Kray twins, who had dominated organized crime in the 1950s and 1960s. Both of the old thugs were pensioners and would probably get a heavy sentence due to their previous convictions, quite apart from the fact that they had used an old sawed-off shotgun. Moran suspected that as he was a good half an hour late the lads would already be stuck into the lager, and he had asked them to order him a vindaloo. He was just crossing Mare Street when he saw her. Janet Brown wasn't wearing her usual blue rabbit fur coat, but instead she had on a thick, brightly colored Mexican poncho and a leather cowboy hat. She had her little boy in a pushchair, laden down with bags of groceries on the handles. Moran zigzagged behind her.

"Not working tonight, Janet?"

She whipped around to face him.

"What're you doing scaring the effin' life out of me?"

He laughed. "Just checking you're OK."

Moran bent down and rested back on his heels as he touched the little boy's face.

"You got anything for me?"

"No . . . I'll be in touch, though."

"Good girl . . . you look after yourself." He had slipped a five pound note into the little boy's hand. Janet gave him a brief nod and hurriedly walked away.

Moran was now in the mood to get hammered. He pulled off his tie, undid his shirt collar, and sashayed down the road toward the Star of India for a good night out with the boys.

* * *

By the time Jane arrived at the Dawsons' flat Lawrence had been there for a while. She rang the bell for the top flat and heard the loud buzzer allowing her entry. She carried two takeaway coffees and two bacon sandwiches and headed up the stairs. The flat door was open.

"Hi there, it's me . . . and I've brought breakfast."

Lawrence was bending over an upturned table, carefully brushing the black fingerprint dust around the underside of the rim.

"Great, I'm starving. Just hoping whoever did the cleanup here might have just done the top surfaces and forgotten to test the underneath of the table. The table was pushed away from the ironing board, right?"

"I think so, yes. We got no prints off the iron, taps, bath or basin. I mean, they did quite a cleanup job."

"Telling me," he said, as he continued to dust the underside of the table with fingerprint powder. He found nothing, and broke open his sandwich wrapper.

"Tell me about Spencer Gibbs . . . is he all right?"

Jane was opening up her sandwich too.

"How do you mean?"

"Well, totally off the record . . . and by that I mean this is between you and me . . . he's been drinking heavily and was out of his head last night. I know that DCI Bradfield's death really hit him hard and he's not getting himself back together. What do you think?"

Jane couldn't look him in the face and simply shrugged her shoulders.

"I didn't think he was going to have a drink last night."

"Well, he came into the pub, and he'd already had a few."

"I think we all took it hard . . . but you know Spencer is a big character and they always backed each other up."

"Maybe that's it, but he should get back singing with his rock band to let off the steam . . . last night he was completely out of it."

Jane was unable to finish her sandwich and her coffee tasted tepid. She wrapped them up in the plastic bag ready to dump in the bin later. She didn't want to think about DCI Bradfield now, didn't want to feel that awful pain in the pit of her stomach. She changed the subject.

"We need to time exactly how long it takes to walk from here to St. Thomas' and to get a taxi. I have a rough idea . . . but then it is possible that if Katrina was here and they are in this together she could have driven him back to the hospital in good time."

"Yeah . . . Get some photos of a Mini the same color as Katrina's—we might get lucky. But then again we might not . . . we've not had much going for us on this one."

They worked well together. Lawrence instructed Jane to check through all the family photo albums to search for any pictures that might have been taken of Katrina. She found none, but there were numerous photos of Shirley wearing the gingham scarf like Audrey Hepburn, tucked in a little bow just beneath her chin. Jane was moved as Shirley had been such a pretty young woman, her thick curly hair sometimes worn in braids and sometimes in a top knot. She wore very fashionable thick black eyeliner and pale pink lipstick. In a number of photographs she was wearing white knee-high boots and a mini-skirt, and Jane thought she looked like one of The Supremes.

There were other photos that were not as glamorous, but Jane decided that Shirley was probably quite aware of her good looks as she played up to the camera and was very coquettish with her lips pursed. Even when she was pregnant she was wearing pretty smock dresses. All of the images were a far cry from that sad wretched drowned woman Jane had lifted out of the bath.

"Can you do me a favor?" Lawrence asked, making her jump. "I'm about ready to go back to the station but I just want you to do something for me. Act out the scenario I'm trying to piece together, will you?"

"Yes, of course. I haven't found any other photos of Katrina in the albums."

Lawrence asked Jane to stand at the ironing board. It was positioned in the exact place they had first found it and its position meant that Jane's back was facing the front door. Lawrence spoke quietly to himself as Jane stood still and he walked around her. He stopped by the high chair and touched the playpen.

"Shirley was ironing. Maybe she intended to wear the blouse that was on the board. She had prepared the baby's bottle, dressed her and laid out the food for her breakfast on the high chair. She was expecting her mother-in-law to babysit so that she could go to the hairdresser."

Jane turned and touched her head.

"The scarf . . . she could have put the scarf on to keep her hair back while she took a bath."

Lawrence nodded and then turned to the bathroom.

"She could have been running a bath ready for herself, which would mean she was not wearing underwear, just the dressing gown."

Jane agreed. "Yes, if she had been wearing underwear it would not have been on the floor beneath the dressing gown but on top of it."

Lawrence frowned in concentration. "If she leaves the iron on, the doorbell rings and she clicks the buzzer, expecting it to be her mother-in-law. Then she goes to the bathroom to turn off the taps and in walks Katrina, who she knows is having an affair with her husband. So seeing her walking into their flat would be like a red rag to a bull."

Jane sighed. Yet again there was no proof that this was what had occurred.

"Jane, listen, there has to be something in this bloody place. We've searched drawers and wardrobes but you start again. I am going to move inch by inch over that bathroom . . . I won't give up."

Jane started searching through a stack of magazines left piled up in the bedroom. They were teenage magazines and nothing glossy or expensive. She sat on the bed flicking through them but nothing was stuck inside, or any articles even earmarked or turned down. She glanced at the bedside clock. It was coming up to almost 8:30 a.m. and she placed the stack back beside the bed. She had already searched beneath the bed and on top of the wardrobe. The flat was not very clean or hygienic, and she felt dirty and frustrated. She told Lawrence that she wanted to get out for a few minutes and take a breather.

He looked at her in surprise. "Sure, go ahead."

"I just want to make a call." She used it as an excuse but then decided that she had not been very professional in failing to return Marie Allard's call, so she would do it now.

"Fine by me. I'm coming up with bugger all in here . . ."

Jane took her purse out of her handbag to get coins for the phone on the landing. As she headed down the stairs she heard a loud crash and hurried down to the landing to see the landlord, Mr. De Silva, standing next to a builder who was chiseling the call box loose from the wall.

"What are you doing?" Jane asked, concerned.

"Having this phone taken out . . . waste of bloody money as I have to pay the rental on it. I'm putting a landline in the flat below and they've got their own on the ground floor. This is hardly used up here anyway, and I want to redecorate the hallway."

There was an ominous creaking sound as the wooden surrounds of the payphone were wrenched from the wall. Jane headed back up the stairs.

"Well, that was a waste of time . . . the landlord is ripping the phone out of the wall, said it wasn't worth the rental he has to pay and that it's hardly used."

Jane picked up her purse ready to put the coins away when Lawrence grabbed her wrist.

"Coins! If Katrina used the phone to call Dawson, she would have had to put coins into the call box and then left her fingerprints on them."

Jane didn't really hear all of what Lawrence was saying as he charged out of the flat and leaped down the stairs. There was a lot of raised voices and unpleasantness from De Silva before the entire piece of equipment was removed from the wall and wrapped in a sheet. Jane watched DS Lawrence carry it carefully down to the waiting patrol car. He was eager to work on it in the lab and he drove off with a squeal of tires, not even saying goodbye. Jane locked the Dawsons' flat and returned to the station.

DI Moran felt terrible. He was very hungover and was sick to his stomach. The vindaloo had been hotter than hell and he had had to drop his suit at the dry cleaners on the way to work that morning. DC Edwards was back at his desk and looked over at Moran who was standing holding a glass of Andrews Liver Salts for his hangover.

"I heard it was a good night, sir?"

Moran frowned. "Ruined my bloody suit . . . that idiot Ellis spilled an entire pint down the back of it."

"So you're not feeling too good then, sir?"

"No, I am bloody not."

"I'm feeling better . . ."

"Obviously, now that you are at long last back at work," Moran replied grumpily, as he headed toward his office.

"Have we had any news regarding the Allard trial yet, sir?"

"No, we have not. And your last report, Edwards, which you left unfinished . . ."

"Yes, sir, you told me to check out any previous assaults and rapes that might match Allard's MO . . ."

"Yes?"

"I didn't find any."

"Terrific."

"So I was about to check from when he lived in Maidstone . . ."

"Maidstone? Well, how far back is that? He'd be a bloody teenager?"

"Not quite, sir, he's twenty-nine years old now. It was only five years or so ago."

"And?"

"Well, I wasn't feeling very well . . . had a high temperature . . . so I had to go home, sir."

"Yes, I know that, Edwards."

"We need to check with a DS Victor Bethell."

"Who?"

"I was told we needed to talk to him regarding a missing persons case . . ."

"In Maidstone? What's the connection to Peter Allard, for Chrissakes?" Moran was becoming very impatient.

"Allard was questioned because the missing girl was a Filipino friend of his wife. They never found her . . . her name was Susie Luna."

Moran downed his Andrews Liver Salts and belched loudly.

"Well, let's get onto him then."

* * *

"I wish I could be present at one or other of the interviews," Jane said.

"I doubt it. As I keep on telling you, we are invisible, underpaid and totally unappreciated. Right, I'm going to take these files in to the boys so that they can get started."

Shepherd walked in and Edith flushed, hoping he had not overheard.

"I want DC Tomlinson in with me. And Tennison, I want you in with DI Gibbs. We're one man down with Paul being over at the labs. Pity . . . but when he gets back let's see if he's uncovered anything. Edith, if Lawrence gets a result you interrupt, but we'll be a while before we get started. The longer time we've got the better, as Harcourt is waiting for her lawyer."

Edith handed Shepherd the files and as he walked out she turned and looked at Jane.

"Do you think he heard me having a go? But you know I am telling the truth . . . you got lucky. Can you do Gibbs a favor? Get him to suck one of these Polo mints—he stinks of alcohol."

Just as Edith returned to her desk there was a call from reception to say that a Richard Blake was there to speak to his client, Katrina Harcourt. Edith walked out and Jane went back to looking over her notes. Gibbs appeared and asked where Shepherd was, and Jane said he had just taken all the files to his office.

"Spencer, do you mind if I say something? It's just that you might want to suck one of these . . . you know what Shepherd is like."

He cocked his head to one side as she passed him the half-opened pack of Polo mints. Gibbs shrugged as he left the room and didn't appear to be at all embarrassed by her comment.

Gibbs and Shepherd worked on cross-referencing all the statements taken from Katrina Harcourt and Barry Dawson. They underlined and discussed their different approaches and made detailed notes. They were deep in discussion when Edith knocked on the door and entered.

"There's a Richard Blake here to talk to his client, Katrina Harcourt. He has asked for any disclosures to be discussed with him."

"Disclosures? What is he talking about?" snapped Shepherd.

"Well, he has been hired by her family and he is unaware of why she is under arrest. Despite having been asked by Katrina, the Harcourts have refused to pay for any representation for Barry Dawson and he has now claimed he does not want a solicitor present."

Shepherd smiled. "Well, thank you, Mr. Dawson . . . makes my life a lot easier."

"I think yours might as well, DI Gibbs," Edith said. "I ran a check on Mr. Blake and his chambers are in Victoria, but they are not criminal specialists and deal mostly in property development frauds. Blake is semi-retired and lives in Hove, so he might be a family friend of Miss Harcourt's parents."

Shepherd smiled again and thanked Edith, joking that "The Taming of the Shrew" might not be too problematic. However, when Edith closed the office door he glanced at DI Gibbs.

"You don't have much to go on, so I suggest you kickstart the interview on a tough line. She is going to be a difficult one to break."

CHAPTER TWENTY-ONE

Jane sat at the Formica-topped table, an empty chair beside her. The dank green walls of the partly tiled interview room smelt of stale sweat and nicotine. There were two plastic beakers of water on the table and Gibbs's thick file, with his notebook and pen beside it.

Katrina was brought up from the cells by a uniform officer. She had been allowed a twenty-minute interview with her solicitor, Richard Blake. He had subsequently had another fifteen minutes with DCI Shepherd and was brought into the room by the duty sergeant.

The two hard-backed chairs in front of Jane were close together and she noticed Katrina move hers further apart, as if she didn't want to sit too close to Richard Blake. Unlike his client he appeared very nervous. He placed his worn briefcase beside him as he took out a legal pad and pen. Without makeup Katrina was very pale, her skin translucent. Her green eyes were devoid of mascara and black liner and were red rimmed with blonde lashes. She was wearing the same suit she had been wearing when she had been brought to the station.

Richard Blake introduced himself to Jane but Katrina totally ignored her, and the uniform officer remained standing by the door, which was slightly ajar. Gibbs made his entrance, crunching on the Polo mint Jane had offered him earlier as an attempt to disguise the smell of booze from the night before. He patted the officer's shoulder in a friendly way and then gestured for the door to be closed. He circled around the table, then in a flamboyant manner drew out his chair and swung it round for him to sit, leaving quite a space between himself and the table. He had long legs and Jane edged further away as he stretched them out and crossed his feet at the ankles.

"I am Detective Inspector Spencer Gibbs, and this is Detective Constable Jane Tennison, whom I believe you have met before. Mr. Blake is acting as your solicitor. Basically all I really need to do is make sure you understand the serious charges that are leveled against you, Miss Harcourt, and ask you to answer the relevant questions—"

"Oh, just get on with it," Katrina interrupted him, as she crossed her legs and then ran one hand through her hair. "I know that you don't have a shred of evidence that can prove I even knew Shirley Dawson. I never even went to her flat and this is all preposterous. I do apologize for my crumpled suit, but it is linen, which always creases, and I have been forced to wear the same underwear, and have no makeup or even a hairbrush."

She looked at Spence hoping he'd respond, but he ignored her obvious attempt to win him over.

"According to WDC Tennison, you told her that, to begin with, you were astonished and surprised at yourself for considering having a sexual affair with an ill-educated porter like Barry Dawson. Especially after you were previously engaged to an accomplished and highly qualified doctor. Sadly you were unceremoniously dumped after the wedding banns had been read out in preparation for what would have been quite a society wedding."

Blake leaned forward.

"I really don't see that anything in my client's past has a connection to whether or not she knew Mrs. Dawson."

"Mr. Blake, I feel that there is a strong connection to the humiliating experience of being dumped by one man, and then setting her sights on a much lower level porter, who claims that not only was she just a one-night stand but that he never had any intention of marrying her . . ."

Gibbs had taken advice from DCI Shepherd to keep his questioning low key. Jane knew what he was after but it was not having the effect he was hoping for, as Katrina wasn't rising to the bait as she had done before. But her lawyer was.

"This is completely unacceptable, and purely supposition. My client would never have admitted to a relationship with a man you suggest she felt was of a lower level."

"Oh shut up!" Katrina said. "Can't you see what he is trying to do? If you can't think of anything better to interrupt with then keep your mouth shut . . . he's just trying to goad me into admitting I was connected to that woman's death."

Katrina crossed and uncrossed her legs, then folded her arms, glaring at Gibbs.

"Go on, Detective Gibbs, try and find some other ulterior motive that you think I might possibly have. I have been totally honest with you at all times. I have admitted that I did have an affair but I have also clearly stated that it was over as soon as I knew he was married. He also lied about the fact that he had a child, so I ended the relationship and left St. Thomas' Hospital."

Gibbs leaned forward and drew his file closer as he thumbed through page after page, all the while speaking quietly.

"Yes, this is all nice and tidy and I am sure you think totally believable. But you are a known liar, Miss Harcourt. You were fired from St. Thomas' Hospital, as you have been on numerous previous occasions from various care homes, due to your unprofessional conduct. You have even been quoted as disliking having to work with dementia patients. So let's go back to just how important this so-called fling with Barry Dawson was, because I believe it was pretty desperate on your part."

"Desperate?" Katrina snapped. "Why don't you take a good look at me . . . do you think I look like a desperate woman? You've got a bloody nerve. Take a look at yourself in the mirror. Has anybody ever told you that you stink of BO, and crunching peppermints doesn't hide your beer breath?"

Katrina then looked over at Jane.

"And as for that dull, flat footed Detective Tennison . . . I would describe the pair of YOU as being pretty desperate."

Gibbs ignored her and continued.

"In my estimation, a woman who gets herself into debt buying a designer wedding gown and having herself photographed as a bride before the actual ceremony, and then gets jilted before getting to the altar, must be more than just desperate. Barry Dawson made promises, marriage proposals, and you also knew he owned their flat in a very nice location. All this must have sounded very enticing for a woman whose qualifications restricted her to agency work instead of full-time nursing staff."

"Rubbish, you have no idea just how good the wages are for agency staff."

"I am very aware; you were sharing a bedsit with another nurse, and you don't even own your car."

Katrina pursed her lips and Jane was sure Gibbs was turning the tables as he continued.

"You have a record of unprofessional conduct and abusive behavior working with the elderly. And to still be dependent on your parents . . . All of this would have been a very cumulative build-up to—"

"To what exactly?" Katrina interrupted.

"Getting rid of the woman who stood in your way."

Jane was impressed as Gibbs kept going, but Katrina remained unperturbed. She crossed and uncrossed her legs again and sighed as he continued.

"You couldn't let his cheap little wife stand in your way . . . you wanted him to get a divorce. Mr. Dawson says he ended the affair with you as he knew he had made a gross mistake. So he confessed to his wife about the one-night stand he had with you."

"It was *not* a one-night stand!" Katrina spat. Jane could see that at last there was another small crack in her composure.

Gibbs was now stepping up the game, his voice louder and sharper as he leaned forward at the table.

"Shirley didn't quite believe it was over. So she followed her husband and took photographs of the woman he says was just a cheap one-night stand. Some woman . . . *you* . . . who worked at the hospital and was proving to be desperate and hard to get rid of. You'd been rejected and burned before by someone you rated a lot higher than a porter, so you took it into your own hands and decided you would call on Shirley Dawson."

"I did not."

"We have a witness. You paced up and down outside the building, didn't you? Was that to work your temper up, or in the hope that nobody saw you going inside the Dawsons' flat?"

Katrina looked at Blake. "Why don't you interrupt?" She then turned back to Gibbs. "Nobody saw me . . . as I have said before, if you have a witness then put me in an ID parade."

Gibbs knew he was flying by his shirt tail, but she had just slipped up and he needed to up the ante.

"The point is, Shirley Dawson was not the silly woman you wanted to believe her to be. In fact, she was quite the opposite. Let's face it, she was not only a lot younger than you, and very pretty, but she had something Barry would never let go—his daughter."

"Heidi . . ." Katrina said, in a surly and dismissive manner.

"Ah, so you know the little girl's name? So you must have been aware that Shirley was not about to agree to a divorce or let Barry bring in the 'one-night stand.' So, Miss Harcourt, you were going to be left in the lurch one more time and you were not prepared to take it, so you went to talk to Shirley yourself—"

Katrina interrupted. "I know the child's name because Barry told me. I resent the way you keep on referring to me as a 'one-night stand,' and you . . ." Katrina turned angrily and pointed at her lawyer. "Why are you allowing this to continue? I am getting sick and tired of being shown such disrespect, when the reality is that as soon as I knew Mr. Dawson had lied to me and we had no future together I ended the relationship. Whatever he has subsequently been saying about me are yet more lies. I did not wish to discuss anything with Shirley Dawson, and I never met her."

Mr. Blake nodded and then pointedly looked to Gibbs.

"I think my client does have a reasonable query as to why you persist in this line of inquiry. She has stated that her relationship with Mr. Dawson was over for some time before the unfortunate incident occurred, and at no time discussed anything with the victim or visited her at her home."

Jane wondered if Gibbs was losing it as Katrina was nodding overconfidently. Then he opened a file of photographs. He picked up an enlarged image of the shaven-headed Shirley Dawson, with the clear head wound in the shape of a V which they had matched to the iron she had been using. Next he took out the same-sized photograph of the wound to Shirley's forehead.

Blake looked shocked as both pictures were placed down side by side in front of Katrina.

"Miss Harcourt, we know you were at the Dawsons' flat on the morning of her murder. She let you in through the main building door thinking you were her mother-in-law, and you went up to the top floor. She was very surprised to see you.

Whether or not you intended to, you picked up the red hot iron and slammed it into the side of her head."

"I was not there! This is all lies!"

"You have been lying, Miss Harcourt, and Mr. Dawson has given us details of exactly how the murder of his wife occurred. I sincerely think that this is now the time to start telling the truth. You have to be aware that we have enough evidence to charge you—"

"Whatever he has told you is not the truth! He is a liar! He is a two-faced LIAR!"

Jane felt her stomach lurch as she observed Gibbs's progress. Katrina's fists were clenched tight and her face was twisted with rage. As her lawyer reached out to take her hand she snatched it away.

"Don't start trying to help this situation now! If Barry is implicating me in something I did not do then I am not going to be framed and made to be the guilty one. I am totally innocent . . . I never touched her, I swear on my life . . . I never did that to her."

Katrina pushed the photographs away from her, and one slid onto the floor. Jane bent down and picked it up, placing it back down on the table.

"Take that out of my sight!" Katrina shouted.

"But this was what was done to her, Miss Harcourt. Someone, either you or Mr. Dawson, slammed the red hot iron into the side of her head and then—"

"I didn't do it!" she screamed.

Gibbs kept his voice low.

"So what exactly did you do, Miss Harcourt? Because now is the time to tell us the truth. Barry Dawson is so confident that he is innocent that he didn't even request any legal representation."

Katrina's face creased into a snarl as she leaned forward.

"I'll tell you what that two-faced liar did."

* * *

Barry Dawson had his head bent low as tears streamed down his cheeks. In front of him on Shepherd's desk were the two identical photographs of the injuries sustained by his wife.

"So help me God, I didn't do that! I swear to you. I would never have hurt Shirley! It was Katrina . . . she's crazy, and because of her it was all getting messed up . . . she wouldn't leave me alone. I can't lie anymore."

Up until now he had claimed that the first he knew about his wife's drowning was when he had arrived home and found her in the bath. Now he changed his story, and the tears flowed as he sobbed.

"Take me through exactly what happened on the morning of your wife's death, Barry . . . get it all off your chest, it will make it easier for you if you talk it all through. Come on, son, start telling us the truth." Shepherd spoke calmly, coaxing Barry to confess.

Barry nodded and took a deep breath.

"I was on duty, at work, and I was in the porters' rest room when they put a call in to me. That's how we get instructions to go to where we are needed, via the phone in the porters' room. It was Katrina—because she knew the extension number, she could call directly. She was hysterical . . . she said she was at my flat and there had been an accident."

"What time was that?" Shepherd asked quietly.

"Be about eight o'clock . . . maybe a bit later. I had been on since six thirty and was due for a break. I took the short cut out of the hospital, going through the mortuary then across the courtyard. I left my porter's jacket in the mortuary."

"Why didn't you just ask to leave?"

"Because of what she had said . . . that Shirley didn't look good."

"You mean she described what she had done?"

"In a way yes, I mean, I dunno . . . she just said they had been fighting and she had hit out at Shirley."

"You mean that she said she was unconscious, or bleeding, or what?"

"Yeah, that she couldn't get her to come round."

"But isn't Miss Harcourt a qualified nurse?"

"Yes, and that's why I was so freaked out because I was desperate to find out if Shirley was all right. I mean, she would know because she is a nurse, and then I got into a panic about my daughter being there."

Katrina was sitting with her hands folded in her lap. She had explained that Barry had called her very early on the morning Shirley died. He told her that he was not going to be on duty and wanted her to come round to the flat to talk to Shirley about the divorce.

"Well, I was not very willing to agree because I had finished with him and I'd left my job at the hospital to get away from him. He begged me to meet him there, so I agreed and drove to London. I think I got there about eight in the morning. I mean, I was really worried about going up to the flat and I walked up and down the road a few times outside before I rang the bell."

Jane watched intently. Katrina spoke very clearly and without any emotion, only occasionally lifting her hands in a theatrical manner to emphasize a point. It was as though she was performing to an audience, and Jane was certain she was lying.

"When I got to the top floor Barry came out, in a terrible state. He said that he had fought with Shirley over him leaving her and that she had refused to ever leave the flat, and told him he would have to pay the mortgage and all child maintenance. He was in such a rage that he had struck her with the iron, and now he thought she was dead . . ."

* * *

Barry had straightened out, as if spilling out the whole story was making him less tense. He explained that he had caught a taxi back to his flat and arrived at about eight thirty. He had run up the stairs and found Katrina in a state of panic, with Shirley lying on the floor still unconscious, or so Katrina had told him.

"She was lying by the ironing board, face down and not moving at all, and Katrina was crying, saying over and over that it wasn't her fault."

Barry had to gather himself before he could continue. He seemed overwhelmed with shame.

"She had run a bath. Katrina said that she was dead and what we should do was put her in the bath and leave her. But I said we couldn't do that as Heidi, my daughter, was there and I couldn't leave her alone. Then I remembered my mother was coming to babysit at nine, so I agreed to do what she wanted me to do."

"I helped Barry carry her into the bathroom. She'd been running a bath before I got there and he said we should just leave her in it. He was expecting his mother to come, so the baby wasn't going to be left for too long."

Barry lifted his arms to demonstrate how they carried Shirley to the bathroom and put her down in the water, which was overflowing. He then became very agitated.

"But she wasn't dead . . . she jerked up in my arms and the next minute I lost my grip of her . . . Katrina started screaming that she was alive, and then she fell forward and hit her head on the water tap, and the next minute there was blood pouring from her nose and I couldn't hold on to her."

* * *

"Can you explain to me exactly how Shirley fell forward?"

Gibbs was making copious notes.

"Barry put her in the bath, head to the right, feet facing the taps, and he lowered her into the water. But it started overflowing and I don't know if it was because it was too hot or what, but the next minute Shirley jerked upward and forward. She was alive, but he lost grip of her and she fell forward and slammed her forehead into the tap. She started to pour blood from her nose and I was screaming as she flopped back. Then the kid was screeching, and the dog was running in and out barking, and Barry had to grab it by its collar and drag it out."

Shepherd tapped his notebook.

"Just let me get this clear, Barry, because it is very important I understand exactly what you are saying. Shirley was placed unconscious into the bath, her feet toward the taps, and the bath was overflowing. Then she suddenly came round?"

"Yes, she sat up but flopped forward and hit her head on the main tap. It cut her head and then she sort of made this snorting sound as blood poured from her nose and then she slid back and went under the water."

Katrina crossed her legs.

"It was just terrible . . . I mean, Barry was totally losing it and crying, and with his wretched child screaming as well, and he had hit the dog with the leather lead so it was howling. I was trying to make him calm down because it was obvious that she was still alive, do you understand? I told him to look after her and said that I would go and see to the baby and give her a bottle."

* * *

Barry was weeping again as he explained that Heidi had started screaming and crying for her mummy, so he had gone out of the bathroom to settle her down and give her the bottle of milk that Shirley had left on the high chair. His dog had been running back and forth all the time, as Shirley usually took him out for his morning walk.

"I put him in his cage, but he was barking and I had to really restrain him. It was only a few minutes but Katrina came out of the bathroom and said that Shirley was dead, and we should both get our stories straight."

He was wringing his hands.

"You see, I knew my mum was coming over because Shirley had a hair appointment, so I knew the baby wouldn't be left on her own for too long. Katrina dropped me off at the mortuary. I had to get back to the hospital and look like I had never left. I called home but there was no answer, and I knew by this time that my mother should have been there to babysit. So I called her and she said that she was waiting for an engineer to fix her washing machine. She had tried to call Shirley, got no reply, but told me not to worry as she had probably taken Heidi to the hair salon with her. But I knew she hadn't . . . I borrowed some change off a mate and kept on acting like I was calling, and then I went home."

Katrina leaned back in her seat.

"It was obvious she was dead . . . there were no more bubbles from her mouth, and her eyes were wide open."

Barry kept his eyes to the floor and his voice sounded hoarse.

"I knew she was dead. Katrina said she wasn't breathing and there were no bubbles coming out from her mouth or nose, and her eyes were wide open."

* * *

The two suspects had now been charged with the murder of Shirley Dawson and had been taken back to the cells. The following day they would be taken before a Magistrates' Court for the charges to be formally heard and a trial date set.

It was five o'clock when DS Lawrence had a match of Katrina's thumb and forefinger print on one of the coins from the payphone taken from the hallway. However, by the time he had relayed the information it was all over. The evidence would be used to prove that Katrina lied about not calling Barry Dawson from the flat.

It had been a long day and everyone was tired, but satisfied at the eventual outcome. Jane had heard Gibbs relaying Katrina's behavior to DCI Shepherd, and how she had tried to put the blame on Barry. Shepherd had laughed, saying that Barry had done exactly the same with his story.

"Which one held her under?" Gibbs asked. Without hesitation Shepherd said he would put his money on Katrina. But in reality it didn't matter because they had both committed murder and would go down for it.

Jane was walking along a corridor on the ground floor as Richard Blake approached. He had his raincoat folded over his arm. Jane had watched his interaction during the interview with Katrina, and had witnessed how ill-equipped he had been to handle the situation or control his client. Jane acknowledged Mr. Blake and he hesitated. His face looked gray with fatigue, and he seemed to be fighting to say something about the awful afternoon he had just been forced to sit through. When he did speak he surprised Jane because it was something so inadequate.

"I play golf with her father every first Sunday of the month."

Jane was now officially off duty. She collected her coat and popped her head into the incident room to see Edith still there.

"You're here late, Edith? Are you coming over to join us at the pub? Everyone's celebrating."

"Listen, with the amount of work I've got to type up from DCI Shepherd I could be here all night . . . I have to say, I didn't think the husband did it, did you?"

Jane shrugged. "I don't know. I mean, Katrina Harcourt was a real piece of work and I was very impressed with Spence . . . he really handled her well and sort of cornered her. He constantly referred to her as being a 'one-night stand,' which she hated, but it took a long time."

"Yes and all his notes have to be typed up. It's going to be a lot of work checking and double-checking all the statements, you know . . . he did this, she did that, and they blamed each other so that's all got to be investigated and ready for the trial. It'll be months of work."

Jane nodded. "One of them held her under the water. Katrina says that Barry held her and he says she did, but what's interesting is that they both describe the same thing about waiting until there were no bubbles . . . so they both had to be in the bathroom."

"Well, they deserve what they'll get. It'll be a big trial with lots of publicity . . . there's already been a press release. Headlines will be 'Murder in the Bath' by tomorrow, and with it being a twosome even more press will be hungry. That redhead'll love it."

Jane put on her coat. She felt confused. Barry had appeared to be so emotionally distraught when she had first met him in the neighbors' basement. He had also appeared to be very honest when she had taken his statement and the tears seemed genuine when he had identified his wife's body. She remembered watching him as he walked away from the mortuary, and how bereft he had seemed . . . And all the time he knew what he had done. Jane realized she was a very poor judge of character and wouldn't make the same mistake again.

"Jailhouse Rock" was playing on the juke box. The CID team had pushed three tables together and there were bottles of wine and beer, and similar to the fare served at the Warburton Arms there was an array of shrunken sausage rolls, curling sandwiches and packets of crisps. Gibbs passed Jane a glass of wine as she sat down next to Lawrence.

"Well, I got there eventually! The fingerprints were confirmation that Katrina Harcourt lied about the phone call. It will be useful evidence in the trial for the prosecution—two fingerprints on the same coin. The coins from the machine at the Dawsons' building all had to be checked by eye match print. Each one had to be carefully laid out on white paper and dusted—"

Jane interrupted his overly detailed description. "Congratulations. As you said, it was a long shot."

"Well, it's going to be one hell of a schlepp to the trial. But we all got there in the end. It was seeing you with the coins in your hand about to use the Dawsons' phone box . . . it just clicked! As you said, it was a long shot. But it paid off, and . . ."

Jane realized that DS Lawrence must have been in the pub for quite a while and it sounded as if he was about to detail the entire forensic department's discovery of Katrina Harcourt's fingerprints to them all.

Gibbs pulled over a chair and took out his wallet.

"Right, everybody, place your bets. Which one of them held Shirley Dawson down in the bath?"

As the rest of the team took out various coins and notes, Jane had a second glass of wine. Gibbs nudged her.

"Come on, Tennison, who are you betting on?"

"I think they both did it."

"No, no, no . . . you've got to bet on one or the other!"

"I think it was Katrina . . . I'll put a fiver on it."

"Fiver on for Katrina!" Gibbs shouted loudly.

"Make that another fiver," Lawrence joined in. "I say it was Katrina too. As you know, with my scientific prowess, I was able to provide the vital evidence from the coins in the phone box . . ."

Gibbs looked at Lawrence despairingly. "Oh God . . . here we go again!"

By the time Jane left the pub it didn't look as if there were going to be any winnings as the bets were all being spent on drinks.

It was already 9:30 p.m. so she decided that, as she hadn't yet managed to get through to Peter Allard's wife, she would ring her again. She wondered if perhaps Marie just wanted to get in touch to find out if a trial date had been set. She made a mental note to be very careful about exactly what she was going to discuss as she was using the payphone in the reception area of the section house. Jane dialed the number in her notebook. The phone rang for a long time before Marie answered.

"Hello?" Her voice wavered like a child's.

"Is this Marie Allard? This is Detective Jane Tennison . . . I understand you've been trying to contact me?"

"Yes . . ." There was a pause.

"Are you all right, Marie?"

"I need speak with you . . . but not on phone . . . to your face, please. I need your help, but it private."

Jane didn't think it was wise to go and see her straight away as she had consumed three glasses of wine in the pub.

"I'm off duty in the morning . . . how about I come to your house at nine o'clock tomorrow?"

"Thank you . . . thank you very much."

Jane replaced the handset and headed toward her room. It had been a very long day, but one she had learned a lot from. She would be careful how she approached Marie, and mindful of what she said as she didn't want any repercussions from DI Moran. She had made a mistake in talking to her at the Magistrates' Court and had been reprimanded, so at the meeting she would not take any chances.

DI Moran still felt very queasy. He had ordered some chicken and sweetcorn soup as he couldn't face anything too solid. DC Edwards was tucking into beef chow mein and crispy sweet and sour pork with fried rice. They were dining at the Golden Dragon, a small Chinese restaurant in the outskirts of Maidstone.

"I think this is him, guv . . ." as the bell tinkled, signaling a customer entering through the door.

Moran turned to see a very broad-shouldered, ruddy faced man with gray-streaked hair, who almost filled the open doorway.

"Ahhh, Moran? Victor Bethell." He walked over and held out his huge hand, shaking Moran's hand vigorously.

Moran gestured to Bethell to sit down with them. "This is DC Brian Edwards. Nice to meet you. Glad you found the place."

Bethell turned to a hovering Chinese waiter.

"I'll have a whole crispy duck, pancakes, plum sauce and fresh vegetables."

Bethell took off his thick duffle coat and pulled out an old notebook from an inside pocket, tossing it on the table. The waiter took his coat to hang it up and Bethell sat his large frame down rather precariously on a small chair.

"You were lucky to get hold of me . . . I retired two years ago. I put my pension into a motor home. Me and the wife are driving to Folkestone for a very carefully planned six-month tour of the Continent."

If Moran had had a headache first thing that morning, he now had what felt like a severe migraine. Bethell's booming voice was like a hammer in his head. A few Chinese customers kept darting fearful glances toward their table.

"I am very grateful you agreed to see us," Moran replied, taking a slurp of his soup.

"When your young DC contacted the station they immediately got on to me because I handled the case. It's all packed up in the cold files, and if needs be I can get one of the detectives there to get it out." He looked at DC Edwards. "But this youngster wanted to have a chat about it first."

Moran took another spoonful of soup, then pushed the bowl aside.

"So what can you tell us about Susie Luna?" The big man opened his notebook.

"Well, for starters it's such a simple name . . . you never forget it."

"She was missing?" Moran asked, wanting to get on with it.

"Yes, she was. She was a Filipino who worked as a chambermaid in one of the hotels . . . pretty little thing."

"So what was the consensus?"

"Foul play—she had one and a half thousand pounds in the bank, she left all her clothes in the room she rented, she gave no notice at the hotel, and she was liked. We had a couple of sightings around the town, but then she just disappeared off the face of the earth."

"Do you think she was abducted? Kidnapped? Murdered . . . ? Did you find her passport?"

"Nope. She was last seen leaving the staff exit at the hotel where she worked, then a few unconfirmed sighting, and then nothing."

Moran leaned to one side as the waiter brought Bethell's order. He was impatient to get to the point of why they had asked to meet, but he waited until the various dishes had been laid in front of the retired detective before he quietly spoke.

"You never found a body. But did you have a suspect?"

With great dexterity Bethell placed a pancake on his plate, spread the plum sauce, then used his fork to shred the crispy duck and carefully laid it onto the pancake.

"His name was Peter Allard. His wife, Marie Allard, was Filipino and worked at the same hotel."

CHAPTER TWENTY-TWO

Jane rang the doorbell for the second time, and waited. She stepped back from the porch and looked over to a side window where she saw the curtain drawn back for a second. Jane had already doubted her reasons for coming all the way to Walthamstow, and it was much further than she had calculated because the previous time she had been at the house was as a passenger in a patrol car. It really did seem such a long time ago. She had still been in uniform as a probationary WPC, and the Allard case had been her first introduction to CID.

"Who is it?" Marie asked nervously from behind the front door.

"It's WDC Tennison, Mrs. Allard . . . you wanted to talk to me?"

Jane waited as various locks and a chain link were undone. Marie opened the door and gestured for her to come in, then quickly closed the door and replaced the chain.

"To stop my mother-in-law from getting in. She very trying and is making my life a misery."

Jane was ushered into the kitchen and Marie offered her tea or coffee, but she declined both. Without taking her coat off she asked if there was anything wrong that Marie wished to talk to her about, and apologized for the delay in returning her call.

"I given up on you," Marie said, and pulled out a chair to sit down. She pointed to the one next to her for Jane to use.

"I have no one else . . . well, I not mean I not know anyone . . . I not have anybody that I can talk to about it and now I am very anxious, and my mother-in-law ask me lots of questions and I am frightened to answer the phone in case it is her, and . . ."

Marie started to take deep breaths and wave her hand in front of her chest.

"I sorry, I get this panic and my lungs not work properly . . . I sorry . . ."

It was a few moments before Marie calmed herself down, and then started to cry, getting up to fetch a box of tissues. Eventually Jane was able to ask why Marie needed to talk to her, and bit by bit she opened up about the blackmail phone calls, the money drops, and that her mother-in-law had discovered the £1,000 missing from the joint account with her husband. She was sobbing.

"I cannot see my husband because of the stress . . . I had to lie about the last five hundred pounds . . . he was becoming very angry with me . . . He tell me what to do, but I not see who take the money wrapped in the newspaper."

Jane had asked if she could take down some details, so as the story unfolded she made pages of notes, trying to ascertain exactly what the chronological order was, as sometimes Marie jumped back and forth as she tried to explain.

"Do you mind if I just go through everything you have told me? I need to understand clearly exactly what has been happening. First, you received a phone call from a woman, who you say sang a song to you and said she wanted five hundred pounds in cash or she would go to the police with incriminating evidence that proved your husband had committed the rape he has denied?"

"Yes, yes . . . that's it. I very scared because she said that if I not pay he would go away to prison for a very long time, and I not know what to do."

"Yes, you said . . . so you went to the prison and visited your husband, and you told him that you paid this woman and she then called again for the second time blackmailing you into paying five hundred pounds?"

"Yes. She gave me time to go to bank and said she would call me again. And I told Peter . . . I told him this."

Jane nodded, and turned a page in her notebook.

"Just repeat to me what he said, will you?"

Marie nodded.

"That it was the police . . . that it was Detective Moran who lied and fitted him up . . . that it was him doing blackmail and that I should just pay to get rid of him as he was bent copper. That how he describe the detective, as bent copper . . . because he had framed him and he did not do the rape."

Jane showed no reaction, but it was very difficult not to be shocked by the accusations against DI Moran. Marie continued describing how she had done as instructed and left the money wrapped in newspaper but she had not seen who collected it. She continued by detailing how the next call came from the same woman, and she wanted another £500. She told Jane how Peter had instructed her to place the money in the litter bin, get on the bus and then jump off to see if she could follow or identify who collected the money.

Marie started to cry again, and Jane had to wait until she calmed down before she falteringly described the ginger-haired boy and how she had seen him getting into a taxi, but had not seen who else was inside. Jane felt herself becoming deeply involved as she was certain the boy that Marie had seen fitted the description of the young red-haired boy with the gapped teeth whom she had questioned about Janet Brown.

"Can you go over the phone call again, Marie?"

"I told you . . . she sings this song 'Angie' something, and she keep repeating it over and over, I don't know if she is Angie or she is singing about someone else. It horrible. That's why I not pick up the phone at night no more."

Jane felt herself becoming increasingly tense as she was certain that Angie was Janet Brown, with her connection to the red-haired boy. She asked Marie again if the woman had ever described just what evidence she had to implicate Peter Allard in the rape. Marie said that she had laughed and said that it was enough to find him guilty.

"How did Peter react when you told him that you paid another five hundred pounds?"

"He not know . . . I told you, you not listening to me . . . I said the woman never showed so I never paid. But now my mother-in-law find out and she told him that I had withdrawn it from our joint bank account. She will make threats to me about the children. She is very interfering, she tries always to dominate me. Peter will go berserk when he knows I never saw who collected it . . . he certain it was that police detective because he swears that he is innocent and they set him up."

Marie was going into repeat mode, and she was becoming more and more distressed. She started gasping for breath, then weeping uncontrollably, plucking one tissue after another out of the box.

"Marie, let me go away and think about all of this and I will get back to you in the morning. I really think you did the right thing in contacting me, but for now can you keep this just between us until I can establish what should be done?"

The front door was rebolted and the chain locked behind her as Jane left. She had been with Marie Allard for more than two hours, and felt exhausted by this new development. She didn't look at her lengthy notes but leaned back in her seat on the top deck of the bus and ran it all over in her mind.

Jane had already been warned once for working solo by DCI Shepherd, and even Gibbs had given her a tough talking to and reprimanded her for blowing his cover in Soho and wasting time on what he considered a piece of lowlife scum like Peter Allard. Jane decided that perhaps the one person she could talk to would be DS Lawrence.

* * *

DI Moran and DC Edwards had returned to Maidstone Police Station and were awaiting the release of Bethell's old files on the Susie Luna case. As impatient as ever, Moran paced up and down the small reception area of the 1950s station, checking his watch.

"How much longer do you think they're bloody well going to keep us waiting?"

Just then a very neat, chisel-faced officer introduced himself and handed Moran a worn cardboard box full of files, photographs and assorted evidence.

"I'm afraid nothing can be taken off the premises without my signature, but you are most welcome to use an interview room to sort through and select what items you require."

"Thank you very much," Moran said curtly.

"Follow me." The detective led them down a dark corridor, up a flight of stairs and opened a porthole-windowed door to an interview room.

"There's a canteen upstairs if you want any refreshments. I'll be in the incident room next door if you need me."

"Thank you very much," Moran said, eager for the detective to leave.

He placed the worn cardboard box on a Formica-topped table as Edwards pulled up a hard-backed chair. Moran looked around the sparse room, taking in the grimy windows. Even the yellowing walls reminded him of Hackney Station, and yet this was a relatively "new" building. He shook his head as he sat down at the table.

"Do you think every police station built in the fifties and sixties gets a bulk discount on pots of crappy paint?"

Edwards pulled the packing tape holding down the flaps of the dusty cardboard box and peered inside. Face up, in a cheap frame, was a photograph of Susie Luna. He took it out and held it up for Moran.

"Pretty little thing . . . Got a rose in her hair . . ."

Moran stared at the photograph, then placed it to one side.

"Right, let's see what else they've got . . ."

Jane had spent a great deal of time on Sunday writing up Marie Allard's complaints and accusations against DI Moran. She knew that the following morning, she would have to have a serious conversation with a senior officer, as what Marie Allard had told her was a very grave allegation against Moran. If there was any truth in it then there would be some significant repercussions. Peter Allard had accused DI Moran of planting evidence in his rape case, and now he was inferring that he was part of a blackmail scam using a prostitute to collect a lot of money, now up to £1,000.

On Monday morning, Jane was glancing through her file when Gibbs appeared.

"Penny for 'em," Gibbs said, as he stood by her desk. He looked smarter than usual, wearing a gray suit and white shirt, with a striped tie and loafer shoes.

"I'm sorry, I was miles away." She looked up at him as he sat on the edge of her desk. "You look very smart."

"Yeah, well, had to look my best as all the press were there, the tabloids are loving it. I'd say we'll all be running around like blue-arsed flies when this bitch Harcourt gets to trial . . . Man, is she a piece of work. She was lapping it up in court this morning, while Dawson was on suicide watch last night. He looked pitiful in court. Apparently he was heartbroken as his mother had had his dog put down."

Jane licked her lips, then made the decision.

"Spence, can I have a private word with you about something? I don't know who else I can talk to about it, but I really need some guidance."

He shrugged. "Sure, fire away."

"Do you mind if we go into your office? It's just quite, erm, sensitive and I need your advice . . . but I don't want anything spread around."

Gibbs cocked his head to one side, then slid off the desk and gestured for her to follow him. His office was smelly and an overflowing ashtray sat in the center of his desk, surrounded by used cups and paper plates.

"Why don't they clean it up in here? Where's Edith?"

"She was here earlier, but she had to go over to the comms room. I'm not sure she'd appreciate you thinking of her as a cleaner, Spence."

"I wasn't! It's just that if you want to have a private conversation, she's got ears on elastic." He shut the door. By the time he had tossed everything into a waste bin Jane was getting cold feet.

"Right, WDC Tennison, I am all yours."

"I was going to talk it through with Paul Lawrence but, as you've said, he's very busy . . . and I don't have enough confirmation to talk to DCI Shepherd."

"Well, go on, Jane, spill it out . . ."

Jane hesitated, then took a deep breath. Keeping it as succinct and direct as possible, she told him the entire story. Gibbs was rather unnerving as he didn't interrupt, but laid his head down on top of his hands on his desk.

"And I think I should question this Janet Brown . . . Remember, she was the prostitute who wore the blue rabbit fur coat that Moran gave me to wear when I was being a decoy. I know she has used 'Angie' as one of her aliases . . . what do you think?"

There was a short pause before Gibbs slowly lifted his head and looked at her.

"Jesus Christ, Tennison . . . talk about kicking over a hornet's nest. There's stuff there that'll rise up and sting you."

"But I'm not repeating anything that I haven't given serious thought to. That's why I needed to talk it through with someone."

"Talk it through with someone? Unfortunately, that's me," he snapped, and turned away, folding his arms across his chest.

"Right, just let me get this straight . . . I'm going from the fuckin' beginning so that I get it right. That night after the Marquee Club, I told you to forget about this whore in the blue rabbit fur coat. You pay no attention to my warning about playing solo, and you totally disobey me . . . and that same night you chase after this Janet Brown, or Angie, who's singing down the phone to Peter Allard's wife. Is it the Rolling Stones song?"

"I don't know. I had no intention of following her, but I saw her getting into a taxi and this boy being paid by her—"

"Yes, yes . . . so Janet/Angie goes off in a taxi and you take after the kid?"

Jane nodded. "Yes, exactly. I saw him going into this adult bookshop."

Gibbs held up his hand.

"Now, you said a guy wearing a cowboy outfit called Stevie ran the shop, together with a big-titted blonde whose name you didn't hear, and the boy worked in the back room?" Jane opened her mouth to interrupt and he snapped, "No, let me finish."

He stood up and started pacing around the room.

"What you don't know is that Stevie Bishop and his wife Ada are virtually the Soho King and Queen of Vice. They have brothels and strip joints all around the red light district. They run the dirtiest sex rackets and are making a fortune. We know that Stevie has big clout with some very senior Metropolitan police officers, and he can buy his way out of any charges . . . I am talking about paying over tens of thousands of pounds . . . and you walk in with your DC card because you just want to speak to some red-haired kid?"

"I had no idea," Jane said sheepishly.

"No, you very obviously didn't. I will have to check out if you stepped into a surveillance operation because they will have been royally pissed off if you did. The drug squad are also being brought in as Stevie and Ada are not satisfied with rolling in the money from the whores—they are starting to deal with international drug operations too. But it'll take a long time to bring down the King of Soho and his dirty grubby wife the Queen of Vice. Right now they are making elephantine fortunes on their dirty book trade, so they lavish big favors on the bent cops . . . and I mean *huge* favors—cars, cash, holidays abroad . . ."

Jane hesitated and asked nervously if Gibbs was explaining the Soho sex trade business and police involvement because it was possible that DI Moran was behind the blackmail with Janet Brown.

"No I'm bloody not! I am simply warning you about treading into dangerous areas that you know fuck all about. This gap-toothed kid that runs for the whores, we need to snatch and grab him without it looking like we are in any way connected to the police."

"You'll help me? Because he has to know where Janet Brown lives, and she is who we need to talk to. Because if she does have this evidence . . ."

Gibbs opened the door.

"I doubt she has, but we need to clear up this shit about DI Moran." He barged out, leaving Jane to follow.

Gibbs booked out a plain patrol car and he and Jane headed for Soho.

On the way they stopped at a "Hot Tea and Pie" cabin and Gibbs bought them both a sausage roll and a cup of tea. Jane was unsure about being seen eating and drinking in a police car and Gibbs laughed.

"Don't be dumb, you're not in uniform, and I've had more hot dinners in the front seat of a car than I have at home."

Gibbs drove erratically, his coffee balanced precariously in the seat divide between them, while he held his sausage roll in a napkin in his right hand. They drove down Wardour Street, then left into Old Compton Street before doing the loop again as they passed numerous strip clubs. They crossed Berwick Street, which was filled with fruit and veg stalls, then into Beak Street and did yet another slow loop around into Shaftesbury Avenue where there was bumper to bumper traffic. Returning to Wardour Street, Jane suddenly spotted the red-haired boy, this time with a very young blonde girl who was carrying a bag of feather boas.

"There he is!" Jane said.

Gibbs stopped the car.

"OK . . . take over the driving and park up in that wasteland car park opposite the Windmill Theatre, and leave the back passenger door open."

With his hands dug deep into his overcoat Gibbs got out of the car and took off down Berwick Street. His head was lowered as he gained momentum to walk directly behind the boy, who was laughing and chatting with the blonde girl who looked no more than fifteen or sixteen. They stopped outside "Pretty Pussies" and the girl turned to go inside. As the boy was about to follow Gibbs used his right finger and thumb to snap a tight, painful hold on the nerves in the back of the boy's scrawny neck.

"You walk quietly along with me, son, or I cuff you and make out you're my informant and you're squealin', and everyone is gonna know . . . I'm a Vice copper, sonny."

The boy was in agony but he could only shrug his shoulders higher to relieve the pain in his neck. To anyone watching it looked as if Gibbs just had a friendly hand on the kid's neck. They continued down the road and then took a side turning to come out by the Windmill Theatre's stage door. Crossing the road, Gibbs could see Jane waiting in the patrol car.

The car park was an old bomb site that had been developed as a parking facility. It wouldn't be for much longer as all the land in the West End was being used for more and more office and retail building. There was an elderly man sitting on a camping stool outside a crumbling wooden sentry box. In front of him was an upturned wooden wine crate with a tin box for selling day-long parking tickets. When he had glanced toward the open car Jane had shown him her ID and he gestured for her to park by a crumbling brick wall on the far side of what had been a crater. She watched Gibbs walking toward her, guiding the red-haired boy. It looked as if they were simply having a chat. Gibbs was smiling, and then as they reached the rear open passenger door he kept his hold of the boy's neck with his right hand but took out his handcuffs with his left. He pushed the boy forward, face down, into the back seat and drew his arms up painfully high to cuff his wrists. He kicked out at the boy's legs as he wriggled and swore and said that if he didn't pull his knees up he'd slam the door on his ankles and break them.

Jane was not exactly comfortable with Gibbs's heavy-handedness, but she had seen it all before when they had been at Hackney together. He had the nickname "The Slapper." But as he was doing her a favor she sat silently watching as he slammed his fist hard into the boy's head, warning him to stay very quiet. She was now sitting in the passenger seat of the plain patrol car.

"Right, we have Philip Jackson, aged twelve. Lives on the Kenworth Estate, and his mother's a junkie called Wanda. Have I got this all correct, Philip?"

"Yes, sir."

"You'd better not be bullshitting me . . . I know where you work and I'll come back and beat the living daylights out of you. I could get you locked up and let Stevie and his wife know you're my informant, so . . ."

"I don't fuckin' know nuffink. I just earn a few quid from the girls when I look after their gear backstage. I swear before God, I'm not running drugs."

Gibbs leaned over the front passenger seat and slapped the boy's head hard, and he moaned.

"Right, this is what's going to happen. I'm going to ask you a few questions and I need you to answer honestly. If you don't, you'll be arrested for living off immoral earnings, you'll be held in the cells overnight to await transportation to a reform school, and this lady here will contact social services to arrest your mother, and any other kids she lets work the strip joints."

The boy started sniffing and Gibbs slapped him again. He then began asking Philip quietly about Janet Brown, wanting to know where she lived. At first he denied knowing her, but as soon as Gibbs mentioned the name "Angie" it was obvious that he did. Gibbs waited as he muttered that he didn't know her address as she just worked the strip clubs in the afternoons, and other times at night, and all he did was look after her handbag as the other tarts were known to steal each others' belongings.

"I need her address, Philip . . ."

"I dunno it! I never been to her pad, honest!"

"So, tell me about the time you picked up a bundle for Angie from the bus stop by the Grosvenor Hotel on Park Lane."

Philip hesitated, then blurted out that Janet had asked him to come with her one afternoon after she'd done a gig at the "Dirty Girls" and he had got into a taxi with her. He had to get out and go to the bus stop and wait to see an oriental-looking lady. When he saw her put a package into the litter bin and get on the next bus he had to retrieve the package and take it back to Janet in the taxi. He said she gave him a ten pound note, then they took a taxi to Carnaby Street, where he bought some shoes.

"Did she tell you what was in the package?" Gibbs asked.

"No, but I knew it was cash . . . I saw it in the envelope."

"Did she tell you why she was getting it?"

"No, just that she was owed it by some piece of scum."

"Where does she live?"

"I dunno! I honest to God don't know!"

"Does she have a pimp?"

"No . . . well, I never seen one with her. She's very tough and I just sometimes work for her, but she don't work for Stevie. He calls her dirty black trash . . . she's got a weird accent, you know, like it's a made-up one . . . like American."

Gibbs sighed, then after a moment he turned and rubbed Philip's head.

"This is important, son. Do you know if Janet or Angie is used by the CID?"

"I don't understand what you mean."

Jane turned to look at the boy, whose face was now pressed down into the back seat.

"Well, does she give a freebee once in a while, to uniforms or detectives? You know anything about that?"

"What you sayin'? She's a grass, like a tipster?"

Jane wanted to ask the boy a few questions but Gibbs wasn't allowing her to say a word, and in some ways she felt as if he was protecting Moran, never mentioning his name.

"No, I am asking if she screws around with the Old Bill."

"No. She don't talk much. She knows what she wants me to do and I just look after her gear. She's a got a kid, I know that. He's brown like her, but I never seen him . . . she had pictures of him in her wallet."

"How do you know that?"

"Cos she takes it out and counts the money in it, in case I filch any. Like I said, she's tough and knows the ropes . . . and she don't mix with the other slags."

Gibbs climbed out and walked round to the rear passenger door behind Jane. He opened the door and Philip cowered away, but Gibbs just yanked him out by his legs. He unlocked the cuffs and then pushed the boy to stand upright, leaning toward him.

"I'm letting you go, son, but you had better not be lying to me because I will come back to get you."

Jane looked through the window of the patrol car as Gibbs gripped the boy's chin, making his mouth purse open like a goldfish. They had words, then the boy scuttled away, passing the sleeping parking attendant who would get more customers later when the shows started their evening performances. Gibbs climbed in beside Jane and started the engine.

"OK, we need to find this bitch. So far Marie Allard's story that she was being blackmailed pans out, but it could be a load of lies. Or this Angie, or Janet, might have something that could prove Allard was the rapist. I don't think DI Moran is involved . . . he wouldn't be that crazy. The kid's just said that Angie is often around the clubs later when it gets dark . . . she collects the money for the numbers game and takes it over to the big man in Chinatown. So tonight I think we should check out the strip clubs. You up for that?"

Jane didn't reply. Deep down she began to feel that perhaps Gibbs wanted to keep on trying to trace Janet Brown because he was also unsure about Moran.

"Why don't we meet back here in a couple of hours and get something to eat until this place hots up? Do you fancy some Italian? Luigi's is around the corner from here."

Moran was sitting in the CID office at Hackney Station. DCs Ashton and Edwards, alongside two other detectives, watched as Moran pinned up the photograph of Susie Luna, which he had taken out of its frame. He proceeded to put up various smaller photographs, some black and white, and numerous Polaroids. He then chalked on the board "Susie Luna—Aged 17, Filipino,

Chambermaid/Waitress/Barmaid, Majestic Hotel, Maidstone. Missing since March 15th, 1969." Two more officers came into the office and perched on the edge of a couple of desks, eager to find out what was going on.

Moran tossed the chalk aside and stuffed his hands into his pockets.

"Brian here was doing some checks into previous possible assault cases in connection with the Peter Allard case. The reason I'm questioning this is because there have been a few queries from Allard's defense council about his confession. It might stand firm, I bloody hope it does, but in the meantime Perry Mason here came across this case."

Moran pointed up to the board.

"Susie Luna, the girl with the rose in her hair. Her body was never found. We have four statements from the officer leading the inquiry . . . Guess who he was questioning?"

"Peter Allard!" Edwards exclaimed.

"Well, I know you know that, you bloody idiot, but these lot didn't. Allard was living in Maidstone—pin that up, Edwards."

Moran pointed to a photograph of a two-up, two-down terraced corner house. "Right, we know Allard rented this property with his Filipino wife, who had also worked at the Majestic Hotel and was close friends with the victim, Susie Luna."

Looking over the information board, Ashton reacted. "Bloody hell! You think Allard killed her?"

"He has a watertight alibi, provided by his wife. He wasn't arrested because there were three sightings of Susie Luna: on a bus, at a bus stop, and outside a fish and chip shop."

"So he's not connected then?" Ashton asked.

"No . . . on the contrary. I think he *is* connected, and I need to find more evidence that'll get me authority from the Kent Constabulary to have the garden in Maidstone excavated," Moran replied.

* * *

At Luigi's that evening, Jane had ordered a *salade niçoise*. Gibbs, however, was wading through a very large dish of lasagna and had already consumed two glasses of Chianti.

"Did you always suspect that Barry Dawson had murdered his wife?" Jane asked.

"Not to begin with. I mean, I was there when it was recorded as a non-suspicious death. But later, you know, when suspicions were flying I remembered something about him."

"Like what?"

"The dog . . . he was snapping and growling at everyone, and was shut in his cage. I wasn't that keen on it being brought in the car with me. His mother kept going on about it being nice tempered, then when Barry got the lead and opened the cage the poor thing cowered back and was terrified of him."

"Yes, I remember . . . and I also recall his mother saying that it was a sweet-natured dog."

"When those two were carrying Shirley's body to put it in the bath they said the dog was barking and running around, and it woke up the little girl. In a statement to DCI Shepherd Barry admitted that he had whipped the dog to be quiet and had put him in the cage."

Jane glanced at Gibbs. He never ceased to fascinate her because the more she got to know him the more sides of him he allowed her to see.

"I knew something was bad about Dawson then—a dog only cowers in fear for a reason, especially as it was normally well behaved."

Jane nodded. She wondered at what point she herself had been suspicious and was concerned that it hadn't been for a considerable time.

"I didn't immediately think he had any connection as he was obviously so emotionally distraught . . . I felt that he was very genuine. To see him cradling his little girl in the neighbors' basement, having just found his wife, was deeply distressing for me to witness. It wasn't until there were small pieces of the jigsaw that didn't match up . . . his lies about Katrina, and his attempts to give himself an alibi with the phone calls. He suddenly transformed from being a compassionate, loving husband to a weak, blubbering man."

Gibbs interjected. "But he wasn't bad-looking, and Katrina obviously thought he was a good catch . . ."

Before Jane could respond Gibbs signaled to the waiter for the bill and glanced at his watch. It was almost 9:30 p.m.

"Right, the tarts should be out, and we should go and find your girl . . ."

CHAPTER TWENTY-THREE

Jane and Gibbs had walked along Wardour Street twice and were now heading toward Berwick Street.

"There she is!" Jane exclaimed.

The blue rabbit fur coat stood out in the neon lights from the various sex shops and strip clubs. Jane was very mindful of the red-haired boy appearing, but there was no sign of him, and maybe they had scared him enough not to get back to work straightaway.

Suddenly there were large groups of men standing outside the strip clubs, as the hustle and bustle of the seediest part of the West End kicked in. Heavy muscle men stood outside the strip joints stopping any customers they didn't like the look of from coming inside. Deafening music played loudly from every doorway, in competition with each other.

Gibbs stopped. "Where the hell did she go?"

Jane shrugged and shook her head.

Taxis dropped and picked up girls and customers, and the hookers moved along the street showing off their figures and backcombed beehive hairstyles. They wore an assortment of red plastic macs, high-heeled patent shoes and miniskirts that were so small they looked like curtain pelmets. Some had on silver and gold hot pants, showing off their bum cheeks in fishnet stockings. They wore glittering earrings, bracelets and necklaces, and many of them revealed too much cleavage to be decent in skintight boob tubes. These were the street girls, and hurrying from one venue to the next were the strippers. They carried their costumes and wigs in tote bags, their faces plastered with thick makeup and false eyelashes, as they ducked and dived between the strip joints. Many of them were doing three to four shows a night.

Incongruously, as Jane and Gibbs moved nearer to the high-priced revue bars, smartly dressed men and women mingled with the crowd. The most famous club, the Raymond Revuebar, was very popular. The narrow road was filling up with classy cars, while women in glamorous long dresses and furs were escorted by men in evening suits. They were greeted at the entrance of the bar by a suitably attired doorman.

Gibbs was getting pissed off. "Well, she must be around here somewhere . . . I need a leak, so I'm popping into the pub." He went into the Queen's Head, leaving Jane waiting outside.

Having done the business, Gibbs ordered a bottle of Coke, and drank three quarters of it before asking the barman to fill it up to the neck with vodka. He then went back out to Jane, who was clearly very frustrated that Janet had disappeared.

"We lost her," Jane said.

"Terrific! Listen, the kid, the red-haired boy, he said she hangs out in Chinatown. Let's go back and get the car and head over there."

Gibbs started up the engine and they began to reverse out of the car park. The old parking attendant removed the rope from the cratered area, hoping for a tip, but he didn't get one.

"It's unbelievable watching the real lowlife cheek by jowl with the fancy people getting out of their flash cars, all dressed up to see the fan dancers and sequined strippers," Jane commented.

"Grow up, sweetheart . . . most of the hostesses in those swanky places are on the game and charge a fortune for a glass of cheap fizz and a feel up. But I doubt your Janet is in their league, or she wouldn't be working that patch over at London Fields. She might be working in one of the brothels . . . hard to know. They use plain white, nondescript doors and the girls are out the back in all the shitty little partitioned bedrooms. The entrances are more'n likely in Wardour Street. You'd be amazed how many smart-looking Private Members' clubs are fronts for seedy brothels. I can do a drive past, but then I'm calling it quits for tonight."

They drove up the entire length of Wardour Street and right onto Oxford Street, before heading back south around Soho Square and into Greek Street, but there was no sign of Angie. Determined to keep looking, they crossed over to Dean Street and back up to Oxford Street, before returning down Wardour Street. Reaching the end of the road they were about to turn left into Shaftesbury Avenue when Jane was sure she saw the blue rabbit fur coat. Directly across the road was the start of Chinatown, with all the lanterns swinging on ropes across a pedestrianized area. There were numerous small, lit-up restaurants and noodle bars, with flashing lights and throngs of customers. The streets were filled with people buying Chinese food in takeaway cartons, and there was a strong, slightly sickly sweet smell of frying chicken and fish.

"It's her, I'm sure of it! D'you see her, Spence? She's outside the restaurant with a blue neon sign above it . . . her blue fur coat's obvious."

Jane started to open the car door and clamber out.

"Hang on, just hang on. You don't go out here alone."

An irate driver behind them sounded his horn as Gibbs made a hand signal for him to overtake. He then mounted the pavement and reversed a few yards. As soon as the engine stopped, Gibbs and Jane were both out and running beside a theater with huge posters advertising the big hit musical *Joseph and the Amazing Technicolor Dreamcoat*. The main entrance for Chinatown was now a few yards ahead. Gibbs was moving faster than Jane, turning out of her sight for a moment. As she caught up he held out his arm for her to stop beside him.

"Stay back a minute, Jane . . . she's heading straight toward us . . ."

Gibbs stepped forward, saying Angie's name. Jane, almost directly behind him, moved to try and block her from passing saying, "We just need to talk to you."

Without missing a beat Janet side-stepped and made a run for it, heading straight into Shaftesbury Avenue. A bus missed her by a terrifying few feet and, with traffic moving both ways beside her, she tried to make it across the road. Gibbs was dodging oncoming vehicles and held his hand up in the air as if it was some kind of warning that he was a police officer. Janet made the mistake of turning back to look at him. The oncoming green Mini estate screeched to a halt as it clipped her left hip and she flipped up into the air and sprawled over the bonnet. Jane made it to the pavement as the distressed driver climbed out, shouting that the woman had run directly into him. Gibbs dragged Janet up onto her feet and gripped both hands on her fur coat, hauling her away.

"She's fine . . . just get back into your car and drive off. Move it."

Jane picked up Janet's tote bag, which had fallen from her hand when she was flung over the bonnet, and she was beside Gibbs as he dragged Janet to their patrol car. She didn't scream and seemed to be in a state of shock, heaving for breath. As Gibbs opened the passenger door she started kicking and punching, and then snarled as she tried to bite his hand.

Gibbs backhanded her hard and, shoving her into the car face forward, he chucked the keys to Jane and instructed her to drive. He had his whole weight on Janet as he pushed her face down and told her she was under arrest, and that they were CID. She seemed to deflate like a punctured rubber tire, then swore at him.

"You fuckin' arseholes! I need a doctor . . . you bastards . . ."

Jane was shaking badly as she drove through the West End and headed toward a multi-story car park that Gibbs suggested they use to ask Angie some questions. The car park was regularly used by the Met and the attendant lifted up the barrier and asked no questions. They went up to the fourth floor where it was partly open, with only a few cars parked. Gibbs gestured for Jane to drive to the furthest corner, then instructed her to reverse and park up.

Janet had grown quiet and Gibbs allowed her to sit up beside him. She was complaining about the pain in her hip and had rubbed it, then pulled down her elastic skirt waistband to check it out. Only as they parked up and Jane switched off the engine did Janet show she was scared. She had a deep, rasping, husky voice that sounded part cockney and part American.

"I don't like this . . . I want to know what you two are after. You got to show me some fuckin' ID cos I don't believe you are coppers."

Gibbs took out a packet of cigarettes and offered her one. She shook her head, and he lit one for himself. He gestured toward Jane who turned to face her.

"That is WDC Jane Tennison. She was stationed at Hackney until recently, and was part of the investigation into a series of sexual assaults. She was subsequently on the arrest of the perp, who is also being accused of rape. WDC Tennison was given your coat to wear. Why was that?"

"I dunno"

"Why did she need to wear something that made her look like you? It's a very distinctive coat, Janet, or do you prefer to be called Angie?"

She shrugged and gestured for Gibbs to open the window as the smoke was wafting in her face from his cigarette.

"The arresting officer was DI Nick Moran . . . you know him?"

"No."

"You know anything about the rapist?"

"No."

"He was caught trying to assault WDC Tennison in your coat, so shall we start again?"

"They sell 'em in Brick Lane. They also come in pink, and three different sizes . . . small, medium and large, and you can call me any name you like, you bastard."

"Don't make me angry. I am going to give you one last chance to give me some answers. Firstly, about the severe beating you took; secondly, about DI Moran's relationship with you; and thirdly, how your coat was used in a CID covert operation and then you got it back, as you are still wearing it."

He slapped Janet hard on the back of her head and she jolted forward and then rocked back. Jane decided that enough was enough and leaned over from the front seat.

"Please, Spence, will you let me talk to her? There's no need for you to get physical . . ."

"Oh, I see . . . we're going to play good cop, bad cop, are we? You lot make me sick."

Gibbs gave Janet another hard slap, took out his handcuffs and gripped her wrist. He clicked them on and then attached one end to the door handle.

"She's all yours, for ten minutes."

Gibbs reached into the front seat shelf and pulled out his Coke bottle, then opened the door and slammed it shut. Jane turned her body round in the front seat and pulled up her legs so she was raised higher and was able to lean toward Janet.

"Please don't make him angry . . . we're trying to get to the truth. It is a very serious offense to withhold evidence, and for an officer to be connected to that offense will have severe repercussions that will give us reason to arrest you."

"I haven't fuckin' done anything wrong! I don't know what you are bloody talking about. Just what offense am I supposed to have done? I tell you what is an offense, you two almost getting me bloody run over and then kidnappin' me, and bringing me to this shit-hole."

"A bigger offense will be you leaving your son on his own while you are in Holloway, because that's where you are going to be sent for a long time."

"Pleeease don't try that one . . . you're fishin' and you ain't gonna catch me, because I've been around far longer than you ever had hot dinners. If you had anything on me I'd be down the station banged up, instead of being handcuffed with an amateur DC who looks like a teenager let out by Mummy and Daddy for the night."

Jane felt her hackles rising.

"You listen to me . . . I was the officer that got attacked, wearing your coat stinking of your perfume. He tried to rape me, split my lip open, but it is nothing compared to what he did to that poor kid he raped and left for dead. I have to be honest that I was not sure about him committing the rape of that seventeen-year-old, but if you have evidence to prove he is the rapist then you are letting him walk free . . . Why? Just tell me why?"

"Money."

"What?"

"He owes me, that's why."

"Owes you? But that doesn't make any sense . . . You would let him off the hook because he owes you?"

"He did this to me . . ."

Janet pulled open her shirt and there was a deep scar just below her throat and across her breasts. It was shocking and Jane couldn't think of anything to say as Angie did up her blouse.

"Screwed me up for stripping in any decent club. Besides, I just wanted to get some compensation. I'd have given it up in time, before his trial anyway."

"Given what up? I mean, do you really have incriminating evidence? Come on, start talking to me, I know about the phone calls to Allard's wife, I know you were blackmailing her into paying you a lot of money and I am asking you now to be honest with me."

"Yeah, I admit it, and I reckon that piece of garbage knows I could get him on the rape, otherwise why let his slitty-eyed wife pay up the cash? He knows I'm Angie, but he doesn't know my real name. I've got him by the short and curlies."

"What evidence do you have?" Jane asked.

"I had the knife that he cut me up with."

Jane took a deep breath.

"Did you give the knife to DI Moran?"

"Mind yer own fuckin' business."

"It *is* my business. It is very important—was the flick knife in your possession after he attacked you?"

"Maybe it was, maybe it wasn't."

"I wore your coat, and I was attacked because of it. He thought I was you, didn't he, *Janet*?"

Janet laughed and leaned back.

"Just goes to show, doesn't it, darlin'? In the dark all cats are gray. He had such an adrenalin buzz, he was stinkin'. Let me tell you something else . . . there's no way that little slitty-eyed bitch of a wife didn't know what he was getting up to. He must've gone back to her reeking of sex. He's hung like a horse!"

Jane almost recoiled.

"The only person that's been half-decent to me is Nick Moran. After Allard cut me up I couldn't work. I was badly in debt and I needed money for my son . . . I'm not making excuses."

"Take me through exactly what happened when he attacked you."

"I was up by the Lido, waiting for a punter. It was about 11 p.m. and I was getting cold. I was passing under a load of big trees, and the next minute he's behind me, grabbing me by the neck and saying that he was going to kill me."

"Can you remember the exact words he used?" Jane asked.

" 'You thieving whore . . . I'm going to kill you.' Next minute he's lifted me off my feet. I fight him off, punchin' and kickin' him, and I grabbed his balaclava . . . I was trying to pull his hair, but the hood came off in my hand. I spat at him, but he was too strong. He pushed me down on the ground, ripped open my blouse, and slashed at my neck and my breasts with the knife. I thought I was gonna die, so I kneed him in the balls and he dropped the knife. Then he heard the uniform copper shouting, cos he heard me screamin'. By the time they got to me Allard had jumped up and run off."

"You had the knife?"

"Yes, in me pocket."

"And as you had taken his balaclava it meant that you could recognize him—did you also take that?"

"No, I fuckin' didn't."

"But you saw his face?"

"Yeah, of course I fuckin' did!" Angie shouted.

"And that was all you used to blackmail Marie, that you could identify him and you had no other evidence?"

"For Chrissakes, I've told you now. I wanna get out."

At that moment Gibbs opened the passenger door and peered in.

"Are you all right, Tennison?"

"Yes, I'm fine . . . close the door, please."

Angie continued. "Anyway, they took me to hospital, stitched me up, but my face was a mess, I mean, I was in a bad way."

Jane leaned closer to her. "You made out a report at Hackney Station, didn't you?"

"Yeah, I did . . . they photographed my injuries and took a statement after I'd been to the hospital."

"Let's just go back. I need to know when you knew that earlier that night a young teenage girl had been raped in that same area."

"I heard about it when I had to make out the report."

"Who interviewed you at Hackney?"

Janet turned away. "I don't remember, I was in bad shape, I just wanted to get home. I had to go back cos I didn't want to take it any further."

Jane leaned closer. "When you went back to Hackney Station did you give the knife to DI Moran? It's very important you tell me, because the young rape victim remembered her assailant held a knife to her throat."

"Yeah, I did . . . but if it gets him into trouble I'll deny it."

Outside Gibbs got to the butt of his third cigarette and tossed it down on the ground impatiently. He had seen that Janet was talking so had kept his distance, his back toward the car. He turned as he heard the car door open and saw Jane getting out of the patrol car. She walked toward him, pulling the collar of her jacket up as the wind was whipping around the open section of the car park.

"Moran is in the clear for the connection to the blackmail. That's all down to Angie, aka Janet . . . but we need to talk to him as soon as possible."

Gibbs glared at her. "Really?"

"Yes. She was attacked later on the same night the young girl was raped. She was almost killed and fought like a wild cat. She would have been dead if a uniform officer hadn't found her. The rape victim wasn't discovered until early morning as she was unconscious and hidden in bushes."

"How much longer is this gonna take? I'm freezing my bollocks off up here."

"Don't you understand, Spence? The two cases were not connected straight away. The rape victim is an innocent seventeen-year-old. It was Moran who sifted out the possibility that the attacks were both committed by the same man, but it took him two weeks before he brought 'Mary Kelly,' Angie, who we now know to be Janet Brown, in for questioning."

"What evidence has she got, Jane?"

"She snatched the balaclava off his face . . . she recognized him."

"And that's it?" Gibbs asked.

Jane hesitated and decided against repeating to him that Janet had admitted giving the knife to Moran to use as evidence. If, as she had said, she were to deny it, it could create even more of a problem for Moran.

"So she admitted the blackmail?"

"Yes, she lied about having evidence so that she could black-mail Marie Allard."

Janet began banging and shouting for them to let her out, and they both started to move toward the car.

Gibbs stopped and turned to her.

"Listen, Tennison. This is not my case . . . I've already done my part tonight. I was only interested in checking out Moran, and that's what I've done. He's not a bent copper, as I knew he wouldn't be. I'm not involved, all right? You were on this busi-ness at Hackney, so now it's down to you to do the run around and report to Moran in the morning."

Jane was in a quandary. She really hadn't expected Gibbs to just leave her to handle all the new information, but she had no option. They drove Janet to a high rise council estate, where she was staying with her mother who was caring for her little boy. She had grown very quiet in the car and moaned about her hip hurting. Gibbs helped her out of the rear passenger side and she walked very slowly toward the entrance of her block. He stayed with her as she got into the dirty lift, which stank of urine, and the floor was littered with cigarette butts.

"Which floor?"

"Six . . . the button someone has stubbed a cigarette out on."

He watched her press the button, and as the gates started to close he stepped out.

Gibbs was silent as he drove Jane back to the section house. She had attempted to be a team player, but she really felt as if she was on her own again.

He parked up and decided to go across the road to the Warburton Arms, where he knew he could get a drink even after closing time. The first person he saw, playing snooker, was DI Nick Moran.

CHAPTER TWENTY-FOUR

The following morning Jane was in the ladies' locker room and hadn't even taken off her coat when Edith walked in.

"You'd better get over to Hackney—DI Moran has called three times. He says he has an update on the Allard trial. I'll make a note in the schedule that that's where you'll be."

"Is DI Gibbs in?"

"He's in, but he's having a meeting with DCI Shepherd and left instructions that he didn't want to be disturbed."

Jane had a terrible sinking feeling as she left Bow Street. She was sure that Spencer Gibbs had gone behind her back and spoken to Moran. Her fears were confirmed when, on arriving at the reception in Hackney Station, DC Brian Edwards told her that DI Moran was waiting to see her in his office, and he wasn't a happy man.

Moran was perching on the edge of his desk, his office door open, as Jane approached.

"Sir . . ." Her stomach was churning.

"Shut the door behind you. You know, Tennison, if you were a bloke I would grab you by your collar and throw a punch at your smug little face. I don't know what you think you've been playing at, but I am going to hear what you've got to say before I get you back in uniform directing traffic."

"I am not in any way smug, sir, I'm just very nervous. I never had any intention of acting on my own, it was just circumstances and my need to double-check before I brought my findings to anyone's attention, especially yours."

Moran leaned forward, pulling his loud tie loose from his shirt collar.

"I'm all ears . . ."

"May I refer to my notes?"

Moran gave the go-ahead with his hands. Jane opened her bag and took out her notebook.

"You can obviously verify the dates, sir. On the night of the twenty-third of August uniform officers brought in a prostitute called Janet Brown. She had been badly beaten and had a deep knife wound to her chest and left breast, which required hospital treatment. She was photographed and a report made out but she refused to press charges, claiming that she was unable to identify the man as he had worn a balaclava."

Moran stared at her, his blue eyes holding hers, and acted as if what she was saying was obvious.

Jane continued.

"The CID were brought in to investigate the rape of a young girl who was found semiconscious on the morning of the twenty-fourth of August. She had suffered a terrible beating and was unable to identify the rapist as he had worn a black woolen mask covering his entire face. But time wise it was possible that she had been raped earlier the same night as Janet Brown. But the two cases were not, to begin with, linked as having the same perpetrator."

He banged his chair to sit forward. "I linked them."

"I know you did, sir, because you brought in Janet Brown, under the assumed name of Mary Kelly, and requisitioned her. But this was two weeks later, when you organized a CID operation and used me as a decoy. I believe you gave me the blue rabbit fur coat as it was probable that the rapist intended Janet Brown to be his victim, and not the young girl."

Moran leaned forward, and flicked through a statement, not looking at Jane. He then sighed and picked up a pencil.

"The prostitute—Janet Brown, Mary Kelly, Angie—was unable to identify her attacker and refused point blank to assist my operation, which was why I held her in the cells. She was released the following morning after we had arrested Peter Allard."

"I know that, sir. I also know that she is capable of identifying him. She pulled his balaclava off when he was attacking her."

"Perhaps what you don't know, Tennison, is that Janet Brown, aka Mary Kelly, aka Angie, had stolen a bag of takings from a taxi around about a month beforehand . . . it was a lot of money, nearly four hundred quid as he had been doing airport runs. He had argued about paying her after sex, so she stole it and did a runner. So now we have a known hooker who steals a load of money from Peter Allard. When he did catch up with her he beat the shit out of her, because she was a thief. Are you following me, Tennison?"

"Yes, sir . . . I didn't know that it was Janet who had stolen Allard's money . . ." She swallowed and took a deep breath.

"No, you didn't know . . . but I did. So you tell me, what a jury are going to believe? A known tart with a long list of previous arrests for prostitution, or are they going to say she deserved what she got and that he didn't rape her? He's a hard-working man with a wife and two kids. It was the first time he had ever been arrested . . . look at how he behaved in court, head hanging down and weeping, all innocent. He even admitted that he did fondle a few women, but he denied rape."

Jane couldn't look at him.

"I wanted him for the rape of that innocent seventeen-year-old girl. I wanted him charged with sexual assaults that I had no evidence to prove he did, but I knew he did them. Look at the way he attacked you and how he acted in court and what you were subjected to by his council. So you tell me, why would I not use Janet Brown as a witness?"

"I don't know, sir."

"She is a tart . . . but she's also an informer and has been for years. One court appearance and she's no use to us. You have no idea just how useful she has been. And you think after one conversation with her that you know her?"

"But she was blackmailing Marie Allard, sir."

Moran threw up his hands and laughed, becoming increasingly impatient.

"That's how she survives, Tennison! Allard cut her breasts and scarred her . . . he would have killed her if we hadn't stopped him."

Jane was unable to hold back.

"So you *knew* what Allard had done to Janet Brown, and yet you made me wear her blue fur coat and planted me as a decoy, *knowing* that he had almost killed her?"

Moran lifted his arms up again.

"Yes, I own up to that. We lost sight of you for a few minutes. But it was only a few minutes . . ."

"So, I'm wearing Janet Brown's blue fur coat . . . you want Allard to think I am her and for him to attack me, so that you can arrest him? Because you already had the knife he used in the rape, and when he slashed Janet."

Moran folded his arms. After a long pause he spoke. For the first time she could see he was uneasy, eventually choosing his words carefully.

"What choice do I have? I'm pretty certain he may be connected to a murder that occurred five years ago. If I don't put him away he's going to kill again."

Moran stood up and opened his office door. Jane didn't know how to react to the fact that he had just virtually admitted to planting evidence. As if he was reading her mind Moran gently touched her shoulder.

"It was all on the level, OK? Now, come with me. I want to show you something."

Moran walked ahead of her and went into the incident room. DC Brian Edwards was standing in front of the information board.

"It's not positive news from Maidstone, guv. The Chief Superintendent there said we would need a lot more incriminating evidence to excavate the garden at the house the Allards used to rent."

Moran sighed as Edwards moved away from the board. Pinned up were the photographs they had pulled out from the cold files at Maidstone. Moran tapped the board with his pencil.

"This is what we're looking into, Tennison, and we need to question—"

Jane interrupted as she saw the photograph of Susie Luna with the rose in her hair.

"Marie Allard?"

Moran hesitated. "What did you just say?"

"That's a photograph of Marie Allard."

"No, it isn't, it's the missing girl from five years ago. Her name is Susie Luna."

"Oh, sorry . . . they look so similar."

Moran glanced at Edwards, then back to Jane.

"Marie Allard gave her husband a cast-iron alibi for the day Susie Luna went missing. I think we need to go and have a chat with her."

"I would really appreciate it if I was allowed to accompany you—Marie Allard trusts me. In fact, she called me personally to tell me she was being blackmailed by Janet Brown who referred to herself as Angie and sang a song and—"

"Did she now?"

Edwards raised his hand. "Can I have a quiet word, guv, in your office?"

"Sure. DC Ashton, show Tennison the files we've got on Susie Luna."

Edwards closed Moran's office door behind them.

"Did everything go all right, guv?"

"Yes. Just a misunderstanding. What did you want to talk to me about?"

"Two things . . . we received confirmation this morning of a trial date for Peter Allard, in two weeks' time."

"That doesn't give us much time to investigate the Susie Luna connection, does it?"

"I'm afraid there may be another problem, sir. Apparently the barrister who represents Allard has raised doubts about his confession and has requested an independent forensic examination of the interview notes. In particular, the confession that Allard supposedly signed."

"Shit . . . that's all I bloody need. I'm going to take Tennison with me to interview Marie Allard. The last time we were there with SOCO we pulled the bloody house apart, so I'm taking Tennison along to give the gentle touch . . . maybe have a woman to woman chat with her." Moran smiled.

"I wouldn't mind coming along after all the new information we've uncovered . . ."

"No, I want you to man the fort here, Edwards. I'm only taking Tennison with me to keep her sweet."

"Gone sour on you, has she, sir?"

"You could say that."

CHAPTER TWENTY-FIVE

Moran parked up outside the Allards' house.

"She's very nervous, sir. It might take a while for her to come to the front door."

"Take as long as you like, I'll be here."

"Thank you."

Moran watched Jane walk away, then down the small pathway leading to the doorway where she rang the bell. He saw her step back and look up at the first-floor window, and then move closer to the door. It was another few minutes before the door opened and Jane stepped inside.

Marie replaced the chain lock. Jane waited for her to turn, and was taken aback by the way she looked. Her hair was lank, she had lost even more weight and seemed shrunken and shaking with nerves. Jane dropped her bag to the floor and held out her arms, hugging Marie. "I am so sorry not to get back to you before now, but it has taken such a long time and I wanted to come to see you personally as I didn't want any of the officers here when I tell you what I have found out. I know how much it will affect you."

Marie stepped away, her eyes wide with anxiety. Jane put an arm around her shoulders and suggested that they went into the lounge to sit down. Marie seemed to calm down as Jane sat on the sofa opposite her.

"I am so sorry to be the one to tell you, but the woman that was blackmailing you is not connected to the police. She was attacked by your husband and suffered a terrible beating that has scarred her for life. She was not prepared to identify him before, but she is now prepared to go to court."

Jane was surprised at how easily she was able to lie, because in reality she knew that Janet Brown would not go to court.

Marie pressed her body back in the easy chair and clasped her hands together.

"He has lied to you, terrible lies . . . the rape victim was just a young, vulnerable teenager. She won't ever recover from the ordeal, and you know that he also attacked me, and if the police officer hadn't been there . . ." Jane's performance was getting better by the second as she lowered her head and ran her fingers over her lips, reminding Marie about when she had first seen her with her lips cut.

"Oh my God," Marie said, clasping and unclasping her hands.

Jane left a long pause, taking out a handkerchief from her pocket and blowing her nose. Marie seemed unable to look directly at her; she was so tiny and vulnerable and trembling, but even though Jane felt sorry for her she had to use that to get some answers.

"How long did you know, Marie, that he was leaving you and your two children and going out to attack and rape women? How long have you known he was evil? Do you realize that you made the reality invisible to yourself, refused to smell the sex? You could smell them on him, couldn't you?"

"No . . . no . . . that's not true."

"Yes, it is, Marie, don't lie. You kept that room upstairs locked. You said it was to protect your children but you knew what was in there, and you used to go into that room when you were here alone . . . didn't you?"

"No . . . no, I did not. He would never . . ." She stopped.

"What did he do to you when he found out you were look-ing in that room, seeing those disgusting pornographic maga-zines? You knew when he was on steroids and behaving like a crazy man . . . you knew and you kept quiet because you didn't want to know the truth. But he will be out soon, Marie, and he will come back here, and you will have to live with it all over again."

Jane knew that some of what she was saying was getting through, as Marie bent forward, clutching at her stomach.

"He will get out, Marie, he will come back unless you stand up and face the truth. You said to me that you couldn't have sex and that was the excuse . . . that is *his* excuse. He blames *you*—it's all your fault that he went with those women and raped and assaulted them. It's your fault because he says you couldn't have sex. You lied about it to me, but it isn't true, is it? What did he do to you, Marie?"

Her face crumpled and she began to sob uncontrollably. Jane felt for her but she knew she had to plow on because Marie had not yet admitted knowing the truth about her husband or if he had, as Jane suspected, abused her.

"Why don't you tell me, Marie, because I am really trying to understand why you appeared to be adamant your husband was innocent, when I can see the pressure you have been under with the blackmail and the threats . . ."

"I been frightened of him, always frightened. He made me do things, always he threatened to take my children from me, so I stay, but if I make him happy he would not beat me. If I not do what he want he would lock me up and take children to his mother. Always he threaten me so I do what he wants."

Jane got up and gently laid her hand on Marie's shoulder. As she turned back she noticed a photograph of Marie with her eldest child as a toddler. Jane pointed to it.

"Was that taken when you lived in Maidstone?"

Marie seemed relieved to be changing the subject. She wiped her eyes.

"Yes . . . yes."

"And you worked at the Majestic Hotel when you were there, didn't you?"

"Yes, I did," Marie replied.

Jane waited a moment before saying quietly, "I need to ask you about your friend, Susie Luna."

Marie reeled back in her chair, visibly shaken by the reference to Susie Luna.

"Five years ago you gave your husband an alibi, confirming that he was at home with you on the afternoon and evening that your friend went missing. If you lied about that, and we find out, do you know what that means . . . committing perjury? You could be sent to prison for six years. But if you want to tell me the truth now, I might be able to help you. Did you lie for him, Marie?"

Marie was expressionless. Very slowly she stood up, and with no emotion she began twisting strands of her hair through her fingers. It was strange, but it seemed to calm her.

"He says he will take my children if I not do or say what he want me to. But I have plan now . . ."

Jane was confused by the complete change in Marie's demeanor.

"I have something for you," Marie said calmly. She started walking toward the door as Jane stood up.

"Where are you going, Marie?"

She walked out of the room. "Follow me . . ."

Jane hurried after her, down the hallway and into the kitchen. She was horrified as she watched Marie pulling a large knife out of the knife block on the counter. Marie knelt down, opened a cupboard door, and used the knife to release a worn envelope that had been stuck to the inside of the cupboard with Sellotape. She then stood up, put the knife back in the block and laid the envelope on the kitchen counter, placing her hand on top of it.

"This is proof . . . but you not send me away from my children."

Moran looked up as Jane came out of the house and gestured for him to come inside. He hurried from the car and followed Jane into the lounge. Marie was sitting calmly on the sofa, staring into space and twisting her hair between her fingers.

"Marie has given me this, sir. It's Susie Luna's passport. She has also admitted that she posed as Susie, wearing a rose in her hair, at a few locations, including a bus stop and outside a fish and chip shop."

Moran took it, then flicked through the old, dog-eared passport and glanced over at Marie.

"So when you were posing as your friend, where was your husband, Mrs. Allard?"

"I don't know . . . when I go home, Susie had gone. I never saw her again."

Moran held up the passport. "So where did you find this?"

"It was in her handbag," Marie replied.

"We're going to need a statement from you at the station, Marie," said Jane gently. "I'll stay with you throughout."

Jane stayed with Marie for two and a half hours as she gave a statement. She admitted that she had introduced Susie to her husband. Their son was three years old, and Marie was pregnant with their daughter. Under pressure to recall how well her husband had known Susie Luna, Marie became very distressed and said that he had sex with her, but he made Marie deny it when the police in Kent questioned them both as being the last people to see Susie Luna alive.

Marie admitted that, because of her pregnancy, she had felt very sick at work and had returned home early, walking in on Peter raping Susie. He was very angry and Marie had run out, afraid that he was going to beat her up. Marie never saw her friend again. Susie Luna had always worn a red rose in her hair and Peter had told Marie to put it on and walk around obvious places for two hours. Marie went and stood for twenty minutes at a bus stop and then outside a fish and chip shop for a further half an hour, eventually standing outside a pub. When she returned home, Peter was working out with his weights and never mentioned Susie Luna again. A few weeks later, Marie found Susie's handbag, went through it and took out the passport. Peter used a leather strap to beat her, snatching the handbag from her, and she thought he must have thrown it in one of the industrial bins outside the hotel. Marie kept Susie's rose and used to always have it by her little statue of the Madonna. She looked at Jane.

"I saw it every day when we move here, so I never forget her, but Peter, he sometime frightened the children, and Kim, my little boy, when they arrested Peter, he ask me if he was bad boy, would he be punished like Susie Luna? I could not believe my boy even remember her, because he was only three year old. But Susie was always so sweet and kind to him. I took the rose as my daughter want to put it in her hair. Susie Luna has been a ghost in my heart."

Jane was exhausted and remained sitting in the interview room with Marie. "You have been very brave, Marie. And you know if you ever need to talk to someone, please call me."

Marie nodded.

"Today I feel better than I have for as long as I remember. I won't go and visit him but if he call me, Detective Moran said I not mention Susie Luna and I won't. I will keep secret until he pay the price for her murder." By mid-afternoon Marie was taken home. Moran knocked on the open door, and leaned against the door frame as she turned toward him.

"She will make one hell of a witness for the prosecution . . . well done, Tennison."

"Thank you, sir. You were always right about Peter Allard and hopefully we will now have enough to legally make sure he gets a long sentence."

Moran watched Jane pick up her bag, put away her notebook and walk past him. He had previously thought of her as a waste of space. A female probationary officer of no consequence . . . but he now knew she was a force to be reckoned with, and not to be treated lightly.

CHAPTER TWENTY-SIX

Jane was off duty at the weekend, and she had agreed to go home to visit her parents. Mrs. Tennison had made roast chicken with all the trimmings, roast potatoes, carrots and broccoli, and her usual gravy from the roasting tin. Jane's sister Pam and her brother-in-law were at some hairdressing function in Birmingham as Pam had been doing a special hair tinting course and wanted Tony there for the weekend.

"That's good news. Is there anything I can do to help with lunch?" Jane said.

"No no, dear, everything's done but the dessert. Pam's back at work and might even win the coloring competition as they have to cut and recolor and style with models. I doubt Tony will be all that interested, but they have a double room at a very nice hotel," Mrs. Tennison said proudly.

"That's good," Jane said, as her attention was drawn to a newspaper placed on the sideboard while her mother added the finishing touches to lunch. She picked it up and took it into the sitting room, never having time to read the newspaper while at work. She was shocked at the headline, "Murder in the Bath accused couple to stand trial," and the press coverage was extensive, with photographs of Katrina Harcourt being led into the court. The redhead was smiling as if enjoying the moment, unlike the photographs of Barry Dawson who had a blanket covering his head. By the time Jane had finished reading the article her father had opened a bottle of wine.

"That's a shocking case, isn't it?"

"Yes, the CID at the station investigated and it was a very complicated case as the young wife in the bath was wrongly diagnosed as being a non-suspicious death, but when we had a second post-mortem it revealed another wound had been inflicted. The suspects were having an affair and it was a very complicated inquiry to be able to charge them with murder. The trial will not go ahead for months."

"Good God, and she looks such an attractive woman! So were you involved in the investigation?"

Jane hesitated and then nodded, but not wanting to go into details she collected the newspapers and stacked them ready to be thrown out.

Her mother, who had overheard the conversation, found it difficult to ask Jane about her work as a police officer. She gave her husband a shake of her head as a warning not to continue. Her father steered the conversation back to safer waters, but after a couple of glasses of wine, while Mrs. Tennison tried to make a crème brûlée, her father topped up her glass and asked quietly, "So it must have been quite a time for you at Bow Street?"

Jane raised her glass and took a sip. How could she even begin to explain about the tragic murder of Shirley Dawson, or the forthcoming trial of Peter Allard? To tell him about the time spent in and around the sex shops and strip joints of Soho, or even the interaction with the beautiful Janet Brown? It was all so far removed from the warmth and normality of being at home with her family.

They sat down together and enjoyed the main course but her mother was in a state of anxiety as the toffee crisp on top of her crème brûlée had hardened like cement and her father was worried he'd break the denture plate in his mouth.

"I must have used too much sugar; it's not that bad is it, Jane?" her mother asked.

"No, it's fine," she said with clenched teeth.

"It's supposed to just crack when you tap it with a spoon."

"You should have used a hammer!" her father said.

This made Jane smile, and as they were trying to chew through the very hard topping, all three of them suddenly started laughing.

"It's so good to be home," Jane said, feeling emotional.

Her father screwed up his face again as he chewed and then swallowed.

"Well, it's perfect for us to have you safe and sound, because we miss you."

The phone suddenly started ringing in the hallway. Mr. Tennison stood up and went to answer it. A moment later he called out to Jane.

"It's for you, Jane."

"For me?" she asked, surprised. She walked over and took the receiver from her father.

"Hello?" she said into the mouthpiece.

"Jane, it's me, Spence. I'm in a callbox at the end of your road . . . I need to see you. Can you come and meet me?"

Jane laughed. "Are you asking me out on a date, Spence?"

"No . . . we've got a nightmare on our hands, Jane. Peter Allard's been released."

"Give me five minutes, all right?"

Jane didn't want to show her parents how disturbed she was by Gibbs's phone call.

"I'm sorry, but I have to go in to the station. There's some confusion about one of my reports."

"Oh, don't you have time for a coffee?" her mother asked.

"No, Mum, I'm sorry but if I can I'll come back later."

She walked down to the end of the road and found Gibbs standing beside a patrol car parked next to the callbox.

"Is this a joke, Spence?"

"No, it's deadly serious. Moran is going crazy. Apparently Marie got a call from him from the prison, and even though she was warned not to mention anything or refer to the present inquiry about Susie Luna, she told Allard she wanted a divorce, that she knew about Angie."

"What?"

"Yeah, her idea of revenge, but the stupid bitch has really screwed up because he's fucking got bail until his trial."

"I don't believe it, not after what we uncovered about his connection to Susie Luna."

"You don't understand, Jane . . . that's an entirely separate investigation, and if they find a body they can arrest him straight after the trial."

"But you're not even working on Allard's case. What do you want me to do?"

"I know I'm bloody not, but Moran wants protection for Janet Brown. He contacted me because he knew that we had taken her to her mother's flat at the council estate. So I need you to come with me to go back there again and get her into protective custody."

When DI Moran found out, he was apoplectic with fury. He had only just returned from Maidstone where Scenes of Crime officers were waiting for permission to lift the paving stones from the small patio garden of the property that had been rented by Allard. They had run into a problem as the actual owner of the house had sublet it and they would require his permission to begin working. DC Edwards had also discovered that the garden had only been paved over during Allard's occupation. They had no option but to wait for permission to start digging.

Moran's blood pressure was going through the roof. He had contacted Detective Chief Superintendent Metcalf and wanted to update him on the Susie Luna case and he had agreed to come into the station, but he had to wait for over an hour.

"Sir, all I was told when I was at Maidstone was that a trial date had been set for two weeks' time. I've now been informed that they have released Peter Allard on compassionate grounds. They've just let a killer walk out, sir."

Metcalf gestured for Moran to calm down.

"I can't do anything about that, because this is a very complex situation, Nick. I don't want to have to underline this to you but it is the inconsistencies in Allard's confession that have given the barristers and the judge the opportunity to release him. Apparently his wife wanted to divorce him and take his children and he begged to be given the opportunity to see her."

"Yes, I know that, sir, and I want her and their two children put into protective custody, because if he is on the loose God knows what he is going to do. And we now have a strong witness that has agreed to identify him with evidence on the rape charge and in my estimation he's going to go after her."

Metcalf flicked through the statements and notes.

"The prostitute Janet Brown?"

"Yes, sir."

"She used the name 'Angie,' among others, but he must now know she is a valuable witness if his wife told him she knew about her."

Metcalf continued to read the reports as Moran waited impatiently.

"This Susie Luna situation, you don't have enough evidence. She was reported missing five years ago, and these accusations from an aggrieved wife are not enough. But if you want them protected, go ahead . . . and just keep your powder dry. I'll leave you to handle it."

"Thank you, sir."

Peter Allard, carrying a small overnight bag, stepped out of the prison gates. Unshaven and already over-anxious because of the wait he had been subjected to before he was released, he hurried to get to the nearest phone kiosk. He had only a small amount of change which had been taken from his pocket when he was brought in to the prison.

DC Edwards drove DI Moran in a patrol car to the Allards' house. They parked up outside, and DC Ashton approached the car and opened the back passenger door. "He hasn't shown yet, guv . . . We've got her and the kids in a safe house. When I told her he had been released, she was terrified. I thought she was going to collapse."

"This is bloody unbelievable, isn't it? They let a killer out on the loose, they don't tell his wife, and even I wasn't told until this morning."

"We don't yet know for sure if he is a killer."

"Yes, thank you, Edwards. Either way they've bloody released a man accused of indecent sexual assault, a man who's also been told the name of the key witness in the case against him."

"How did Allard manage to get out?" Ashton asked.

"His confession was thrown out due to inconsistencies, and as he has been on remand for some time, and the only firmed-up evidence we've got is sexual assault, he was granted bail. He just needs to go back for his trial in two weeks. If he finds out that we're on to him regarding the Susie Luna case, he'll do a bloody runner. You go back to the station and keep in contact on the radio if you hear anything."

"Yes, sir, I'll get the Underground then. I've been here since early this morning."

"Get back any way you can, go on, but stand by as we might need you, I've only got a handful of officers."

Ashton, rather disgruntled as he was also supposed to have the weekend off, walked off down the road. He was tired out having been up all night with his new baby girl and his wife was exhausted. She would be really pissed off with him as he was now on standby at the station.

Moran lit a cigarette and checked his watch. Edwards saw a black taxi pull up in front of the house. Peter Allard stepped out of the passenger door.

"Shit, here he is, guv," Edwards said.

"Let's see how he reacts to an empty house."

Allard was wearing a pair of jeans and a denim shirt. They saw him leaning into the taxi driver's window, and he appeared to be having a conversation. He then went up the path to the front door and rang the doorbell. He stepped back and looked up at the windows, then rang the bell again. When there was still no answer they saw him reach up to the top of the door frame and take down what was obviously a spare front door key.

Allard opened the door and replaced the key before he slammed the door behind him. Moran gestured to Edwards.

"That's Allard's taxi cab, isn't it? Go and check the driver out and get rid of him."

Edwards climbed out of the patrol car, crossed over to the taxi and tapped on the driver's window.

"Are you waiting for someone?"

The driver answered, "Yes, I'm booked."

"No you're not. This cab registered to you, is it? You got your cab driver's license?"

Moran saw the driver move off as Edwards returned to sit beside him.

"He moved off fast but it's Allard's taxi, didn't even have to show my warrant card."

Allard stood in the neat and orderly lounge. He went out into the kitchen and immediately became suspicious as a meal had been left half-eaten on the table.

He headed up the stairs and saw the wooden slats nailed across his gym door. He placed one hand on either side of the door frame and kicked the door open. The room was in the same state of disarray as it had been when Moran and the SOCO had searched his house. The knives were all gone, but he picked up a nunchuck, swinging it by the chain. He then went into the children's bedroom. The beds were unmade and the floor was strewn with toys.

"Bloody untidy," he muttered, as he made his way to the master bedroom. It wasn't like Marie to leave the house in such a mess. If nothing else she had always kept the place spick and span and even his mother had agreed with that.

"Bitch!" he exclaimed, as he saw that the wardrobe doors were wide open. Some of the clothes were lying on the bed and it was evident that Marie had packed in a hurry. He twisted the chain in his hand and swung the nunchuck down hard on the bed.

Gibbs and Jane stepped into the stinking lift of the council block and went up to floor six.

"Which flat did she go into?" Jane asked.

"I dunno . . . I just saw her into the lift and she asked for the sixth floor. I didn't go up with her, so we'll have to try them all. I'll start at 600, you start at 640 . . ."

Moran looked at his watch. "He's been in there over an hour."

Edwards yawned. "Maybe this is a waste of time. It doesn't look as if he's going anywhere."

"Yes, he was. He asked that taxi to wait for him."

Inside the house Allard pulled on a black tracksuit and a pair of Adidas trainers. He looked out of the window and swore when he saw that the taxi had gone. "Bastard!" he muttered. He then put in a call using the phone in the hallway. He needed cash, as he'd not found any in the house.

He went into the kitchen, put two slices of bread on a plate, buttered them, and opened the cupboard to take out a jar of Marmite.

* * *

Gibbs and Jane had no luck with their door to door inquiries. Nobody had heard of Janet Brown, Mary Kelly or Angie, and no one had seen a black girl with a toddler. By now they had knocked on every door on the sixth floor. Two flats had not answered so the residents could be out. In most cases the occupants were abusive, slamming their doors shut. No one wanted to admit to knowing anyone when the police were involved.

"Well, that's it then," Gibbs said.

"You know who I think might know where she is, and if she's working one of the clubs? That ginger-haired boy, Philip."

"Christ! Does that mean another trek into Soho?" Gibbs moaned.

"You don't have to come with me, Spence. I'll find her on my own," Jane said tetchily.

"Listen, Jane, I've already explained about Moran. I just covered my arse, all right? I didn't drop you in it, but you have to learn you can't just hurl dirt at a good officer like Moran without severe consequences. I was looking out for him, OK? I didn't even intend talking to him but he was in the pub and asked what was going down . . ."

"All right, all right. Are you going to come with me, or not?"

"Yes . . . but it's my day off as well, you know," Gibbs said, reluctantly.

They returned to the patrol car and Gibbs radioed in to Moran to say they had not been able to warn Janet Brown so they were now going off to see if she was working one of the strip clubs.

Moran was becoming impatient. After receiving the call in from Gibbs he had hoped they would be able to follow Allard and see if he led them to Janet Brown. As there was no show, he was not going to wait any longer but would go into the house and check it out. He slammed out of the car, and Edwards hurried after him. He kicked the door in and shouted, "Police . . . POLICE!"

They moved from room to room, unsure if Allard was in the house. Not finding him downstairs, Moran went cautiously up to the landing, while Edwards looked in the cupboard under the stairs. The door to the room used by Allard as a gym was half open, the splintered wood all over the carpet. Moran eased the door open wider with his foot before entering but it was empty; he then went into the bedroom. All the wardrobe doors were wide open, and disturbingly there was an array of women's clothes left torn and shredded over the bed. Moran then hurtled down the stairs as Edwards yelled from the kitchen, "He was onto us, he's just legged it."

The kitchen window looked out over the small back garden. It had a low fence; each property had a similar type, and the end of terrace had a high brick wall. Edwards and Moran watched Allard climbing up and taking two attempts to make it to the top.

"Get out, cut him off," Moran shouted.

As Edwards raced down the road, Moran hurtled out of the front door and threw himself into the patrol car. He started up the engine and did a fast U turn, the tires screeching as he drove to the end terraced house.

Edwards was bending over, panting and gasping for breath, and they could both see the black taxi disappearing down the road.

"Shit." Moran hit the steering wheel with his hand as Edwards got in beside him.

The numerous small turnings up ahead gave no sighting and Edwards radioed in to Gibbs to inform him they were following a black taxi with Allard as passenger.

Moran shook his head. "We're not following, we've bloody lost him."

"There it is, up ahead," shouted Edwards. Moran put his foot down and at speed overtook the taxi and swung the car to stop directly in front of the vehicle. There was no passenger, just a very startled cab driver who put his hands up in the air, terrified.

Gibbs and Jane were walking down Berwick Street. They had stopped by various strip clubs, some closed and not opening until the evening. At one small dingy club, Gibbs had removed a photograph of Janet, and the bouncer was very unpleasant and abusive, saying she had not worked there for weeks, that she was black trash and a loud-mouthed bitch.

Armed with Janet Brown's photo, they continued moving along the road, and stopped at the adult bookshop. The blinds were down, and the "closed" sign in the window. Gibbs hammered on the door but no one answered as it was too early in the afternoon, and Berwick Street was almost empty.

"Let's do another round of the clubs," Gibbs said, as they moved off. They were just turning into Wardour Street when Peter Allard got out of the Underground station in Oxford Street. He did not go via Wardour Street but walked down Regent Street, turning left into Argyle Street and passing the Palladium Theater, then Liberty and the Magistrates' Court to head into Berwick Street from the opposite direction. He was very tense, constantly looking over his shoulder.

He got to the adult bookshop, but made no attempt to try to gain entrance by the shop's front door; instead he eased warily toward the small white door beside it.

It was chipped and peeling and had no number or door knob, but a substantial key hole, and just above it was a small eye hole for anyone on the other side to check who was at the door. He gave two bangs of his fist and waited; he then repeated it, and pressed closer.

He heard the key turning, and the door was inched open by Stevie, the pot-bellied owner, who was wearing a pajama top, stained trousers and slippers.

"Hello, Stevie, lemme in."

"Shit, we're not fuckin' open."

"Yes you are, lemme in."

Stevie begrudgingly unhooked the chain and opened the door. He knew Allard because he was a regular customer and bought his porno magazines and steroids from the shop, but he didn't like being forced to open up. He walked along a dirty, bare-boarded narrow hallway, passing the door that gave access into the shop, Allard following behind. Above were the rooms the girls used for their clients and where Stevie had been sleeping. They continued into a small back room with racks of stacked magazines, some of them still boxed and some in an old locked cabinet as they were pornography with more graphic content. There were also drugs bagged and tagged, and bottles of extremely potent steroids.

"What you want? Take your pick, but make it fast."

Allard said he wanted the pills, not any magazines, and Stevie unlocked the cabinet, selecting the usual container and held it in his hand.

"You got the cash?"

Allard dug into the deep pocket of his tracksuit jacket with his left hand as if he was about to hand over the cash, but he used his right to bring out the nunchuck he had tucked into his waistband at the back. He was so fast, Stevie didn't see it coming, and the crack against his scalp was so vicious he sank to his knees. He tried to grab hold of one of the racks containing the magazines and it toppled over onto him. Allard stepped over the unconscious man, and picked up the container before turning back and out into the small corridor.

He knew this area, knew the girls rented the squalid rooms upstairs. This was where he had first met that tart Angie, and this was the place the red-haired kid worked—the kid Marie had described, that took his money. Just thinking of his wife made him tense with rage. He'd find her and when he did, he'd beat the living daylights out of her.

He went up the stairs and checked each dingy room before he sat on one of the dirty sheets, opened the container and took a fistful of small yellow pills.

It was getting dark and Soho was coming alive. Gibbs and Jane met up with Moran in the car park they had used previously. By now Moran had assigned a few uniform officers to search for Angie as well as Allard. There was one positive piece of news, and that was they had now been granted permission to start lifting the paving stones at the Allards' previous residence. As they had his passport they knew he could not escape abroad.

"Allard will be looking for Janet, and as we've not been able to trace her, maybe he's having the same problem."

Jane said nothing. They were sitting in the patrol car and the smoke was making her eyes run as the men were all chain smoking.

"She's a wily lady. I mean, she took me inside that estate, I saw her get into the lift, and she was lying. Press the sixth floor, she said, it's the one where someone stubbed their cigarette out. I saw her do it and then left. I never went up with her . . ."

Jane agreed. "We knocked on every door on the sixth floor, apart from two. Maybe we need to go back. None of the residents were that helpful, they just slammed the doors in our faces."

Gibbs sighed. "Listen, this is not my case, pals. I've been legging it around all afternoon and it's now getting dark; the tart could be anywhere, and so could Allard."

Moran stubbed out his cigarette and turned to Jane. "You want to give it one more try at that estate, and I'll do another round of the clubs? Spence, just drop her off, and Jane, radio in if you find her."

Gibbs drove Jane out of the car park as Moran and Edwards started to head toward the red light district. They stopped to buy a hot dog each and then heard the ambulance approaching with the lights flashing and bell ringing. A uniform officer approached and said that there was an altercation in Berwick Street at the adult bookshop and the woman who owned it had called in the police.

Moran watched as the still unconscious Stevie was carried on a stretcher into the ambulance and the paramedics began to try to resuscitate him. His wife was sobbing and swearing at the same time as she said she would find the bastard. Her husband had only one dried wound to the side of his head; apart from that there was no other physical sign of violence. She said it had to have been some pervert after money but she had already locked up the cabinet of drugs.

Moran was standing in the corridor where the rack of magazines still lay on its side as Stevie's wife became very agitated and wanted him to leave as she was going in the ambulance.

"I got to lock up . . . you can come back another time."

"Shut up," Moran snapped.

"I am not leaving without locking the doors, it'll be an open bloody invitation, there's stuff in here worth a lot of money."

Moran turned on her and told her to be quiet again, when he saw a trail of blood, not from beneath the rack but closer to the small staircase. She tried to interrupt him again but he ordered her to go and get in the ambulance.

"I can't leave this place open," Ada wailed.

Moran ignored her and began to slowly move up the stairs. Spots of blood could be seen, and then as he reached the landing there were blood splatterings against the wall. He pushed open the door and could see the small figure curled on his side, his red hair matted with blood, his face badly beaten, blood bubbles gathered at his open mouth. Moran went over to him. The poor kid was terrified, his eyes wide, and he even tried to ward off Moran.

" 'S'all right, I'm not going to hurt you. Do you know who did this to you? Look at me, come on, I've got an ambulance outside. You know who beat you up?"

Ginger started crying and then nodded his head. "Big guy . . . he hit me wiv this thing on a chain. Oh God, he done me head in."

"Listen, you are going to be looked after, but tell me why he did this to you."

Ginger spat out blood as Moran held him upright in a sitting position.

"Angie, he wanted to know where Angie lives."

"Did you tell him?"

"What you fuckin' think, he was crazy. I told him."

It was another few minutes before the boy was able to give Moran the address.

Moran picked the injured boy up in his arms and carried him out.

"Oh Jesus God, that's Ginger. Ginger, who would want to do something like that to him, he's just a kid!" Ada began screaming in hysterics as Moran carried the boy out into the street to the still waiting ambulance. He spoke urgently to Edwards.

"We get the car and get over to Janet Brown's estate. It has to have been Allard. Radio in to Gibbs that we're on our way."

* * *

Jane got out of the car and slammed the door.

"I'm going," Gibbs said.

"Fine, Spence, you go, or just wait until I come out and you can take me back to the section house. It's my day off as well, you know."

"It's not my bloody case," he moaned.

He watched her heading up the pathway to the estate entrance. She had the photograph of Janet Brown in her hand. She turned back and gave him a smile as she went in through the main doors. He felt a bit guilty. He knew he wouldn't drive off and leave her, he was just pissed off at losing almost an entire day off.

Inside Jane stood in the lift and looked at the floor numbered buttons. Floor six did have a burn mark, as if someone had stubbed out a cigarette against it. The lift was rank, smelling of urine, and dried white chewing gum covered the filthy carpet. It moved slowly upward, clanking and grinding. Once it lurched and she thought it was going to stop, but it continued upward.

The lift door opened, and Jane stepped out. She headed for the two flats where previously there had been no answer. She rang 615 and waited but there was still no one at home. She moved to flat 620 and was about to ring the doorbell when a thin-faced woman with a trolley bag came toward her.

"Excuse me, I am trying to contact this woman, she has a young child. Can you look at the photograph? I was told she lived on this floor."

The woman moved closer and stared at the photograph of Janet Brown.

"She's round the corner by the stairwell, go through the doors."

Jane smiled. "Thank you very much."

"That's all right. I live here." She took out her keys to flat 620, and Jane moved down the corridor. They had made a mistake, presuming all the flats were located along the landing. They had not considered there was another flat by the stone stairwell.

Jane, annoyed at all the time they had wasted, pushed open the double doors. They had cracked panes of glass and graffiti on them, and where the old carpet stopped there was a stone floor leading onto the stairwell. The flat's front door was painted green, chipped in places, and the brass letter box was in need of a polish. Jane had her hand on the old bell cemented into the wall. It also had brass surrounds but the button was missing. She put her hand out to push the letter box flap instead of knocking, but the door slowly opened a few inches. She hesitated and gently laid the flat of her hand to open it wider.

Still being very cautious, Jane moved a few steps into the hallway. A child's pushchair and toys were left on the floor. A large red tin toy double-decker bus lay on its side. The carpet was threadbare but the hallway was clean, an old upright hoover was propped against a wall with a full basket of laundry beside it. Hanging on a hook was the blue rabbit fur coat, and with relief Jane knew she was in the right flat, so she walked more confidently toward an open door that led into the sitting room. It was worn but comfortable, a sofa and an easy chair with a big throw rug in front of an electric three bar fire. Jane was about to call out for Janet, but stopped as she could smell a strong sweet unpleasant smell of body odor.

Allard had seen Jane enter. He was in the kitchen at the far end of the hall, the door open just a crack. He'd beaten the hell out of the ginger-haired kid to get the address and he'd been waiting for Janet. By now, Allard was sweating and hyper, and he eased back toward a cabinet to open a kitchen drawer. It made a scratching sound as it opened and it contained dishcloths and tea towels. He tensed up, listening, and then eased back another drawer that contained kitchen knives.

Jane heard the noise as her heart began pounding. She was sure that someone was in the flat and the fear made her freeze, because she was certain it was Allard. She tried to control her nerves and think where the sound had come from, but as she didn't know the layout of the flat, she couldn't be sure. It felt as if she was trapped in the room. She took deep breaths, telling herself that the sound had to have come from the left at the end of the hallway, and she would have to get out of the room and run to her right to escape.

Gibbs lost his attention on the road for a moment, as Moran was on the radio saying they would be there in minutes, so he missed Janet Brown walking into the estate with a bag of shopping, only catching her as she walked into the reception area.

"Nick, I think I've got her, she's here at the estate," Gibbs said into the radio, getting out of the car. He ran into the flats' entrance as the lift began to move upward. He looked at the old dial, which didn't work, unable to tell which floor it was moving to. He pressed the call button again and waited.

Jane had looked around the room for anything she could use as a weapon, but there was nothing. She decided to run for it, and as she got to the hall the kitchen door flew open and Allard came at her, holding the knife up above him, making stabbing motions, and then slashing down toward her body. As she backed into the room, the knife wedged into the wooden door and he began dragging it loose.

When Janet got to her front door she was immediately suspicious as it was half open. She kicked it wider as she heard Jane screaming, and hurled the bag of groceries aside. Allard had his back to her and, turning to face her now with the carving knife free, he switched from attacking Jane and went for Janet. She picked up the old hoover and swung it at him. She didn't release it, but swung it again and this time it knocked him into the door frame. He was screeching like a crazed animal and

Jane came out, kicking at his legs, but he got back up on his feet screaming with rage. Janet now rammed him hard in the groin with the folded child's buggy. He dropped the knife and yelped in agony. She grabbed the knife and was on top of him, holding it at his throat.

"You want to know what it feels like, you scum. I'm gonna cut your throat, you bastard."

Gibbs had done a frantic run, unaware as Jane had been about the flat by the stairwell; he now heard the screams, hurtled through the double doors and ran into the flat. Janet was losing her fight as Allard was able to push her aside—his strength was frightening. It took the three of them to get him down. Gibbs was punching and stamping on his prone body but Allard still attempted to get up. He was clawing at Gibbs and then punched him in the chest and he was by far stronger and starting to stand.

Jane was gasping for breath as she picked up the little boy's tin bus and rammed it down on Allard's head, knocking him face down and giving Gibbs the chance to drag his arms up and cuff him.

Janet was crying and laughing at the same time. She slumped against the corner and then started to sing in a screeching voice "The wheels on the bus go round and round, *round and round.*" She picked up the knife wanting to have another go at Allard. "He could have got my boy, he could have hurt my boy."

"Just knock it off, will you. Gimme that *now.*"

Gibbs had tied a towel around Allard's head, so he was disoriented and cuffed, but still using his body like a ram and kicking out at anything as Jane and Gibbs hauled him into the lift.

Moran and Edwards screeched to a halt beside the patrol car. Edwards immediately went to assist Gibbs and get Allard in the car. Moran went directly over to Jane, and held her, asking quietly if she was all right. She nodded, and he gently touched her face.

"You come back with me, Edwards will go with Gibbs and lock the bastard up. Come on, let me put you in the car. I won't be long."

Jane sank into the passenger seat, and closed her eyes. Moran had a few words with Gibbs and Edwards and then headed into the estate.

Moran found Janet sitting on the sofa, shaking and drinking from a bottle of brandy. "If she wasn't here, he'd have killed me, I just thank Christ my mum took the kid to a friend's cos I got to work and . . ."

"Shush, shush," he said, sitting beside her. "We got him and you're safe."

She nodded. "You want me in court, Nick, I'll do it, do whatever you want. She knocked him for six with the double-decker bus."

"Will you be all right?"

She nodded, taking another swig of brandy. "You make sure she's all right because she was in here alone with him."

"I will, but you muddied the waters, Janet. What the hell were you doing blackmailing the bastard?"

"I couldn't work, I'm still red raw from where he sliced me, an' I wanted to get something out of it. I had to get my mother over from Jamaica to look after my son, I was broke, Nick."

He sighed. "Is it true you have evidence, I mean apart from being able to identify him?"

She took another mouthful of brandy.

"Tell me, I am looking out for you, for Chrissakes, and I always have, but this is you pushing the limit . . . was it a lie?"

She hesitated and then slowly got to her feet. "It might mean nothin', but when those coppers found me, I stuffed it into me bag along with you know what."

Janet went to a cabinet and opened a drawer. She took out something wrapped in newspaper. "You can smell him on it, and I know he raped that young girl because he thought she was me, and I know you used that blonde copper in my fur coat because it was me he was always after."

Moran frowned as she slowly placed the newspaper-wrapped parcel on the coffee table. As he reached over to open it she put her hand over it.

"It's all been my fault, Nick, cos I stole his money out of his cab and I know you was protecting me and couldn't use me as a witness, and to be honest you have always been about the only person I could trust."

"You've certainly screwed me over, so what is it?" Janet slowly opened the newspaper. It contained Peter Allard's balaclava that she had ripped from his head. He didn't touch it but rewrapped the newspaper around it. He knew it could not be used as evidence as it was too long after Allard's arrest.

"Will you still look after me, Nick?"

He got up and smiled, saying he would make sure she was taken care of. He had no idea what she had meant by the double-decker bus but he would find out.

CHAPTER TWENTY-SEVEN

DS Gibbs drove Jane back to the section house and as she attempted to get out of the car he had touched her arm.

"Listen, I need to apologize to you, I behaved like an arsehole, and I just want to clear the air between us. To be honest when I did that run into that estate I had a few seconds when I didn't think I would be able to deal with stuff, you know, the tension and all that crap. I've had these recurring sweats and panicky feelings, but when I saw you with that bastard I never felt for a minute I couldn't cope. Maybe it's over, you know, I've come through it." Jane was taken aback when he leaned toward her and kissed her cheek, before he gave an embarrassed wave of his hand for her to get out of the car.

Jane was back on duty on the Monday morning. DCI Shepherd had been informed of the arrest of Allard, and told her that she was to be at Hackney Station to make a formal report. He didn't appear interested in discussing what had occurred, having already had a lengthy conversation with DI Gibbs.

Jane was not disappointed. In fact, she was partly relieved as she had been very traumatized, and had hardly slept after she had left Gibbs. However, like Spence, she had been somewhat comforted by the fact that she had remained in control and had not suffered from nerves.

Peter Allard had been charged with assault and battery and held in the cells at Hackney. On his arrival at the station, Moran had received a call from Maidstone. The stones from the patio had been lifted, and using arc lights, as the soil beneath was being carefully sifted, they had partly uncovered a roll of carpet.

The body was inside the carpet, covered with plastic, and thick duct tape bound her from head to toe. As a result of the tight bindings there was little decomposition. It was without doubt Susie Luna, as in the pocket of her overall was a name tag from the Majestic Hotel where she had worked.

After clearing her absence with DCI Shepherd, Jane arrived at Hackney Station and went into the incident room where DC Edwards gave her the update on the discovery of the body. Moran was waiting for the formal identification but it was pretty conclusive. "He wants to see you, and he's had DCI Shepherd on the phone, so he'll no doubt fill you in."

Jane felt nervous, wondering if this was going to be a severe reprimand over her suspicions about Moran. She was not that eager to go and see him, but she had no option. She checked her appearance in the ladies' locker room and then went to his office, which she still thought of as Bradfield's. She knocked on the door, and it was a moment before she heard Moran say "come in." He gave almost a curt nod of his head, to indicate for her to sit in the chair opposite his desk.

"We need to discuss a few things just to clear the air a bit. I have given DCI Shepherd a rundown. He started off being a bit tetchy about your professional conduct, saying that you were not a team player—he already seems to think you were acting without backup on the Shirley Dawson case." Jane chewed her lips.

"Shepherd said he had discussed this with you previously, about some unethical procedure. Apparently, despite the coroner's report that it was a non-suspicious death, you and DS Lawrence continued to investigate. You went without authority to question Katrina Harcourt and introduced evidence of the black patent leather shoes but—"

Jane interrupted. "It was a good job we did."

"Hang on, Tennison. Although he disapproved of what he described as unethical procedure, he did express his admiration for the way you triggered the investigation into the murder of Shirley Dawson. What was it that made you suspect foul play?"

Jane hesitated before answering. "I found it very distressing because I was alone in the flat with the victim, her eyes were open, and I had to lift her out of the bath to be taken to the mortuary. Something just didn't feel right. She was the same age as me, and she had a small child, and it was seeing the baby food, her bottle ready to feed her."

"As a detective, you're going to find an awful lot of cases of non-suspicious death and of victims as young or even younger than you. What was it that made you believe Shirley Dawson's death was suspicious?" he asked her again.

"It was an intuitive feeling that something didn't add up. I think the position that her body was found in, in the bath, was not quite right. That was all really."

"But at that point you didn't have the evidence. Would you have ever considered the need to find something that would implicate them?"

Jane knew he was testing her with regard to the fact she knew he had planted the knife. She looked at him directly. "There was no need to uncover evidence that wasn't there because my finding of the photographs was enough."

"What did you feel when you were proved right?" Moran asked quietly.

She turned away, unable to answer.

"It made you feel good, didn't it?" he asked, and she nodded.

"And how did you feel about the two suspects being charged with murder?"

"Good, they deserve to be given life sentences."

"How would you feel if they had got away with it?"

"That I had failed."

"I suppose you know why Allard was given bail and was let out of prison?" Moran stood up and put his hands in his trouser pockets, and moved from behind the desk.

Jane was becoming more uneasy, suspecting he was going to bring up the fact she had been suspicious of him doctoring the confession and planting evidence of the flick knife, which she now knew had been given to him by Janet Brown.

"Allard will be put away for the rest of his life. He hid the murder of Susie Luna for five years, hid his disgusting perverted sexual urges and appeared on the surface to be a decent honest husband and father. The current trial will go ahead because the other criminal offenses, the assault on the owner of the adult bookshop, the kid Ginger, the attack against you and Janet Brown, and even the murder of Susie Luna, are not what he is on trial for, they will be a completely separate arrest. Do you understand? The law let him loose, and we got him back, and we won't let him out of our sight, but it's all down to the correct procedure in the courts, understand?"

"I find it hard to believe," she said and he nodded. He began to unnerve her even more as he moved behind her, still with his hands in his pockets. She was sure this was now going to be a reference to the knife.

"Make you feel positive, does it?"

"On the one hand, yes, that we caught him. On the other, very confused that the trial will get him on one set of charges and that he could then be free unless we have the evidence to get him on something else."

"Right, because his legal team will not allow the new charges to be read at the same time, so the jury will not be privy to them. There will have to be a completely new trial."

She swiveled her head round to see him because it sounded unbelievable.

"What do you feel about Janet Brown? Or Angie, as she calls herself?"

She was taken off guard and shrugged. "I don't know what I feel about her."

"She saved your life?"

"Yes."

"She has agreed to give evidence at Peter Allard's immediate trial, but I am unsure if we will need her. What do you think about that?"

"If it will jeopardize her as an informer, and it is possible to keep her identity safe . . . then she should not be called."

"But you know she blackmailed Marie Allard?"

"Yes, but in reality if she hadn't we might never have got the details and information about Susie Luna."

He nodded and moved back to the desk. "So that is something you would not deem necessary to expose?"

"Yes, sir."

"Good, OK, WDC Tennison. I think we've cleared up a lot, apart from . . ."

Oh God, she thought, now it's coming, but he leaned down behind the desk and brought up a large package wrapped in a Hamleys carrier bag. "This is for you. I don't think it is necessary to put it in the report. DC Gibbs organized it, and we all chipped in."

He swung the handles in his fingers. "WDC Tennison, you are one of us. So take it and we'll see you tonight for a good knees-up."

Jane left with the carrier bag, and went into the ladies'. She opened it up and took out a very large, very expensive replica of a red double-decker bus. She couldn't keep the smile off her face, tucking it under her arm, loving the fact he had said that she was one of them. It made up for everything she had been through. She'd make sure Peter Allard was put away when the time came, and if that failed, she would make sure that she would be the one to arrest him for murder.

Shortly before the trial of Peter Allard began, DS Lawrence had a meeting with Moran. The newspaper was still wrapped around the black woolen balaclava, and as he carefully opened it to reveal the hood, he placed it onto a sheet of white paper on the lab table.

He leaned in closely and sniffed, as he could detect a strong sweet smell.

"I can smell some kind of aftershave."

Moran nodded. "Yeah, I know, it's Aramis . . . I use it, but I won't be as from today . . . Anything else? Any bloodstains?"

Lawrence used a spatula and took his time examining it, turning the hood around, pressing it down and checking every inch. He detected that on the area where the assailant's mouth would have been, the wool was in part stuck together.

"This could be his saliva, but I can't detect any blood. I can test if there is a residue but I doubt it, and with it being black nothing shows up. Your rape victim wasn't cut, was she? Besides, you won't get it into the trial now—how long ago was this found?"

"He was wearing it on the night of the rape, so it's quite a substantial time, although it was kept wrapped in that newspaper. But I'm certain his defense council won't accept it . . . I just needed to know for certain."

"Sorry, but like I said I can do some tests . . ."

Moran shrugged and checked his watch. "I got to go. Thanks for your time, Paul."

Just as Moran reached the double doors leading out from the lab, Paul called out to him.

"Hang on . . . come back."

Moran hurried to the table. Lawrence was using a pair of fine long tweezers and had placed onto the white paper a thin, pale blue woolen strand. He now teased out a second strand and held it up.

"Is that blue rabbit fur?" Moran asked.

"No, it's wool, just caught inside the rim of the hood. What was your rape victim wearing?"

Moran took a deep breath. "A shaggy blue mohair jacket."

"Shit . . . it's a pity this wasn't brought in earlier because I could have checked it out with the actual jacket."

"Thanks, Paul, but I don't hold out much hope that we can use it."

By the time Moran returned to Hackney he was anxious to discuss the findings from the balaclava. He felt that the results confirmed, without doubt, that Peter Allard had committed the rape. But he was concerned about the late discovery of the vital evidence and after a heated discussion with the defense lawyer they were refused permission for it to be used in court.

Disappointed, Moran put more pressure on confirming that the body found at the Allards' rented house was Susie Luna. The body had still not been formally identified when the trial began. All he knew was that they were hoping to gain a result from dental checks, and there had been delays caused by trying to trace a dentist in Maidstone who had had Susie Luna registered as a patient.

As the trial commenced Jane witnessed the hidden depths of Peter Allard's sick mind. He constantly made direct eye contact with the jury and said very clearly that he pleaded guilty to the assault charges. When the rape charge was read out he said loudly, "Not guilty."

Jane held her own in the witness box. She was controlled under questioning by the defense council, who accused her of deliberately encouraging the defendant by wearing sexually suggestive attire that would have been an attempt to lure the defendant into making a sexual approach. Jane denied the allegations and said that her intention was to safeguard any other women from being attacked. It was all very uncomfortable and by the time she returned to sit in the court to listen to the rest of the trial she could hardly contain her anger. Moran winked at her to indicate that she had held her own. He then sat with his head bowed, refusing to look at Allard who stood in the witness box looking very handsome, wearing a suit and a pressed shirt his mother had brought into the prison for him to wear for his court appearance. Allard had the audacity to keep his head held high, and then lower it in a gesture of submission when he said softly that he was ashamed of having assaulted the women but he was under such stress because of his wife's medical predicament.

The defense were able to argue that his confession was taken under duress and was therefore not admissible evidence. They argued that his signature and that of WDC Tennison were also not acceptable.

The prosecution asked why, as innocent as he professed to be, he was wearing a stocking mask and Allard bowed his head.

"Because I am a foolish, stupid man. I was desperate for some kind of satisfaction, and I am deeply sorry."

The jury filed out as DC Edwards approached Moran and passed him an envelope. He ripped it open and then leaned back, closing his eyes. Jane was sitting directly behind him and he turned to face her whispering, "We just got confirmation . . . Susie Luna's dental records match the body found at Allard's house. We bloody got him!"

The jury returned half an hour later. The foreman handed the judge the result and there was a palpable tension in the courtroom. When the judge read out the verdict there was an audible murmur from everyone present. Peter Allard was found not guilty of rape and, as he had pleaded, guilty of the assaults. As he had already spent time in prison on remand he was released and free to leave the court.

Allard walked out into the marble reception area of the Old Bailey. He was smiling as he shook the hand of his barrister. It was extraordinary and it felt as if he was in total denial about the second knife attack on Jane and Janet Brown, and the brutal assault of the young boy Ginger. But he suddenly straightened and looked afraid, his eyes like a trapped animal.

DI Moran was clearly enjoying the moment, and he made a point of having WDC Tennison by his side. He looked across at Jane.

"He's yours, Tennison . . . it's your arrest."

They approached Allard and Jane's voice echoed around the old courthouse reception.

"Peter Allard, I am arresting you on the suspicion of the murder of Susie Luna. You do not have to say anything unless you wish to do so, but what you say may be given in evidence."

It was as if everyone was caught in time, moving in slow motion as Allard stepped back. But an officer had already moved in behind him. Moran handcuffed him, then stepped to stand beside him as Jane moved to walk on the other side. As DI Moran and WDC Tennison escorted Allard out of the court, the press photographers suddenly realized that something very newsworthy was happening, and the flash bulbs began popping as the cameras clicked in quick succession.

Allard was still handcuffed as he was pushed into the waiting police van and the caged doors locked behind him. When the doors slammed shut he let out a howl like a wolf.

Jane and Moran got into a patrol car together. She had expected him to show some kind of emotional exuberance but instead he was quiet. He eventually turned toward her.

"It's over. I'm going to give you a nudge for a commendation, because you've shown persistence and good team work as a trainee CID Detective . . . surprising for . . ."

She was about to thank him when he added, ". . . a young woman."

Jane laughed. It was a backhanded compliment but she was now more determined than ever to move up the ranks in this, her chosen career.

Want to find out what happened to WPC Jane Tennison?

Turn the page for an extract of Lynda La Plante's

GOOD FRIDAY

PROLOGUE

In March 1976, Jane Tennison successfully completed her 10-week CID course at Hendon and returned to Bow Street, while awaiting a transfer to another station as a fully-fledged detective constable. She was still under the strict watchful eye of DCI Shepherd, nicknamed "Timex" due to his almost obsessive time-keeping schedules. DI Gibbs had frequently not seen eye-to-eye with DCI Shepherd, and he had been posted away from Bow Street. Jane hadn't heard from him, and wasn't sure whether he had managed to curtail his excessive drinking.

It wasn't long before Jane's posting as a DC came through and to her dismay she was offered a place at Hackney. She requested a private discussion with Shepherd to ask if she could remain at Bow Street. Although she knew that he could be tricky and controlling she never the less admired his tenacity.

Shepherd knew, intuitively, the reason behind Jane's appeal. Several officers who had been stationed at Hackney at the time of the abortive Bank raid, which had tragically killed DCI Leonard Bradfield and WPC Kath Morgan, had been transferred. Jane gave no reason for her request, but encouraged by her previous performance at Bow Street DCI Shepherd agreed that she could return there.

Jane was in a catch-22 situation. Although Shepherd had agreed for her to remain with the CID at Bow Street, he gave her very little opportunity to prove herself and she was becoming increasingly frustrated. She was due to attend a court appearance for a drunk driver. Usually this kind of case would have been handled by a uniformed officer, but Jane had been driving an unmarked CID car when the drunk driver had driven straight into the back of it. He had been belligerent and quite abusive.

On arriving at the court she was annoyed to find that there was a backlog of cases being heard, so she went to get herself a coffee. As she headed back to the waiting room she was almost sent flying by a DC bounding through the door.

"God, I'm sorry," said DC Brian Edwards, then, recognizing, her gave a wide smile.

"Jane! It's good to see you!"

"Hello Brian. You got a case here this morning as well?"

"Yeah, Flying Squad job. Committal hearing on a three-hander for armed robbery."

"You're on the Flying Squad?" Jane tried to hide her surprise. Edwards was young, and almost as inexperienced as she was.

"Yeah, it's completely changed my life. The blokes on the squad are a great bunch of guys. We work all over London investigating armed robberies. The adrenalin buzz when you nick an armed blagger on the pavement is incredible."

"Congratulations! I must say, you look good."

Edwards had always been rather untidy and scruffy looking, with his thick curly hair worn long, and his shirt always hanging out of his trousers. Now he was wearing a trendy leather jacket, a white t-shirt, and dark trousers with side zipper boots.

"Are there any women on the Flying Squad?" Jane asked.

"No way. I doubt they'd ever bring in a woman. It's tough work, Jane, and we get results." Before she could respond to his arrogance and chauvinism, Edwards glanced at his watch, "So, what're you here for?"

"Just a traffic offense. a drunk bloke rammed into me while I was driving the CID car."

Edwards laughed. He turned to look over at two men dressed in similar clothing to him, as one gestured for him to join them.

"See y'around," Edwards said, as he sauntered over to them.

* * *

By the time Jane got to the CID office three hours later she was in a foul mood. Edith, the CID's clerical officer, who had worked alongside Jane since she started at Bow Street, smiled warmly when she saw her.

"Everything go all right in court?"

"Yes. Guilty, banned for two years and a hefty fine. When you think how much paperwork I had to do to get him into court . . . He wore a smart suit and tie and said it was out of character, blah, blah . . . Considering the lip he gave me, he got off lightly."

"Well, you've got a load of shoplifting crime sheets on your desk from DCI Shepherd. There's been a slew of clothes nicked from Oxford Street stores today."

"Shoplifters? That's a uniform crime investigation, not CID!"

"Not when they all happened within an hour of each other. Shepherd reckons it's an organized gang who sell the stolen goods on market stalls."

"Well that sounds a lot more interesting than the stuff I usually investigate."

Edith sipped her tea. "He wants you to get statements from all the shops, and an inventory of exactly what was stolen, along with the value."

"Oh my God," Jane muttered.

"Don't shoot the messenger," Edith retorted, resuming her typing.

Jane began to sift through the crime sheets and statements on her own desk. "I met DC Brian Edwards at court. Remember him from the Susie Luna murder?" Edith looked blank. "The rapist, Peter Allard? He got a life sentence, and—"

"Oh yes, I remember. long time ago, now . . . Over a year . . ."

"Edwards is on the Flying Squad now."

"Really?"

"He said they never take women on the Squad."

"Well, I doubt any decent woman would want to be on it." Edith's tone sharpened. "They're a bunch of chauvinistic bastards! Ever since that TV series came out, 'The Professionals,' they act like they're film stars, the lot of them, think they're God's gift . . . There've been a lot of unpleasant rumors about corruption, too, but far be it from me to name names . . ."

Jane processed the Oxford Street reports for the rest of the day, drawing up charts of the shops, times of the thefts and a description of the suspects. She then filed everything methodically, just as DCI Shepherd liked, but she was finished by three thirty. She sat drumming her fingers on her empty desk and at four o'clock decided she would approach DCI Shepherd. It was ridiculous that she was sitting around when she was now qualified to investigate more serious cases.

She knocked on his office door and waited.

"Come in."

Jane walked in and stood by his desk. Shepherd gave her a cursory glance.

"What is it, Tennison?" Shepherd's pale blue eyes and boyish looks belied not only his age but also his professionalism.

"May I speak freely, sir?"

"Yes, of course. Sit down."

She drew a chair up in front of his desk.

"I don't feel that my time here is being utilized properly. I've gained a lot of experience since I've been here, and I know that you are aware of my participation in previous cases—like the apparently non-suspicious death that resulted in two murder convictions."

Shepherd didn't answer right away. He paused for a moment, then picked up his fountain pen, unscrewed the top, examined the nib, then slowly screwed it back together. "Yes, of course, I am aware of the case you are referring to . . . Katrina Harcourt and . . . er, Barry Dawson . . . correct?"

"Yes, sir. I was also part of the investigation of the rapist Peter Allard when the body of Susie Luna was discovered, and—"

"Yes, Tennison, I'm more than aware of those investigations, and the part you played in them. But I don't see why you're bringing them up now, all these months later?"

"Sir, I'm grateful that you agreed for me to return to Bow Street but now that I've passed my CID course and been made detective I'm concerned that my training is not being used to its full potential."

"Really?"

"Yes, sir. I was wondering if there was any possibility that I could apply for a transfer to the Flying Squad?"

Shepherd laughed. "Tennison, with your length of service and experience there is absolutely no possibility of your being transferred to the Flying Squad. You are welcome to apply but I doubt the application would be taken seriously. But let me think about what you've said and we can talk in due course about some possible alternatives."

Edith was getting ready to leave when Jane walked in to the CID office and sat down at her desk, in a glum mood.

"I'm off home now," Edith said.

"Edith, do you think DCI Shepherd's got it in for me? He keeps his distance from me, and I get all the dross. I'm investigating dead-end crimes that none of the other detectives are allocated. I know that he was very complimentary to me, and agreed for me to return to Bow Street . . ."

"As I keep on telling you Jane, the Met really don't like giving women the kudos they deserve. They're old-school, and Shepherd is as well . . . although he maintains that he's a forward thinker, in my opinion he plays by the rules—and those rules don't include female detectives."

On returning to the section house Jane sat on her bed, feeling thoroughly depressed. She had been thinking of moving out and renting a flat of her own now she was earning a sufficient salary. She had saved a considerable amount living at the section house. The time was right for her to be independent.

Later that evening she called her parents and told her father that she was contemplating moving. Mr. Tennison encouraged her to think about buying rather than renting. He even offered to help by paying the deposit, saying that in the long run it would be much better for her to own a flat and pay a mortgage, as it would be an investment.

Jane's morale was boosted. If she couldn't improve her working schedules at Bow Street she could at least change her personal life style, and be more independent.

DCI Shepherd didn't approach Jane after their meeting, so she carried on working on the low-level investigations she had been assigned to. She was disappointed, but at least she now had another focus, spending her days off looking at possible flats. She was unsure how she was going to manage financially, as she had only just bought a second-hand VW Golf. However, Jane's father actively encouraged her and produced a list of areas that he felt would be suitable.

"I don't want to jump the gun, Daddy. This is really going to stretch my wages . . . so far I haven't seen anywhere suitable."

"It takes time dear, and you won't be jumping the gun. I'll look into everything with you. If we find a place that needs fixing up you can call on your brother in law, Tony, to help with the carpentry, and I can do the decorating."

Mrs. Tennison was not quite as enthusiastic and was anxious about Jane moving into a flat on her own and taking on such responsibility. She had even suggested that Jane might want to go back and live at home with them again. She constantly worried about Jane and felt that, if she wasn't living at home, it was safer for her to be in secure accommodation like the section house, along with other police officers.

"It sometimes feel's like I imagine a school dormitory, would be, Mum, with no privacy . . . and I hate the communal bathrooms. I really want to find my own place."

"Well, in my opinion if you get your own place there'll be no incentive for you to meet someone, get married and set up a home together. Just like Pam and Tony did."

After years of being compared to her sister, Jane had learned not to argue with her mother, or to listen to her opinions. Mrs. Tennison was still unable to cope with Jane's career choice, and would far rather that she had been more like Pam and had chosen a safe "homely" job. She had always been prone to anxiety, and if she had known of the horrors that Jane had been subjected to during her training and at her various attachments since then, she would be even more neurotic.

On her days off Jane and her father scoured the estate agents' windows viewed endless properties and made arrangements for a mortgage. She had a file of estate agents' particulars and spent her breaks in the canteen having coffee and sifting through them all. Edith, was very supportive of Jane buying her own flat, although she was quick to dismiss one property after another as being too far out of the West End, or in an unsatisfactory area. Edith owned her own small terraced house in Hackney but constantly complained that the neighborhood was going downhill and that it was not a good investment for her future. Her elderly mother suffered from dementia and she was dependent on social welfare carers to be able to look after her. Jane had once asked Edith if she had considered placing her mother into a care home.

"I wouldn't dream of it! She might be the bane of my life but she's my mother . . . even though she often doesn't know who I am, and she's a constant worry, but when she is lucid it makes it worthwhile. I'm sure if you were ever in the same situation Jane, you would do the same."

Jane nodded in agreement, although the thought of losing one or other of her parents and having to care for them by herself was too much to even contemplate.

As she was pondering, DCI Shepherd summoned her into his office.

"Detective Tennison, I have been giving your request for a transfer some serious thought. You are, as I have said to you before, far too inexperienced a detective to join an elite squad like 'the Sweeny.' But they have a sub-division known as the 'Dip Squad' . . . if you do well there it could be a stepping stone toward the Flying Squad. They're quite keen for a female to join them, and I can get you up on an attachment, if their DCI agrees."

"What exactly is the Dip Squad, sir?"

"Well, they deal with professional pickpockets . . . there's shed loads of them descending in force from overseas, most notably Italy, Chile and Colombia. The Dip Squad are working right now with teams along Oxford Street, Regent's Street and Piccadilly, as well as teams covering underground stations at Victoria, Embankment and Oxford Circus. So, how does that sound to you?"

Jane wasn't at all sure, but at the same time if this might be a possible route to the more glamorous Flying Squad then she knew she should accept.

"Thank you very much, sir."

Shepherd stood up, dismissing her. "Good. I'll let you know as soon as I get confirmation."

Jane was beaming when she went back into the CID room and Edith swiveled around to look at her.

"I may be transferred to the Dip Squad."

Edith shrugged and turned back to face her typewriter. "Rather you than me, dear . . . it's a dreadful, dirty little office and they don't even have any clerical staff. Oh, by the way, I meant to show you this."

Edith handed her an advert from *The Job*, the Met's official newspaper.

"I think it sounds really interesting . . . an ex-clerical worker based in Scotland Yard is offering her flat for sale. Good location, just off Baker street, a minute from the Underground. It's got . . . two bedrooms, and I think it's a very reasonable price."

Jane jotted down the information. As she was off duty that afternoon she arranged to go and see the flat in Melcombe Street. She walked the short distance from Baker Street underground station, and liked the location as it was so close to Regents Park. Melcombe Street was a small turning, with a row of shops on one side and narrow three-story houses opposite. There was no front garden as they were built back from the pavement, but the houses were white washed and looked well kept. The door to number 33 was freshly painted with a row of brass bells on one side. She rang the bell for the top flat and waited.

After a short while a very pregnant woman opened the door and introduced herself as Mrs. Taylor. Jane could immediately see why she wanted to sell the flat. She followed the woman up three flights of narrow stairs, and reaching the top floor Mrs. Taylor she had to stand and gasp for breath.

"Are you all right?" Jane asked, concerned.

"Yes, I just get so breathless. I used to run up these stairs before I was pregnant . . . they never bothered me. But I've only a month to go and it feels like I'm carrying a sack of coal in front of me!"

Jane followed her into the hallway of the flat. It was mostly all white walls, newly painted. She showed Jane a small, well-equipped kitchen incorporating a dining area with high stools. Straight opposite was a bathroom with new bath, washbasin and toilet. It had fresh flowered tiles, and a heated towel rail.

"My husband has just finished doing this place up. We've moved to our new house in Barnes so we're ready to sell and can exchange right away."

Jane loved the flat. Although it was small, it was so clean and bright and the two bedrooms, one much larger than the other, were freshly painted and decorated with Laura Ashley wallpaper.

"That's it!" Mrs. Taylor said, as Jane looked around the larger bedroom, which had fitted wardrobes.

Jane had hoped for a larger flat, with a communal sitting room. But this flat wouldn't need anything done to it, and she could rent out the smaller bedroom straightaway.

Jane inquired whether any of the furniture was included.

"Yes, everything! I mean, I'll be taking the bed linen, cutlery and china, but I'm leaving all the furniture as is. And it comes with a new washing machine, fitted fridge and cooker."

Jane rang her father as soon as she returned to the section house and told him that she thought she had found the flat she wanted to buy.

While she was at work the following day her father went to view it, and during her lunch break she called him to see what he thought.

"Well, you can't swing a cat in it . . . I mean, there's no dining room or sitting room, and it's quite a walk up. Your mother had to have a breather halfway."

Jane hadn't realized her mother was also going to look at the flat. She doubted that Mrs. Tennison would approve and was starting to feel disappointed, as her father continued discussing the finances.

"You know it's only a 22-year lease?"

"Yes, Daddy, but I think the price is fair, and it includes all the furniture . . ."

"There's no garden. It's a top floor and there isn't even a small balcony."

"Yes, I know that . . . but it's close to Regent's Park."

"And it's a bit too bloody close to that siege that went on in Balcombe Street, which is just up the road you know, Jane?"

"Yes I do know that, Daddy, but the IRA are hardly likely to target the same area twice and the IRA gang were arrested and awaiting trial . . ."

"Your mother wants to talk to you. . . ."

Jane sighed, certain she would get a negative response.

"I like it dear," her mother said. "It's so clean, and has lovely big windows so it's very light and airy. But don't you think it's going to be too small? I mean, you said you were going to need two bedrooms. You could make that the big one into a sitting room, because otherwise you have nowhere to sit and watch the TV so, taking that into consideration I think it will be too expensive to just be there on your own . . ."

Jane was forced to listen to her parents' pros and cons regarding the flat, as they handed over the phone from one to another. Eventually Jane had had enough.

"I like it and I prefer it to any other flat I've seen. I know it may be small, but it's ideal, for me. I don't need much space."

"Where will you park your car?" Mr. Tennison asked.

"There's residents' parking outside the house, and when I don't need the car I can park it in the small lane behind your flat."

"Well, that's fine by me. It's in a good position for the underground station and then Marylebone Station is just up the road. But I doubt you'll be able to rent out that small bedroom."

Jane was becoming increasingly argumentative and now insisted that she wanted to go ahead.

"Well it's £24,000, and with that short lease I'm not sure it's a good prospect. But I'll talk to the mortgage broker in the morning. We've made a file of your income and future earnings, and if I put down £10,000, let's see what they think about it."

"That's very generous of you, Daddy."

"Well you'll eventually have to pay me back, but if you really want this flat then in the end it's your choice."

As she put the phone down Jane felt relieved, and grateful to her father.

"Everything all right, luv?" Edith asked.

"My father's OK about me buying the flat. I can't wait to move in and have my own independence . . . no more section house rules and regulations . . ."

"Well, don't get too excited yet, Jane, everything has to be signed on the dotted line before the purchase goes through."

"I know, I know . . ."

"And then there's the police regulations to follow: your move must be approved by a Chief Super, neighbors have to be checked out for criminal records . . ."

"Yes I know Edith." Jane sighed, wishing she hadn't said anything in the first place.

"And you need permission if you want to get married."

"I've no intention of getting married yet Edith, but I might take in a lodger."

"Well you'll need permission for that as well."

"God, this job wants to know the ins and outs of everything, even my personal life."

Edith put her straight, tapping the side of her nose. "Listen dear . . . it feels like they want to know the color of your knickers, but just make sure it's all reported in line with police regulations."

* * *

As she was about to leave the station DCI Shepherd called Jane into his office again. He was quite abrupt, saying that he had been in talks with the team and the DCI heading up the Dip Squad at Vine Street Police Station, and she could start there immediately, from the beginning of the following week.

"You'll work with a splendid officer, DCI Church. There's about ten or twelve officers on his team and you'll work shifts, 9 a.m. to 5 p.m. mostly or 2 p.m. to 10 p.m. I've arranged a six-month attachment and at the end of it the DCI will make the decision regarding whether you will continue with them or not."

He stood up. "Good luck Tennison. I hope you'll find this attachment more to your liking. I've arranged for your replacement, a male officer, to start next Monday. You can spend the rest of this week completing any outstanding reports and paperwork."

"I really appreciate this, sir. If my replacement needs me to go over anything while I'm still here then I will be only too pleased to do whatever is necessary."

He shook her hand. "I am sure he will be quite capable Tennison."

"Yes, sir."

Instead of feeling excited by the prospect of joining the new team she felt a little nervous and wondered if perhaps she had been over enthusiastic. DCI Shepherd's attitude had not been very positive, in fact the reverse. She had also noted that he had made it clear her replacement would be a male officer. But it was too late to change her mind now, so she concentrated her thoughts on arranging the final details of her mortgage with the bank and making the final purchase of the flat.

Jane's last day finally arrived and Edith bought Jane a housewarming-leaving present, of a table cloth and matching napkins. It was thoughtful of her but Jane doubted she would ever use them as the folding table in the kitchen had a Formica top.

"I'm going to miss you, Jane." Edith said.

"I'll miss you too Edith. You've always been such a good friend to me, and I hope we'll stay in touch."

"I'm sure we will. Please keep me updated on how it's all going with the Dip Squad. When do you start?"

"Next week. And tomorrow I'm picking up the keys to my new flat so it's going to be a busy weekend."

Edith watched as Jane filled up a cardboard box with her personal items. She suspected that Jane would be in touch sooner than she expected, because from what she had heard about the unit Jane was in for a big change. The Dip Squad sounded like a bunch of hooligans.

The next morning, Jane unlocked the door of number 33 and walked in to the flat she now owned. Her parents were helping her move and she could hear them panting their way up the stairs with suitcases of clothes and the few boxes of personal items that she'd accumulated during her time at the section house. Jane walked into the small kitchen. The previous owner had put fresh flowers in a jam jar on the kitchen table, and had left milk, sugar and a loaf of bread on the side. She'd also left Jane a note wishing her good luck and hoping that she would like living in the flat as much as she had.

Eventually her parents left and Jane was alone for the first time in her new home. She carried her suitcase into the bedroom and sat down on the bare mattress on the bed. She hugged herself, feeling as though she had made the right decision.